THE MERCHANT'S DAUGHTER

Rebecca Hardy was born and raised in London, England and has lived between Sussex and London all her life. Writing since an early age, she is a regular contributor to photographic publications and blogs as well as short works of fiction, and shares love for books on her Instagram profile **@Rebecca_readsbooks**. She now lives in West Sussex with her two lively boys, two equally lively cats and her husband.

By Rebecca Hardy

The House of Lost Wives
The Merchant's Daughter

THE MERCHANT'S DAUGHTER

REBECCA HARDY

ꕥ

First published in 2023 by
HEADLINE ACCENT
An imprint of HEADLINE PUBLISHING GROUP

Cataloguing in Publication Data is available from the British Library

ISBN 978 1 0354 1060 6

Typeset in 10.5/14pt Sabon LT Std by Jouve (UK), Milton Keynes

Printed and bound in Great Britain by Clays Ltd, Elcograf S.p.A.

Headline's policy is to use papers that are natural, renewable and recyclable products and made from wood grown in well-managed forests and other controlled sources. The logging and manufacturing processes are expected to conform to the environmental regulations of the country of origin.

HEADLINE PUBLISHING GROUP
An Hachette UK Company
Carmelite House
50 Victoria Embankment
London EC4Y 0DZ

www.headline.co.uk
www.hachette.co.uk

For Mum & Dad
Cochairmen of my fan club

Author's note

Although some of the occurrences in this book are loosely based on true events and circumstances, this author wishes to inform the reader that, aside from the liberty I have taken with one or two names, every element is entirely fiction.

Chapter 1

ꟸ

THE M WORD

It was a week before my world was turned upside down that the subject of marriage was first mentioned.

I had overheard my parents discussing my future in the drawing room late one evening, when they thought I was in my room curled up with a book. I had, in fact, left said book on the window seat downstairs and was just coming to retrieve it when the fateful M word was overheard, causing me to stop outside the open door and eavesdrop. My mother and father's heads were just visible over the backs of their armchairs, and although it was too warm for a fire, the candles placed in front of the hearth glowed before them, stretching shadows towards my hiding place as though they might be reaching for my bare toes. Aristotle, our King Charles spaniel, snored quietly in his usual spot before the empty fireplace.

'She must marry, my dear,' repeated my father. 'It is imperative that we find her a suitable husband.'

My mother made a sound that indicated she felt equally humoured and frustrated by the idea.

'You know our silly girl and her notions,' she chimed. 'Jenny is terrified of men after what that young lord did to her.'

'*She* is terrified, or *you* are, my dear? For it seems to me that you have barely let her out of your sight these eighteen months, since that regrettable incident,' my father replied, not unkindly.

It was true enough, for my mother, Katherine Miller, was indeed as protective of me as any lioness might be of her cub, particularly if that cub had been abused and publicly ruined at the hands of another.

She tsked in reply and ploughed on. 'Mark my words, I know our girl's heart better than anyone and she will not form an attachment. Unless she falls in *love*,' she added, as though the word were sickly on her tongue.

'She will not marry if she does not meet someone, and she will not meet someone if she does not venture outside these walls,' my father pointed out.

'But she does go outside on occasion.'

'To visit the bookshop,' came my father's resigned reply.

'Yes,' my mother agreed thoughtfully, 'though I don't believe that she would wish to marry at all. She would no doubt rather run off with a character from one of her books.'

'You cannot marry a fictional character,' my father replied gruffly, as though my mother were not already aware of the fact. 'And although there is nothing wrong with *love*,' he added, making the word sound a little sweeter than my mother had, 'there are practical reasons for marrying. George Talver's offer still stands.'

I suppressed a shudder at the name. I would not marry my father's business partner if he were the last man on Earth.

'How romantic of you, Mr Miller,' my mother replied drily. 'I can assure you that as charming as George may be, I do not fancy him for a son-in-law.'

My father paused, and I could see the bob of his head in agreement at that. Thank goodness.

'I have to agree with you, my dear. I am only thinking of her future. If she marries a nice man soon, she will have time enough to bear us a few grandchildren before we are too old to enjoy them. Our son-in-law could take on my role in the family business, and you and I could visit all those old houses and gardens you so enjoy speaking of.'

As horrifying as the thought of bearing children was to me, I had to smile at my father's gentle barb in my mother's direction. She gave an amused harrumph in reply, but he was not finished.

'If she does not find a suitable partner soon, I worry what might happen to you both if some tragedy were to befall me.'

And so it began again, reminding me why I hated this discussion so. Although both of them had tried on several occasions to convince me that next season would be *my* season, I truly had no interest in finding a husband for the sake of an heir for the business. If only my parents had had a son, then no one would have to worry about the family fortune falling out of our hands.

'Do not speak like that,' my mother retorted. 'I could not imagine a life without you, Mr Miller.' I stifled a chuckle, knowing she only referred to him thus when she was particularly vexed. 'After all, what would I do with the house, the business? Never mind that to lose you would be most impractical.'

'Oh dear me. Impractical, would it be?' There was the hint of humour in my father's tone at that.

'Quite a nuisance indeed.'

'Be that as it may, my dear, the truth of the matter is that we cannot have our sweet little girl grow up to become a spinster, no matter what her poor experiences have led her to believe.'

There was a moment's pause while my mother chose her best

response, and I willed her to come to my aid even though she had no notion that I stood only feet behind her.

She settled on a sigh, before resting her hand on my father's arm. 'She's no longer the bright and impulsive girl she used to be, Jacob. Yes, at first it was at my insistence that she stayed home and waited for the world to forget the unfortunate incident, but now it is she who digs her heels in at the mention of social engagements. When that blasted man ruined her, he crushed her spirit too, and I cannot bring myself to put her through the pain again.'

This conversation would replay itself in my mind in the days and weeks following while I searched for its meaning in the events that came after. How poignant and somehow full of foreboding it had been, though seeming so innocent at the time.

What more was said between them I do not know, for I felt the presence of someone behind me and turned to find Marcus, my father's manservant, looming over me like a spectre, his face as unreadable as ever. I promptly scurried back to bed empty-handed, without either of us saying a word.

She's no longer the bright and impulsive girl she used to be. My mother's words still stung a little, though it had been a year and a half since my fall from grace, and I clenched my fists in protest, standing before the sack of flour that hung in my closet. It was barely disguised with an old blanket that I had now yanked off, pushing my clothes to one side so that I could stare at the garish face I had painted on the front. My maid had accidentally unveiled my punching bag once while cleaning, and her scream had sent the other staff running to her aid. Only Marcus, who had followed the commotion, and myself had laughed at her discovery. Lord Buckface, we called him, and although my artistry left much to be desired, I thought it was an apt likeness of the man who had wronged me.

The bag had been Marcus's idea, and in recent months I'd found myself more and more grateful for having something to hit, to release a little of the anger that I held inside, relishing the sting of canvas against my knuckles. I was always careful to wear gloves in the day, as any lady should, and if my mother noticed the wear on my hands, she refrained from comment. I had begun to believe that she was afraid to have the conversation with me, knowing what demons it might unleash.

After a few well-aimed hits to the target, I found myself already drenched in sweat and gave it up for the night, concealing the source of my nightmares behind his shroud and closing the door to the closet. I lay on top of the blankets, the room too hot and stifling to burrow underneath them, and stared at the ceiling, fingers twined over my chest as my parents' conversation and thoughts of marriage filled my mind. It had been a long time since I'd even entertained the notion, so outcast had I become from society. It worried me that Father thought it suddenly urgent that I find a husband.

My mother knew the truth of it. Unless I could spend the rest of my days with one of the heroes from my stories, I would rather remain alone. Fictional men were far better company and were not so vulgar as real ones. But to be a heroine of one of my novels, I would have to be either devastatingly beautiful or unwaveringly brave. I was pretty enough, I thought, yet perhaps I did not have the breathtaking looks of a princess in need of rescuing. And although I was not brave, I did not consider myself a coward, despite my mother's sentiments. After all, there were not many opportunities to be brave while cooped up in a London town house.

I propped myself up on one elbow and reached over to the bedside cabinet, opening a small drawer that contained a bundle of pictures and postcards. Retrieving my keepsakes, I sat up and undid the frayed string, worn thin from all the occasions I had done just this for years. To anyone else, these bits of card and paper held little value: sketches of ships that my father had given me as a child, tokens he had sent me on his various travels, letters describing far-off places that I could only imagine. I had once begged him to take me with him on his journeys, but he had always refused, stating that a ship really was no place for a lady. I traced the lines of one of his rough sketches, a group of men in some tavern, each one suspended in laughter. The drawing itself was not particularly detailed, but I often looked at it and transported myself to that mysterious place where strangers became family over the course of a journey, and where you knew the man you worked with better than perhaps you did your own wife. With heavy eyelids and a sigh, I stacked the pictures and stowed them away, lying flat on my back in my bed.

The germ of an idea formed in my mind as I lay in the drowsy heat – thoughts of bravery, of travelling and sightseeing, of discovering places other than the same streets and parks that I had known all my life. For if I were to marry as soon as my parents wished, there would be no opportunity for that. No, instead I would be running a house and having children, attending parties as a married woman. If it was perhaps an impossible dream, in my half-asleep state it seemed like rather a good one.

I'd not always recoiled from the thought of marriage. Growing up, I had been the absolute model of a daughter, pursuing every possible avenue for a proper courtship, and at one point had even had *three* proposals, all of which I had rejected based on my feelings, or lack thereof, for the men in question. My parents had not pressed me on the matter, for there had been time enough, they thought, to find a suitor. But then had come two moments of my life in which the topic of love was truly ruined for me.

The first was only a few months after I had first come out at the age of seventeen.

My mother had ensured that I attend every cotillion ball and party from Belgravia to Knightsbridge, in the hopes of finding me a suitor among the high aristocracy, and that I might come away with a taste for balls and dancing as well as a husband. The former certainly came about. My appetite for pretty gowns and dances, social discussions and meeting others of my age knew no limits. I swiftly fell for a young man by the name of Nigel, although even now when I look back on it, I believe I fell in love with what he represented and not the boy himself. I had felt that everything about him was soft and caring, his compliments always sincere. He was a poet, and like so many others of his talent, he loved and hated with passion and honesty. He seemed genuinely enchanted with me also, and we always danced once or twice at any social gathering at which we met over the first weeks of the summer. I waited in vain for him to ask me for a third dance, where our attachment might be confirmed, or to call on me the day after and at the very least leave his card. Instead I found him a month later dancing with another girl of slightly wealthier stature, a lock of her hair twined around his finger, any unspoken arrangement between us ending as abruptly as it had started.

The second ruination had been far worse, even the reminder of it sending goosebumps across my hot skin. Somewhat disillusioned by Nigel, I had attended a party where the host had been only a few years older than I. A Lord Darleston, who had inherited his wealth at the young age of twenty-two.

I am still uncertain how we came to be alone that night, or where my friends and parents had disappeared to, leaving me with the young lord in his rose garden, the fresh blooms filling my nose with heady perfume. I had sensed the danger when it was already upon me, moments too late. My stomach turned at the reminder of it, Lord Darleston's words echoing through my mind.

'I am grateful we find ourselves alone, Miss Miller, for I can show you my favourite garden statue. I think you'll quite enjoy it, having a fondness for the Greek tales as you do.'

The words had been inconsequential in themselves, but the lie had rung through me as loud as any alarm bell. Yes, there was a small likeness of Athena in the garden amongst the roses, her shield and spear in her hands, her robes draping evocatively from her marble form, but that was not what Lord Darleston had wanted to come here for.

Even as I lay in bed now, I could feel the phantom press of his fingers on my arms and his stale breath upon my neck. The imprint of his hand on my bodice, the look of rage in his bloodshot eyes when I slapped him, the low growl in his throat as he forced me into the grass and pushed my skirts up. The rip of fabric, the scramble as my silk gloves failed to find purchase on anything that might stop him from having his way with me. I think I screamed, but it was muffled by a hot palm pressed over my face. Then the champagne flute that had fallen to the ground was in my hand. Only a swift swipe of it into his head, the glass erupting like violent crystals in my fingers, had stopped him from doing his worst. I could still recall the blood dripping down his temple, black as ink in the moonlight. The nightmares had almost abated a year ago, when I found out that the lord in question had been imprisoned for gambling debts, but still he haunted me, the memories an indelible scar upon my mind and heart.

Rumours had circulated quickly afterwards, undoubtedly straight from his very lips. They varied from me throwing myself upon him to some ridiculous idea that I had been plotting to be seen compromised by him so he would be forced to propose, but despite my protests that none of it could be true, society had rejected me, and I, in turn, had lost my faith in it. I spent many months in a dark place after that night, unwilling to leave my room for more than meals, my books the only thing keeping me sane. My large bedroom, with its attached bathroom and closet, was my safe haven, the four walls my sanctuary. I saw little more than the pretty blue wallpaper, the elegant furniture, and the view of the square from my balcony. I became a quiet echo of myself for what felt like a very long time.

Finally, fatefully, my mother insisted I attend the birthday party of a young girl who had suffered equal misfortune at the hands of the very same lord. The family was poorer than ours, and she had lost her sister almost immediately after the assault, and yet there she was, communing with people as though she were fearless, daring anyone to say anything against her. I could still see her descending the staircase of their bare home on her father's arm, defiance in her eyes. I had told myself I would not mention the torment we had both experienced, but as she spoke to me with kindness, I could not help but ask how she retained the will to carry on, to be seen in public.

One conversation with Lizzie Dawson had changed my resolve and given me the strength to put Lord Darleston behind me. She had decided that nothing would stand in her way or break her, and the proof of it was that she was now happily married to a captain and running a manor in Sussex.

'He's already taken a part of us we'll never get back,' she had said. 'Don't let him take the rest.'

They were words I now lived by.

I had implored Marcus to teach me to fight. He had refused in his own silent way at first, knowing that my parents would disapprove of their daughter indulging in fisticuffs like a common brawler, but soon enough I persuaded him to at least teach me to defend myself against an assailant so that I might never be caught out again. So it was that Lord Buckface was created – any resemblance to persons living or dead purely a coincidence – and though I had never had to put my skills to any real test, I felt confident that I could land a punch or two given the opportunity.

As my tired eyes traced the faint cracks in the paint on the ceiling, my candle flickering despite the night being stiflingly still, I wondered how Lizzie was and what she was doing now. I should write to her and perhaps invite her here, or ask her if I could impose and stay in Sussex for a week or two. Maybe the change would do me good. Wanderlust had sometimes tugged at me when I disappeared into the pages of a story, wishing to see the places I had read about for myself; to taste exotic foods and smell the rich scents of an alien land. Slowly a plan began to form in my mind, even as weariness tugged at me.

I fell asleep that night on top of the mattress with Lizzie's words rattling around my head, the prospect of an arranged engagement looming over me, and what I might do to change that fate.

No, despite my parents' insistence, I was not about to marry the next eligible bachelor who came along.

The following morning, after penning a letter to the woman who had inspired me so, I announced to my parents that I wished to leave London for a short while.

'What is she saying, Jacob?' my mother asked my father, as though I had spouted some foreign tongue and she had not in fact heard me perfectly.

'I believe she is requesting leave of us, my dear,' he said with a sigh as he sipped his tea. 'It seems she has grown tired of her parents after all these years.'

'I have not grown tired of you, Papa,' I huffed, aware that he was teasing me and succeeding in his fun. 'I merely wish to know what the world is like outside London.'

'I hear Bath is very pleasant at this time of year,' he said, passing a crust of his breakfast roll to Aristotle when he thought my mother wasn't looking.

'I do not wish to go to Bath. My intention is to begin in Sussex, to visit Mrs Blountford – you remember her, Mama?'

'Ah yes, although she's a lady now that her husband's uncle is dead. Remarkable young woman,' my mother commented, narrowing her eyes at the dog, who, having swallowed the crust whole, was now making a dramatic coughing noise beneath the table.

'I have written to her just this morning in the hopes that she will have me for a few weeks. I realise I should have asked permission, Papa,' I interjected when I saw my father open his mouth to protest, 'but I know that Lizzie – Lady Blountford – won't think the request improper coming directly from me.'

I didn't mention the fact that I also intended to speak to Lizzie's husband, Captain Blountford – or perhaps Lord Blountford now, if he had taken his late uncle's title. He had travelled the world with the navy and might be able to advise me on how to proceed with my plan. Although I hadn't particularly thought it through, there was the notion that from Sussex I could take a coach to Plymouth, and thence a ship to France if I had the courage to pursue my idea of adventure. The captain, who had fought all the way across the far reaches of Egypt and Africa, might be able to guide me better. And if bravery eluded me and I decided not to embark on the trip, at the very least I would have escaped from under my parents' feet for a while.

'The wilds of Sussex, eh?' said my father. 'Are we certain that the countryside will cope with the likes of our daughter?'

'I am not sure she is ready for it,' my mother argued. 'Going to a strange place to stay with people we've barely met.' I might have been inclined to agree with her had I not been so eager for the opportunity to travel. For it was not men and parties I wished to seek out, but rather new sights and experiences that might give me the resolve I needed to return to society. I imagined that my father, joint owner of a large merchant company and seasoned traveller himself, would sympathise with me.

He smiled warmly at his wife, sharing one of their silent, private conversations that I was so accustomed to, which mostly involved my mother scowling and my father waggling his eyebrows plaintively until she said, 'Oh, very well. If Lady Blountford will have you, then I suppose a few weeks away will do you no harm. But you'll be taking a chaperone.'

I felt a thrill through my very bones at the thought of escape.

Adventure. It called to me even as I sat at the breakfast table, absently sliding some of my egg onto the carpet so that Aristotle would cease whining for food. I was but an invitation away from new sights, countryside and the possibility of salty open air.

But then my father died, and everything changed.

Chapter 2

ꟾ

THE WILL

The death of my father, Jacob Miller, was as sudden as it was painful to our family. He had been sitting with us at breakfast one Friday morning, and was gone by the afternoon. We were told later of the unhappy circumstance of his demise, and even then it felt as though it had happened to someone else, and not the man I admired and respected. While attending a luncheon with his business partners, he had simply dropped dead, face first into the main course. The doctor suggested he might have had a sensitivity to something in the food, which had our cook blanching at the thought that I might have inherited any similar reaction.

It is a peculiar thing to lose someone you love, for it is always more than just the person that dies. Their voice, their mannerisms, even the stories they had yet to tell all disappear, leaving a person-shaped hole in the world. Our house, previously a vibrant and happy place for our small family, turned into a hollow shell where the air was thick with nothing but grief.

My first wish was that we had had more time together, as though the past twenty years of my life had been an inadequate amount of time to truly know my father and appreciate everything he had accomplished. The sketches in my bedside drawer and his handwriting in his ledgers, our family portrait in his study, his clothes hanging in his wardrobe – all of these things made up the man he had been and yet none of them replaced the deep loss of him from our lives.

My second wish was that it had not affected my mother as greatly as it had, for when he died, it felt like a part of her had gone as well.

Heat settled over the city, summer's stifling blanket, enveloping the streets in sunshine and humidity. My father had been swiftly buried because of it, the funeral attended by very few. Only Mother and I, our staff, Mr Osborne and Mr Talver, my father's business partners.

Those first days after his wake my mother sat in her armchair and barely moved, as though if she waited long enough her husband might stroll through the door and take up his place beside her. We all felt the loss keenly in the household, but it was worst for her. She forbade anyone to sit with her, or to move his chair or adjust the cushions. More than once, I climbed out of the window onto the balcony of my room and read there until the heat became unbearable, but more often than not I stayed with her, perching in my usual window seat with a book. Even the sound of turning pages that she had complained about so profusely before seemed to no longer bother her, or perhaps it was that she was too numb to care.

Marcus, now the household steward without my father to attend to directly, had taken it upon himself to stand vigil and bring her food even when she left most of it untouched. He had met my father as an adolescent, and was deaf by some accident of birth. When I was only five or six – my curiosity outweighing my manners, as was so often the case with children – I had asked my father if he had ever heard Marcus speak. He could have called me impertinent and ignored the question, but that was not the way of Jacob Miller. Instead, he sat me down and told me of the young, ambitious man whose only desire was to see the world from the deck of a ship. Having been left a sizeable inheritance by his deceased parents, he had bought a vessel, swaggered into the first tavern he saw, and promised riches to any man who wished to join his crew. Marcus, discarded by his own parents and considered good for nothing except carrying barrels and wiping tables, had seized the opportunity to work for this brash but determined young sailor.

That first voyage had been tough on all of them, particularly a young man who had more money than sea legs and no idea how to run a ship, but through their joint naïvety and lack of knowledge of the sea, they formed a friendship. When my father, by some miracle, gained more and more contracts, he spent less time at sea himself, preferring to leave the voyages to those with more experience, and hired Marcus as his personal steward. In their time spent together, Marcus had only vocalised once, warning my father when a boom almost took his head off during a strong wind on that first voyage. He was either unable or unwilling to speak, but was perfectly capable of reading lips and signalling his responses.

Where others mistook his lack of speech as stupidity, my father, only a few years Marcus's senior, saw someone observant and intelligent, with the strength and value of ten men. They developed their own sort of language, using their hands, and my father taught it to me and my mother so that the steward never felt as though he could not communicate if he so wished. In a time when society looked down upon those who were not oralists, my father resolutely disagreed with this form of thinking, and Marcus became more than simply part of the household staff and more like the uncle I'd never had. Now nearing his middle age, he was a tall and imposing figure who could communicate more with a simple expression than most humans could with a dozen words. But without my father's constant company, even he seemed unmoored somehow.

Jacob Miller had been the axis upon which our house had spun. Now Marcus, my mother and I were all planets around a sun that had winked out. My mother's grief seemed to eclipse my own, for although I too needed time to come to terms with my loss, in her inability to carry out daily tasks and run the house I found myself more and more taking her place. Loss became a blade lodged in my chest, the pain ever present even as my body tried to heal around it, made doubly hurtful by the lack of my only surviving parent.

Despite knowing that he would never come back, I heard my father's footsteps in every creak of the floorboards, in the faint scent of tobacco that still clung to the furniture. I sensed him in every room he'd ever frequented, and it felt as though, if I just willed it hard enough, he might walk in the door with his briefcase in hand, telling us what a day he'd had at his offices. But of course that never came to pass, and the days bled into weeks and still my mother didn't move, and still my father was gone.

A letter had arrived from Ambletye Manor, Lady Blountford's place of residence, but her cheerful words and invitation went unanswered. I was unwilling and unable to put into words the change of events that had occurred since my original writing. Stacks of condolences, some addressed to my mother, others addressed to me personally, arrived and sat in a dresser drawer, unread. Silence fell over the house like a fog, punctured only by the sound of the doorbell occasionally ringing with well-wishers and friends bringing flowers and their sympathy. We turned them all away.

That was, until the executor of my father's will arrived.

I had the vague notion that it must be nearing the end of July. Mother was in her chair, her body angled away from me, her constant silence more unnerving than if she were screaming. I sat fanning myself at the window, too hot even to read, watching the ladies outside in their many layers of skirts sweating beneath their parasols. Men mopped their brows with limp handkerchiefs. The scent of rotting sewage wafted in through the small opening, but any breeze was better than none at all, even if it gave the house a stench of dustbins and full chamber pots. Edith, my mother's maid, was busy arranging vases of lilies around the room to counteract it, but it only reminded me of the funeral, making everything smell of death in all its forms.

I watched as a fat bluebottle flew at the window in heat-drunk stupidity, its repetitive *tap tap buzz* the only significant sound. Even Aristotle, who was sleeping in the solitary patch of shade in the corner, refrained from barking when the doorbell rang.

I spied the stranger on the stoop from where I sat, unfolding myself from the seat and wandering over to the doorway to listen in as Marcus answered the door. Aristotle rose to his feet and languidly followed me across the room, his nosiness getting the better of him.

'Good day! I am Mr Gallows of Gallows & Enwright Solicitors. I am the appointed executor of the late Mr Jacob Miller's will and I am here to meet with Mrs Miller, if she would be available to see me. I sent letters and left my card several times.' His voice was far too bright and cheery for such weather, and I peered through a crack in the hinges to see that Mr Gallows was a man with an unfortunate name and an even more unfortunate moustache. It crawled across his top lip like an emaciated caterpillar, twitching peculiarly when he spoke.

Marcus gestured something that I inferred to be a dismissal.

'But she must see me, man!' the solicitor protested. 'It is of the highest importance that I read her the will, lest she be left with nothing!'

'Mama,' I said quietly, turning to find her with her eyes closed, the gentle rise and fall of her chest indicating that she had fallen asleep. I touched her arm gently and repeated myself. 'Mama, a man has come to see you about Father's will.'

'Jacob? Is that you?' she said with a start, confusion and worry etched on her face. It broke my heart to see her like that, a forthright and intelligent woman reduced to an addled shell of her former self. It was as though my father had constituted half of her personality, and without him here she had forgotten what it was like to be alone, no longer able to counteract his playful humour with her severe but well-intended berating.

'No, Mama, it is Jenny. There is a man wishing to speak with you regarding Father's will,' I pressed, fanning her even as I pulled her up from the seat. Her hand felt small and frail in mine, forcing me to take it gingerly, wrapping it over the crook of my arm as I guided her across the room. 'We must make ourselves ready. I shall tell Marcus to see Mr Gallows to the parlour, yes?'

The steward came in, his face giving no indication as to whether he was surprised or alarmed to find my mother standing.

'Marcus, please show the gentleman to the parlour and ask Cook if she can arrange some refreshments. We will be with him as soon as we can,' I said.

With a brief glance at my mother, he nodded and turned on his heel, giving us free passage upstairs to our rooms.

I made haste to find Mother another dress, practically throwing it at Edith when she poked her head around the door of the bedroom.

'Make Mrs Miller presentable for our guest, Edith, while I change my clothes,' I ordered, finding myself slipping easily into the role of lady of the house after the recent weeks of mourning.

In my own room, I removed the summer dress I had been wearing and donned my mourning dress. Then I pinned my dark blonde hair up with an unadorned clasp and went to escort my mother downstairs, Aristotle leading the way.

In the few minutes we had been gone, the doorbell had rung once more, so that we were greeted by not only the solicitor, but also Father's business partner, Mr Henry Osborne, shortly followed by the sorry sight of Mr George Talver. Something cold writhed in my belly at the sight of the latter, even in the heat of the day.

'Katherine, I am so sorry once again for your loss,' Mr Osborne said, opening his broad arms to embrace my mother as we entered the room. 'Jacob is sorely missed in the office, I can tell you.'

Henry Osborne was a sizeable man with an appetite to back it up, as I had discovered whenever he came for dinner. As he was my godfather, we had attended almost every party and ball he and his wife had thrown, and Marie Osborne had never missed one of my mother's salons. They had three daughters of their own, some years my junior, all exact copies of their mother. Osborne had always been kindly towards me, and my father would sing his praises as a friend and colleague, but I occasionally had a sense of unnerve around him. As a child, I had once convinced his eldest daughter to steal biscuits from the kitchens with me. He had been furious, and although I had been but seven at the time, I could still recall the angry shine of his black eyes, his ruddy nose pockmarked and bulbous like a deformed strawberry above his yellowing moustache. Though it was superficial of me I had never quite forgotten that feeling of being perturbed.

He and George Talver, a much smaller, quieter man, who reminded me of a serpent with his slicked-back hair and flattish nose, had been my father's business partners for longer than I had been alive, and his closest friends. When Jacob Miller had chosen the lucrative business of trading, mostly in spices and foodstuffs, he had needed adequate funds to combine with his own in order to purchase more ships and pay for offices in the City. The two gentlemen before me now had been the solution. Both were from wealthy families, with a keen mind for business, and despite my dislike of Talver, something that only I appeared to have a sense for, they had made Miller, Osborne & Talver Merchanting Ltd into the trading name it was today.

'And you, Jennifer, how are you managing, my dear girl?' Osborne turned to me.

'I am well under the circumstances, sir,' I replied with a weak smile.

'The business just isn't the same without your father,' Mr Talver said in that strange, monotonous voice of his, and I hid my slight revulsion as he placed a wet kiss on my hand, cursing myself for leaving my gloves upstairs.

I knew I ought to have more tolerance for a man with whom my father had worked for two decades, but the recollection that he had made an offer for my hand had me recoiling.

I nodded curtly, turning my attention to the solicitor. 'Mr Gallows, I apologise for keeping you waiting. Had I known you were visiting, I would have ensured you a warmer welcome.' I gestured to the round table in the parlour and gave Marcus a meaningful look to indicate that the refreshments should be brought through. My mother said nothing, taking a seat at the table like a spectre.

'Not to worry, Miss Miller. I did send a letter in advance. Well, er, a few actually,' he said cheerfully, though his general disposition was of someone quite nervous, his moustache quivering as he spoke. 'I received no reply, and it could not wait another day, I'm afraid.'

'Horrible business,' Osborne interjected loudly, 'having to divvy up a man's belongings after his death.'

I glanced at Talver, who only nodded along, his grey eyes emotionless as ever.

'My apologies for my ignorance, good sirs, but I did not expect to find so many of us in attendance . . .' I left the sentence hanging with the unspoken question: *Why are you all here?*

'The last will and testament of Mr Jacob Miller involves both of his partners, I'm afraid, due to the nature of their business contract with each other. It appears that there are very specific clauses that relate to the shares of the partnership. We really have waited as long as possible for this.' Mr Gallows opened his bulging briefcase, sending paperwork scattering into the air. 'Where is it now? Oh yes, here we are,' he said, unfolding a document several pages long.

'Mama,' I whispered, grasping her hand under the table, 'can I get you something to drink?'

My mother said nothing, only blinking dazedly at me. I sensed the shift in Talver immediately, his feigned concern turning almost imperceptibly to understanding and delight. If my mother was not of sound mind, there would be no argument over the will, no contention here about the results. He looked like a competitive gambler who knew he had already won the game.

The solicitor began to read, his voice far louder than was necessary for the table.

'. . . and the house and internal possessions, the coach, horses and all of my homely belongings, as well as my savings shall be bequeathed to my wife, Mrs Katherine Miller, or, in the case of her absence or death, my daughter, Jennifer Miller. My shares in Miller, Osborne & Talver Merchanting Ltd shall be returned to the company and divided equally between my business partners, or their heirs in the event of—'

'What?' I asked incredulously, cutting the man off. My hold on my mother's hand tightened, and I realised she was gripping mine in return. Her face had drained of colour as the words began to sink in.

'Where would you like me to repeat from?'

'The last bit,' I said urgently, ignoring the serpentine smile on Talver's face and the unmistakable brightness in Osborne's eyes.

'Uh, ah, here. My shares in Miller, Osborne & Talver Merchanting Ltd shall be returned to the company and divided equally between my business partners, or their heirs in the event of their deaths.'

An icy chill slid down my spine despite the heat. Heavens above, we were going to be cut out of my father's business. His savings might be enough to allow us to continue living here for some time, but certainly not for ever. Without his steady ten thousand a year, I did not know what would happen to us, the servants, or my plans of adventure. I urged my mother to say something, anything that would not result in us being left destitute, but it seemed she had gone into an even deeper shock. She blinked rapidly, slowly digesting this new information.

Mr Gallows continued, oblivious to the fact that he had just turned our lives upside down. 'The only exception being if, at the time of my death, my only daughter, Jennifer, is married, and her husband is willing and able to replace me adequately. In the event of this, my shares will remain with my family.'

My heart sank. I thought of my father, only a few months

ago, speaking of finding me a husband. Was it because he had known all along that without one, my mother and I would lose our livelihood? Had he foreseen his death somehow? I felt the sting of tears and blinked them away quickly.

Mr Osborne took the opportunity to let his feelings on the matter be known. 'It is such a shame that Jenny never married, is it not, Mr Talver?'

'Indeed,' was all the small man replied, quirking an eyebrow at me. His gaze held mine for a little too long, and I fought the urge to squirm in my seat. I could almost sense the plan forming in the back of his mind. If he were to marry me now, he would have the largest share of the company.

'That is a great shame indeed,' Mr Gallows said, sounding a little impatient that he had been interrupted so many times. He cleared his throat to continue reading, but was cut off once again.

'She is engaged,' my mother said, croaking out the first real words she had spoken for days.

The room fell silent but for the sound of the clock on the mantel marking out the seconds that stretched around us. I tried to catch her eye, to get a sense of what she was thinking, but she stared levelly at the solicitor as though daring him to challenge her.

'I beg your pardon, Katherine, but this is the first I have heard of the matter,' Osborne protested once he had recovered from his surprise.

'I did not think to inform you, sirs, as until this moment I did not know it had any bearing upon your lives,' my mother said sharply. 'But that is the truth of it. She is due to be married in six months' time.'

My jaw almost fell open at that news, and I had to remind myself to close it. What was my mother saying? The lie had come so easily to her, and yet she refused to meet my stare, her fingers still firmly gripping my own the only acknowledgement that she knew what she was doing. I could usually sense when someone was being deceitful, had felt drenched in that very feeling the moment the solicitor had begun to read the will, in fact. These men wanted to take the business for themselves, and it would have been a foregone conclusion if it were not for my mother's lie. The realisation sent another wave of chill down my back.

'Six months! We cannot have the business abandoned for so long. It is already feeling your husband's loss,' Talver complained.

'Ah, that is quite true,' Mr Gallows said, seizing the opportunity to contribute to the conversation and fishing around in his briefcase for another set of papers. 'Here we are, the terms of partnership, which state that if the position of executive or partner is left abandoned due to death or sickness, the remaining partners are permitted to find a replacement after two months.'

'Two months! What if Jenny's fiancé is not able to accommodate your rules, gentlemen? Then you shall take my husband's life's work for yourselves, is that it?' It was as though my mother had been asleep these past weeks and suddenly awoken, such was the fire in her voice and words.

'Well, I'm afraid they do have the right, Mrs Miller, considering that your husband passed in May and it is now July . . .' Mr Gallows began, but quietened down at a glare from her.

'So that is the truth of it. I must forgo our wedding arrangements and force my daughter upon this poor man because you cannot grant us any leniency in your contracts and rules,' my mother replied coolly.

I felt a bubble of maniacal laughter rise up at her sudden

invention of a fiancé who was now being forced to take over my father's business, but quickly squashed it down.

'Well, as this is the first we are hearing of it, Katherine, I'm afraid we will have to insist that the young man begins his apprenticeship as soon as possible. If he cannot agree to the terms of our contract, then perhaps he would not be suitable to fill your late husband's shoes after all,' Osborne said, his concern genuine.

'Oh, he's suitable,' she replied with a confidence I couldn't match.

'We will allow you this week to make arrangements for the wedding, but would expect the young man to be in our offices on Monday so that we can test his mettle, as it were. High season has already begun, and it would be best to have your future son-in-law learning the ropes.'

I gave him a weak smile in response, not trusting myself to speak. I was doubtful that I could lie as artfully as my mother.

'It would be most improper to host a wedding when we are still in mourning,' my mother snapped, brushing a hand down her skirts as though to remind our company that she was still wearing black.

'Of course, it is a most unusual circumstance,' Mr Gallows said, trying to be helpful, 'but if the celebrations are kept to a minimum, it would not be out of the question for your daughter to come out of mourning a few weeks early.'

My mother harrumphed – actually harrumphed – at the poor man while she considered his words. She, a widow, would be expected to observe mourning customs for at least a year. As my father's only child, I was held to no such restrictions. Expectations were anywhere from a month to half a year – whatever length of time I saw fit. I was already wearing dark purple, and although I had not been out in public since the funeral, I had not intended to stay in mourning for much longer.

'Would you consider extending the two-month deadline?' I asked, finding my voice and trying to keep it steady.

Mr Gallows frowned at his papers before looking to the other two gentlemen for confirmation. 'I'm afraid that if we go by the contract, Miss Miller, you would have until the end of July. There are no clauses that permit an extension.'

My mother, who had no sense of what day it was, let alone what month, looked to me to clarify.

'That gives us less than a week, sir. Six days, in fact,' I pointed out, trying my level best not to sound alarmed. My mother blanched at that, and I worried that she might quickly relapse into her depression, knowing how impossible the task now was. Mr Gallows, Osborne and Talver all nodded at the same time.

She made a final effort to compel the gentlemen to feel some sort of remorse for the position they had put us in. 'Six days, you say? And you will not grant any leniency to the widow of the man who built the company with you? Well, my daughter will not even have time for a honeymoon.'

Honeymoon? Who could worry about a honeymoon when I did not even have a fiancé yet?

'I am sure that we can allow him leave once we are certain the company will be in capable hands,' Osborne said, as though he were doing us a favour, 'and if the expenses to move the wedding are so great that you cannot afford them, I would be happy to assist.'

I flinched at the barb, but Mother remained composed, though the glint in her eye towards my godfather was murderous.

'You are most kind, but there will be no need for that,' she replied flatly.

'Please understand that we do this out of no malice,' Talver added, his lie dragging like sharp nails across my now clammy skin. 'We only have the best interests of the company at heart. It is not just your own livelihood at stake now that Jacob is gone, but our own as well.' I sensed that that, at least, was true.

'As you say, Mr Talver,' my mother replied, unimpressed. 'Now, gentlemen, I have much to do. Will that be all?' she continued, looking to Mr Gallows, who seemed all of a fluster at her sudden change of temperament.

'I-I believe that *is* all, Mrs Miller, yes. I shall return next week to oversee the bequeathal of your husband's shares to his successor, but otherwise I simply require your signatures.'

Moments later, the paperwork was signed and my mother rose from her seat, sending all of the gentlemen to their feet.

'Well, now that I have six days rather than six months to arrange a wedding, I will have to take my leave of you.' Katherine Miller had a way of speaking that could either make people feel like the most important in the room, or the least significant thing she had laid eyes upon. In this case, her tone indicated, it was certainly the latter.

Mr Osborne turned to us in the entrance hall even as the door stood open, letting in the afternoon heat. 'Does this young man have a name? I should like to ensure that my dear goddaughter is marrying into the right family.'

'William,' my mother replied without hesitation.

'Ah, I see,' he said, slightly disappointed that he had not caught her off guard. 'And does William have a surname?'

'None that concerns you, Henry. Good day, gentlemen,' she said dismissively, nodding to Marcus, who ushered them out.

As he closed the door behind them, I exhaled, almost collapsing on the floor with relief that they had gone.

'Jenny, this is no time to loll about. We have work to do.'

'Work?' I replied, looking up at the woman who had

managed to lie flawlessly for the past half an hour. Despite her black dress and pallid complexion, she stood ramrod straight, her blue eyes, so much like mine, alight with an energy I hadn't seen from her in weeks. Her face still held soft lines of grief, but there was fierce determination and purpose there too. I had to admit it both frightened and awed me a little.

'Yes, work, girl,' she said, taking me by the arm and pulling me towards the parlour. 'We must find you a husband.'

Chapter 3

ഇ൫

SEEKING A GENTLEMAN

It was as though the past several weeks had not happened, and my mother had not spent every waking hour sitting in an armchair, so grief-stricken that she was unable even to cry.

Barely hours after our visitors had left, she was almost back to her usual vibrant self, tearing about the house giving orders, writing letters to arrange meetings, and, most significantly, eating.

'I have written to Mr Granville, Mrs Chambrey and the Ellisons, all of whom have sons of the right age for you. Hopefully they are not all already engaged or married. Just one of them will suffice,' she said between mouthfuls of bread. It seemed the necessity to find me someone to marry had suddenly given her a purpose. Even though I wished to take her by the shoulders and shake this silly idea out of her, I couldn't help but feel relieved that she was up and about. I did not wish to disabuse her of her plans, even if they were terrible.

'We shall have to see if they will come to us, for it would be most improper for me to leave the house whilst still in mourning. I may need to find someone to present you, in fact. Perhaps

Marcus could fill the role of guardian. You would have to do the talking, naturally, but for those families we are more acquainted with, I am certain they wouldn't mind.'

I was beginning to recover from the shock of it all, but instead of rallying to the cause, I could only feel an all-consuming dread at the story she had conjured.

'Mama, I cannot possibly marry someone within the week. I have barely been seen in public this past year and a half, and I am certainly in no state to start socialising now.' Not to mention that I was terrified of the idea, though I kept that to myself.

She waggled her fingers at me as though dispelling my complaints.

'Do not fret, my girl. There is no great science to being out and attending balls, and socialising is much like riding a horse. One is absent from it for a few months or a few years but can easily get straight back on and remember it all as though it were yesterday.'

'I cannot ride a horse,' I said exasperatedly.

'Well, you understand my meaning. There is nothing to it really. Putting on dresses, saying things that people wish to hear, flirting. You won't have to do it for long, after all. It will not be like before,' she added, looking away from me momentarily. She had caught me flinching at her use of the word 'flirting' and no doubt suspected what had crossed my mind.

Parties. Lord Darleston. The whispers and sneers, the laughter and derisive glances hidden behind a flutter of fans and gloved fingers. Heaven only knew how much I hated the idea of circumnavigating that landscape once more.

'And what if I don't like him, whoever he may be? William, was it?'

'Oh please, Jenny, do not be so naïve. Many a marriage has been built on less. I did not love your father when we first married. It took months for that to happen. Luckily he has . . .' she corrected herself calmly, 'he *had* a sense of humour and a tolerance for being told what to do.'

'And that is how my life shall be? Married to a stranger in the hope that one day we might love each other? What if he turns out to be an awful person?'

'Have a little faith, my girl. It is our livelihood at stake here.' When she saw my eyes widen with hurt, she softened her tone, reaching out to squeeze my hand before letting it go. 'I will not let anything bad happen to you, Jenny. I promise. But I do need you to at least *try* to cooperate.'

I slumped in my chair, somewhat crestfallen. Not so long ago, as the daughter of a rich merchant, I had thought I would have the luxury to travel the world. Make a name for myself beyond simply becoming some young gentleman's accessory. That was what all the heroines in my books had done. Aristotle, who had made himself scarce during the meeting but had now hopped onto my lap in sympathy, gave a whine. I stroked his silky head and fussed with his droopy ears, making his tail swish appreciatively against the armrest.

'And what do we do when we find someone who isn't called William?'

'Oh, that is simple enough. We shall pretend it is his middle name or some such thing and no one will be any the wiser,' Mama said with a wave of her hand, sending crumbs flying. Aristotle leapt from my lap to salvage them, so I knitted my hands together on the table and watched her. The colour was back in her cheeks. Her eyes were bright and purposeful. How could I refuse her this? Adventure would have to wait, at least until I came up with an alternative plan.

'Now, is it the Earl of Morberry who has a boy about your age?'

'Frank is fourteen, Mama!'

'Oh, well that is too young, I suppose. I must write to the archbishop immediately and seek an audience with him,' she continued, pulling out a fresh piece of paper and setting down her bread roll so that she could pen another letter.

'You know the Archbishop of Canterbury?'

'Not personally, but we will need him for a special licence if you are to be married before the week is out.'

The expense did not bear thinking about. How she would navigate the fact that we did not yet know my husband's name did not seem to concern her. I rested my chin on my hands and contemplated our predicament. Stunned as I was at my mother's transformation, I could not see how her scheme would work.

'I cannot truly believe you are going ahead with this, Mama. How on earth are we going to find someone willing to marry at such short notice who is also suitable to take on Father's business and not leave us in a worse state than we were when we began?' I was trying to be the voice of reason, but I could see that my mother was not even half as concerned as I was.

'Stranger things have happened, Jenny. Romeo fell in love with Juliet in just four days.'

'Yes, and look what happened to them!' I shook my head. 'What of my travels? I have not replied to Lady Blountford's invitation to visit. She will think me rude and peculiar if I don't go now.'

'Nonsense. You must write back to her and explain our change of circumstances. She will be understanding. Invite her here the next time she is in town if you wish.'

Frustration and something akin to fear built up in my gut as I argued with her and had every reasonable excuse immediately rejected. I did not see how I could possibly marry a stranger in less than a week. Of course, I had read stories of couples for whom love had come immediately. Love at first sight. I had thought myself one of those fortunate and rare folk when first I had met Nigel, in fact. But if the past almost three years since I came out were anything to go by, I knew that love was not such a simple thing. Why did my mother think she could work some miracle and find me a husband, something I had not been convinced I actually wanted, in six days? And what luckless fool would agree to such an arrangement?

Later, in my room, I would cry angry tears. I would punch Lord Buckface until my knuckles were raw and my shoulders ached from the exertion, furious that the men in our lives had so much power over us. And then there was the marital bed to think of.

I had been so naïve before Lord Darleston's party, with just the barest understanding of what went on between husband and wife. I had educated myself a little more since then, understood how children came about and so on. The thought of doing any of that with some stranger filled me with sick dread.

But for now, I kept my distress to myself and listened to my mother. She had an answer for all my complaints, unwavering in her resolve in the matter. Every attempt at reason was countered with the simple statement that if I didn't go through with it, we'd be living on the streets in a year or two. Oh, it would not be immediate, she explained. We might need to tighten our purse strings a little at first: employ fewer staff, simplify our meals, abstain from extravagant purchases. But within weeks we would need to seek smaller lodgings and perhaps rent out the house in order to provide us with an income. Before long, we would need to refrain from new clothes and – she exaggerated the point – *new books*. That, combined with her sudden vigour and purpose, had me keeping my feelings on the matter to myself. Tears threatened in the corners of my eyes and burned my throat, and I looked out of the window while my mother's pen scratched across paper as she wrote letter after letter.

What was worse? I wondered. Marrying a man who was a stranger to me, or being the person responsible for us losing everything that my father had worked to provide for us? And what would he have wanted? To that question I already knew the answer. Had overheard it, in fact, just a few short days before he died. He had wanted me to marry to protect not just his legacy, but myself and my mother as well. With painful realisation, I knew that I would be the last person to go against his wishes.

So it was that I found myself the next day attending appointment after appointment, dinner after tea after luncheon, at various aristocratic houses.

My mother had been discreet in her requests, knowing just how much information to reveal, or not, as the case might be, and had instructed me on what to say and do down to the very last demure smile. I was to gather information, determine whether the son was eligible and, more importantly, whether he would be able to convince Osborne and Talver that he was my fiancé without baulking. Marcus, who was chaperoning me, had his own orders, and as observing others in lieu of conversation came naturally to him, a simple nod or shake of the head on his part would be all I needed to confirm or deny my own thoughts.

I suppressed my nerves as we took the carriage on a merry route through the nicer parts of London. It had been so long since I had had to do any social performing that I had almost forgotten what it was like – the parts I loved as well as the parts I hated.

The dressing up, the soft touches of make-up, the silk gloves all had me feeling a little like a princess. But the prospect of conversations with men, and their parents, filled me with dread. One of these men, I thought as we pulled up outside the first house, in Belgravia, would be my husband. Once married, he would lay his hands on me. I would be owned by him. And if my previous experiences were anything to go by, those encounters might not be all that pleasant.

My fists bunched in my lap and I closed my eyes, gathering myself. A hand gently placed itself on my arm, and when I looked up, Marcus was smiling at me, his large, warm presence better than any tonic. *Breathe*, he gestured, taking in an exaggerated breath through his nose and blowing it out through his mouth. I copied him, breathing in for the count of three and out just as slowly. It did help, and before I could change my mind, I told him I was ready.

We both knew the plan. We would spend half an hour on niceties, leaving a trail of crumbs to see if the young man in question, or his parents, might bite. It would not do to make our case immediately – we didn't want word getting back to Osborne and Talver that I was actively seeking a husband, after all. I was to smile and woo them to the best of my somewhat limited abilities. As soon as it became obvious that we had not found what we were looking for, Marcus would signal to me, I would make some excuse, and we'd go on to the next appointment.

Much to my relief, the first young man was already engaged; the second had just joined the Royal Navy and would be away for a year. The third had been married this past month, and the fourth, the son of the Ellisons, was so vulgar in his manner that Marcus repeatedly shook his head at me when they weren't looking. Thankfully we were forgiven for some of our more abrupt exits by my pretending that I suffered from headaches after my father's passing. It was a lie of sorts, but our hosts would usher us out as soon as I mentioned it, for which I was grateful.

Each encounter became a little easier. The knot in my stomach loosened, and Marcus's reassuring presence reminded me that nothing bad could happen to me while he was there.

By the third day of pandering to the wealthy parents of young men, I concluded that there were no eligible bachelors left in London. At the end of each day I would give a full account of the meetings, and my mother, I found, agreed with my sentiments.

On the morning of the fourth day, we began to despair.

'Who are we scheduled to visit today, Mama?' I asked politely as I sipped my tea. My mother's appetite had almost completely recovered, I was glad to see, but I refrained from touching food until absolutely necessary, given how many occasions I had had to eat in recent days. I was relieved to see colour in her cheeks as she too poured herself tea.

'I could only secure us two appointments at such short notice, I'm afraid. The first is with Lord Everington,' she replied, glancing at her agenda.

'I didn't realise he had sons,' I said with a frown. She hesitated for only a moment as she stirred a spoonful of sugar into her cup.

'He doesn't. He's recently widowed, in fact.' Although her tone was light, I sensed her daring me to challenge her. I contained a splutter of surprise as my tea almost went down the wrong way.

'Isn't he fifty? Mama, really—'

'It's not ideal, I'll grant you that.' She set her cup down so that it clinked firmly in its saucer, and sighed. 'But he is a good man, and was a loving husband to his late wife. Someone a little older, with more experience, might work in our favour. Being titled he may not have any interest in the business itself, but I am sure the extra income could tempt him.'

I said nothing, swallowing my shock and instead seeing the war that my mother seemed to be fighting with herself on the matter. I waited for her to speak, and eventually she did. 'To be honest, I blame myself entirely for having to put you through this ordeal. If only I'd had more children – a son – perhaps you could have been spared all of this.'

I couldn't argue with that, though I would never agree to place the blame on her shoulders. If I had just found an appropriate suitor a few years ago, we'd not even be having this conversation.

'I wanted more children, you know,' she continued, her gaze turning wistfully towards the place where my father used to sit. 'I lost two before you were born – my miracle child, I called you – and then one more afterwards.'

I sucked in a short breath at the revelation. Now that I thought of it, there had been a time when I was small when my mother had been very ill, but I had not connected it to any particular condition.

'I had no idea, Mama,' I murmured. It was so easy to forget that my mother was a person in her own right. A wife, an excellent mistress of the house, and a loving but firm parent were all roles she had undertaken, but beneath them she was a woman, and I had never known of the pain she suffered. To think I might have grown up without her, gone with one of her children, and that she had dedicated her life to raising me, was humbling. I felt an echo of fear that I could have lost her and wouldn't have understood why or how.

'The doctor said we should stop trying to have another child and content ourselves with raising you. And I have never, ever taken you for granted, Jenny. Not one day has gone by when I did not thank God that he blessed me with you.'

The grief she had been hiding so well these few days was

beginning to creep into her features once more, and my heart ached for her. It edged into the lines around her eyes and threatened to steal her words away. I stood up and moved to her side of the table, placing my arms around her shoulders from behind and pressing a light kiss to her cheek.

Even through the hurt of learning this news, fury simmered beneath my skin, and I tried to smother it quickly as I gave her shoulders a gentle squeeze. Anger at the situation, at Osborne and Talver for putting us through this, even at my father for agreeing to such a nonsensical contract with his business partners. I felt a quiet rage that my own coming out had been marred by the poor excuses for men that I had encountered. Was it my fault, or my mother's, for us being in this predicament? Hardly. But as usual, we women bore the burden of solving the unsolvable, and I wouldn't let us fall into destitution because of it.

'We'll solve this, Mama. I promise.'

Even if I had to marry a man thirty years my senior, or someone I'd never met.

Lord Everington was pleasant enough. He had a great white moustache that I struggled to avert my gaze from, imagining it tickling and scratching my skin. But when I tactfully broached the subject of remarrying, he paled considerably, spluttering something about how there had only been one woman for him, and though his late wife had borne him no sons, his title and money would go to his nephew.

The meeting left me feeling deflated and yet grateful that those scratchy whiskers on his upper lip would not be a part of my immediate future.

At least he had been honest.

My skill at detecting lies had come into its own these past few days, but I was growing weary with the constant social untruths and feigned friendship offered by these people we were visiting. I had never told my parents of my ability, nor did I know from where it had manifested. There had never been an appropriate moment to confide in them about it, and now my father would never know.

'I have an idea, Jenny, but I will have to ask you to trust me implicitly,' my mother said after Marcus and I arrived home, subdued after yet another failed liaison. The day's second appointment had been with Master Hebworth, the son of a physician, who spent the entire tea talking of his experiments in preserving rodents and their young in formaldehyde, and how this could further the interests of science and the study of diseases. Feeling slightly green around the gills by the end of it, I was inclined to agree with anything my mother might ask simply to avoid yet another ordeal such as that one.

'I do trust you, Mama, of course,' I said, beginning to fan myself in an attempt to dispel my lingering queasiness from the afternoon, 'but you make it sound as though we are going to embark on something . . . unconventional.'

'Indeed,' my mother said, gesturing for me to join her in the parlour, where she had laid out a map of the area surrounding my father's offices. There were the docks, where our fortune had been made, and the busy City square mile that my father had often walked through and met with associates. My eyes quickly darted away when they fell upon the address of the chop shop where he had died, an ache like pressing on an old wound flaring in my chest.

My mother picked up her own fan as she assessed the map. The heat had not let up, and it had taken all my willpower not to strip off as soon as I had arrived home.

'Well, are you going to at least give me some indication of what we are to do?'

She looked from the map to the window, her eye caught by a passing carriage as it jostled over the cobblestones, the parlour loaded with a suddenly fraught silence. I imagined she was searching for the best way to communicate her idea without startling me. Her lips were pursed, as though she didn't like what she was about to say.

'It occurs to me that we require a merchant to ensure that your father's business is maintained in our best interests. We could pick any man off the street who wished to marry into money, but,' she added quickly when I began to open my mouth, 'that would not help us in the grander scheme of things. And yet I am beginning to believe that in seeking out wealthy young men, I have been going about this all wrong.

'It occurred to me after you recounted your conversation with Master Hebworth,' she continued, 'that we have yet to speak to a single man who has any experience in your father's field of expertise.' She trailed off, momentarily lost in thought, before seeming to make up her mind about something. 'No, at this point we no longer care if he is wealthy and eligible, or handsome and charming. Our priority should be to find a gentleman with sound business sense and an alacrity for doing as we wish.'

'You want us to find someone ugly who can lie for us?' I replied dubiously.

'His looks have nothing to do with it,' she waved her fan at me, 'but yes, a man with a malleable temperament, who can think on his feet and knows his way around ships and commerce, would be preferable.'

Perhaps I should have stopped her there and then. If we were not narrowing our selection down to the gentry, how on earth were we to find the right sort of man amongst the thousands who resided in London? I bit my lip as I pondered how best to pose this question. Perhaps she had some plan? She had become quite the force to be reckoned with on the subject, and having seen her, in her darkest moments, become a lifeless shell of her former self, I had neither the desire nor the gall to contradict her. But this was my future. My life. My happiness. My thoughts of travelling, of seeing the world, felt so far away from me now, as though the person who had conjured those dreams was another Jenny, from another time. In some ways, I supposed she was.

'We shall have to exercise extreme caution, of course,' she said thoughtfully, as though reading the unanswered questions in my mind. 'After all, Jenny, you are far more important than any business or livelihood. If we find a suitable gentleman with knowledge enough to take your father's place in the business, he can become your husband in name and nothing else, unless you yourself desire it.'

I released a breath and nodded, feeling a little appeased. When we had been visiting society's finest families, I had been looking as much at the parents as at the men themselves. Were they happy? Had the young man in question been brought up by good people? Did I sense deceit or lies in any of them? Most of them had been pleasant enough, but families like that had only one thing in mind – heirs for their fortune, grandchildren, the importance of their lineage. And I knew how those things came about. But to have a husband in name only, who might otherwise leave me alone, content with his portion of money and less interested in me as an actual wife, would suit me very well indeed. I was not averse to falling in love, but under the circumstances, it was quite unlikely. I gave my mother a smile. 'Very well, Mama. What would you have us do?'

'Ah, the idea is still half formed in my mind at present,' she replied, a finger tapping the map absent-mindedly. 'But when I have it complete, I will lay it all out for you. I am too warm to think now.' And with that, she closed her eyes and spent the rest of the afternoon in silence, busy plotting a very different outcome for me than the one I had envisaged.

On Friday, three days before we were to deposit my so-called husband at the offices of Miller, Osborne & Talver Merchanting Ltd, I found myself travelling to the docks. My mother, resigned to taking matters into her own hands, had changed out of her mourning dress and was to accompany me on this occasion, though the need for discretion was at its greatest because of it.

'When you said we were looking for a merchant, Mama, this was not quite what I had in mind,' I said, hastening to keep up with her brisk pace. We had dressed in the plainest clothes we could find so as not to draw attention, and Marcus, at my mother's behest, walked three paces behind us at all times. She had chosen a plain dress in green that was still likely more expensive than an entire dockworker's wardrobe, but I hoped that our lack of silk and satin might allow us to be overlooked by most. She had kept her face away from the carriage windows in the hope that no one we knew would see her out of doors, and both of us had donned bonnets in the style of common women before we had stepped down. It was a little like going out in disguise, and I didn't entirely hate it.

'I have thought about it long and hard all week, Jenny,' she called over her shoulder as we weaved through the crowd, 'and this is the best place to find someone who might be experienced enough to do your father's business proud.'

The docks were a crossroads of civilisation, swarming with gentleman merchants and ship's captains, labourers, loaders, deckhands and sailors, all of them slick with sweat and many of them smelling as though they had not seen clean water in a very long time. As we rounded the corner and took in the lines of vessels moored at the riverbank, I couldn't help but be impressed at the sight. Some were as tall as buildings, some as small as carriages, each with its weathered canvas sails and vibrant standards in red and green, gold and blue snapping in the faint breeze. Gulls swooped down to perch on abandoned crates, eyeing the day's imports hungrily, while the calls of workers and sailors mingled with their cries to create a cacophonous din.

I paused as I took it in; the madness and magnificence of it all. Adventure, my silent companion that had been buried since my father's death, pulled at me like a rope. How many people began their journeys here in this very place?

A nudge at my elbow signified that Marcus had caught up with me, prompting me to find my mother, who had already located someone to accost.

'Merchants, you say? Well, they usually gather at the Hand and Anchor over on Ship Street, madam.' A gentleman dressed in a worn pea coat and britches pointed her in an easterly direction.

We had barely reached her when she was off again, and I was forced to scurry behind once more.

The Hand and Anchor was, as the name perhaps suggested, a tavern for sailors, merchants and all those who wished to do business with them. The Tudor-styled public house stood on a corner across the road from the riverside, a sign in the window suggesting that not only did they serve the best ale, and that there were rooms available above for anyone desirous of them, but that one was required to wear a shirt *and* shoes, should one wish to be served. Who, I mused as we stepped through the low door and into the smoky darkness inside, would wander around without a shirt or shoes on? Evidently more than one person, if the landlord had deemed it necessary to add it to his sign.

Pipe smoke and the scent of old ale filled my nose, as my eyes adjusted to the dim interior. Every public house I had ever been to, although that was not very many by ordinary standards, had that same smell of musty furniture, aged wood and tobacco mixed with alcohol, so thick you could almost bottle it and sell it as a cologne to lower-class gentlemen.

A brief silence settled over the establishment as we walked in, the patrons glancing over at us to take our measure. Women weren't common in public houses unless they were working, and despite dressing down, I doubted we looked like mussel-sellers or flower girls. Determining that we were no threat and less interesting than their drinks and current companions, the clientele resumed their conversations and I allowed myself to breathe again.

I was surprised to find that my mother did not turn around and leave as soon as she set eyes on the place, as I had expected her to, but instructed me to find a seat somewhere while she went to the bar to reconnoitre. Marcus hesitated only for a moment, but I waved him towards her, believing, perhaps foolishly, that she required more protection than I. For a moment I wished we had brought Aristotle with us, but he was very much a house dog and would have likely been more alarmed than I at these new surroundings.

I lost sight of them in the bustle almost immediately and instead contented myself with eavesdropping on the conversations around me as I settled onto the hard bench, worn smooth with use and indented slightly with the shape of the buttocks of patrons past.

There were gentlemen of all shapes and sizes, colours and accents, and a smattering of women too, although they were in the minority. Most of the ladies looked as though they were working, either as barmaids or prostitutes, and I averted my eyes from them. I knew of such things, of course. I read books, and books told you everything you needed to know about the world. Experiencing those things was another matter.

The tables nearest me were the easiest to listen in on, and I singled out threads of conversation as I breathed in the smoky air and waited for my mother and Marcus to return.

'. . . and they told me I would get ten pounds for a successful voyage, yet I've not seen a single coin since I returned. Been sailing for a year and barely a penny has crossed my hand . . .'

'You've never seen the sun set until you've been to the West Indies, I tell you . . .'

'You should have seen the women over there, John, breasts the size of . . .' I quickly fixed my hearing on another conversation, stifling my blush.

'. . . a dozen slaves. That's right. Supposed to be ferrying sugar and coffee, wasn't he.' I glanced out of the corner of my eye at the speaker – a rough-looking man who looked like a dockworker from his bulging arms and clothing.

'What did he do with them?' another gentleman asked, younger and brighter-eyed than the first, taking a swig from his pitcher.

'Apparently they all died – each and every one of 'em. Thousands of pounds' worth of workers gone, just like that.' The first man clicked his fingers to demonstrate the point. 'He claimed the crew had the pox, which put off the inspectors and the navy. But I heard they might've been let off somewhere on the Continent instead.'

The drinker's companion scoffed at the notion. 'Fairytales and fables, is that.'

The conversation piqued my interest. Slavery had been abolished just in the last few years, and yet that did not stop those in that devil's trade treating humans as though they were things and not people. My father had held strong views against the practice, and I wondered what he would have made of the story.

I imagined, for a moment, what such a mysterious captain might look like. Closing my eyes, I pictured myself in a jacket of deep green with gold brocade trim, soft leather trousers and knee-high boots, a cutlass threaded through my belt and a tricorn set atop my head, smuggling workers into the hold of my ship under the cover of night. It was a ridiculous fantasy, of course. Sailors didn't seem to dress nearly as well as my imagination had me think, and I knew of no captains who were women, but I felt a little thrill at the idea of it while I listened to the strangers discuss the merits and shortfalls of such an enterprise as freeing slaves.

'Captain Hodgson, they call him, although I don't believe it to be his real name . . .'

The scrape of the bench opposite me pierced my fantasy, and my eyes shot open to find a bullish man leering at me, his tankard nearly spilling over onto the table as he staggered. What teeth he had left were yellowed and worn, his sour breath enveloping me as he leaned forward.

'I'm afraid these seats are taken,' I said firmly over the din.

If he was disappointed, he didn't show it, merely hooked the bench with his foot and pulled it out further.

'Excuse me, but I said these seats are taken,' I repeated, not bothering to hide my affront that he was obviously ignoring me.

He slapped his drink down on the uneven surface of the table, sending beer sloshing across the wood, and made to sit down, hitching up his trousers somewhat theatrically. I balled my fingers, wondering how his flabby jowl would feel as my fist connected with it. Having only hit Lord Buckface, his floury insides nothing compared to the flesh and bone of a real man, I knew I was no trained combatant – I'd just as likely end up making a fool of myself if I lashed out. I narrowed my eyes as he gave me a garish smile that had no mirth in it.

'Sir, I beg your pardon, but if you sit down, I will have to remove you!' I stood up, ready to fling his drink from the table if nothing else.

'And I beg *your* pardon, miss, but I don't see how you could,' he growled, not taking his eyes off me, daring me to make good on my threat.

I found my mouth opening in protest even as his descent was stopped abruptly by something slapping across the bench. A hard cane of black polished wood blocked the seat, and he was forced to stand upright, eyes widening in surprise as he came face to face with a man. Well, he would have come face to face if the man had not towered over him, so that he was more face to chest.

'What do you think you're doing?' my tormentor exclaimed angrily.

The newcomer, withdrawing his cane from the bench, looked down his aquiline nose. Black hair fell in waves around his tanned face, cut level with his sharp chin, while his eyes were so dark they looked black and pupil-less in the dim light of the tavern.

'I believe the lady said that those seats were taken,' he replied simply, his voice deep and slightly accented so that I could not place its origin.

'I don't think that's for she or you to decide! 'Tis a free tavern and no one gets to tell me where I can or cannot sit,' the leering man spat.

I watched the two of them size each other up, wondering who would win if they came to blows. What the tall, dark stranger had in height, the shorter man had in girth. There would be fists and elbows involved, but also sheer muscle and brute strength. Even as shock and fear smothered all other senses, I was acutely aware of how interesting things were about to get.

'I believe it is exclusively for the young lady to decide with whom she shares her table,' the tall man replied, tapping his cane once on the straw-strewn floor for emphasis. I heard the snick of a blade. Some dull part of my brain registered the danger, but I reacted too slowly, failing to force the words of warning out of my mouth. However, the weapon did not belong to the shorter fellow as I had assumed. It was in fact protruding from the end of the tall man's cane. In one deft motion he had flipped it around and it was now pressed just under his opponent's chin.

'All right, all right!' the bullish man exclaimed, trying to pull back but finding that he was pinned in place by the strength of the other man's hand on his arm.

'I think you owe the lady an apology, don't you?' The stranger said it so quietly I was sure only the three of us could hear him.

'That won't be necessary. I would rather prefer to be left alone, thank you,' I rushed to say.

But to my surprise, the shorter man looked at me apologetically and said, 'S-sorry, miss. I meant nothing of it.'

The other man finally glanced at me, dark eyes catching my own, and I felt a blush rise to my cheeks. He quirked an eyebrow, as though to determine if the apology was satisfactory, and I nodded in reply, finally permitting him to let the ruffian go. As he staggered away, his drink forgotten, I noticed the swell of noise. It was as though the Hand and Anchor had been holding a collective breath and now exhaled, the babble of voices filling the air and patrons carrying on as if nothing had happened.

'Are you all right, miss?' The question was spoken softly, without a hint of the animosity it had carried before. Gentle, like the caress of a feather, even as I caught the click of the knife retracting into his cane.

'I am well, thank you, sir,' I replied, allowing myself to take in the gentleman's full features. He had a striking face. Thick eyebrows over those dark, shining eyes, a strong jaw softened by the length and cut of his hair. Although he looked down upon me as well, it felt more chivalrous somehow now that there was no immediate threat.

'Are you without a chaperone?'

'No, sir, I have company.' I nodded in the direction of the bar, invisible behind the sea of bodies, but the meaning was obvious, as he seemed satisfied. With a short bow, he turned to leave, and for some reason the question burst forth from me before I could stop it. 'May I know the name of my saviour?'

He smiled, a flash of teeth that reminded me somewhat of a wolf, so brief and almost savage was the gesture.

'Erasmus, miss,' he replied, and with that he disappeared into the crowd, the tap of his cane drowned out within moments.

'Erasmus who?' I murmured to myself, sitting back down. Erasmus who, indeed.

Chapter 4

A CURIOUS DINNER PARTY

The entire exchange between the gentlemen at my table could have lasted no more than a minute or two, but when my mother joined me, I felt as though she'd been gone an hour. Márcus carried mugs of what was probably ale, but none of us touched them as I told her what had occurred, speaking as quietly as possible while still being heard over the din.

'How terribly exciting,' my mother said, wide-eyed, when I described the stranger. 'Do you happen to know if he was a merchant? A bachelor?'

'Mama, we barely shared more than ten words between us! I'm sorry that my first thought wasn't to ask if he'd like to marry me and take over my father's business.' I rolled my eyes even as she scoffed and tutted, muttering something about my attitude and how our plan would fall apart if I failed to take advantage of every opportunity.

'Well, while you have been getting yourself in trouble, my girl, I have been arranging a meeting, of sorts. We shall be dining with the most eligible merchants this very evening in a private room of the tavern. If all goes to plan, we will have a husband for you before the day is through.'

I should not have been surprised at my mother's single-mindedness, nor that she had managed to orchestrate such a thing in only a short space of time. She was like a hurricane when she had her heart set upon something, and it did no good to argue with her, lest you be caught in the force of it and swept away. If dinner with a group of men was what I must endure to save us, so be it.

'What on earth did you tell them? Oh, my daughter needs a husband post haste and I need a list of your unmarried qualified merchants and sailors?' I mimicked, causing her to frown.

'I am not so incautious as you might think, Jenny. I merely said that my husband had recently passed, then mentioned the company's name and that I had a business proposal.' She sniffed a little haughtily. 'I may also have told the landlord only to mention the meeting to young, unmarried captains and merchants,' she added, pulling off her gloves slowly, not meeting my stare.

'Oh, good grief!' I slapped a hand down on the sticky table and immediately regretted it. Marcus passed me a handkerchief to wipe my fingers with as I ranted, 'Honestly, we might as well have advertised in the papers. If word gets back to Osborne and Talver, we'll be done for.'

'I have paid for his silence very generously, girl. They all know what will happen to them should they be indiscreet.' She looked pointedly at Marcus, who merely nodded.

Glumly, and somewhat resignedly, I acquiesced. There was little use arguing with her. All that was left to do was wait.

My mother and I retired to a private room, and she sent Marcus to fetch a small case of accessories from our carriage. Our dresses, plain as they were, were still expensively made, and required only a few touches to better their appearance. A pearl necklace and earrings for her, an onyx charm on a gold chain for myself. She arranged my hair with a clasp decorated with black beads and real opals, pinning it back from my face so that the length of it fell down my back over a silk shawl. It was remarkable what one could achieve with just the slightest of changes, making the transition between the middling and wealthier class, and from day to night-time attire almost effortless.

By six, the dining room above the tavern was ready, and I sat, feeling a little like a rare animal on display, as men were shown in one by one. Marcus gave each an appraising nod, communicating his initial impressions with a flicker of his eyes. For someone who spoke so little, he had a way of saying a great deal. A quick frown here, a surprised raise of the eyebrows there, and even a grimace as one man entered, the stench of alcohol so thick on him that he was quickly shown the way out.

The circular table had been set according to my mother's instructions, overseen by Marcus, even if it was no fine dining experience. A white tablecloth had been found from somewhere and seven places had been laid; five for our guests, with myself and Mama placed strategically between them.

With the inebriated gentleman gone, there were only four contenders, which was hardly surprising considering the haste with which the party had been assembled. As I looked around the room, I noticed that they were very different from one another, and wildly varying in age despite my mother's instructions to the innkeeper. I was positioned between two such contrasting men. On my left, Philip Squire, a twenty-year-old blond-haired, blue-eyed boy who from the age of thirteen had steadily worked his way through the ranks of his ship to first mate. On my right, a forty-year-old who had recently lost his merchant business when his entire fleet had sunk. I tried to give each of them equal attention.

My mother sat on the opposite side of the table, questioning the two men flanking her with equal vigour and sending me confusing eye and hand signals when she thought they weren't looking.

'Jenny! Mr Botham here has four ships of his own,' she called across. Mr Botham was also twice my age and looked as though he regularly frequented the bottom of a wine bottle, if his permanently reddened nose was anything to go by.

'Fascinating,' I replied non-committally.

'And Mr Arthur's father is a merchant also. Isn't it peculiar that we have never met?'

'Most peculiar, Mama,' I said.

Mr Arthur was a pretty man in his twenties, but from the way he was eyeing Philip Squire, I had the distinct impression that he found the young blond more interesting than me. Whether anyone else at the table noticed, or they were simply ignoring it, I could not say, but it soon became quite clear that neither man was husband material, what with the small smiles they shared and the way Mr Arthur flushed a little when my mother asked him why he had not yet found himself a wife.

So that left the forty-year-old Oliver Crispin to my right and the unfortunate Mr Botham beside my mother. I sighed inwardly and wondered which of the two would be the lesser evil: the one down on his luck who had just lost his fleet, or the one who would probably be happy to marry me in exchange for a bottle of single malt.

As the latter engaged the party in tales of his journey to the Americas, there was a commotion outside that I could only just hear over the clink of glasses and cutlery. Footsteps thundered overhead, doors slammed, and shouts came from a few rooms away. Marcus sensed it at the same time as I did, and was about to step outside and investigate when the door burst inwards.

What did I expect to see? Someone flustered and panting from having just given chase, or possibly even a special constable looking for his quarry?

What I did *not* expect was to find the tall, dark stranger from earlier entering the room with a thud of his cane, adjusting his blood-red cravat, his hair tied back elegantly from his face. He did not appear to have been running, or shouting, or any of the things that had been happening outside the room, and yet from the way he glanced behind him, I could not shake the impression that he might have had something to do with the ruckus.

He cast his eyes about the party until they found mine, inky black irises meeting sky blue, before setting his sights upon my mother, sensing the lie of the land and who was truly in charge here. He gave a brief bow, and her eyes lit up brighter than a bonfire at the sight of him.

'My apologies, ladies and gentlemen, for my tardiness,' he said in that deep, resonant voice of his. 'I received the invitation only this past quarter of an hour and felt that I must change for the occasion.'

Mother immediately lost interest in the two men who flanked her, motioning for him to sit down.

'Not at all, sir, not at all. It is kind of you to attend at such late notice, Mr . . .?'

'Erasmus, madam, Erasmus Black.'

The name rang in the air, vibrating like a tuning fork when it has just been struck. *Erasmus Black*. There was something intense about the single-syllable surname, and it suited him. I wondered why he had not given it to me earlier, unless he had something to hide.

'How do you do, Mr Black. I am Mrs Katherine Miller, and this is my daughter, *Miss* Jennifer Miller.' I ignored the excessive emphasis, wondering if it would be more discreet for her to simply paint a sign with the words *Looking For a Husband* and hang it around my neck. 'We are most grateful for your presence at this late hour,' she continued, waving at Marcus to fetch the wine, while I restrained my eyes from rolling.

As we had only just begun to eat, a plate was quickly brought for the newcomer, and despite Mr Botham's attempts to steer interest back to his last voyage, all Mother's questions seemed very specifically aimed at my saviour from earlier.

What did he do? she asked. He was a shipowner, his vessel in dry dock for repairs, and after three consecutive voyages, he intended to stay in London for a while to re-establish connections here. He had, in fact, been looking to take on contracts from some of the well-known merchants in the area.

Did his family have a maritime background? Indeed, his father had been in the Royal Navy but was killed in action, while his younger brother was still an officer, currently in Plymouth awaiting orders. And his mother? Died in childbirth when his younger brother was born.

Was his family wealthy? At this I shot her a look that would have withered anyone of a weaker constitution. But Mr Black answered without hesitation. Yes, modestly so, with a ship to his name and a little property.

Had he a wife? Someone he was promised to? Indeed, no. Regrettably, life at sea had not found him fortune in love or marriage.

What was his interest in the merchant trade? After this question, which might have been the tenth or twentieth, I would have kicked Mother under the table if I could have reached. But if Mr Black was perplexed by it, he showed no emotion, only replying that he had some experience in dealing with merchants and reiterating his hope to acquire a new contract while in town.

Mr Botham managed to interject something about the lucrative nature of being a merchant, drawing Mother's attention away from Mr Black for long enough that I could have a conversation of my own with him.

I had been studying him while he suffered the inquisition, and had noted how he was never flustered by a question, nor used more words than necessary to provide a satisfactory reply. It was difficult to age him; with his impeccable clothing and tanned, weather-worn face, he could have been anywhere from five-and-twenty to five-and-thirty years, but I assumed it was somewhere between the two. Yet whenever I had caught his eye, which was infrequently, as he had given my mother almost all his attention, the glimmer there suggested someone younger and perhaps more roguish than I was allowing myself to believe.

'I am surprised to see you again so soon, sir,' I said, as I paused between mouthfuls of game pie, roasted potatoes and string beans.

'Again? Jenny, do you know this fine gentleman?' Mother interrupted. The woman's ears were better than an owl's. My nostrils flared at the interruption.

'Indeed, Mama. Mr Black saved your seats from that uninvited patron earlier this afternoon,' I said, at which she made a girlish sound somewhere between a squeal of delight and a giggle.

'It was no trouble at all, Mrs Miller,' Erasmus said, smiling congenially at her before casting his eyes back to me. 'I did what any gentleman would have done in my position.'

'Do you regularly go around saving distressed ladies, sir?'

'Your daughter did not appear distressed, madam; indeed, if

I had not been there, I am certain she could have handled matters herself. I only saved the gentleman from losing any more face, being rejected by a beautiful woman in front of his peers. It was more a kindness towards him, I think you will find.' He jested, I was certain of it, but if there was any irony in his words, he concealed it well and Mother did not notice.

'Indeed? Well, you would be thrilled to know that Jenny adores a knight in shining armour, should you change your account of events.'

'Mama!' I gasped, mortified that she would say such a thing in public.

'She reads more books in a week than the average person does in a year, I'd wager,' she continued.

'Never thought it was very wise for women to read books.' Mr Botham took the opportunity to assert his opinion.

'On the contrary, sir, I believe that reading expands the mind and allows one to travel beyond the frontiers of one's own imagination,' Mr Black said pointedly. I felt a thrill at those words despite myself. A fellow book lover? I quickly reined in my excitement. I knew of vipers that paraded as men, throwing compliments at you like sweet buns and waiting for their moment to strike. Lord Darleston had been one such, handsome and congenial on the outside but an entirely different beast underneath.

I looked at the men assembled around the dinner table. How could I possibly know after just one meal which would be a good husband and which the ruin of all my happiness?

'Well, I suppose it's the only way a woman *can* travel, through the pages of a book,' Mr Botham replied, 'for they are about as useful on a ship as a slave is at a cabaret, what?' He clutched his stomach, laughing at his own joke, even as I felt the air in the room crackle with animosity. Although his expression remained neutral, Mr Black's knuckles had whitened on his cutlery, he was clutching it so hard.

Messrs Squire, Arthur and Crispin all shifted uncomfortably in their seats, eyes darting from one to another, while mine found Marcus's. With the raise of one eyebrow, our man was at Mr Botham's elbow, glaring at him with a look that could easily be construed as an invitation to leave.

'But I have not yet finished my dinner, man! Can it not wait?'

The venomous expression and a gesture towards the door indicated that it certainly could not. With a grumble, the offending guest excused himself and was shown out, easing the tension at the table with his exit.

'Mr Black,' Mother said a little too brightly, 'would you do us the great honour of joining us after dinner for a drink? I have a business matter I would like to discuss with you.'

Mr Black inclined his head and the meal continued, the remaining men making attempts at conversation while my mother skilfully steered them towards more sociable topics. I always marvelled at her ability to do that. To be the hostess no matter what an evening might bring. I supposed having Marcus on hand to get rid of unwanted guests was always useful.

I found my appetite diminished after that exchange. For it was quite obvious to me, even if to no one else in the room, that my mother had found what she was looking for, and she would not stop now until it was hers. If she had her way, Erasmus Black would become my husband.

Chapter 5

ꙮ

AN ARRANGEMENT

The table had been cleared and the other gentlemen courteously escorted out, leaving Marcus at the door, while my mother had moved to sit beside me. Mr Black remained across from us, an untouched glass of rum in his long fingers.

The cane, which I knew to secretly be a weapon, was propped on an empty chair, and I studied it as they spoke in low voices. The black wood was polished to a shine, with a silver lion's head fashioned into the top, but there, just below the animal's jaw, was the most discreet of buttons. The trigger for extending the knife, I thought as I examined it from a distance. A family heirloom, or made to order to his requirements? Either way, there had to be a reason for a man to carry such an object. As practical as it had been earlier today, I once again felt questions on the tip of my tongue.

'. . . it is a most unusual predicament, but you would be well rewarded,' my mother was saying. That almost innocent charm with which she had smothered everyone at dinner had slowly ebbed away the longer she spoke, revealing the astute business-woman underneath. 'Her dowry is not inconsiderable, and although she is perhaps an unconventional beauty, she is well behaved and will keep to herself much of the time.'

I tore my gaze from the cane and glared at her. Of all of the traits I considered to work in my favour, being well behaved and quiet was not one of them. And what was a 'conventional beauty' anyway?

'It is fortunate for me, then, that I do not adhere to conventional standards myself,' Mr Black replied smoothly, sparing me a glance. I dropped my eyes and frowned at the tablecloth. His words might have been sweet enough, but I felt an arrogant undertone beneath them that made me altogether uneasy. 'As honoured as I am that you have considered me for such a proposition, I really do wonder if I am the more fortunate of us in this arrangement.' He twisted the glass between his fingers, the candlelight glinting off it as he fidgeted. It was a nervous gesture, I thought, although his face remained composed. 'You have offered me a portion of your late husband's business, a room in your town house, and your daughter's hand, and in exchange only my cooperation in your ruse. The deal appears too good to be true.' I felt his eyes upon me again as he spoke, but I remained unmoved. There were those obfuscating compliments again, throwing me off the scent.

I had been trying to get a sense of him for over an hour now, and still I could not feel a single alarm bell of a lie. Every word that came out of his mouth seemed to be truth, and that alone worried me. Perhaps I was getting rusty, my knack for feeling people out wearing down and becoming unreliable.

'It may seem to be an unbalanced agreement to you, Mr Black, but in all honesty, we have little choice now. Jenny must marry this weekend or our livelihood will be taken and distributed amongst my late husband's partners. If it is any consolation, they are not the easiest gentlemen to work with, so it won't be painless, and you will have to remain alert at all times lest they try to catch you off guard. How and why Mr Miller tolerated them for so long, I truly cannot say.'

Mother was right, of course. Both Osborne and Talver suspected that my fiancé was a ruse, that much I had ascertained. I was certain that if I did not produce a husband before their agreed date, Talver would see it as an opportunity to propose again himself. I could refuse, of course, but either way my father's portion of the business would be out of our reach. No doubt he knew that we would choose the lesser of two evils; giving him a larger portion of the business as my husband would at least provide us with some income. To turn down a proposal from him without an alternative solution would only guarantee our loss. Now that Mr Black sat before me, though, I wondered if both Talver and my godfather would feel cheated to find that we had conjured up a living, breathing husband, and if they would make his life incredibly difficult for it.

'What we are asking of you is no small thing, Mr Black,' my mother continued. 'I shall have to ask you to dedicate yourself to the business until you have proven that you are capable. I refuse to relinquish everything Jacob worked for to someone inexperienced, hence my interest in your work as a merchant sailor and shipowner.

'Besides,' she added with a wave of her hand, 'I do not give you my only daughter's hand lightly. I would have liked a full courtship between you to ascertain your suitability, and I must stress that your marriage is merely a business arrangement until my daughter expresses any other wish.' She looked at me pointedly, and I felt myself slide further back into my chair, hoping for it to swallow me up. What would this worldly sailor think of that? Surely having a wife in name but in no other aspect would put him off the idea? My mother's voice brought me back to the conversation. 'Believe me, Mr Black, if I am given any cause as to doubt your intentions towards her or our family, you will be dealt with.' She glanced at Marcus, and I was amazed that Erasmus did not squirm in his seat when our man nodded, nor took offence at my mother's tone.

'That is quite fair enough,' he replied reasonably. 'It is the greatest fortune that you found me when you did, for I was due to move lodgings tomorrow in search of better contracts. Perhaps there is a higher power at hand that has drawn us together?'

His dark eyes glittered and my mother raised an eyebrow in reply. I had the distinct impression that she considered *herself* to be the higher power, on account of the fact that she had worked so tirelessly this past week for us to arrive here.

'Perhaps,' she said dismissively before changing the subject. 'Your father was a naval officer, you said. Do you have property in the family?'

'A country house by the name of Crawbridge, near Plymouth, madam,' Mr Black replied. 'A modest fifty-roomed house with some sixty acres of land.'

Her eyes lit up briefly and she flicked a meaningful glance at me. A man could be forgiven multitudinous sins of character if he boasted ownership of a house and land. 'Very good. You rent it now, with all your travelling, I imagine?'

'Indeed I do. I split the rent between myself and my brother in case he should ever take an early retirement.'

'Your accent is not from the south, though, if you do not mind my remarking.'

He flashed one of his feral smiles before replying. 'My mother was from Greece. I was born there and spent a considerable time in that country in my youth. I have not completely forgotten my roots.'

I met his gaze at those words, for they were so weighted that

I sensed the undercurrent of emotion in them. He looked right back, unblinking. There was sadness there, and something else – an intensity that vanished within a moment.

'Perhaps Miss Miller would like to ask me some questions,' he suggested. 'She has been rather quiet this evening.'

It was true that I had barely spoken, my mother characteristically absorbing all of the attention, but now that I was faced with the opportunity, I struggled.

Who are you really, Mr Black? Why do I get the sense you are hiding something from us? Why do you carry a knife in your cane?

None of those questions seemed appropriate for a first meeting, and when I had finally settled on something innocuous about his family, the door burst open for the second time that evening.

'Kit, I told you I mustn't be disturbed,' Mr Black said gently to the newcomer.

'Apologies, Mr B, but there's a special sniffing around the cargo, and Ayche says you must come at once,' Kit choked out, even as Marcus planted a hand on his collar to stop him from taking another step into the room. His accent was thick, and it had taken me a moment to understand what he had said. He was just as difficult to age as his master, hair shaved so close to his head that he could pass as a man in the dim light. But his voice had not yet deepened, and not a whisker or scar marred his face.

Mr Black stood abruptly, sketching a shallow bow to myself and my mother.

'Apologies, Mrs Miller, Miss Miller, but I have business I must attend to. Sir, I would appreciate you unhanding my ward – he will do you no harm,' he added to Marcus, who released Kit's collar at a nod from Mother.

'Of course, Mr Black, but I have not yet had your answer,' she said as she stood.

Picking up his cane from where it rested, he gave her a final smile, but turned his eyes upon me again as he answered, like a wolf hunting a lamb. 'Yes, I agree to your terms. I shall meet you at St Mary's church at lunchtime tomorrow, as requested.'

The tavern was still bustling when we left. Mr Black and Kit were nowhere in sight, and there was no sign of trouble by the docks as we stepped into the cool night. The heat of the day had vanished, and once again it was fireplace weather.

I wondered what the cargo could be that would cause a special constable to be interested. And who was Ayche? I hadn't picked up every word of that brief exchange, the boy's accent difficult to fathom, but now that I thought back on it, there was a similarity between his and Mr Black's own voice. And Erasmus had referred to him as his ward, so there was every possibility that Kit was also of Greek descent.

It was nearly eleven o'clock when we trailed back to the waiting carriage, Marcus keeping close in case any unsavoury characters spied two well-dressed women sauntering through the streets at this hour.

The docks took on a very different character at night, the bustle and vibrancy of daytime replaced by something far more sinister. Masts reached up into the night like bobbing sentinels, black against the inky blue sky. The air was filled with the creak of ropes and the gentle lapping of water against weathered hulls. One or two ships were guarded, their precious cargo still aboard, the pipes of their wardens glowing in the dark, yet if Mr Black's ship was amongst them, I could not tell.

Perhaps it was a bout of paranoia, for I had not been out this late since my last party two years ago, but I could not shake the feeling that we were being watched. I looked at the buildings and storage houses around us; their windows were blank and dark. But I felt hostility emanating from the depths of a nearby alley, a shadow observing us.

Hurrying to the carriage, I sank down into the plush seats as my mother, silent until now, launched into a list of all that had to be done tomorrow.

'This is marvellous news, Jenny. I shall have to send Marcus to collect the licence first thing, and your dress should be ready – I took the liberty of ordering you one. If any alterations need to be done, Edith can manage it after breakfast. We shall have to keep witnesses to the minimum, I'm afraid, but perhaps we can throw a party once everything has settled down. And we need to ensure that Mr Black keeps his story straight when you are out in society.'

'And what story is that, Mama? That we picked him up in a public house by the docks the night before we married?' Even I was a little surprised at my tone. I had not intended to sound so angry, and yet the reality of what I was about to do had begun fraying at my nerves as the evening progressed.

'Don't be silly! We shall tell them that you met when Mr Black was last in London, perhaps a year ago so as not to make things seem so rushed. You courted, he proposed, and we have been waiting for his return ever since. He will have to grow accustomed to being called William in front of Osborne and Talver,' she added with a snap of her fingers, only just remembering that part of the lie. 'We will of course tell our friends that the wedding had to be brought forward after your father's . . . unfortunate passing, but they will be understanding, I am sure.'

She was incorrigible, and I did not have the energy to argue. A headache began to form behind my eyes and I pinched the bridge of my nose in an effort to ease it. When would the lies stop? It was exhausting trying to remember all the tales she had conjured about my mystery fiancé. Now that he had a face and a name, I felt no better for it. If anything, I felt worse.

I was about to marry someone I knew very little of and had spoken directly to only twice.

'You are not losing heart now that we are at the final hurdle, my dear?' she asked softly, finally noticing my discomfort. 'We are so very close to everything working out as planned, and Mr Black seems an amiable fellow. Successful marriages have been built on less.'

I shook my throbbing head gently. It was not that Mr Black seemed awful or cruel. Indeed, of all the gentlemen I had met in the past week, he certainly appeared to be the best of them. But I could not rid myself of the sense that he was hiding something beneath his pretty words and subtle arrogance. And becoming someone's wife . . . well, it added complications.

'I only met your father twice before our parents arranged for us to be wed,' she offered, though I knew the story already. 'He was the son of one of my mother's friends, and they spoke of his ambitions at every ball we attended. When your father's parents tragically passed, I met him at their funeral and exchanged a few words. He proposed on our second meeting, and the first had been shorter than ours here with Mr Black.'

'Why did you agree to the proposal?' I wondered aloud.

'My parents were keen. Your grandfather had already agreed on my behalf and I had no real cause to decline. It all worked out for the best, after all.'

It was supposed to make me feel better, and I gave a murmur that could have been construed as agreement.

'I shan't let him near you alone, if that is what you are worried about,' she added, perhaps sensing my trepidation.

I looked into her anxious face, for marrying me off to a near-stranger was not something to be considered lightly, even she knew that. Particularly after my previous experiences. The tension in my head eased a little at her assurance.

'You won't leave me alone with him even . . . after the wedding?' I asked as tactfully as I could.

'Of course not. You are far too precious to me for that. No one need know that the marriage hasn't been consummated,' she said delicately, taking my hand in hers and patting it. 'As I said before, he will be husband in name only for now, until we test his mettle, but otherwise you can see as little of him as you wish. Of course, should you fall for him in earnest, you can do as you see fit, but only once we are sure.'

Was that what I truly wanted? To be a wife in name but not in any other respect, and to have a husband who was little more than insurance against us losing our fortune? Whatever the answer to those questions might be, I was too tired to think of it now.

'Very well,' I said with a defeated sigh. 'Just tell me what I need to say, and when, and I shall do it.'

Chapter 6

ꕥ

A CHURCH, A RING AND A BIT OF PAPER

The following afternoon, I stood at the doors of St Mary's church dressed in a gown of pale blue that Edith had deftly trimmed with white lace and blue ribbon just this morning.

I felt such a quivering unease in my stomach that I wondered if I had swallowed a moth in the night and it was now trying to escape. I'd slept little, so Mother had insisted on extra powder to cover the dark smudges under my eyes, my hair ringleted around my face and pinned up from my neck against the heat.

Unlike many other girls my age, I had not spent hours imagining what my wedding would be like, although I had often thought of my husband. Even as a young girl, the adventurer in me had wanted to marry a pirate, an explorer or the captain of a vessel. When I had been a debutante, I'd conjured up images of a handsome, wealthy man of my own age who wanted nothing more than to see me happy. But whatever I had imagined, I was not certain that Mr Black was it. Marrying a mysterious shipowner seemed an interesting prospect on paper, but in reality? Well, it was frankly terrifying.

The object of my uncertainty stood at the altar obediently awaiting my arrival, even as my mother poked me in the back to make me walk faster. He inclined his head to us as we walked, and the moth in my belly spasmed.

'Stop dawdling, Jenny,' whispered Mama as I tripped over my feet for the second time. I held a posy of forget-me-nots and white roses in my clammy fist, the stems already wilting in the heat. She had chosen them to match my dress and the colour of my eyes. Like everything else today, even something as small as my bouquet had been entirely out of my control.

I took up my place beside my husband-to-be and glanced at him uncertainly. The suit he wore was immaculate, but different to the one he had worn the night before. He had an impressive wardrobe, I noted as I took in the navy jacket and embroidered waistcoat. His boots were polished to a high shine.

'Do I please you, Miss Miller?' His voice was deeper than a whisper, but still only I could hear it. I looked up from his boots to find his eyes gleaming, not black in the daylight, but a deep mahogany brown, as they met mine.

I swallowed and somehow managed to keep my composure.

'You will do, Mr Black,' I murmured seriously.

He laughed at that, giving me a delightful glimpse of the muscles in his neck and jaw. I pressed my lips together to stifle a smile and continued to examine him unabashedly. His dark hair had been tied back, exposing tanned skin that looked darker against the white of the silk cravat. Yes, this was a man who knew how to dress. Even standing still, his hands resting on the polished lion's head of his cane, he emanated a kind of strength and confidence. It did nothing to settle my nerves.

Perhaps he was a little like I had imagined my husband might be, I mused, tilting my head away from him and allowing myself a small smile. He was quite handsome in a more earthy, rugged way. Not with the refined, gentle looks of the wealthy I was accustomed to, but possibly more alluring because of it.

'Do you believe in fate bringing us together?' I asked as I fixed my eyes upon the cross hanging above the altar.

'Why do you ask?' he replied softly.

'Well, you mentioned it last night – that some higher power had brought us to you. I just wondered if you thought it to be true, or if it was purely a platitude to please my mother.'

'I am many things, Miss Miller, but a liar is not one of them,' he replied simply.

'Oh? And is that not just the thing a liar would say?'

The grin he gave did not reassure me. Neither did his next words as he bowed his head so that the approaching vicar could not hear, his breath warm by my ear. 'I suppose you will have plenty of time to find out.'

I turned my head away so that he would not see the heat creeping into my cheeks at his closeness.

'Dearly beloved, we are gathered here today to witness the joining of this man and this woman . . .' the elderly vicar began, barely sparing either of us a glance as he proceeded with an abbreviated version of the ceremony. I turned to our witnesses. My mother hovered behind me as I had expected, but I was surprised to see that the young man from the night before was standing as Mr Black's witness. I gave him a friendly nod, but he looked fretful and quickly averted his gaze. Tension rolled off him in dark waves, prickling my senses. I glanced at Mr Black to see if he mirrored the boy's unease, but as always he was the picture of calm.

A loud throat-clearing brought my attention back to the vicar, who had apparently asked me a question.

'What? Oh. I will,' I replied hurriedly, not sure if it was the correct moment to say such a thing. Erasmus huffed a laugh, but no one made any comment that I had misspoken.

'Very well. And will you, Erasmus Bartholomew Black, take this woman, Jennifer Katherine Miller, to be your wife according to God's holy decree; do you promise to be to her a loving and loyal husband, to cherish and keep her in sickness and in health; and, forsaking all others, to be faithful to her as long as you both shall live?'

Even knowing what was to come, my stomach still gave a lurch. 'I will,' he replied, the words echoing in the empty church.

There was a finality to those words, and a sense of foreboding. I looked up at him, wonder and perhaps bewilderment on my face. He smiled at me in response. Not the wolfish smirks I had seen before, but a full, joyous grin. My heart did a little somersault at the sight and I smiled back uncertainly. This was my husband. For better or for worse. What a wonderfully terrifying prospect.

Satisfied with our vows, the vicar turned to the boy behind us. 'Have you a ring?'

'No, but I do,' my mother interjected before the young man could speak. She removed her glove and slid a ring off her finger that I recognised as having belonged to her own mother, a gold band with a sapphire set in the centre. She placed it gingerly in the vicar's palm, and something like regret passed across her face.

'Are you sure, Mama? It is your most cherished piece of jewellery, is it not?'

She smiled, fixing her gaze upon the man beside me as she answered, the warning clear in her eyes.

'It is certainly precious to me, but so are you, my girl. May it be a sign of a long, happy marriage between you.' *For if it isn't, there will be hell to pay*, said her eyes.

Unperturbed, Mr Black took both of my hands in his and gently slid off my gloves, passing them to my mother without removing his eyes from mine. I held very still as the ceremony continued, my skin tingling at the contact of his fingers wrapped around my own. Callused palms, worn smooth and hard, gripped mine gently. I could guess so much from those hands – had they fought and laboured, saved and perhaps taken lives? There was a strength in them, and I wondered fleetingly what it would be like to feel them on other parts of my body.

I blinked away the thought almost as quickly as it had come, seeing something darken in Mr Black's face as he looked down at the redness on my knuckles from the bout with Lord Buckface in my closet last night. With a few promissory words from him, the ring was slipped onto my finger and we were pronounced husband and wife.

That was the totality of it. Not even an hour had passed between me entering the building as Jenny Miller and stepping out as Jenny Black, and if marrying was supposed to make me feel any different, it did not take effect immediately.

For what was marriage but an agreement? A church, a ring and a bit of paper? I mulled over it as I stared out of the window of our carriage, trundling over the cobblestones back to the house.

'Are you happy, Mrs Black?'

It took me a moment to realise I was being addressed, and I turned to my husband, who had asked me the question. My mother was trying very hard not to listen, but as she was sitting opposite us, it was next to impossible.

Was I happy? Perhaps only that the whole thing was over, not because I did not like him, but more for the fact that I was in a state of shock.

But there was a hopefulness in his words that I did not wish to disappoint.

'I think I could be,' I replied, fidgeting with the ring on my finger, and we rode the rest of the way in silence.

It was like any other Saturday when we sat down for a late lunch, even if the cook had added my favourite cakes to the dessert in silent celebration of becoming a new bride. Aristotle, who had given our newest resident an approving sniff when we entered, sat upon my slippers waiting for leftovers. No, nothing had truly changed at all.

'As agreed last night, Mr Black, the decision to stay here at our town house rather than remove yourselves to Crawbridge still stands,' my mother said as we ate. 'We have much to do before your arrival at the offices on Monday, and you must be given time to be properly acquainted with the business.' She was sitting opposite me, my new husband to my right, and my father's empty spot at the head of the table to my left. I helped myself to gravy and tried to block out thoughts of moving away from home.

'Indeed, Mrs Miller. Crawbridge still holds tenants and I currently have no intention of leaving London. It is more than just the business with which I need to be acquainted,' he added, looking at me.

My mother swept past the last statement without acknowledging it. 'Have you a man I can send for to unpack your things?' she asked. 'That young boy – Kit, is it? He disappeared rather quickly after the ceremony. Will he require space in the servants' quarters?'

'No, indeed, madam. I do not hold with keeping slaves or servants.'

I glanced at Marcus standing in the corner, but if he'd spotted Mr Black's lips moving, he gave no sign, even if he did seem to be blinking a little pointedly.

'But he works for you?' Mother continued.

'Kit is part of my crew, yes, but I would consider him more my ward than an employee. He is not my servant on land or sea.'

'In that case, will you require a room for him also?'

'Thank you, but no. He will stay with my crew, who all have lodgings arranged for them. It will just be myself staying under your roof.'

'Good gracious. Well, you must be accustomed to doing things yourself, I suppose,' she breezed on, 'and it is a fine thing to have a wife to take care of such matters. Now that you are a married woman, Jenny, you will have more responsibility. An image to uphold at the very least. Perhaps finally you'll be able to put that peculiar notion of travelling from your mind.'

'What?' I said, dropping the contents of my fork, which Aristotle quickly retrieved from the floor. A smile tugged at my new husband's lips as the dog whined for more, and I caught him slipping a sliver of venison off the side of his plate when my mother wasn't looking. They would get along fine if he carried on that way.

'Do you mean "pardon", my dear?' Mother replied pointedly.

'No, Mama, I mean "what", as in "What do you mean, I won't want to travel now that I am married?"'

'You wish to travel?' Mr Black asked, and his genuine curiosity had me looking at him rather than my disgruntled mother.

'Why, yes. I wanted to see—'

'Fantasies from storybooks, I'm afraid, Mr Black,' Mother interjected.

'Please, Mrs Miller, you must call me Erasmus . . . or William if it makes things easier,' he added with another smile that seemed not at all innocent.

'William, thank you,' Mother replied. 'You must understand that due to some . . . misfortune, we were forced to prevent

Jenny from courting in recent years. She has long contented herself with the company of books, but recently she has got it into her head that she must leave London. Not something she should be doing on her own after . . . everything.'

I pressed my lips together, partly grateful that she had not completed that thought, but equally frustrated that she had chosen this moment to show my weakness. I wanted to correct her, to tell her that her protective instinct was no longer necessary. That just before Father died, I had been planning my own escape and did not need defending from the things that lay outside our town house. But not only would that have been insensitive and ungrateful of me, it was not entirely true. Her desire to ensure my safety was not unmerited, after all. She had not been the one to keep me cloistered – it was I who had decided to relinquish the company of society.

'It was not books that made me wish to travel, Mama,' I gently protested, disliking that she made me sound like a child in front of our guest.

'Where would you like to go?' Erasmus interjected, looking to me again. Taken aback by the sudden attention, I floundered for a moment while my mother huffed at the interruption.

'I-I thought I'd quite like to see the coast. When I was a child, we visited the seaside once or twice. I once wished I could visit Paris. Oh, and Africa. I would love to go there. I should so like to see a real giraffe,' I replied, unable to stop myself from smiling at the idea.

'I've had that privilege – they are truly beautiful creatures,' he said, his deep voice turning wistful for a moment.

'Really? Are they as tall as houses, as I've read?'

My mother, no longer able to put up with our chatter, interrupted before he could reply. 'But you have *responsibilities* now, Jenny,' she emphasised the word as though by doing so she could erase all my dreams. 'For one, you will be helping me to run the house, won't you?' I closed my mouth, which had opened in excitement at the prospect of giraffes. Real giraffes, that Erasmus had seen himself, with necks as long as trees.

I looked between them, feeling helpless. I wanted to talk to Erasmus about travelling. If he had sailed as far as Africa, there was no telling where else he might have been and what stories he might share. But my mother's eyebrows were raised almost to her hairline, and I did not want what little favour my new husband had curried with her to so quickly dissipate. Not out of any particular loyalty to him, but rather to keep the peace in the household that had undergone so much change in such a short length of time.

I thought of my father with a pang of sadness. He had always been so good at tempering my mother's stormy moods. This was to be my life now. I'd had a glimpse of it while she had been in mourning, organising the servants in her stead when she had been unable to eat or sleep or move.

'Yes, of course, Mama,' I replied quietly, feeling Erasmus's eyes upon me.

'And you, William, we must get you settled and caught up with Jacob's affairs before Monday morning. I have his ledgers, and Marcus has kept all of his journals so that you might familiarise yourself with them. We don't want to give Osborne and Talver any excuse to cut us out of the business due to ineptitude,' she said, the firmness in her voice unmistakable.

'Very good, Mrs Miller,' Erasmus replied flatly, though I sensed a sliver of exasperation in his tone. 'However, I must see my crew this evening. They're as good as family to me, and would expect to celebrate such an event, and meet my new wife.'

I blinked, a jolt of surprise running through me. I was a

wife. *His* wife. And I couldn't even remember my husband's real middle name. It certainly wasn't William, as my mother was going to insist upon from now on.

'But Jenny doesn't want to go out and celebrate, do you, my dear? No, indeed,' she ploughed on without allowing me to answer. 'We shall hold a gathering for you once you have been to the offices. A ball to celebrate, perhaps in the autumn, would be most appropriate.'

Erasmus's restlessness grew palpable, even from a few feet away.

She was protecting me from him, just as I'd wanted her to. But inwardly I found I didn't want to be protected quite so much. I wanted to sit and talk to him about his travels, to find out why his tone had warmed when he'd mentioned his crew.

'It is no trouble, Mama. I should like to meet Mr Black's associates. Perhaps they might come here to save me leaving the house?'

Erasmus gave an abrupt and unintentional splutter, patting his mouth with a napkin theatrically before saying, 'I'm afraid they might not be comfortable in such a . . . formal setting. But we have a perfectly safe meeting place where I would gladly escort your daughter, and you can send your man as chaperone if you wish.'

My thoughts immediately jumped to visions of gentlemen's clubs, smoky and mysterious in their masculinity. These were the safe havens of men, where women would not dare set foot. Surely he wouldn't suggest taking me to such an establishment?

If my curiosity showed, it was quickly wiped away with my mother's shrill question. 'You would leave me here alone?' she asked, alarmed, even though I had not said I would do any such thing. What I had construed as protectiveness was perhaps not just for my benefit, but because she didn't wish to be by herself.

I felt a pang of guilt at the thought of abandoning her, and shook my head.

'No, of course not. I'm sure I can find an occasion to meet your acquaintances in a week or so, Mr Black. I am . . . quite tired, after all,' I said, reassuring my mother as much as myself.

'You are certain?' Erasmus asked, his disappointment quickly hidden, though I caught it all the same.

'Yes,' I replied with more certainty, 'yes, I think a quiet night in would be better. But I would very much like to meet your crew,' I added, laying a hand gingerly on his arm.

It was the first contact I had made with him since the church, and I ignored his surprise when he looked down at my hand before meeting my eyes. I saw my own conflict reflected there. The desire to do what I wanted in direct contention with what my mother insisted; in contention with my own fears too. *The story of my life*, I felt like telling him.

'The pleasure will be all theirs, I am sure,' he replied, even as his expression shuttered, the light in his eyes dimming as he looked away.

'If you do plan on taking Jenny out anywhere, I will insist on Marcus accompanying you, for her safety, of course,' Mother said, waving a hand for the plates to be removed.

'Believe me, madam, no one will ever lay a hand on your daughter, whether Marcus is with us or not.'

And although there was little chance that she would let me go with him alone, I believed him, for every single word was true.

Chapter 7

ꕥ

ESCAPE

'Mrs Miller has made it quite clear that she does not trust me,' Erasmus said as I watched him from the doorway of his rooms.

All afternoon I'd tried to read, while the two of them had pored over ledgers and paperwork, but most of the time I had been listening to the sound of their voices from my window seat and staring fruitlessly at the page. I had forgotten how much my mother knew of the merchant business, and was taken back to a time long before I had come of age, when my father would consult her on his decisions and they would spend their evenings studying the market prices for the wares we imported. It must have been strange for her, I thought as I watched their heads bowed together over a table littered with paperwork, to share this thing that she had previously only ever participated in with my father. I doubted she was through her mourning, so the businesslike way in which she had conducted herself these past few days was a sign either that she was slowly recovering from the loss of my father or, as I suspected the more likely case, that she had learned to hide her grief masterfully.

As the day drew on, I had grown more and more accustomed to the deep timbre of Erasmus's voice, with its subtle Mediterranean inflection. I still clutched my book now, thinking I might read to ease me to sleep. Not precisely how one might expect to spend one's wedding night, but a comfortable substitute under the circumstances.

As I had eavesdropped on this afternoon's conversation, I'd discovered a few things about my new husband. He was polite almost to a fault, although not afraid to speak his mind and make his opinion heard, which was impressive in itself around my mother. He was also a very quick study, for he had made rapid progress through my father's journals. There was little he did not already know about trade routes, high season and the values of our most precious trading commodities: sugar and spices.

Despite his alacrity for understanding the merchant trade, Mother had only let him go when I gently reminded her that he would need to unpack and make himself comfortable in his new rooms. This was where I now stood, in the hope of stealing a few moments alone with him.

But not truly alone, because of course Marcus waited in the corridor like a guardsman, watching his every move.

Erasmus had a trunk open at the foot of the expansive bed and was finding homes for his clothing as he spoke. There was something rather intimate about seeing him in his shirtsleeves, his jacket and waistcoat hanging on the back of a chair, as he moved from one side of the room to the other to stow his garments. He had refused all offers of a servant to do it for him, and I wondered if he would do the same if I volunteered my assistance. Was it help he was averse to? Or just maids and stewards?

'She will trust you, given time. She does not know you, that is all,' I replied, taking a step into the room and feeling Marcus's eyes upon my back.

'I sense you do not seem to struggle with the idea, and we have been acquainted just as long,' he pointed out, retrieving a second, smaller trunk and dumping the contents onto the bed. Books and clothes appeared to be the totality of his possessions, with very few trinkets. We had that in common, I noticed.

'Who says I trust you?' I asked pointedly.

He paused very briefly and spared me a bemused glance. 'There is something about the word "trust" that is altogether misleading. There are degrees of trust, I would say.'

'Indeed? And how have you come to that idea?' I asked with a frown.

'Well,' he said, waving a book in my direction before placing it on the desk, 'take our situation. Your mother was sufficiently assured of my character to let me into your home, your confidence and your family. That is a large amount of trust to place in an individual. In turn, I have given you my life.'

'Your life?' Something about the way he explained it made me feel quite uneasy.

'Yes, my life. I was not a purposeless character waiting to be written into one of your stories, Mrs Black,' he said, gesturing towards me with another volume. My breath hitched again at the use of my new name. 'I have friends, a crew, a livelihood of my own. A ship and more than twenty mouths to feed, and I have surrendered my life as I knew it in order to help you.'

I failed to suppress my anger at that statement.

'And what about *my* life, Mr Black? You are part of our home, our confidence and our family now, most certainly. You will be in control of my father's portion of his business first thing on Monday, the thing that determines our very livelihood. And you also have been given *me*, so let us not pretend that you are poorer for this bargain.'

He arched a dark eyebrow at my sudden outburst. 'I never

proclaimed myself poorer,' he replied, turning away from me to place some of his things in the desk drawers. I glared at his back, wondering why the conversation vexed me so.

'*Can* you be trusted?' I asked. I saw him stiffen momentarily before quickly concealing the motion by standing up straight and turning towards me.

His dark eyes flashed in the candlelight. It was these things, these small physical tells, that allowed me to judge whether someone might be lying. But it was also something in their tone of voice. An altered pitch, or maybe something more supernatural than that. Sometimes it was a feeling, at other moments it was almost a taste, as though every one of my senses had been honed to detect dishonesty in others.

'If I said yes, would you even believe me?' he asked, cleverly obviating the question.

'As your wife, I would have to take you at your word,' I said carefully, 'but if you spoke a lie, I would be able to tell.'

'Is that so?' There was scepticism in his tone, and I felt challenged to prove myself.

'It is, and I can prove it.'

'Very well, I should like to test this lie detection of yours, if you will indulge me.'

I straightened and rolled my shoulders, knowing that there was not a person I had encountered with whom my peculiar ability did not work.

'I shall make three statements about myself. I would be intrigued to know which one you think is not untrue.' I nodded for him to go on, feeling a little thrill rise in me. It had been a long time since I had been so challenged. 'I have visited fifty-two countries. I speak two languages. I am technically an orphan.'

The false statement was as clear as a bell to my ears. 'You do not speak two languages,' I said proudly, though it pained me to hear him mention the loss of his parents, in some echo of my own recent bereavement.

He appeared mildly impressed. 'Correct. I speak three.'

'Another lie,' I interjected.

He nodded, allowing me a small moment of satisfaction. 'Indeed. It is four. An interesting trick, I must say, though it must be exhausting to have such an ability in society, where everyone is busy telling some lie or another.'

He had turned his back again as he spoke, so that I was faced with his broad shoulders.

'It is no trick, and just because I know someone is lying does not mean I have to act on it,' I said.

'True. But people can deceive without lying.' He wiggled an eyebrow at me as he scooped up a few more books and began stacking his collection on the writing desk. I moved closer to try and spy the titles, but they were so well worn it would be impossible without picking them up.

'I can usually tell that too,' I said, putting my own book down and walking over to pluck the top volume from his pile. *Canterbury Tales* was embossed on the broken spine in faded gold lettering. A work I had read many times.

'Even if the deceiver is as devilishly good-looking as myself?' he replied in feigned seriousness.

I rolled my eyes and shook my head. Would he always be this vain? Or perhaps it was all an act.

'Yes, even then. For men who know they are good-looking are far easier to read than those who are not aware of it,' I replied, looking up at him as I flipped through the yellowed pages. He really was extremely tall; it was more noticeable with only a few feet between us.

'The same must be true for your sex, I am sure. One must be

cut off from the fruits of observation indeed to be so unaware of one's charms,' he replied, his expression serious.

'Are you being coy with me?'

He placed a hand upon his chest in mock offence. 'What cause does the lion have to be coy with the mouse?'

I scoffed, frowning at him accusingly. 'Are you always this insufferable?'

'I have been told so, yes. But back to the matter at hand. If you really can tell a lie from the truth as infallibly as you suggest, I'd not mention it to my crew if I were you.' He gave a quirk of his mouth that was not quite a smile.

'You say it as though they are all liars and thieves,' I murmured, sparing a glance at Marcus, who had possibly caught some of the conversation from where he stood. He would report every word back to my mother, I was certain of it, but without her breathing down my neck, some of my husband's assurance was rubbing off on me.

'Well, Mrs Black, based on your skills, it would do me no good to tell you otherwise.'

'Oh, please. Call me Jenny, if you can bear me calling you Erasmus, otherwise holding a conversation with you will be even more exasperating than it already is,' I replied, perching on the corner of the desk and selecting another volume, *Aesop's Fables*. It was filled with the most remarkable etchings. I had not seen an edition like it, and was tempted to ask if I could borrow it.

I had become so distracted by the book that I did not notice he had stepped closer.

'Jenny,' he rumbled, grinning as he pulled it from my hands, 'my crew are harmless enough, but they do not like strangers, and one who can tell if they are lying will be even more unpopular.' He glanced to the doorway, leaning closer still. 'If Big Don finds out that you can sense a lie, he will refuse to play cards with you. Which is a shame, for he is a terribly bad loser and rather amusing when he is drunk. There is good money to be made there if you can catch him out.'

I could not tell if he jested, for he turned away to return the book to his pile, but I sensed a seriousness in his words.

'You will introduce me, though, when my mother arranges a party?'

He stiffened at the question. 'I do not entirely understand why you must wait for her permission,' he replied quietly, 'but I promise you'll meet them as soon as we are able.'

I too looked at the open door before edging nearer.

'I'm sorry if she is a little . . . overbearing sometimes,' I whispered, which gained me a wry chuckle in reply.

'Overbearing? Jenny, you are a mouse around her, allowing her to speak for you and sway your every decision.'

I frowned. 'I do not take kindly to being called a mouse all the time, so don't make it a habit.'

'Well, I think underneath it all you might be a little lioness,' he purred, nudging another small trunk under the desk with his foot as he spoke, masking the words with the scrape of wood on floorboards. 'I only hope I get the opportunity to find out without having to steal you away from her all the time.' It was the strangest compliment, barbed as it was with a criticism of my mother.

I felt my cheeks redden in her defence. 'That is quite unfair. You do not know what it was for her to lose my father, or to be threatened with the loss of our income. She is protective, yes, but she has every reason to be after what happened to me . . .' I paused abruptly, realising too late where my words were taking our conversation. I was not ready for that yet.

The room felt stifling, Erasmus too close, and I backed away towards the door.

His expression softened. 'I apologise if I came across as unfeeling. The circumstance in which we find ourselves is more than unusual, and your mother is doing a remarkable job of keeping you safe. Though it seems she is not the only one confining you indoors.' He took my hand before I managed to register it and rubbed a thumb over my reddened knuckles. 'What happened to you, little mouse?' he asked gently.

My eyes narrowed at the nickname, but I saw it for what it was: an effort to lighten the sudden turn of mood. I returned one of his not-smiles – merely a flash of teeth.

'A story for another time, perhaps. Sleep well, Erasmus.' I extricated my hand and turned to leave before he could keep me back, nodding to Marcus on the landing and entering my own rooms down the hall.

I leaned against the door when I closed it behind me, sucking in a ragged breath. This subtle dance, each of us prying into the other's life step by step, was exhausting.

It was only then that I remembered I had left my book in his room.

As was typical for London in summer, the temperature had dropped with the sun, and a breeze finally wafted through my open window. I took my time preparing for bed, mulling over the abnormality of my circumstances and all that had passed between Erasmus and me since we met. The fact remained that I knew little about him, and at the pace we were going, I might still be as mystified a year from now.

I suffered a bone-weary nervous energy after the day's events, too agitated to be truly tired. I paced in the dark for what felt like hours, willing myself to relax.

I hadn't wanted to remove my wedding dress, and I'd sent my maid to bed telling her I would ready myself. It was foolish,

I knew, for there really hadn't been anything overly special about it, but a part of me was unwilling to acknowledge that the day was over. I was still fully dressed when I heard the slide of a sash opening a few windows down. It could only be him, for my mother slept on the other side of the house, facing the garden.

If I had fallen asleep as planned, I would not have been aware of it, nor the movement of someone hoisting themselves over the stone balcony. I would not have peered through the net curtains to find my husband descending the trellis, cane wedged under his arm, with all the skill of a burglar. Wisteria branches were his footholds, and he landed on the street in a confetti of white and purple blooms.

I hesitated for only a moment, barely thinking as I dashed across my room, prising the door open and peering into the dark corridor. Marcus had been replaced at his station by one of the younger male servants, who was contentedly snoozing in a chair outside Erasmus's door. The house was quiet other than the gentle sound of the clock ticking in the hall downstairs, and I was an experienced night-time wanderer.

On stockinged feet I crept downstairs, avoiding the steps that creaked, just as I had done as a girl when going in search for a midnight biscuit or a glass of milk.

Curiosity had got the better of me, and I didn't want to miss my chance. I pulled on a pair of walking boots that my mother had left by the door for polishing and, forgoing a coat, slipped through the front door, stepping over Aristotle. Splayed on the front doormat, snoring, he barely twitched an ear as I passed. What a pointless guard dog he was; more likely to lick an assailant to death or search them for food than stop them from attacking us.

The night was very cool, and I immediately regretted my

decision to leave my coat behind. I was contemplating going back for it when I caught sight of Erasmus, cane in hand, at the end of the square. He kept to the pools of light that spilled from the lamps dotting the street, while I dashed after him as silently as I could, hugging the shadows.

What on earth was he doing climbing out of his window? Although the servant stationed outside his door would have prevented him from coming into my room, a precaution no doubt put in place by my mother, no one would have stopped him from using the front door as I had.

He walked with a confidence that could only come from knowing he was tall, formidable and armed. He did not peer down alleys as he passed, or look over his shoulder once, safe in the knowledge that if he were attacked, he would be the better off in a fight. I wondered what it would be like to have that sort of boldness.

I managed to remain out of sight all the way to the William Shakespeare, a public house that I had never once entered but had passed many times, due to its proximity to home. So *this* was where he wanted to go. Such an establishment was not where I had expected him to conduct business with his crew. Unless he had come here for different reasons entirely. I had seen those working women in the Hand and Anchor yesterday. I was aware that men had . . . needs. That perhaps he had not expected to spend our first night of marriage separated. But even knowing that did not appease me, and I felt a twinge of betrayal.

Clenching my jaw against the desire to call out to him, I watched as he approached the tavern, sliding myself into the darkness of the alleyway beside the building.

The lights were on inside, and noise spilled out as patrons came and went – some of them with female company, I noticed with a surge of despair. Erasmus placed a gloved hand on the door handle before pausing and looking up.

'Have you come to meet my compatriots, little mouse?' he said gently, without looking at my hiding place in the shadows.

'How long did you know I was following you for?' I asked, stepping into the light with all the dignity I could muster.

'I heard the click of the front door as you left home,' he said, keeping his voice low.

I sighed with a mixture of relief and frustration. 'You could have used the front door yourself, you know.'

He shrugged. 'Force of habit. I hope you're not planning to stand out here all night,' he added, holding out his arm to me. 'Shall we, Mrs Black?'

I hesitated. There truly was no going back now, was there?

'Promise you won't bite?' I asked as I slipped my arm through his.

'No, but if it helps, I'll make sure no one else does,' he replied with a chuckle. With that, we stepped inside.

Chapter 8

ꝏ

THE CREW

It was unusual to find myself in a second tavern in as many days, although this establishment was quieter than the Hand and Anchor, bereft as it was of sailors and dockers.

The furnishings here were less tired and more comfortable-looking, consisting of wooden chairs with cushioned seats, assembled intimately in small groups, rather than trestle tables and long benches. As I scanned the room, I found every spot to be taken. A line of men stood shoulder to shoulder at the bar, speaking in low tones to one another. The susurration of voices, punctured occasionally by laughter, gave the place the air of a clandestine meeting room, and pipe smoke hung above our heads, mixed with the scent of hops and the tang of harder alcohol.

My husband led us through the tables until he reached a large one in the far corner.

'There he is! We thought you'd stood us up, Mr B,' called a high-pitched voice. The speaker had short black hair and the fine, narrow features of someone from the East.

'My apologies,' Erasmus replied, waving a hand. 'It takes time to look this good, you know,' he added, which earned a round of groans from his crew. 'Ladies, gentlemen and vagabonds, may I introduce my wife, Mrs Jennifer Black.' He stepped to one side and spread his arms as though I were a prize racehorse that he had just bought.

'How do you do,' I said, giving them a small curtsey before the boy I recognised as Kit pulled out a chair for me to sit down.

'How do you do,' replied a large man, his tone slightly mocking. He was barrel-chested, bald and almost twice the breadth of my husband, and I had already guessed who this might be before he introduced himself. 'Donald Fletchley is the name, but these ruffians call me Big Don, if it please you.' He proffered a large hand, which I was about to take when it was batted aside by a tiny porcelain fist belonging to our original greeter.

'Lei at your service, madam,' she said, for now that I could see her closely, she was indeed a young lady managing very cleverly to disguise herself as a man. Her gentleman's jacket parted as she leaned forward, hinting at her curves, and her dark hair fell over half her face, but her fierce grip on my hand was anything but delicate.

'A pleasure to meet you, Miss Lei,' I replied, trying to extricate my fingers from hers.

'Just Lei will do,' she replied quickly.

'You'll have to forgive the excitement of my compatriots here,' Erasmus said, settling into the chair beside mine so that his leg was pressed against my own under the table. It was unavoidable, for we were a party of eight crushed around a table designed for five, and I found myself unable to move away. Or perhaps unwilling. I wasn't yet certain.

'Oh, come on, Mr Black. Less than a week ago you didn't even have a lady friend, and today you have a wife. You have to allow us a little fun,' said a young man with a shock of red hair and a missing front tooth.

'No fun will be had at the expense of Mrs Black, thank you,' Erasmus replied with mock sternness.

Not wanting to be spoken on behalf of for the entire evening, I thought of my mother, and how she managed to win over guests at dinners and parties.

'Perhaps you would be willing to introduce yourselves one at a time? I won't promise to remember everyone's names on my first try, but I will certainly do my best,' I said, looking around at the faces all turned in my direction.

'A splendid idea,' Erasmus said before waving Kit towards us and palming some coins into his hand. 'Would you be so kind as to refill the mugs, Kit?' The boy scooped up the empty tankards on the table and went in search of refreshments.

Big Don and Lei I now knew, and Kit, of course, while the red-headed gentleman was Gar O'Brian, a young Irish sailor. Then there was Carl Hansen, whom everyone referred to as 'the Viking'. Last of all came Mr Atkins, a serious gentleman who looked as though he had reached the age of sixty a long time ago and had not aged since. He allowed me a grimace every so often, but save for his own gruff introduction, he was quiet. Faded tattoos marked his wrinkled hands, and his fingers shook slightly as he raised a cup to his lips, but there was still a sinewy strength to him that spoke of long, hard glory days at sea.

'And this is all of you?' I said when the introductions had been made and Kit had returned with the drinks.

'Oh no,' replied Lei with a light laugh. 'We're just the ones allowed off the ship to roam London without supervision.'

'Although I'm beginning to regret that decision already,' Erasmus replied, giving us a wink. 'Ode and the captain are still on the ship?' he asked.

'The others are there too, Mr B,' Big Don supplied.

I leaned towards my husband, tugging on his sleeve so that he brought his ear down to my mouth.

'I thought *you* were the captain?'

He angled his face so that our noses were almost touching, his smile conspiratorial. I pulled back a fraction in surprise as he answered, 'Not really, no. But I am when the need arises.'

'What does that mean?'

He patted my hand, still on his arm. 'All in good time, little mouse. I wouldn't want to give away *all* of my secrets in one evening, now would I?' His eyes shifted from mine to something behind me, his expression changing in a moment. 'I'll be right back.' He turned to the large man beside me. 'Big Don?'

'Yes, boss.'

'Look after my wife while I'm gone, and *please* don't let Lei get too close to her. I know what she's like around pretty young things.'

I began to protest, but Big Don was already turning his giant body to mask his master's retreat across the tavern.

'Where is he going?' I demanded of the gargantuan man, who was a head taller than me even sitting down. I really was a little mouse beside him.

'Ah, Mr B is always working, Mrs B. Even on his wedding day he's got business to attend to,' Big Don replied, taking a swig from his tankard.

I shot a wary glance at Lei, whose attention remained firmly on her ale, avoiding my stare. Frustrated at being left in the dark, I pressed the two crew members closest to me.

'What's this cargo you're all so protective of?' I had not forgotten Kit's sudden arrival at our meeting last night, pulling Erasmus away to attend to urgent business. If the Captain, whomever he was, remained on the ship, it must be important.

Big Don looked down at the table, his scarred hands splayed on the polished surface like a pianist about to play. He mumbled something, but when I asked him to repeat himself, it was old Mr Atkins who answered.

'Best not to enquire into matters you don't understand, madam. You'll end up wishing you didn't know the answers,' he growled.

My eyebrows shot up of their own accord, and I struggled to school my features into something that resembled innocent curiosity. Unaccustomed as I was to being told to mind my own business, I took the hint. There would be no information forthcoming unless I remained nonchalant. I looked at my beer mug to distract myself, wondering when it had last been washed. Throwing caution to the wind, I took a draught from it and winced as warmth slid down my throat. I took another, just to give myself time to collect my thoughts.

'Very well, sir. An easier question to answer then, perhaps: how did you all come to meet my husband?'

That was a tale that Big Don was more than happy to tell, his features becoming animated again as he spoke.

'It's not my place to say everyone's story of course, Mrs B, but I'll tell you that the boss saved my life twice in the space of a week. It was New Guinea, seven years ago now if memory serves.'

'Oh Lord, not the New Guinea story again,' the red-headed Gar said, downing his drink in a single gulp.

'You'll get your turn, Irish,' Big Don replied, before continuing. 'We met at a gambling den. I'll be the first to admit that I've lost more times than I've won.' His cheeks flushed red at the admission, which I found strangely endearing. 'Mr B paid off the owner when he saw I was down on my luck. We'd sat at the same faro table for the evening and become quite friendly, us both having naval fathers, and the owner was upset when he found out I couldn't pay. Would have ended up in fisticuffs or worse if it weren't for the boss. The second time was when the very same owner found me abed with his wife. Beautiful, she was, with skin the colour of coffee and hair as smooth as silk. The fellow was chasing me down the street with nothing but a sack to cover my—'

'Thank you, Big Don, for that delightful tale,' Lei butted in, attempting to save me from a mental image that would not be easily erased. 'Mr Black challenged the husband to a duel on behalf of Big Don here. He won, then told the stupid lump that he'd better join his crew lest he get himself killed.'

'It was a wise choice, I think,' I replied, giving the big man a friendly nudge with my elbow. 'What about you, Lei?'

The girl shrugged, as though her story would be nowhere near as interesting. 'I was the slave of a Chinese merchant. Mr Black freed me, and I came to work with him.' Her tone was so bored that one might think she had just referred to the weather or an uninteresting book. She fingered a thin, pale scar around her wrist and I wondered what sort of a reminder it served as.

I opened my mouth wanting to ask more, to comfort her or to tell her how sorry I was, but one look from the woman had me closing it again. Nothing I said could change the past, her expression told me.

Erasmus returned, slipping something inside his jacket, the glimpse of a green wax seal on the outside of it. It was there and then gone the next moment as he sat back down beside me, the heat from his body seeping into my side.

'I hope they've not been scaring you too much, Mrs Black. They can be quite an alarming bunch when left to their own devices,' he said, resting his arm on the table so that it pressed against my own.

'Oh, I don't know about that. They've been telling me how they met you, no doubt in the hope that I'll realise what an awful person you are and run away at the first available opportunity,' I said with a smile, forcing the unease from my mind. He was hiding something, for certain, but evidently he was not about to whip out the letter and reveal its contents here in the middle of the tavern, so I would have to push it from my thoughts until we returned home.

'Dear me. Well, I hope you don't plan on going anywhere so soon,' he replied, his voice a rumble in my side.

'Do let me know if you're planning to run away,' Lei piped up, her tone light again, a wide grin on her face. 'I'll come with you.'

'As kind as the offer is, Lei, I don't think I'll be leaving just yet. Not until I've heard about the giraffes.'

'Giraffes!' Big Don exclaimed, waving his empty mug in the air until someone came along to refill it.

'And elephants,' Gar proclaimed from the other side of the table. 'Don't forget the elephants.'

'You must tell Mrs Black about that lion, Mr B, and how when you saw it you nearly sh—'

'Yes, thank you, Big Don,' Erasmus cut in, pinching the bridge of his nose in exasperation.

The smile that crept onto my face with each new tale, each faux pas on the part of Big Don or wink from Lei grew wider and wider as the evening went on.

More drinks were brought to the table. Erasmus told me of a trip across Africa to bring rum to a tribe of natives in exchange for precious stones when he and four of his crew were nearly attacked by hyenas (although I doubted the true merit of the tale as, even a little merry as I was, I could sense the hint of a lie). Gar and Carl gave their stories of being rescued when their ship was hit by a storm between Ireland and Scandinavia. On and on it went, until the edges of my vision became fuzzy from drink and my throat hoarse from laughter. I could not remember the last time I had laughed so deeply and so often.

'All right, you bunch of vagrants, I think I must take my wife home before I have to carry her,' Erasmus finally said, to the protests of his friends. Or family, I mused, for that was what they really were. A family of mismatched personalities that somehow fitted together perfectly. As we stood, my husband's hands firmly on my waist to save me from falling, I felt a tug of loss for a group I had never been a part of, and sadness for what I no longer possessed.

My father had been the strongest link in the chain that was our family, and now that he was gone, I could feel each of the remaining parts weakening. How long would my mother keep up the strength she'd found when our livelihood was threatened before she dwindled back into the blackness that had consumed her? My thoughts darkened as I waved goodbye, and I made a mental note not to drink ale again, or certainly not in such quantity.

The cool air outside the tavern was like a slap in the face as we walked, and I shivered hard even though my skin was flushed from the alcohol. Warmth enveloped my shoulders and I realised, in a somewhat detached way, that Erasmus had placed his coat over me as I staggered down the road, staying quiet so as not to disturb the neighbours at whatever ungodly hour it might be.

I had not been this inebriated since that night at Lord Darleston's party. I should have felt scared, or wary at least, for that time I had let the unspeakable almost happen. And yet . . . I felt secure and safe in the company of this man I had only met the day before. No alarm bells. No warnings that something bad was about to befall me.

'You didn't happen to bring a key with you, did you, little mouse?' he whispered into my hair when we reached the house. I shook my head and immediately regretted it as the pavement swam before me.

'I didn't think to, sorry,' I said, frowning at the black-painted door looming at the top of the chequerboard steps.

'Well, I suppose it's just as well I did,' he replied, fishing in the pocket of his jacket that I wore. I heard the metallic sound of tumblers falling into place and the click of the door opening.

'Did you just pick the lock on our front door?' I asked. He held a finger to his lips to indicate silence and ushered me inside.

Aristotle twitched in his sleep before resuming his dreams, no doubt involving food, as I shucked off my mother's boots and motioned Erasmus to follow me, pointing to the steps he would have to avoid to remain undetected.

With his hand on the small of my back so that he could catch me if I stumbled, we made it to my rooms without difficulty.

'You have a wonderful family,' I whispered as he closed the door behind us.

He tilted his head as though weighing up my words. 'You didn't find them too awful, then?'

'Not at all,' I said, dropping onto my bed and lying back on the mattress, grateful that the world stopped spinning when I did so. 'I thought they were delightful.'

'You have no idea how relieved I am to hear that,' he said, sitting down next to me. I tugged the back of his waistcoat until he lay beside me on the bed. Moonlight spilled through my window, illuminating the room in a soft light. I felt a gentle buzz in my limbs at the recognition of there being a man in my room, though it might have been the alcohol.

'I feel quite honoured, actually,' I said, stifling a hiccup, 'to be so welcomed by them, considering our arrangement.'

He frowned, turning his face towards me. We were still at least two feet apart. 'How so?'

'It isn't exactly conventional, all this.' I waved a hand in the air to signify the general oddness of it. 'We may be married on paper, but you are not my real husband, are you?'

He huffed into the darkness, and I could not tell whether it was in amusement or ire. 'Do you want me to be your real husband?' he challenged.

Something in my mind flinched away from the implication, and the panic that rose into my throat was sudden and unexpected. I found myself drawing away from him slightly, though even now I recognised it was because of the subject we were discussing and not because of him. If he were to be my real husband, he would own me body and soul, or so the words of our marriage ceremony had stated. I would be giving myself to him, consummating our vows, at this very moment, if it were not all a total fabrication, born from the desperation of my widowed mother.

'If I am to take your meaning as I think it is intended, Mr Black, then no. I am not quite ready for anyone to be my "real" husband at this moment.' Good gracious, I sounded just like her, I thought in a detached sort of way.

'Ah, we are back to our formal mode of address, are we, Mrs Black?' he teased, apparently having taken no offence at my indignation. 'Well, do not worry. I remain content with our arrangement as it is, if you are.'

The edges of my vision were beginning to dim as he spoke, and I wished we had had this conversation whilst I was sober.

'Erasmus, I think you might be just what this house needs,' I said. In my head, it had been a logical thread of my thoughts, though his frown indicated his surprise.

'How did you come to that conclusion, little mouse?'

'Well, for one, I have not felt afraid since the moment I met you.'

He was silent for a while – too long, in fact, for the sound of my heart slowly beating in my ears seemed to fill the room as I waited for his reply.

'Jenny, if I can do nothing else, I will endeavour to make certain you are never afraid of me.'

'You said it,' I said with a lazy smile, my eyelids drooping. I could not help but notice how lovely he was in the dark, the moonlight striking the planes of his face, the angles of his jaw illuminated in silver and blue.

'Said what?' He shifted, and immediately I felt the distance between us.

'You called me Jenny.' I fought to stay awake.

'Ah,' he said, finally getting up and walking across the room. 'Don't get used to it, little mouse.' Even though my eyes were closed, I heard the smile in his voice before the door clicked shut and I allowed sleep to envelop me, wrapped in his coat in my wedding dress.

Chapter 9

ꕤ

MILLER, OSBORNE & TALVER

I awoke on Sunday later than usual, my head thumping from all I had drunk the night before. The maid who came into my room paused when she saw my attire, but refrained from commenting as I washed and dressed for church. I thought to check the inner pocket of my husband's jacket, just in case the letter he had acquired last night was still there. I would not have opened it if it were, but it would have given me an excuse to go to his rooms and ask him about it. As it was, the pockets were empty, save for a set of lock picks and a clean silk handkerchief.

Despite my many burning questions, we shared no more than a few words throughout the day. If Marcus or my mother sensed anything of our escapade the night before, they showed no sign of it, although Mama did ask me why I kept grinning like a fool as we sat in church and my mind wandered during the sermon.

After that, I saw little of Erasmus, unless you counted staring at the back of his head from my reading spot by the window while he worked, poring over paperwork to prepare him for Monday's ordeal.

For an ordeal it was.

Unconvinced that Erasmus would be able to continue the ruse alone, Mother insisted on accompanying him to the offices of Miller, Osborne & Talver Merchanting Ltd, which of course left me with no choice but to attend as well, if only to introduce my new husband formally.

'This must be William!' Osborne said with enthusiasm when we arrived. 'It is a pleasure to finally meet you, lad, considering that we did not know of your existence until only a week ago.' The term 'lad' was an undisguised insult, I thought, but I sensed my godfather was playing the part of substitute father-in-law. 'We weren't certain that you were even real, were we, Talver?'

'No indeed,' Talver replied, giving me a look that signified he *still* wasn't certain that Erasmus was real.

'Well, as my mother-in-law has likely already told you, I was at sea until recently, but you'll be glad to know I am all caught up on current affairs and ready to get to work,' Erasmus replied congenially. He was being far too pleasant, his smile too easy, for the viper that stood before him. No one else seemed to sense Talver's intentions as I did; his hostility and insincerity. Certainly my mother disliked the man, but my father had always spoken so highly of him that any suspicions of hers were assuaged.

I could not explain how my sense for lies and deceit worked, and still my mother did not know about it. My father had suspected, I thought. When I was very small, he had promised me a sweet if I behaved during a particularly important dinner. I had told him I knew he was lying by the way it made my head hurt, but as I could explain no further, we said little about it afterwards. Marcus, with his skills of observation, was perhaps the only person to have detected that I had such an ability. Growing up, every childhood white lie had left me feeling disappointed, the deception coating my tongue like medicine. And at this very moment, the source of these feelings was George Talver, who eyed Erasmus like he was sizing him up for slaughter.

'Henry will no doubt put you through your paces, but he is harmless enough,' my mother had warned Erasmus in the carriage on the way over. 'I believe George Talver, on the other hand, is very likely disappointed that we have not given him the opportunity to take over Jacob's shares. A businessman through and through, that one. Whatever you do, keep your wits about you with them both.'

'Do not worry, Mrs Miller. I have no intention of dropping my guard,' he had replied.

But now, looking at the three of them shaking hands and pretending to be the best of friends, I could not rid myself of the unease that crept into my gut. It was a cold knowledge that something might go terribly wrong if I left Erasmus here alone with Talver, and although I had known my husband only a few days, a protectiveness had stolen over me.

'Ladies, delightful as it is to see you as always, we must take your young man away. We have much to catch him up on before our ships leave at the end of the month,' Osborne said, placing a hand on my husband's back to steer him from us. 'Oh, look at you two – the picture of worry. Don't fret, Jenny, we shall be gentle with your beau,' he added warmly.

'Oh yes, we'll ensure he settles in nicely,' Talver said, the lie slipping easily from his lips.

I frowned, and Erasmus caught it.

'One moment, please, gentlemen. If you wouldn't mind allowing me a moment alone with my wife?'

'Of course, of course. I remember young love,' Osborne said, while Talver gave me a thin-lipped smile that made me want to throttle him.

The high-ceilinged room was bright and airy, the windows set well above the cabinets and desks. I remembered coming here so many times as a child and marvelling at the way the sunlight caught the row of model ships along the right wall just before midday. Several clerks dashed about with piles of paperwork, or sat penning contracts and correspondence, creating enough noise that we could not be overheard.

'What is the matter?' Erasmus asked as soon as the two men were out of earshot.

I glanced at my mother, who stood a few feet away with Marcus at her elbow, her eyes searching the room as though she were looking for something. Not something. *Someone.* The last time she had been here had been when my father was alive. My eyes fell upon the empty desk where he had sat. It would be Erasmus's now, I realised, and my frown deepened.

'I do not like this. Talver is . . . unsettling me. I believe he may give you more trouble than we thought. Allow me to collect you by carriage this evening, won't you?' I said, placing my gloved hands in his. It did not feel so abnormal now as it had two days before.

'You are not worried about me, surely, little mouse?' He bent his head as though to peer under my frown, his dark brows drawing together.

'Of course not,' I replied indignantly, 'but I sense that his intentions towards you are not entirely pure. He may seem jovial on the outside, but I do not trust that he will be gentle or kind. His words are like sugared dainties laced with poison. Perhaps you should work with Osborne exclusively for the day, just to be safe?'

Erasmus tugged me closer and I fought the urge to check if

Mother was watching. I was near enough to see the flecks of black in his mahogany irises.

'Allow me to put your mind at ease when I say I know what I'm doing. I am well aware of the sort of man we are dealing with, and I am on my guard,' he said quietly, so that only I could hear. 'Besides, if it makes you feel any better, Lei is on the roof and Big Don is outside, along with Kit and Gar. If anything even smells like trouble, they'll be in here in an instant.' He brushed his lips against my gloved knuckles and stood back, his smile broadening. 'Dinner this evening?' he asked, louder, so that no one in the room could miss it.

I nodded, my stomach still clenched when he turned away from me. An odd sensation crept upon me as I tried to calm myself. It was not as though I had developed feelings for him so soon in our brief acquaintance, but I wouldn't wish any harm to come to him either. Though it did seem a little excessive to post guards on the street. There was something he was not telling me.

'Come along then, Jenny,' Mother said weakly, breaking my train of thought as she pulled me towards the exit. She had evidently had enough of the painful memories the place conjured. 'I hope William realises he will not be taking you to dinner alone,' she added as I gave a final glance at my husband before stepping into the morning sunlight.

'Surely you don't wish to join us?' I asked, my tone making it very clear that it wasn't what I wanted either.

I scanned the street for Big Don and the red head of Gar. There they were, standing outside a tea room, smoking. Big Don gave me a not-so-subtle wave as we climbed into our carriage, and I replied with a quick nod.

My mother drew her brows together, as though she couldn't quite believe what she was hearing. 'You believe he has already proved his mettle to you after such a short time?'

I blinked, remembering that as far as my mother knew, every conversation I had had with Erasmus had been in her presence, and if that were anything to go by, I knew very little of him.

'Not as such, Mama, but I will admit that he is not what I was expecting when we originally made our plans. He seems . . . sincere,' I said, hoping that it was sufficient.

'Sincere, yes, though I do sense something a little secretive about him,' she observed, fanning herself. 'If it is all the same to you, Jenny, I would not have him taking you out alone when you have only known him a few days. I shall not be joining you, of course, but Marcus can come along. Just in case.'

She was correct, of course. Despite me being a married woman, I didn't truly know my husband or what it was he hid from me. I grimaced, thinking of the letter he had taken receipt of on our wedding night.

My mother gave her own sigh upon seeing my sour expression, thinking that perhaps it was directed at her.

'As much as I am pleased that he is beginning to grow on you, my dear, you must give it a little more time. He is still practically a stranger and he needs to show he can be trusted,' she continued as we pulled away from the offices. 'Otherwise it will be Nigel all over again,' she added with a knowing raise of her eyebrows.

'Really, Mama! Erasmus is nothing like that dandy.' I crossed my arms over my chest and leaned back in the seat.

'Maybe so, but giving your heart to a man you've only known for five minutes is dangerous when there is so much at stake.'

'I am not giving him my heart,' I said, suddenly annoyed at the turn the conversation had taken. 'Besides, this is entirely different to Nigel. We have taken a man away from his own life and thrust him into ours, dangling him before the sharks with no idea what Osborne and Talver might do to him. I just wonder if we're being cruel.'

My mother gave a surprised laugh. 'Your father's business partners are hardly sharks, my dear. Brutal businessmen they are for certain, but having spent a little time with William, I am confident he can take care of himself in this matter.'

It irked me that she used the pretend name she had forced upon Erasmus in private, even if she might be right about the rest.

'That may very well be, but as you say, he has known us but a few days and is placing an awful lot of his faith in us too. I think I am permitted to be concerned for the welfare of my husband. One that you forced upon me, I might add,' I retorted.

'It is a marriage of convenience and don't you forget it,' she replied with the same bite, before softening her tone. 'I'm not saying you mustn't love him, Jenny, for that will be your duty eventually, if it all works out. I am saying that you must be careful, for I could not bear for you to be hurt again.'

With that, the bubble of anger that had grown in my chest evaporated, leaving me deflated.

She was right, of course.

I knew that Erasmus dressed and spoke like a gentleman and came from a proper background, but experience should have shown me that these things did not constitute reliable character. He carried a weapon in his walking stick. I knew that he had a motley crew and a ship, and that he had seen more countries in his lifetime than I had read about in a hundred books, and that every person who had shared their story had told me he had saved them from something.

But I also knew that he had secrets.

I know what I'm doing. I am well aware of the sort of man we are dealing with, and I am on my guard.

What had he meant by that? Whatever it was, he was suspicious enough to have his own crew stationed outside the offices.

My mind was no more settled when we arrived home, and I was grateful that my mother did not ask me for anything more that afternoon so that I could take some time to think.

I paced my room. We had lunch. I paced a little more. Aristotle came up to keep me company for a while until I made him dizzy from treading the carpet and he fell asleep on my bed.

I warred with my conscience.

In the end, my conscience lost, and that was how I found myself stealing down the corridor to Erasmus's room in the late afternoon like a thief in my own home.

I wasn't exactly sure what I was looking for. Clues? Some sense of who he was? His bedroom was much the same as the last time I had seen it. His clothes hung in the wardrobe, his books were piled on the desk. I discovered the waistcoat he'd worn at the tavern and searched the pocket in vain for the letter, but of course it was not there. I sat at the writing desk and ran my fingers over the book covers. Voltaire, Johnson and Smith were among them, but there were also a few titles I had known and enjoyed. *Songs of Innocence and Experience*, *Gulliver's Travels* and *Don Quixote*, as well as the two I had picked up when he had arrived. *Aesop's Fables*, with its ornate illustrations, was still by far the prettiest volume on the pile. As I lifted it from the stack, it fell open to the title page, where an inscription was written in a feminine hand:

When you stand in the face of danger, be the lion. When you stand in the face of liars and thieves, be the wolf. But above all, my son, be the light in times of darkness.

With all my love,
Mama

Guilt washed over me as I read the words, my cheeks burning with sudden emotion. Feeling as though I had stumbled upon something too intimate, I rushed to place the book back on the pile, and in my haste knocked them all off the desk.

I dropped to my knees to pick them up, placing them back carefully in the exact order in which they had been stacked. If I suspected one thing about Erasmus, it was that he would notice if they were not as he had left them.

It was then that my eyes fell upon the small chest that he had slid under the desk the other night. A heavy-looking padlock secured the latch on the front, but everything else about the box seemed old, ancient even. The wood was warped in places, the nails rusted, but it was sturdy and impenetrable when I tried to prise open the lid, thinking I could circumnavigate the lock. Treasure, my imagination told me, even as I cast the idea aside.

The higher likelihood was that it contained something that Erasmus didn't want anyone to see, and that in itself was cause enough for me to want it opened.

I cast about for a key, searching carefully in drawers and pockets, under his pillow, beneath the Persian rug on the floor and, to my own embarrassment, in his laundry.

What was I doing? I admonished myself, standing, hands on hips, in the centre of the bedroom and turning a slow circle. I was about to give up on the idea altogether when something caught my eye: something white peeking out from under the mattress that must have been disturbed when I lifted the blanket. Gently I pulled at it, and as it slid out, I saw a broken green wax seal on the outside.

I tried not to feel too triumphant as I unfolded the letter carefully. This was not the one from last night, I didn't think, for it was aged with stains that looked like wine and something else, but it could well be from the same sender.

The handwriting inside was barely legible, as though a spider had crawled into an inkwell and then dragged itself across the page.

Find an opening in one of two companies, both well established in London. The first be Miller, Osborne & Talver. The second Griegsson Merchants & Holdings. 'Twill be difficult for sure, but you do what it takes to find the funds. Two thousand per month. We trust you will do anything and everything within your power.

I felt a cold fist close around my heart. My father's company was underlined in a different colour ink, and I recognised the other name as direct competition to his business. I had met many of the proprietors and merchants of other companies at parties and balls that he was obliged to attend, and though I could barely recall what Mr Griegsson looked like, I believed him to be a Dutch merchant who had settled his company in the city several years ago.

So what was this letter asking for precisely? It was not signed. I flipped it over to study the seal, but the hardened wax had cracked, rendering it unreadable.

That familiar sense of unease crept up on me as I read it over again, understanding that Erasmus Black had come into my life for one reason and one reason only: he needed money.

Why he had to seek out these two companies in particular, and what the two thousand pounds per month was for, I had no idea. Perhaps it was to look after his compatriots while he settled in London. But two thousand? That was surely too large a sum for just paying his crew.

With trembling fingers, I folded the letter and placed it back where I had found it, wondering how I would confront my husband without revealing that I had been snooping in his room.

All of a sudden I felt a presence behind me and whirled around in panic, only to find Marcus standing in the doorway, one quizzical eyebrow raised.

'I can explain,' I blurted, realising that nothing I said would help. Marcus's expression was almost amused, the corner of his mouth trembling with an effort not to smile. Heady relief flooded me and a nervous laugh escaped my lips at the insanity of the situation. 'In fact, you know, I cannot. I can't explain at all. I came here looking for clues about my mystery husband and now have more questions.' I slumped into the chair at the writing desk.

Marcus signalled to get my attention and then made a clear sign in the air with his hands.

You don't trust him.

I didn't think it was a question.

Shaking my head, I signed back, speaking as I did.

'I don't know. You have known me all of my life, and you know that I can tell when someone can't be trusted.' I paused, rubbing at the ache that had begun to form in my forehead. 'I think the problem is I *do* trust him, but he is not telling me everything. I came here in the hope that I could find something, some shred of evidence that I'm wrong to believe him.'

I looked back at the steward to find him observing me placidly. He was infinitely patient, reading my lips and allowing me to finish what I had to say.

Did you find anything? he asked.

'Yes. Well, I think so,' I replied, retrieving the letter from under the mattress and showing it to him. My father had taught him to read when they were much younger, though he had little chance to practise, and he frowned once or twice as he peered at the writing. When he had finished, I signed, *Please don't tell Mama. I don't know what this is and I want to confront him myself.*

He handed back the letter, then took a step away, as though weighing up whether to keep this secret for me. I hated to think what it must feel like to be everyone's confidant in this household. We had always been happier than most families, I knew, but it couldn't be easy.

This is yours to deal with, he signed, *but I shall watch him for all our sakes.*

I nodded in relief, tucking the chair under the desk and scanning the room once more to ensure I had left nothing out of place.

Your mother wishes you to change before dinner. Carriage is ready.

'Of course,' I replied, shuffling past him towards my own room.

In the carriage on the way to collect Erasmus from the offices, I watched Marcus from the corner of my eye, wondering if he might change his mind and show the letter to my mother.

But that was the least of my worries. The biggest issue at hand was what I would say to my husband when I saw him, and whether he would truly lie to me. For if he did, it would be the first time since we had met, and I wasn't entirely sure I was ready for that.

Chapter 10

AN UNWANTED TRUTH

Despite my trepidation, I was glad that I had decided to collect Erasmus from the office, if only because I was given the satisfaction of seeing the surprise on Talver's face.

'Jenny! Wonderful to see you again,' Osborne boomed when I entered. 'Not letting that man of yours out of your sight, I see,' he added when I marched over to my father's desk, where my husband now sat.

I muttered something about ensuring he was still in one piece before practically dragging him out of there, passing Talver on the way.

'Anyone would think you don't trust him alone with us,' he said with a sneer.

'The exact opposite, Mr Talver,' I replied, ushering my husband outside.

The street was bustling with people on their way home, and the air was oppressive, a heavy blanket of grey cloud overhead threatening impending rain. London changed from day to night, two different cities in the same few square miles. This was the time of day when men returned home from their duties to their families, or to their gentlemen's clubs, and costermongers who just this morning had been offering baked rolls and freshly caught mussels now replaced them with the labourer's dinner fare of meats and pies.

We skirted around one such lady thrusting her wares at us as I pulled Erasmus towards the waiting carriage.

'Are you in such a hurry to leave them behind?' he asked as Marcus opened the door for us.

'You have no idea. Mr Talver unsettles me greatly,' I said, thumping the roof to set the carriage in motion and leaning back in my seat, my arms folded across my chest as we pulled away from the office buildings.

If Big Don, Gar or any of the other crew were still outside, I did not spot them. They likely had better things to do than wait around all day after all.

'With good cause, I'm certain,' he replied, mirroring me but stretching his legs out across the floor, his cane folded into the crook of his elbow. 'Did you manage to stay out of trouble while I was gone?'

I started at the question, hoping I didn't look too guilty.

'I certainly tried. What about you? Did they both behave?'

Erasmus scoffed, folding one booted foot over the other so that his ankle brushed my hem.

'Absolutely not. My new business partners are incredibly nosy. Your godfather questioned me throughout the day, asking where and how we had met, how long we had courted before I proposed and the suchlike. Mr Talver seemed more interested to hear where I had sailed these past twelve months that we were supposedly engaged. Which reminds me,' he said, reaching into his breast pocket and pulling out a tiny velvet pouch, 'I told them that I had proposed to you with my mother's ring. I suppose it would be a good idea for you to wear it in public.' He loosened the strings and emptied a thin gold band onto his palm, holding it out for me to take. It was clearly hand-made, the metal rough-hewn and imperfect, set with a tiny black stone.

This was not at all what I had expected, and I was momentarily thrown. Up until that moment I had assumed that, a little like myself, he had been pretending. We were playing parts in a grander production; one where we did not share intimate details about ourselves or tokens of love. Perhaps I placed too much importance on something as simple as a ring, but it felt significant somehow. I pulled off my glove and took it, my fingers brushing his palm.

It was heavy considering its size, scarred and dented with untold stories.

It was a little loose, but by placing it at the base of my finger and putting my mother's ring on top, it held in place comfortably, the two pieces being so different and yet somehow fitting together perfectly.

'This was truly your mother's?' I asked, thinking of the inscription I had read earlier in his copy of *Aesop's Fables*.

'It was actually my grandmother's, passed down to my mother when she left Greece and given to me after she died,' he said softly, his eyes fixed on the ring.

'Thank you,' I said, feeling a heaviness between us, one that continued to rear its head the more time we spent together.

'Well, if we are to lie effectively, we must ensure that our stories match,' he said with a smile, sitting back and slipping the empty pouch into his pocket. His voice had taken on a lighter tone than it had held a moment before, as if the spell, brief as it was, was undone. 'If they ask, I proposed to you on the deck of my ship before I set sail for Africa, knowing that you would be waiting for me when I returned.'

'How very romantic,' I replied demurely.

'Now, I had better tell the driver where we're going, or we'll end up at another tavern for dinner.' He leaned out of the window to call up to Marcus, who sat beside the driver.

'We are not going home first?' I asked him as he drew his head back in and pulled the curtain against the evening sunshine.

'Oh, I don't think there's any need for that. I don't want to keep you out too late, after all,' he added with an unexpectedly soft smile.

I had been prepared to launch into a tirade of questioning when we had a moment alone, but in typical Erasmus style he had deflected my concern until all my attention was on the fact that he had given me something so . . . personal. Despite him parrying any sentimentality in the gesture, there was something significant in wearing his family's jewellery, and I couldn't quite determine how that made me feel.

I eyed the sword stick that went everywhere with him, and curiosity got the better of me.

'Is it for a particular injury that you carry a walking stick, or just to poke unsuspecting drunkards when they get out of hand?'

He gave me half a smile as he pressed the button to extend the knife, laying it across his knees as he did so.

'I broke my leg as a child and it occasionally aches during the damp weather. It was particularly troublesome when we travelled to the colder northern climes, and I had the stick fashioned by a Scandinavian woodworker some years ago.' He stroked the cane thoughtfully before pressing the point of the blade onto the floor and retracting it with another push of the hidden button. The lion's head shone, and I thought of his mother's written words. For those times when he stood in the face of danger. 'Although I don't really need it much of the time, I find it a comfort to carry with me. What is so amusing?'

The smile I hadn't realised I was wearing faltered. 'I just think it is reassuring to know that even the elusive Mr Black has a weakness, no matter how slight.'

'Oh, everyone has a weakness, little mouse. It is what one does about it that makes the difference. I turned mine into a weapon.'

I wondered what *my* weakness was. Trusting handsome men, perhaps. 'You must lead a rather interesting life to feel comfort in carrying a knife. Is the company you keep that bad?'

His grin in the dimness of the carriage was stark white against his tanned skin. 'The company I keep is as varied in temperament as the ocean itself, little mouse. I find it better to be prepared for the worst while hoping for the best.'

An enigma wrapped in a riddle, I thought to myself.

I was mystified as to where we would be eating, and several minutes passed before we found ourselves at one of the oldest establishments in this part of town. I was pleasantly surprised. Rules in Covent Garden was a popular establishment that I had been to a handful of times with my parents. The decor was opulent, all polished brass, red velvet and varnished mahogany, while the location was near enough to the theatre that actors and playwrights alike were often found at the bar, and the oysters had a reputation of their own as being some of the finest in the city. I could not fault my husband's taste.

We sat in a corner, flanked on either side by high partitions, giving us the illusion of privacy while still being in Marcus's line of sight as he stood, statuesque as ever, by the wall.

I sank further into the velvet-cushioned chairs and allowed Erasmus to order for both of us as I contemplated the letter I had found, attempting to formulate questions in my mind. *Do what it takes to find the funds*, it had said. But what for? And why were my father's and Mr Griegsson's companies the two he had to find an opening at? I had begun to suspect that the fates had smiled upon Erasmus Black if our meeting the other day had truly been a coincidence.

A cold sliver of uncertainty ran down my body as I looked anywhere but at my husband. *Had* our meeting been a coincidence? Or had he been planning something such as this all along? But how could he have known that I would be at that tavern seeking a husband that day? I almost laughed at the absurdity. If I asked him about it, though, I doubted he would tell me the truth after he had taken such pains to hide the evidence of it.

Whatever the letter said, the author would be waiting some time before he had his two thousand pounds a month. Erasmus wouldn't have access to that sort of money so soon.

'I know I gave you that moniker you so delightfully hate, but I did not expect you to take it quite so literally, little mouse,' Erasmus commented after a while. It was true that I had barely said a word since we arrived, so conflicted was I about the letter, the ring and his true intentions.

My eyes met his across the table and I held his gaze.

'Why did you come to London, Erasmus?' I asked, keeping my voice steady.

He gave the slightest frown before shrugging. 'As I said to your mother when we met, my ship is in dry dock and I hoped to pick up some lucrative contracts while here.' A lie carefully concealed within a truth, I thought.

The feeling his words gave me was akin to a small rock in my shoe; I could ignore the slight discomfort they brought, but not for ever.

I nodded, seemingly in agreement. 'And you knew of my father's business before you met us?'

He showed no surprise as he answered. 'Why, yes. Miller, Osborne & Talver is certainly known amongst privateers for its long expeditions and high pay. The company is an excellent source of work for the docks.'

'Of course,' I muttered, scolding myself. The letter could easily have been as innocent as a tip-off from some fellow sailor, telling him where he might find his fortune. It didn't solve the mystery of who it was that trusted him so, but it did make me wonder why my mind automatically jumped to the worst conclusions.

Because you can sense he's not telling you everything, came a voice that sounded an awful lot like my mother's.

He propped his elbows on the table, knotting his slender fingers together and resting his chin upon them as though to examine me closer. 'Something is the matter and you're not telling me what it is.'

I blinked once, twice, wondering how much damage I would cause if I admitted I had been searching his rooms. Our relationship was too new for me to know what his reaction would be, or how he would take such a violation of his privacy.

'Apologies if I seem a little . . . out of sorts, but it occurs to me that I still know very little about you.' I dropped my gaze from his.

Our food was brought by a young serving girl – a plate of oysters and a serving of pheasant that had my mouth watering before it had reached the table. With it came small dishes of vegetables and grains seasoned to be either sweet or savoury. Grateful for the momentary distraction, I tipped back an oyster, its cool sweetness sliding down my throat, followed by a sip of stout.

'So you wish to know more about me, is that it?' Erasmus replied without moving, watching me eat with some sort of delight.

'Is that too much to ask?' I spoke abruptly.

'Not at all. But it seems to me that we know about each other in equal measure. You are just as much of an enigma to me as I am to you,' he replied airily, taking up his glass and turning it in his hands. Once again it struck me as a nervous gesture, a fidgeting that was so at odds with his calm expression.

'How so?'

'Well, I know that you are the daughter of one of the wealthiest merchants in London, that you were prevented from courting so as to land yourself in the lucky position of marrying me,' he flashed one of his debonair smiles at that, 'and that for some reason you desire to see the world but do not venture much further than your own doorstep, preferring to stay cooped up in the house reading of the adventure that you seek.'

I frowned, helping myself to some pheasant and chewing on it thoughtfully. He had yet to touch the food, but I was not complaining. More for me.

'That is all there is to know,' I said eventually. 'It seems to me that I am not an enigma at all, and that you are simply avoiding my questions.'

'I must disagree, little mouse, for although I know that you barely leave your mother's sight, I do not understand why. You are a capable and headstrong woman from what I can tell, and yet you both act as though you were made of fine porcelain. The bruises on your knuckles indicate otherwise, however.'

His index finger tapped on the tablecloth, beating out a staccato rhythm, but stopped when he caught me looking at it.

'Very well,' I said with a sigh, placing down my cutlery and glancing over at Marcus to ensure he wasn't watching and thus able to read my lips. 'But if I tell you my secret, you must share yours, even if you are disappointed with the truth.'

'Deal,' he replied, patting the table as though that was all he had been waiting for, before finally helping himself to the oysters. 'I'm ready when you are,' he said after a few moments.

'What, here? Now?'

'No time like the present. Besides, I cannot sneak you out to a local public house every time I wish to be alone with you, can I?' He was in an awfully good mood for someone who had had to put up with my father's business partners all day, I thought. Though likely he was used to dealing with paperwork and stuffy merchants just as much as sailors and high seas.

I peered around the booth, checking that we were indeed alone. He had picked our table well. It was secluded at the back of the restaurant and enclosed on either side, so it almost felt as though we were dining alone. The nearest tables were empty, most of the patrons choosing to sit near the front by the windows.

'It is hardly a dinner-time conversation,' I pointed out, pushing my plate away from me.

'You would be amazed at the topics of conversation that are occurring in this room as we speak,' he replied, leaning back with an oyster in one hand. 'Those gentlemen two tables over are just now realising that they have both been spending time with the same lady of the night and she has been feeding them each lies about each other.'

'Erasmus!' I hissed, tugging his arm so that he would look at me instead of the gentlemen in question, my cheeks reddening.

'That's nothing compared to the couple by the window. I believe he is just now confiding to his wife that he has lost their entire family fortune on a gold mine venture that turned out to be nothing but iron.'

I let my eyes skim over the couple, the lady's face darkening as her husband spoke in a torrent of whispers that were inaudible over the hubbub of voices.

'How do you know all this?' I narrowed my eyes at my husband.

He gave a shrug before downing the oyster. 'My crew are very good at overhearing what goes on beneath the surface of this city. Whenever we visit a new location, I like to ensure that I know all the facts about the locals before I go into business with anyone. Occasionally, other loose titbits make it back to me, and I've found it never hurts to have a little more information about others than they have about you.'

I shuffled in my seat as I digested this new piece of information. Perhaps it explained the letter: one of his crew simply confirming that he should be seeking work from my father's company or Mr Griegsson's in order to make money. Still, the amount was what irked me – it was not a small sum, and so very specific.

I tried not to let my puzzlement show as I looked around at the patrons, each of them entirely engrossed in their own conversations. There was little risk that I would be overheard if I wished to tell Erasmus about my past, and although he seemed to collect gossip like a magpie gathering trinkets, I didn't see any threat in being honest with him. It was no great secret what had happened to me, after all. I was almost surprised that he had not discovered the truth while he and his crew were doing their research. It was one of the reasons my mother had pulled me from society; at the time, everyone had heard of what had happened at Lord Darleston's party, or some version of it, and for those with long enough memories it would no doubt still be a talking point if I were to attend another ball. Society usually flitted from one rumour or scandal to the next, with little attention span for each one, but my removal from our social circles had been rather pronounced and Lord Darleston's arrest last year had only brought the whispers back to the surface. So no, my story was no mystery for Erasmus to solve, but I felt I would prefer him to hear it from my own lips.

I told him, quietly, as he ate, appreciating that he allowed me the dignity of saying my piece without interruption. It all came out. My love of dancing and dresses. My determination to attend every ball and event north of the river. The party. Being lured to a quiet corner of the rose garden and Lord Darleston's vice-like grip on my arm, pushing me against the statue of Athena and forcing his lips to mine. The aftertaste of buttery pheasant turned acrid in my mouth as I recalled my dress ripping as I struggled against his wandering hands. I knew what he had intended, and only the shattering of my champagne flute against his temple had saved me. Then the nightmares that came afterwards. The hopelessness. The need to fight back against something.

'I was so broken and disabused of the glamour of society that my mother decided to keep me home. Before long it was I who refused to leave the house. I wouldn't have gone out even if she had ordered it. I retreated to my books to keep myself occupied and sane, unwilling to interact with others. She worried for me, of course. Both of my parents feared that I would never marry, and then when all this began,' I gestured towards him with my fork, 'she promised me that I would not have to be a true wife to anyone if I did not wish it.'

I traced lines in the gravy with my cutlery, embarrassed to have admitted such a weakness out here in the open. Erasmus's tanned face had paled, his jaw clenched as I spoke, and I wondered if he thought less of me now that I had told him the truth. I had never seen him angry before. Maybe this was what it looked like.

'If you are offended that we didn't explain my circumstances before we married, I am sorry,' I added, leaning back in my seat. 'Had we courted properly, I'd have told you, and perhaps you would not have wished to marry someone who had been so dishonoured.'

Silence settled as our table was cleared of plates, neither of us saying a word until the waiter was out of range.

'Where is he now, this young lord?' Erasmus finally said, his voice flat.

'Prison, for gambling debts,' I replied softly, trying to read his expression. A small part of me was relieved that he did not seem to be holding the ordeal against me. My so-called friends certainly had. But another emotion had burrowed its way into my chest in the form of disappointment. What had I expected? For him to stand up at once and tell me he would duel Lord Darleston for my honour?

'Are you upset with me, Erasmus?' I prompted when he didn't react.

'What?'

'I asked if you were upset with me.'

That expression I could read – surprise – as he leaned forward and took my hand in his own, my cold fingers pressed into his rough, warm hands.

'No, little mouse. I am not upset with you. Disappointed that I did not meet you sooner so that I could have brought this man to justice myself, perhaps. Furious that there are people shallow enough to hold such an incident against you. To me you have done no wrong. I understand why you didn't tell me at first, particularly right after we were married. I would have done the same in your position. It does complicate things somewhat, though,' he added, as he gently twisted his family's ring on my finger in a slow, thoughtful circle, sending a thrill through me.

'How so?'

'Well, my secret is nowhere near as exciting as yours,' he replied with a smile. It was tentative, as though he were testing me to see if I could suffer a jest after just pouring my heart out to him. Luckily I could.

'Oh, well then you must be *very* boring, for mine was hardly exciting.'

Pudding was brought, and I admired the beautifully arranged sugar-covered flower petals and small spiced confections before tasting them, allowing myself a small moan of pleasure.

'Well, for fear of *boring* you, I shall keep it short,' he said, popping a cake into his mouth. 'It begins with that.' He pointed at the plate between us where our final course was arranged.

'Pudding?' I asked through a mouthful of sponge.

'Well, not just pudding, no. Food, commodities, the trade.' He raised his glass of rum, examining it in the candlelight. 'Sugar, tobacco, rum, cotton. Those come from the West Indies to England on ships like mine. From China and Turkey we have silks and soaps, dyes and spices. From France we get our wines and brandies, rich velvets and fabrics, and from Flanders come our lace and linens, all exquisitely expensive. Saffron,' he added, his voice suddenly heavy, 'comes from Greece.'

I frowned at the list of commodities. I knew little more about the merchant trade than that shipping such items to and from England was the sole source of my family's fortune.

'Have you ever wondered how we obtain it all?'

I nodded vaguely. 'I know that merchants like yourself contract ships to bring it over from such places. But what does this have to do with you being here in London?'

'All in good time,' he replied, a shade quieter. 'Do you understand the principles of supply and value?'

I gave a slight nod. 'I think so. Some things are expensive because they are more difficult to obtain than others.'

'Indeed, or it might be that an item is more costly to produce. Some of our more valuable spices, for instance. These come from plants and other natural sources that are farmed. Let us take cinnamon as an example. The farmer needs to be paid for the production and care of the plant, but then a process is required to turn it into the rich russet powder we find in our most exclusive kitchens. It also comes from Ceylon, which is a difficult journey and at times of the year near-impossible to navigate. Saffron, which has dyed and flavoured these cakes here, is the hardest of all to come by now. There are only a handful of regions that have the climate to grow the flower, and each bloom contains a mere three strands of the stuff. It is like powdered gold.'

'So it is expensive,' I supplied, to which he nodded.

'Exactly. But other than perhaps the king himself, there are scant few aristocrats who couldn't live without it. Sugar, on the other hand, is quite the opposite scenario. Because of the way it is harvested, and the fact that the plantation owners who grow it do not pay their workers, it has become relatively inexpensive and is now prevalent in many English kitchens.'

A slight feeling of discomfort settled over me as he continued.

'Imagine a field under the baking Barbados sun.' He waved his arm as though conjuring the image around us. 'It has to be hoed and fertilised. Sugar cane has to be planted and cultivated. When it is ready, it must be cut with machetes and harvested before being ground in a mill and then boiled, the molasses being removed to make this.' He lifted his glass of rum towards me. 'What you have left is the sugar that we carry over in barrels to feed the sweet-toothed aristocracy.'

'It sounds like an awful lot of hard work for pudding,' I said, looking down at my plate. None of this was truly a revelation, but the way he spoke of it made it sound tainted somehow.

'Indeed. But the worst thing of all is that the people who have to do all of that hard work are never paid and are forced to work for days on end, sometimes without rest. They are unlikely to survive more than a few years in such a place.'

He assessed me as he spoke, his voice growing lower and deeper with each sentence. I could not shake the feeling that I was being somehow tested. I held his stare, hoping that he approved of whatever he saw in my expression, and that it would encourage him to continue.

'For as long as humans have existed, there has been trade of sorts. Unfortunately, there has also been a baser form of commerce. One that deals with matters of the flesh and that in most company is not fit for discussing at the dinner table.'

Perhaps it was my imagination, but there was an edge to his voice, a fervour that I had not heard from him before. A crackle of anger that reminded me of our very first meeting.

'You still haven't told me what this has to do with you,' I said, trying to hide my sudden nervousness while my stomach began to slowly twist at what I suspected he was hinting. His eyes took in the room about us before landing back on me, assessing perhaps the suitability of the subject in our present environment.

'I am getting to it, little mouse. But I'm afraid I must admit to being conflicted at this juncture.' His glass was once again twirling in his fingers, which only demonstrated his own apprehension. 'There is a trade that I would hope a lady such as yourself has no knowledge of. One that deals with women and girls even younger than the one who served us our meal. Have you heard of the skin trade, Jenny?'

I swallowed and simply nodded. I was no expert on the subject, but I was not so shut off from the world as to be blind to its atrocities. Of course, I had never heard it spoken of openly in conversation such as this, but thanks to my varied reading tastes, I had studied one or two essays on the matter.

'This trade is the reason your ship came to England?' I asked, exhaling a pent-up breath. From the way he spoke, I was not led to believe that he condoned the practice, but then why was he here?

'Well, if I'm honest, I cannot tell you the whole story, for we would be here until midnight tomorrow and I would still be talking. But,' his voice dropped to a whisper as he pushed the plate between us to one side so that he could lean forward, forcing me to press closer until our elbows were only inches apart on the table, 'if you promise not to breathe a word of it to a soul, not even your mother, I will find a way to tell you. I promise.'

His face was so close, his eyes dark and glittering in the candlelight as they dropped to my mouth, that I almost forgot to be annoyed that I had not yet heard the secret.

Suddenly the room lit up in a flash of lightning, just as a peal of thunder rattled the windows outside the restaurant, and one of the lady patrons shrieked in surprise. Seconds later, the heavens opened, rain drumming on the pavement and windows outside.

Marcus was at my side in a moment, awaiting the inevitable instructions to bring the carriage around so that we weren't caught in the storm. I sent him on his way and turned back to Erasmus, who was already waving for the bill. Several other diners had the same idea as us, and the restaurant became a flurry of coats being fetched, and fluttering money, and complaints from the wealthy that their outfits would be ruined.

'When are you planning to make good on your end of our bargain then?' I asked him, wondering if the weather had contrived to ruin a perfectly good moment between us.

He stood as I did, taking my shawl from the back of my

chair and draping it over my shoulders. 'I knew you wouldn't let me forget it,' he said with a chuckle, taking my hand and tucking it into his elbow before retrieving his cane. 'Perhaps you would join me for a drink before we retire tonight and I can tell you the rest?'

'As long as you don't try to weasel out of it,' I replied.

'You do yourself a disservice to think you would ever allow me to weasel out of anything,' he said with a sideways glance, leading me to the exit.

You do not know how it can rain in England until you have seen it after three weeks of relentless sunshine, the way it falls in streams so that you can barely see a few feet in front of you. It truly was a deluge, spilling from the restaurant's awning, the street blocked with a throng of bodies, not only from inside, but also passing pedestrians trying to escape the downpour who had found a place to wait it out.

'Would you be willing to make a dash for it?' Erasmus called over the thunder, removing his jacket and holding it above my head.

'I'm not averse to a bit of water,' I called back, taking his cane so that he could cover us better, and huddling closer until his arm rested over my shoulders, his jacket taking the brunt of the storm.

'Just as well considering you married a sailor!' he replied.

I clutched his arm as he forced us through the crowd and onto the pavement, where the rain fell like a river from the heavens. I thought I could make out the familiar tall figure of Marcus waving to us, and my father's insignia three carriages down, but it was difficult to say for certain. Our bodies were almost pressed together as we trotted down the street side by side, my shoes filling with water in seconds despite the extra cover he provided.

'I think I see Marcus!' I said, just as I lost my grip on his arm. Immediately my hair and face were drenched, as though Erasmus had stopped suddenly in the middle of the street and I had left him behind.

But he hadn't stopped. He had disappeared.

'Erasmus?' I called, turning a quick circle, but all I saw were the hazy shapes of passers-by, dashing through the rain or ducking into the cover of nearby doorways. I gripped his cane in my fist, tugging on my sodden shawl with my free hand as a shiver ran involuntarily down my back.

He couldn't have just run away and left me in the middle of the street, could he?

'Erasmus!' I shouted more urgently, taking a step towards a nearby gap between two buildings, my mind illogically searching for his hiding place. I peered into the shadows, the rain obscuring any real details, but as I craned to get a clearer look, a hand clamped over my mouth and another gripped my neck, yanking me around and dragging me backwards into the dark.

Chapter 11

ꟷ

UNEXPECTED LIAISONS

My screams were stifled as I was hauled down the alley, one of my shoes slipping off as I kicked out helplessly. My mind was so panicked that I forgot I still held Erasmus's cane until I was pulled out of the rain and through an open door, my assailant grunting with the effort. I lashed out, thrusting the silver lion's head over my shoulder and connecting with something hard.

It was a man, by the sounds of the voice that hissed an expletive, and his hand slipped so that I could release a cry.

'*Help!*' I screamed into the darkness, my voice reverberating off the walls.

But it had done no good, for the door closed behind us with a definite thunk, the room descending into darkness.

'Unhand my wife this instant!' I heard Erasmus's command from somewhere nearby. 'This has nothing to do with her.'

'Erasmus!' I choked out before I was turned around and pushed violently. I would have collided with a wall or the floor, but he was there, scooping me up in his arms before any damage could come to me.

'How *dare* you,' he said into the darkness, his voice rumbling in his chest. I had never heard him so livid, and it sent a strange thrill through me.

'How dare us?' came a gravelled voice that I did not recognise. 'How dare *you*, Mr Black, or shall I call you Captain Jones?' The flare of a match temporarily blinded me before a lamp was lit overhead, illuminating a dank abandoned storage space and the faces of our captors. Three men, each almost as large as Big Don in height and stature, barred our exit, their faces a mishmash of poorly healed broken bones and scars. None of them was particularly lovely to look upon.

'I think you must have me mistaken for someone else, good sir,' Erasmus said coolly, although I could feel a slight tremor in his arms where he still held me, pressed against him as though he would not ever let me go.

'Oh, that's right, you're going by another name now,' the man in the middle said, shouldering forward. His eyes were like two tiny blue coals, pinpricks in his broad face, a latticework of pink scars across his cheek. 'I hear you've given up your captaincy for a new name. William now, is it?'

'I don't actually mind what you call me, but I believe you are yet to introduce your good selves. It would be quite helpful to know the names of the men who ruined a perfectly good evening in town.'

The scar-faced man smirked, his cheek pulling tight with the gesture and making it more grotesque than appeasing.

'Tommy Barton, at your service,' he gave a mocking two-fingered salute, 'and these here are Little Tom and Medium Jim.' The gentlemen on either side of him gave no indication as to which was which, but with ironic monikers such as theirs, I supposed it didn't matter.

'Well, Mr Barton, so long as we can settle whatever your

grievance is and you allow my lady wife to leave immediately, I would be happy to assist,' Erasmus replied.

'Don't be coy, Captain,' replied Barton, apparently the spokesperson for the group. 'Kaine wants his share of what's owed him and we've been told to extract it from you no matter the cost.'

'Ah, Kaine Clark, I see. And what exactly does Mr Clark think I owe him?' Erasmus asked, even as I felt his hand slip between us and gently prise the walking stick from my fingers. Only I could identify the snick of the blade being released.

'Oh ho ho. Boys, I'm going to enjoy telling Kaine how Captain Jones here forgot that he lost him ten thousand pounds somewhere across the great ocean. It'll make your death so much more satisfying to know you lied until your last breath.'

I stifled a whimper. Even Erasmus, quick as he was with his weapon, would be no match for these three.

In the back of my mind, I ran through possible ways out of this horrendous mess. If Erasmus truly did owe this Kaine Clark ten thousand pounds, I might be able to put at least something together to stave the men off until the matter could be properly dealt with.

'That is quite illogical, sir, for if you kill me, you have no way of obtaining the money you accuse me of owing your master.'

I looked up at Erasmus, his eyes pools of black in the light, and wondered if he knew he was setting us up for disaster. Even Tommy Barton, no genius by appearances, would know what to do if he couldn't kill us.

'Whatever it is you think my husband owes, I'm sure we can come to an arrangement,' I said, hating how querulous my voice sounded. I tried to make up for it by holding my head high and keeping my back straight, but Tommy still barked a laugh at me.

'The lady has money? I should have guessed you would attach yourself to someone wealthy, Captain,' he said, looking from me to my husband with savage delight in his face. 'Well, little lady, I hope you know what you've got yourself into, marrying a thief and a liar.'

'I have been told that it takes one to know one, sir,' I replied with a coolness that would have made my mother proud. That wiped the sneer off his face abruptly.

'I have a better idea. How about I hold onto your wife until you bring us the money, Captain?' Tommy said, reaching a meaty fist towards me so as to take my arm. I stifled a whimper, panic erupting through my body at the thought of being manhandled or touched by this man, burying myself deeper into Erasmus's side.

There was a flash of movement from beside me, the swish of wood and metal so fast that I missed it, and there stood Tommy, the knife end of the cane protruding through his outstretched hand.

Shocked silence filled the tiny space for a short second before several things occurred at once. Tommy bellowed, blood dripping from the wound on his hand and down his arm. His colleagues, alarmed into action, ran towards us just as the door burst inwards and the hulking shape of Big Don filled the room. I had been wrong – he was slightly larger than all three men individually, but still surely no match for them together. A small shape darted into the room behind him and clambered onto one of the discarded crates that lined the walls, before leaping off and launching at one of our captors. Strong, wiry legs wrapped around his neck in a contortionist's hold. Lei flashed me a pearly smile as she pitched her weight forward, dragging the man with her so that his face collided heavily with the concrete floor.

Don took a punch to the side of his face that would have knocked me out for a week, but he shook it off and laid a fist into the stomach of Little Tom or Medium Jim, whichever he was. Doubling over from the gut punch, his face met Big Don's knee, the crunch of bone and blood audible over the scuffle of fighting.

Erasmus had yanked his blade free from Tommy's hand. Holding it against the larger man's throat, he forced him backwards until he hit a wall of crates with a crash.

'Tell Kaine that if he wants something from me, he should simply ask nicely. I would be delighted to speak with him in front of the Saints. They would be *very* interested to hear about the illicit cargo that he's got himself involved in,' he rasped into Tommy's ear.

Tommy made a choking sound in reply, his bloodied hand slipping as he tried to fend off the walking stick. Satisfied that his message had been heard, Erasmus released him, sending the man to his knees gasping ragged breaths. A final sharp rap of the cane across the back of Tommy's head knocked him out cold.

Little Tom and Medium Jim were both on the floor, Big Don rubbing his jaw and Lei dusting off her hands as they stepped over the unconscious bodies.

'Sorry to keep you, boss. The rain made it near-impossible to track where they'd taken you. One moment you were running with Mrs Black to your carriage and the next you had both vanished,' Big Don apologised, wiping his knuckles on a handkerchief that had seen better days.

'Not to worry,' Erasmus replied. He cleaned his blade on the sleeve of Tommy's jacket, then turned to me, his eyes roaming over my face and body, his hands grasping the sides of my face to check for signs of damage.

'Are you all right, Jenny?' he asked, his thumb grazing my jaw.

The slap I gave him caught him off guard.

'What in God's name was that about?' I spat, pulling out of his grasp as his hand went up to his cheek. A flash of hurt across his face almost had me regretting lashing out. Almost, but not quite.

'I can explain everything.'

'You had better start soon, or you can find your own way home in the rain,' I replied, using my trembling hands to lift my skirts, stepping over the prone forms of Tommy and his friends.

'Perhaps that wouldn't be a bad idea, Mr B,' Lei said, her eyes darting between me and my husband. 'No lady should have to witness something like that,' she added with a sympathetic smile in my direction.

Erasmus shook his head regretfully, the slap seemingly forgotten.

'I'm sorry, Jenny, truly I am. I had no idea that my . . . business would catch up with me so soon. But Lei is right, I should stay to clean up here.' He gestured to the unconscious men. I didn't dare ask what he meant. 'If you'll wait up for me, I'll explain everything when I get home.'

An unwelcome feeling of hurt twisted in my chest at the thought of going home and explaining to my mother what had happened. But of course I couldn't do that. She'd never let me out of the house again for as long as I lived. Visions of her threatening to annul the marriage swam before my eyes and I blinked them away.

'I'll have to lie to Mama,' I said, feeling suddenly defeated. My threat to leave Erasmus here hadn't been genuine, and despite what had just transpired, I did not want to go.

'Ah, yes. I'm afraid so.' He took a step towards me, but I matched it with a step backwards. 'I can think of something, I'm sure,' he added, which only made things worse.

'Yes, I imagine you probably could,' I snapped, remembering Tommy Barton's words about him being a thief and a liar. 'I will manage, thank you very much.' With that, I turned and left, ignoring Big Don's worried expression and Lei's hand reaching out to me as I passed.

The rain had eased only a little, but I managed to find my missing shoe and trudged back towards the carriage feeling wretched. Marcus ran to meet me when I emerged from the alleyway, signing frantically.

What happened? I lost you in the rain.

'We got turned about when we came out of the restaurant,' I said, signing back, before allowing him to help me into the waiting carriage. He glanced around for my husband, but I shook my head. 'Erasmus met an old acquaintance and decided to stay. He'll make his own way home.'

Marcus nodded uneasily, clambering in and sitting opposite me rather than riding up top with the driver. He thumped the roof and we were jerked into motion, rattling over the cobblestones. I knew I looked awful; I could see it written all over his worried face. I would have to come up with a plausible lie quickly if I were to avoid my mother's scrutiny.

'Jenny, you're soaked through, poor thing! I shall have Edith run you a bath,' Mother said when we arrived, ushering me through the door. 'I was hoping to have a word with William about today,' she added, searching over my shoulder, her brow creasing into a frown when Marcus closed the door behind us. I plastered on a dizzy smile, pretending as though I had perhaps had too much to drink.

'He met an old acquaintance from a previous expedition,' I said, feigning a slight slur. 'Don't wait up for him,' I added, turning towards the stairs and staggering a little. I was bone-weary after everything that had happened, so it was not difficult to exaggerate it.

'Are you all right, my dear? Your neck is very red,' she said, her keen eyes missing nothing. I froze two steps up and turned, croaking out a false laugh. Having been dragged by the neck into that dingy room, I wouldn't be surprised if I came out in bruises tomorrow.

'Ah, my shawl got caught on something while we ran through the rain. Almost strangled myself with it, silly me,' I replied, disappearing up the stairs before she could notice anything else.

I waited until Edith had brought up enough warm water for a bath, refusing her offer of help when she was done and sagging against the door as soon as it closed. Tears burned in the back of my throat, finally spilling over as I undid my dress with quivering fingers. I held my hand firmly over my mouth, hoping that no one would hear me sob.

That night two years ago I had reacted the same way, shivering from a cold that ran so deep in my body that no amount of hot baths would warm me. The crying had taken weeks to stop then.

I left my clothes in a puddle on the floor of the bathroom, stepping into the tub on trembling legs and willing the warm water to take away the chill, even though I knew deep down that it was shock that was to blame, and not just being caught in the rain. I pressed my fingers against my eyelids, hot tears sliding down my cheeks as I tried to get enough air into my lungs.

My body felt tainted; by Tommy Barton's hand on my neck, by the echo of Lord Darleston's fingers on my bodice, by the words that I feared were true. *I hope you know what you've got yourself into, marrying a thief and a liar.*

As I immersed myself in the water, I tried to imagine it all washing away, fragment by fragment, one hurt at a time. By the time the water was tepid, my crying had stopped and something harder had taken the place of my fear. The pain in my neck did not subside, however, and I imagined I would be wearing a scarf or shawl for days to hide the marks.

Once dry and dressed, I found myself in front of Lord Buckface, my fist curling with muscle memory. I plastered images of Tommy Barton and his colleagues on the sack of flour as I hit it over and over, until my shoulders were knotted and my knuckles reddened almost to the point of splitting.

It was more than an hour later, as I lay in bed, curled in as many blankets as I could find and half awake, half in a nightmare, that I heard a gentle tap at my door. I was vaguely aware of it opening and closing again, and the sound of soft footsteps padding across the room, the dip of the mattress as someone perched beside me.

I opened my eyes, annoyed with myself when my heart gave a small leap at the sight of Erasmus sitting there, his face etched with regret and disquiet.

'I'm sorry if I woke you,' he said softly. His clothes were dry, his cane nowhere to be seen, so I assumed he had changed before coming to visit me.

'No,' I murmured, pushing myself into an upright position but holding the blankets up to my chin. 'I'm glad you came.' I *was* glad, but I also wanted answers.

'Jenny, I . . . I cannot apologise enough for what happened this evening.' He reached out a hand and then seemed to think better of it, resting it on the quilt between us instead. 'I have been in many similar situations in my life, but I never wanted you to experience something like that.'

'That isn't why I'm angry with you, Erasmus,' I replied, although some of the earlier fight had gone out of me.

'It isn't?'

'No. It's not every day a girl is kidnapped and gets to witness a real-life fight between thugs and pirates,' I said with a half-shrug. 'For that is what you are, is it not? A pirate?'

He shook his head incredulously, even if I was sure he could see the pain beneath my bravado.

'I'm not a pirate. Not in the traditional sense, anyway.' He gave a wry chuckle. 'But those men were definitely thugs. Blunt tools rather than sharp implements, working for a man I thought we had left behind in Portsmouth.'

'Kaine Clark,' I whispered. 'Who is he?'

'An already wealthy man looking to become even wealthier off the backs of others.'

'It could be argued that that is how most men become wealthy, taking advantage of someone less fortunate in order to improve their own lot,' I reasoned. 'It doesn't really answer my question though, does it?'

He drummed his fingers on the quilt as I watched him carefully, waiting for some untruth or excuse to evade me.

'The situation is a delicate one,' he said slowly, weighing up his words cautiously. 'I am not used to sharing so much of myself with someone I have been little acquainted with.'

'Neither am I,' I pointed out. 'I would say that I am all the more cautious of sharing because of my experiences with your kind.'

His mouth drew into a line of displeasure at the reminder. 'That is an entirely fair position to take.' He exhaled through his nose, clearly seeing that we had reached an impasse. He could start talking, or I would pester him until he did. 'You must understand that it is not that I do not trust you with the facts, but rather that the more you know, the more danger you are likely to be in. Tonight was a perfect example of that, and I haven't even brought you into my confidence yet.'

I huffed at that, encouraged only by the use of the word 'yet'.

'If it is something illegal—'

'Not entirely,' he rushed to say, 'though sometimes my true work must be funded by means that might appear unscrupulous to others.'

I heard the words, each one careful and measured without a hint of fallacy, all while still avoiding the true question. Erasmus Black was a formidable opponent when it came to wrangling answers out of him.

'So, Kaine Clark is someone you've cheated in order to fund your "true work"?'

Anger flashed in his eyes. 'Kaine Clark is the basest of men, and no victim in this matter, I assure you. We met a representative of his in Tunis, where he had bought two dozen women, intending to sell them at a higher price to brothels in Europe. He commissioned us to transport them for him.'

Something caught in my throat at that. The laws prohibiting the sale of slaves were almost a decade old, and the thought of Erasmus working on one of those ships transporting people made my skin crawl. My father's father had been raised as a Quaker, and had passed on his views against slavery. My father's own opinions had been even more strongly against the practice.

'And did you?' My voice was hoarse with emotion at the thought.

Erasmus looked down at his hand between us on the bedspread, failing to meet my gaze. 'They all died, tragically, halfway across the ocean.'

'That's a lie,' I said, the twang of it in the air between us, as audible to me as an off-key note. There was something familiar about the tale, too – I had heard of a ship that had lost slaves in the middle of the ocean due to sickness, had I not? Though the tale had been accompanied by a rumour that they had been freed.

A muscle in his jaw clenched as I caught him by surprise with my observation. 'Very well, Mrs Black, if you insist on knowing all the sordid details, it is indeed a lie, but it is the official story and if anyone says otherwise I will vehemently refute it.' He clenched his jaw in defiance, the silence stretching out for a heartbeat too long.

'What really happened to them?' I insisted.

He looked away once more, and in the dim candlelight, his throat bobbing as he delayed his reply, I thought how young he suddenly seemed. Vulnerable, somehow.

'To answer that is to bring you entirely into my confidence, Jenny, and although I have no concerns that you might turn against me, these are not my secrets alone.'

As much as I wanted to begrudge him this, what he was saying was understandable and, when I considered it, quite honourable. Despite this, my frustration flared.

'After all I have endured this evening, you would still deny me my answers? What else must I do to earn my way into your confidence, if being kidnapped, threatened and almost strangled is insufficient?'

Chastened by my outburst, he shook his head gently, settling himself a little closer to me on the bed. 'I apologise if I seemed insensitive in any way,' he hastened to say. 'Please rest assured that *my* confidence is already yours, Jenny. You may have a peculiar knack for telling if someone is lying to you, but I have my own methods of reading people.' His eyes roamed my face, lingering on my neck, where the red marks were fading to bruises. 'I will tell you my part in it willingly, and hope that you will not judge me too severely once you've heard it. But I cannot tell you the secrets that don't belong to me, and would ask that you do not push me on this.'

I huffed, letting the blanket fall and crossing my arms across my chest. This was not what I wished to hear, but it appeared that it was all I was going to get. I nodded in acquiescence, not wanting to say more lest he change his mind.

'I don't know how much you know of my home country, or the oppression that my mother's people have endured under the Ottoman rule,' he began.

I knew enough, though by no means all of it. My father had been a great lover of Greek culture, and had studied much philosophy. Our dog, Aristotle, was testament to that, though the philosopher himself may not have appreciated his great name being lent to a long-haired food-disposal contraption.

I made a sound that I hoped was encouraging, and Erasmus continued. 'Well, rather than dissect the inner political workings of it all, I will keep things simple. If you are a boy born to a poor family, you are automatically conscripted to the army. If you are a girl, you are taken from your home and sold into slavery. A very unfortunate few of those girls are groomed for the brothels or sold into the skin trade, often before the age of eleven.'

I swallowed, wincing at the unexpected pain it caused. I both wished him to stop and willed him to continue, tamping down my discomfort.

'I have spent these past years trying to do my part to reverse the fate of some of these girls. I cannot save the young men from the front lines of battle, but as a sailor, I can track down contracts commissioning the sale of these young women and attempt to return them to safety rather than deliver them to their would-be masters.

'Some have nothing to return to and instead choose to join our crew. But others we try to relocate or reunite with their families. Whatever the outcome, it is always their own decision to make, and they do not require my interference beyond giving them a fair chance.'

I was aware of my heart thudding heavily in my ribcage and in the tips of my fingers. Tears once again threatened, burning at the back of my eyes as I took in his words. Not for me, but for the images he conjured, the scenes he described. A parent might try to hide their children if they could, conceal their daughters, send their sons away, anything to protect them from being used. More homely girls could be utilised for menial positions, and parents sometimes took payment for their daughters if they thought they would have a better life in servitude than at home. But if they had a beautiful daughter who might earn more coin as a prostitute, there was no saving them once they were taken. Only the wealthy had protection.

'This happens to all of them?' I asked hoarsely.

Erasmus shook his head, candlelight catching in his irises. 'It is not as bad now as it was a hundred or more years ago, but there is still much work to do. Many lives still to save.'

'And Kaine Clark? What became of his money?' My voice barely rose above a whisper.

He smirked, as though amused at the man's loss. 'I used it to pay my crew, to fund our voyages. Creating believable aliases can cost a fortune, and feeding fifty or more mouths for months on end is no small endeavour. Add to that the medical care that some of the girls required before they could travel, and Clark's money was barely enough to cover our costs.' He turned his gaze to my face, searching it for some sign of my thoughts at this new revelation. It was almost too much to comprehend, this task that he had undertaken.

'Why would you not simply report Clark to the authorities and have him arrested?'

He blew out a breath of frustration. 'It is a tad more complicated than that, unfortunately. Politics, for one thing. And as I said, he used a representative for the sale. It appears he is part of a network of men making such clandestine arrangements; there are merchants in every country willing to ignore their scruples for the sake of easy money. Every time I have taken a contract to help release women in captivity and traced it back to the originator, we have been met by a wall of opposition. I am certain there is a team of them, with money and guile and hidden influence everywhere.'

'They were speaking of a captain in the tavern on the day we met. Are you him?' I asked, trying not to let awe creep into my voice at the realisation.

'Actually, no. Well, I'm not the captain per se, but I do stand in for the real one when it is required of me,' he said earnestly.

That was the truth, I sensed, and he was being more honest and frank with me now than he ever had been before. My body was leaden with tiredness, but I forced myself to stay alert, not wanting the conversation to end.

'Big Don and Lei, Gar, Kit and Carl – even Mr Atkins – they're all in on this?'

'Oh yes, and a few more you haven't met yet besides.'

I nodded, contemplating all I had just learned. It was like staring at a page of words in a different language – trying to decipher the meaning with no dictionary or reference. He was a privateer, and one who put the welfare of others before his own, from what I understood. That had landed him in more difficulty than even he appeared to be admitting, for he was not wealthy enough to fund the enterprise himself and, as I had suspected might be the case when I found that letter, was stealing from others in order to carry out his plan. I wanted to ask him about the two thousand pounds there and then, but it would only prove to him that I was not as trustworthy as I kept insisting I was. I would have to find another way to question him on it.

'How many of these women are on your crew?' I asked instead.

'Half a dozen at the moment. We total twenty, more or less. Some stay for a voyage or two and then find somewhere to settle. Others stay longer. You have met some of our longest-serving crew already.'

I felt an odd swell of pride at that, to have been invited into his inner circle so soon. 'I should like to meet them one day, the women who have joined you.' I wondered what a ship like that might look like. No wonder Erasmus was so protective of his vessel, his cargo and his secrets.

'Give it time and I will try to find a way to make that happen.'

Despite running into his enemies tonight, I felt a grudging respect for all Erasmus was doing. He was trying to make a change, which was more than could be said for most men in this world.

'I am sorry that you have had to bear the weight of this,' I said, meaning every word. My anger and the blame I had laid upon him after this evening's events were minute compared to what he and these girls were being put through.

'My own trials are nothing in the face of what those girls endure, nor the boys that are turned into soldiers before they have come of age,' he said, echoing my own thoughts. His voice had dropped once more. I briefly wondered if there was a personal reason for his involvement in all this, but dismissed it. One did not need a reason to be a decent human being, after all. I felt his eyes on me again, and I met them, seeing concern there, which he tempered with a nervous smile.

'It is not a subject, I think, that your mother would deem fit for a lady, and I am certain I don't need to remind you that what we are doing, whilst altruistic perhaps, is still breaking the law.'

'Then I count myself fortunate that you finally agreed to

confide in me. You know I would never breathe a word of this to another soul,' I promised.

He gave a sad sort of grimace. 'I hope you don't consider me indelicate, but it is because of what you confided in *me* that assured my confidence. You have personally seen a darker side of society that many other young ladies of good breeding might otherwise be ignorant of.'

I didn't like the reminder of Lord Darleston, even if it was given with good intentions. I tried to lighten my tone as I replied. 'It is just as well you did not marry a different well-bred lady then. Although I do wish there were a less dangerous way to continue your mission.' I didn't realise I was rubbing my neck until his expression darkened, and I dropped my hand quickly.

'No amount of apology is adequate for what happened tonight, Jenny. Please believe that what harm came to you is one of my greatest regrets,' he said solemnly.

'Oh, I don't know. We were having a perfectly lovely evening until those men came and ruined it,' I said with a levity I didn't feel, pulling my blankets tighter around me. Erasmus caught one of my hands and brushed a thumb over the back of it, making me wince despite the gentleness of the contact.

'These grazes are fresh. You've been hitting something.'

I drew in a breath, wondering what he would think if I showed him the truth. I would have no secrets of my own left at this rate. I pulled my hand out of his and stood, walking over to the closet before I could change my mind. Pushing my clothes aside and removing the cover of my punching bag, I heard him give a surprised chuckle as he came to join me.

'I suppose as this is a night of revelations you may as well see for yourself. This is Lord Buckface.' I waved at the sack of flour. 'After what happened to me with Lord Darleston, I . . . I was in a very unhappy place. Marcus put it here as a way of helping me to cope with my anger. It's something to release my frustration on and rid me of the overwhelming sense of helplessness that the whole incident brought me.'

'Oh, Jenny,' was all he said in reply, standing at my back, the warmth of him almost too close.

'I thought I was done with those feelings. That by having a target like this and a bit of practice, I'd never feel that fear again. But this evening was a painful reminder that I am not as brave as you, or as strong as Big Don, or as skilled as Lei. It angered me all over again.' I turned to look at him as he stared at the garish countenance of Lord Buckface, before drawing his gaze to my own.

'Actually, I couldn't believe how well you dealt with the situation under the circumstances. Even Lei believes we'll make a pirate of you yet.'

'I thought you said you weren't pirates,' I pointed out with a narrowing of my eyes. I could feel the warmth of his breath upon my face.

'Ah, did I say pirate? I meant privateer,' he replied smoothly. For a second I thought I saw his eyes flick downwards towards my mouth, but the moment was there and gone in an instant. 'Does this mean you know how to throw a punch?' The question caught me by surprise, and I gestured for him to put a little distance between us as I nodded.

'Marcus taught me how, so that I wouldn't hurt myself if I ever needed to, er, defend myself.'

'Show me,' he said, moving back another step.

Suddenly self-conscious, I landed a feeble punch right on Lord Buckface's nose, once, twice, and then a third time with more strength.

'I had better warn my crew not to anger you, Mrs Black,' Erasmus said. 'Though you might like to try this. May I?' With a nod from me, he stepped forward and gripped my wrist gently, angling my fist and lifting my elbow so that it moved in a smooth arc. 'That's it. The force must come from here,' he said, placing a hand on my abdomen. The contact sent a flutter of nerves through me. There was nothing between my skin and his hand other than my thin nightdress, and I realised too late as I looked down that the soft candlelight in the room shone through the fabric, silhouetting my body underneath. Erasmus didn't seem to notice as he instructed me softly, his breath hot against my ear. 'Drive through the motion with your muscles here and you can take down a man twice the size of Big Don.'

He guided me the first time as I did as he suggested, testing how much force I could put behind a thrust of my fist by using more than just the muscles in my arm. The difference was marked. He stepped away once more to watch me practise, and I tried to clear my mind of how good it had felt to have him near me.

'Oh ho, you are a quick study,' he said when I'd left an impressive dent in the sacking that I would have to stitch up in the morning, lest Lord Buckface's insides end up all over my closet floor.

I turned around, cheeks flushed with exertion and even a little pride, seeing his dark eyes filled with something I couldn't quite place.

'Jenny,' he breathed, letting my name hang between us, suspended in a moment weighted with emotion. 'I . . . I never intended for you to be dragged into my mess.'

'We dragged you into ours,' I countered.

'It is not the same.'

True, it was not even remotely similar. We had traded my hand in marriage for a secure position, plenty of money and the promise that he would support us. His mess was betraying criminal merchants by freeing Greek slave girls, taking their money in the process to feed his crew. I could not deny I was impressed.

He searched my face for some sign of trepidation, and found none. 'I worry that things are about to become more dangerous for us. If Clark knows I'm in London, it is possible that others will follow.'

'How many merchants have you done this to?' I asked, alarmed. 'Don't answer that,' I amended when I saw his expression. 'Let them come, Erasmus. We will be better prepared next time.' I wanted to take his hand and tangle my fingers in his, to reassure him that I was here for him. It was a feeling I quickly dismissed before I found myself doing something rash.

The gap between us seemed to close and widen with every word, as though we were dancing.

'Would that it were that simple. Living here with you is a risk. Why I thought I could get away with it, I don't know. I worry that if I stay much longer, I won't be able to protect you adequately, particularly when there is so much at stake.'

'But you cannot leave,' I protested. 'We have a bargain. If you were to vanish suddenly, what would happen to Miller, Osborne & Talver? It would not be long before your new business partners swept in and took our share for themselves. No,' I continued with a violent shake of my head before he could interrupt, 'if you were to suddenly take your ship and your crew and sail into the sunset, we might be able to hold them off for a few months, but before long they would insist that you must have been lost at sea or . . . or that you had abandoned us. And I can tell you now that my mother wouldn't recover if we lost the business.'

Even to my own ears this sounded like a feeble excuse for keeping him near, but it was still true. Perhaps I was foolish for wanting to continue this ruse with him, knowing what I did now. Surely if I had married one of the other men from the other night, my life would have been far less complicated than it had suddenly become. But I sensed in the very depths of my gut that Erasmus Black was a good man, and that despite his choices and lifestyle prior to our meeting, I would be safer by his side.

Whether he read all of this in my expression or drew his own conclusions, his concern quickly turned to mischief. 'Don't tell me you're growing attached to me, little mouse?'

'Pfft, don't flatter yourself,' I replied, making an unladylike sound that had more to do with my nerves than incredulity. 'But we *are* husband and wife in the eyes of the law. It is your duty to stay, and my duty to stand by you. Even if you are an insufferable rogue most of the time.'

'Ah, I see,' he replied quietly, seemingly unconvinced. Several emotions passed across his features, and I could sense his hesitation as he wondered whether staying would do more harm than good.

'Are you a man of your word, Erasmus Black?'

'I like to think so,' he replied with a dip of his head, dark strands of his hair falling forwards so that I had to resist the urge to tuck them back behind his ear. I closed the small gap between us, but kept my hands to myself. His unique smell of old ships, spice and rum filled my nostrils as I looked up into those dark irises.

'Then swear to me you'll not leave me. Us. That you will allow me to help you in whatever way I can, rather than pushing me away.'

He reached for one of my hands and brushed his lips against the back of my fingers, sending a jolt of surprise and pleasure through me. I quivered, wondering if my legs might give way being in such proximity to him.

'I swear I will do everything in my power to protect you. That I will allow you to help me in whatever way you can, and that I will let you rest when you are evidently too tired to remain standing.' Without warning, he pulled me towards him and scooped my legs out from underneath me in one swift motion, depositing me on my bed and pulling the blankets right up to my chin.

'Goodnight, little mouse,' he whispered, brushing a kiss against my brow before taking his leave. That scent of spice and rum lingered in my sheets and on my skin, so entirely Erasmus.

It was only as I lay there on the edge of sleep that I realised he had changed the vow I had asked him to make, and had not promised to stay.

Chapter 12

ᘓᘐ

A DIFFERENT KIND OF ADVENTURE

My sleep was filled with snatches of nightmares. Of shadowed figures grasping for me in the dark and the quicksilver sounds of blades cutting the air. I must have been calling out, for when I woke, I was drenched in sweat and the inside of my throat was coated with needles.

'Erasmus?' I heard myself murmur at a figure beside my bed.

'Shh, my girl, I am here.' My mother sat in a chair nearby, pressing a cold cloth to my forehead. Her gaze was unfocused and faraway, as though she were deep in thought even as she tended to me.

'Mama?' I said thickly, trying to push myself up.

'Don't try to move. The doctor said you should rest. Nothing to worry about, he assured me, just too long in those wet clothes last night. I don't know what that man was thinking, letting you get soaked to the bone and leaving you to come home by yourself,' she added, scolding Erasmus in his absence.

'Where is he?' I looked around the room as though he might

materialise from the wardrobe. The distinct scents of camphor medicine and lavender essence clung to my sheets and in the air, evidence that the doctor had indeed been.

'At the offices,' she replied, and I tried to hide my disappointment. 'He could not be spared with everything going on there.'

Now that I looked at her, my mother appeared more worn than usual. I thought of what Erasmus had told me last night, and panic constricted my ribcage like laces. 'Has something happened?'

She put a pillow behind my head and straightened my blanket, keeping her hands busy as she replied. 'Osborne is concerned that two of our ships haven't returned from the West Indies, and I wouldn't be surprised if he commissions more immediately in case they are lost to us. It would be a costly risk, certainly, but I've told William what he should do if Talver argues against it. Thousands of pounds' worth of cargo at the bottom of the ocean would be a terrible blow.'

Nothing to do with our discussion last night, then, I thought with a little relief. Though lost ships was not something to be happy about.

'You know an awful lot about the business, Mama,' I said, as she dabbed at my forehead once more. I gently pushed the cloth away and, ignoring her orders, sat up fully. I was cold and slick with sweat and my head felt as though someone had stuffed cotton in it, but I didn't want to lie around all day.

'Well, a lady picks things up being married to a merchant for over two decades,' she said, dumping the cloth back in its bowl of water and drying her hands.

Her tone was indifferent, as though it were nothing that she knew the ins and outs of the source of our family's livelihood better than most. But it wasn't nothing. I was beginning to see that if it weren't for the fact that she was a woman, my mother could have easily replaced my father in the business. Her understanding was such that she had been able to teach Erasmus all he needed to know in just two days, and I was reminded once more of the way my parents would discuss work-related topics and trading routes just as other couples might spend their evenings gossiping about their peers or other more trivial matters.

'Anyway, William seems quite competent. Although I still have not forgiven him for leaving you last night, he seems well intentioned enough. You'll have to keep him on a tighter leash, though,' she added with a meaningful look.

I didn't want to tell her that I had no chance of tightening any leash when it came to my husband. If anything, I would be dragged along behind him.

'I should like to visit Oscarson's,' I said, changing the subject, 'for I have entirely run out of books to read.'

She frowned and shook her head. 'You're staying in today, Jenny, doctor's orders, but I can send Marcus for you if it is very urgent.'

It was obvious I would not be able to leave the house without climbing out of the window myself. I would have to be content with going another day. It had been weeks since I had visited the bookshop – I realised with a start that it was before my father had died, in fact – and I was missing the place sorely. But not quite as much as I missed the reassuring presence of Erasmus. A disconcerting thought all in itself.

While my mother fussed and clucked about my room, I replayed the events of the previous evening, understanding now why he had not told me about his true business before, but still feeling as though I were missing some parts of the story. Despite that, there was no denying that he was growing on me. I flushed when I remembered the feel of his hand on my abdomen, his lips on my forehead as he said goodnight. Perhaps 'growing on me' was the wrong way to describe it.

'Oh, Jenny, you're burning up,' my mother said, attacking me once again with the cool flannel as she misread my flaming cheeks for fever. I said nothing, too embarrassed to explain the true reason for my increased heart rate and hot skin.

I spent all of Tuesday resting, forced to remain in bed despite not feeling as poorly as the doctor had made out. My neck throbbed, and a quick examination in the mirror confirmed that I had angry bruises that stung when I touched them. Something about the events of the night had left me with a hollow ache inside that felt all too similar to the aftermath of my last attack, and only reading or going through my father's bundle of sketches by my bed seemed to take my mind off it.

I fell asleep sometime before dinner and awoke in the middle of another nightmare after the household had gone to sleep, suddenly aware of the fact that Erasmus hadn't come to check on me.

Wednesday and Thursday passed without me once seeing my husband, who was working long into the evenings, and by the time Friday arrived, I felt more than well enough to venture outside, but was once again prohibited from leaving the house.

'It seems like it may rain again, Jenny, and I don't want you catching another fever or, heaven forbid, anything worse,' said Mama as I stood in the parlour, fully dressed.

'Mama, I am not an invalid. I need the air if nothing else.'

'Then sit on your balcony,' she replied, unmoved by my pleas. 'When you have had enough air, come back downstairs, for I need to go over some of the housekeeping expenses with you. Perhaps now you can share in the responsibilities, learn the intricacies of running a house?' It was an order thinly disguised as a request, but quite fair enough, I supposed.

I thought of Crawbridge, Erasmus's family estate. Although it was far too early to consider relocating there, some whimsical part of me wondered what it would be like to be lady of a house such as his. A silly notion that followed me back upstairs to my room.

As I sat on the balcony watching the carriages trundle past, the nannies with their charges entering and leaving the communal gardens, a cat stalking a fat pigeon that was pecking for scraps in the gutter, I noticed a dark-clad figure standing against the railings opposite the house, watching me. My heartbeat picked up as I gathered my skirts to return indoors, thoughts of sending a message to Erasmus and putting Marcus on guard running rapidly through my mind.

But then the figure removed his cap and tipped it towards me, a crop of familiar red hair glinting in the sunshine. It was Erasmus's crew mate Gar, and not one of Tommy Barton's thugs, who watched the house.

So Erasmus hadn't left me entirely alone.

During the course of the afternoon, Gar was replaced by the blonde Viking Carl, who nodded amiably at me when I peered through a ground-floor window. I waved back, comforted that I was being guarded by my husband's people, even if he could not be home himself.

As I accompanied my mother throughout the afternoon, inspecting the cleanliness of silverware and selecting flower arrangements for the front hall, I allowed my mind to wander, despite her constantly tapping me on the back of the hand to get my attention. More than once I caught her suppressing a laugh at my distractedness, and I was sure I overheard her murmuring something about newly-weds not having the attention for important practical matters.

I attended her meeting with the housekeeper, and in the process was able to convince her that there was no need for a servant to be stationed outside Erasmus's room. She did not argue, though she looked mildly unconvinced at my reasoning. Surely it would ease any disruption to the schedules of the household staff, I rationalised. I wanted him to feel welcome in this house. He was working so hard, it seemed like the smallest gesture to suspend surveillance of his comings and goings. Without too much coaxing, my mother agreed, and I wondered if Erasmus had been working his charms on her while I had been convalescing.

After several hours of studying the housekeeping books, I was relieved of my tedious duties and permitted to read in my favourite window seat. But the quiet enveloped me, and save for those moments when I could hear Mother speaking with the maids or Marcus, I found my mind drifting back to Erasmus. Perhaps it was a good thing that I had not seen him since Monday, for it gave me time to reflect on all that had happened between us.

He had been so careful around me, but was already so protective. Despite myself, I recalled the way he had gripped me when he thought we were in danger from Tommy Barton and his comrades. The way he had never overstepped or forced himself on me. I wondered what it would be like to feel the warmth of him beside me as I slept, my head resting on his shoulder, his arm draped protectively around me, his hand splayed across my back. But most of all I wondered what it would be like to kiss him. It was an odd sensation, this tiny thread of desire that tugged at my insides as I sat and watched people go about their business outside. It was as though something in Monday night's ordeal had altered the way I saw him, giving me a little faith that not *all* men were careless with women's hearts and bodies. That I now knew some of his true motivations certainly helped. From the moment we had first met, something about him had struck me as different from the other men I had encountered. Not just those who had previously wronged me, but the young men I had been subtly vetting at my mother's behest for much of last week.

All of my prior experience of gentlemen had been tainted. Nigel had treated my affections with wanton carelessness, Lord Darleston had been something far more debased and evil. Erasmus was nothing like either of them. He was serious when he needed to be; fierce, professional and enigmatic. But there was also a softness to him that he had allowed me to see more than once. I thought of his mother's words in his book: *be the light in times of darkness*. It had been so dark before he came into our lives, so bleak after my father died, that I truly felt as though he had indeed been a light for us.

What had I said to him in my alcohol-induced haze on our wedding night? That I had not felt afraid since I had met him. As I took the time to examine my feelings, I found it to be true, with the exception of our encounter with Tommy Barton and his men. From the day of our very first meeting, I had been curious, with a healthy dose of apprehension, but never fearful. Despite the revelations of his life before I knew him, I couldn't fault any of his actions, and I could not deny that I admired his principles.

And when I had told him I was not ready to be his wife in every sense, he had not forced himself upon me. How many other gentlemen would have been so understanding?

I wondered if this was what love felt like.

I closed the novel I had been half reading, musing that

perhaps the stories had been addling my mind with their romanticism.

We took tea, the day dragging on, and still Erasmus did not come home. Concerns that Tommy Barton and the other fellows had pounced on him outside his offices filled my mind. If Kit hadn't called by to say to say that he had been waylaid and would not be back for supper, I would have been tempted to go out in search of him. That thought surprised me, for a few weeks ago I would never have considered leaving the house for the sake of a man. It was with some unease that I realised I was more concerned for him than I was perhaps admitting, enough that I would have put my own fears aside to ensure his safety.

After a quiet dinner, when the household had mostly retired, my mother and I played piquet, my mind elsewhere as she trounced me round after round.

'Jenny, my dear, I sense that your heart is not entirely in this game,' she said, laying down her cards.

'What? Oh, sorry,' I said. I had lost count of my score long ago, and from my mother's handwritten notes, I could see that she had far more points than I. 'Did you send the carriage for Erasmus? It's far too dangerous for him to walk home alone, I think, and it might encourage him to return rather than sleep at his desk, wouldn't you say?' I chewed my lip as I envisaged men leaping out of alleyways and bludgeoning him. Would Big Don be with him at this time of night?

'Jenny,' my mother said firmly, pulling me out of my morbid thoughts, 'what is the matter?'

'Nothing, Mama. Sorry. I just . . . I wish that I had been able to spend a little more time with him before he was embroiled in his work. I worry that he stays too late at the offices and does not sleep enough.'

My mother's smile was almost wistful. 'I remember when I first married your father. I had the house to occupy me, but we had moved so far from my family and friends that I was often alone, as you know. I made new acquaintances, of course, but I despaired when he came home in the dead of night, his head full of numbers, contracts, ships and manifests.'

I did know this, but it was only now that I was grown and married myself that I understood how difficult it must have been for her to be alone, away from my titled grandparents and society in general. They had arranged my parents' marriage, but from my early memories they had not admired my father's work. My mother had married down in status, but my father's wealth had made the proposal too enticing for my late-grandfather to refuse. I realised that she had understood my own removal from society better than I had previously acknowledged.

'What did you do?' I asked, lifting Aristotle onto my lap and giving his silky head a stroke, receiving a wet lick to my chin in thanks.

'At first I was angry. I gave him a terrible time for neglecting me. But before long, I realised that I would have to change some of my own ways now that my life did not revolve around parties and dances. I learned about your father's interests. I studied his trade and became his adviser and confidante, so that rather than stay out late, he could come home and know that I would be there to help him with any problems. By the end of our first year of marriage, I had enough knowledge that I could speak just as well to merchants and their wives as I could to the aristocracy. You would do well to maintain those connections too, Jenny, as much as I know you despise them,' she added with an arch of her brow.

I sat in silence for a moment, pondering what she had said. 'Why go to the trouble, though? I thought you said you did not love Father when you married him.'

My mother gave a knowing grin. 'I did not, but I knew that I could in time. He was intelligent. Handsome, of course,' she said with a nod, 'and so quick of wit. He was like no other man I had met. Charismatic, clever. I was drawn to him like a magnet.' Her voice had taken on a faraway and dreamy tone. I loved it when she spoke like this. She could be as sharp as a knife when she wanted to be, but when it was just the two of us, away from the ladies of society and the constraints of propriety, her manner was soft and vulnerable. It was a rare treat.

Her words put me in mind of my first meeting with Erasmus, how curious I had been about him. Had he felt the same when he had seen me? I wondered.

My mother's hand found mine across the table, and Aristotle snuffled at it in case she was offering him food. She batted him away and gave my fingers a squeeze.

'Love is not something that just happens to people, Jenny. It is made. It is created. It takes work and patience, and above all, honesty. But aside from raising children, I would say it is the most rewarding type of work there is.'

I thought of that later, after we had tidied the cards and said our goodnights. I paced my room in my nightdress, unable to sleep until I knew that Erasmus was home safe and sound.

Just when I thought I could not bear the wait much longer, and was contemplating getting dressed and seeing if one of the crew was still standing guard outside so that I might speak to them, I heard the front door open and close. He was home.

I waited, thinking of all the things I needed to say, hoping that he would come and tell me how his day had been, make some humorous comment about his business partners. He had not seen me since my fever, after all. It had been four days since we had spoken.

But he did not come to my rooms as I had hoped. Instead, I heard him trudging past to his own bedroom, his footfalls and the thud of his cane on the carpet passing my door without a moment of hesitation.

I waited a few minutes.

A few stretched into ten, which became half an hour, until I could stand it no more. I donned my robe and slippers, stepped into the corridor and tapped gently on his door.

He opened it, his face tired and drawn in the candlelight.

'You are avoiding me,' I said, standing in the doorway.

'Ah, I thought it was you who was avoiding me,' he replied with a casual lie, turning away so that I could step into the room and close the door behind me. He had not yet readied himself for bed, and I wondered what he had been doing since coming home. My eyes darted around and I noticed that the small trunk that was usually under the writing desk was now in the middle of the floor, the lid closed but the lock undone. A larger trunk was open, as were a few of his drawers, clothes spilling over the sides. Had he been . . . packing? He removed his jacket, dark green velvet with gold buttons, and placed it on the back of the chair.

I blinked away my surprise at the state of his room and cleared my throat. 'I had hoped to see you this morning before you left for the offices, or yesterday, or even Wednesday. Or Tuesday, in fact,' I said, sounding a little desperate even to my own ears. There was an inexplicable chill in the air between us.

'I checked on you the night after . . . on Tuesday morning,' he corrected himself, 'but I found you were feverish and murmuring in your sleep. I had a maid call the doctor before I left.' He did not meet my gaze. 'I thought it better coming from one of your servants rather than your mother hearing I had been in your room unaccompanied.'

That was fair reasoning, and I couldn't precisely say why it bothered me so. Perhaps it was his stand-offishness, or the fact that he would not look at me.

He rolled up his shirtsleeves to reveal tanned arms marked with a dozen nicks and scars from hard years at sea. The sight sent another wave of heat through my cheeks that had nothing to do with any fever, and I tried not to stare as he loosened his cravat.

'I am conscious of the fact that you and your mother have not known me very long. She made it clear to me on Tuesday that I have much to learn about looking after my *lady wife*.' The last two words were sharp and hard, unpleasant to the ear. 'It is a wonder that I don't still have a guard at my door – something I have you to thank for, as I understand it. Besides,' he shrugged, 'she has every right not to trust me, as do you.'

His voice was steady, his tone careless almost, as if he was not aware of how much damage those simple words could do. It was such a change from our previous conversation, as if he had built a wall between us in the days that he had been absent. I could not quite understand it, and I took a step forward, trying to read his expression as he studiously undid the thong in his hair and let it fall loose around his face.

'Did she give you trouble?' I asked. After our conversation this evening, I doubted she would have meddled. She was well within her rights, but from my understanding, she approved of our match. If anything, Erasmus had gained her trust just as quickly as he had mine.

'No more than I deserve. She scolded me for letting you fall ill, and told me if I did not have more concern for your well-being, we might need to revisit the terms of our agreement.' An empty threat on her part, I knew. 'I'm inclined to agree with her.'

My brows drew into a frown. I had been expecting a little humour, perhaps a casual comment on my mother's nerves. I did not like this change in him. 'What are you saying, Erasmus?'

I noticed the white of his knuckles as he gripped the band of leather before flinging it onto the dressing table, exhaling through his nose in exasperation.

'I'm saying that you've had the briefest glimpse into the life I led before we met, and look what happened,' he growled, his voice full of low anger. 'You were kidnapped! I have never seen you so pale as when I came home to you on Monday night. And the next morning,' he ran a hand through his hair, 'I came to see how you were only to find you fighting some nightmare, burning with fever and clearly unwell. And the bruises on your neck . . .' His eyes immediately found them, and I resisted the urge to pull my robe up to conceal them. '*I* was responsible for those. I thought it only right that I should allow you to convalesce in peace. I am a selfish fool to think I could keep this up while doing what I do. I . . .' He shook his head as if trying to remove a thought. 'I will not be responsible for harm coming to you. If that means I have to keep my distance, then so be it.'

My mouth fell open with surprise. The guilt and fear seemed to be waging a war somewhere very close to the surface of him, and I tried to assuage some of it.

'I thought I had already made my feelings clear regarding Monday's events, but in case I was not definite enough, I will say it plainly. I don't blame you for what happened. Perhaps you think me foolish, but I cannot find fault with your actions or decisions when I understand your motives as I do.'

I strode towards him so that he could no longer avoid looking at me, and planted my feet in front of his, noticing that even without his shoes on, he was still almost a head taller than I.

'Yes, I had a mild fever from being soaked through by the

rain. Yes, I was a little distraught to find my husband had a secret life that I was suddenly a part of, but at no point did I give you the impression that you should stay away from me. I know that we have established you are not my husband in every sense, but at the very least I feel I warrant a place as . . . a friend? Surely with all that we have been through these past few days, you can acknowledge that I have earned that.' I tried to keep my voice low, and level with his, but I couldn't deny that his coldness had irritated me. My senses told me that whatever this was, it was not my mother's doing. His feeble excuses were tiny white lies, and I could sense every single one.

'It is through confiding in you that I have realised my errors, Jenny. I should never have told you my secrets in the first place. It is better that you play your part of the dutiful wife here in the safety of your home,' he replied stonily. That was the truth at least.

I bristled at his words. I was supposed to be upset with him for avoiding me, not him at me for getting tangled up in his messes.

The worst thing was, underneath it all I knew he was correct. I had spent half the day fantasising about a happy life together only to have him come home late and tell me that he wanted me to stay away from him. But he *had* put me in danger. With his secrets, with his past. Tendrils of fear climbed their way up my spine, partly from the thought of him pulling away from me, and partly from the idea that he was right.

That did not stop me from giving a derisive scoff. 'First you criticise my mother for treating me like porcelain, and then you do the same. Who are you to tell me how to carry out my duties? Is it so surprising to you that I do not want you to keep your distance? That I might actually want to be something more to you? More than just a stranger who lives under the same roof?'

Frustrated, I fidgeted with the rings on my finger; his mother's and mine beside each other, glinting gold, black and blue in the light.

'Jenny, you don't know what that means . . .'

'You said you are a man of your word. So tell me, Erasmus – what is your word worth if you push me away at the first sign of trouble? Why even give me this?' I held up my hand, the gold band he had placed there winking in the low light.

He hesitated, emotions flitting across his face. Sadness, regret, frustration, pain, all were there and gone in an instant. A muscle ticked in his jaw, and I saw I wasn't truly the source of his ire; rather he was angry with himself.

'It is not that simple. I thought it could be. I wish that I were just some foppish merchant who had the good fortune to stumble across you and your mother last week in the pub, and that I could spend the rest of my life making you happy,' he said in a rush of words that had my heart beating a staccato rhythm in my chest. 'But I am not, and I cannot. There are so many people involved, and if any of what I'm doing were to come back to you, it could threaten everything your mother is trying to preserve.' His voice was firm enough that I could see he would brook no argument on the matter. But I had heard the hidden meaning in his words even if he had, as usual, been so careful with them. Something else had occurred to give him second thoughts. Something or someone had alarmed him enough to come home and try to pull himself away from me. He took my hand, resting his fingertips on the rings as though they might anchor his thoughts. My heart stuttered with the contact.

'There are real lives in danger. My own life is at risk every day that I keep up this pretence, even with my years of experience. To bring you into this now is not fair on either of us, no matter how much I might wish for it.'

Breath hitched in my chest as I picked apart what he had

said. He was pushing me away, shuttering himself so that I could not get closer to him. I'd had but a toe in the door, and I wanted to wedge it wide open and be let in.

'Are you going somewhere?' I asked, looking towards the larger trunk, open on the floor. His jaw ticked once more, almost in answer, but I waited.

'I thought it best I remove myself from your home. That way I can continue to work for your father's company without drawing attention to you.'

'No,' I said definitely. 'I do not accept that.'

'I will keep one of my crew outside your home until my business here is concluded, but to stay would only draw more danger to your doorstep.'

'Then we face it together, Erasmus. What must I say to make you understand that I am willing to help you, that I *want* to help you?'

He didn't reply, but his expression was haunted. Who had he lost to have caused this reaction in him? I wondered. He was afraid, but rather than match his fear, I found myself wanting to comfort him, to be brave when he could not be.

'Am I a fool for wanting this?' I asked, realising a moment too late that I had asked the question aloud.

'That depends,' he murmured, 'on what exactly it is that you want.'

I blew out a breath, staying otherwise still as he held my hand between us. When was the last time I had been honest with myself, or anyone else for that matter? I sighed, feeling something open up inside my chest that I couldn't name. 'To no longer feel alone,' I began, cheeks flushing slightly. 'To have someone I can confide in. A companion. A . . . true husband.'

He closed his eyes as though it pained him to hear my admission.

'You are far from foolish, Jenny. It is human to want those things.' When he opened his eyes, the candlelight caught in them, flecks of yellow and gold in an inky pool. 'But the heart is a precious thing, and not to be given lightly, particularly not to someone unworthy.'

The sting of his words had me biting my tongue. Did he consider himself somehow unworthy of me, or was it I that was not worthy of him?

'What happened today?' I probed gently when he said nothing further. 'If you explain it to me, perhaps I can help.'

It was his turn to sigh, stirring the hair that fell in front of his face. I didn't hesitate, using my free hand to brush it back, taking heart from the way he almost leaned into my touch.

'I promised you I would let you help. But I also promised myself I wouldn't put you in harm's way. It is best if you don't know.'

'Ah, Erasmus Black,' I scolded, 'you think you know all the right things to say to make a girl forgive you for keeping secrets. But I am not any girl, and I cannot be fooled by pretty words, no matter how clever you are at wielding them.'

His throat bobbed as he swallowed, and I tried not to be distracted by the movement, by the fine column of his neck and the shade of stubble that grew there.

'For a mouse you have awfully sharp claws,' he murmured hoarsely.

'It was you who mistook me for a mouse,' I answered, the room growing warmer as we stood before each other, him trying to defend whatever he was hiding while I pulled away his armour piece by piece.

Another sigh, although at least this one was accompanied by a smile as he realised that I would not let the matter go. 'You are impossible.'

'So are you,' I retorted, extricating my hands and folding my arms across my chest.

'I deserve your rage, and you will understand why soon enough. If you are certain you want to hear the truth of it, I will tell you.'

'I can deal with the truth, Erasmus. What I cannot abide is lies, so if there is something you must confide in me, I would rather know now.'

'Little mouse, there will be no coming back from this once I tell you. Much has happened since we met last week in the tavern, and I do not know how you will react when you learn my real purpose for being here.'

'If it is so awful that I decide you should leave, then you are already half packed,' I said almost carelessly. 'But if you tell me and I do not run from this room screaming, I beg you to stop shutting me out. Please.'

He nodded resignedly, gesturing to the chair at his small desk so that I could sit, while he took his place on the edge of the bed, elbows resting on his knees.

'Very well, I will tell you. But do not say I gave you no warning.'

Chapter 13

ꕥ

ERASMUS TELLS THE TRUTH

'I came to London at the behest of my captain, who has the singular goal of locating someone very important. In the process of finding this person, we have, as you know, been taking on contracts that might put us in a position to free any girls who are being ferried into the skin trade. And sometimes we take on voyages that will make us enough funds to continue our work.' I nodded in understanding. I imagined that this captain of his must be quite the man to have inspired someone such as Erasmus to help him.

'With such a grand mission, did you believe that by marrying me you might access a larger amount of funds to help you?' I asked before I could think better of it. It was quite the accusation, but the idea had occurred in the back of my mind during our dinner that this might be the true explanation for his hidden letter. His wounded look had me thinking otherwise, however.

'Your money did not enter the equation when I agreed to marry you, although I must admit it was the only logical explanation I could provide my crew for entering into such an arrangement.'

I felt not entirely convinced, knowing that he needed two thousand pounds a month for something he had yet to disclose. 'What was it then? You were informed that my father's company might be dealing with these illegal contracts?'

His long fingers steepled in front of him as he endured the frustration in my tone.

'This is where it becomes difficult, for it is so much more than that, Jenny. During my last trip to the Continent, I came upon an excellent opportunity for us. A shipment of saffron that was so lucrative it would fund the purchase of three dozen of these girls. It was money far in excess of what we had had access to previously, and would allow me to acquire their contracts directly, take them aboard our ship and immediately release them. To be clear, this is an impossibility under normal circumstances. I merely needed to pose as an interested buyer, place the highest bid, and they would be free.

'I am oversimplifying the ordeal, of course, for sometimes it takes weeks or months to ingratiate ourselves with the sellers. They must believe that our interest is genuine, lest we give away our entire game.'

I imagined Erasmus playing the part of one of these merchants, having to pretend that he condoned the practice. The thought filled me with apprehension and concern for him.

'I was so close,' he continued, his frustration showing in the way his expression screwed up into a frown, 'but when we thought the deal was already done, we were outbid under the table, after the auction had already completed.'

I gave a quiet gasp. 'Surely that would be . . .' *Illegal*, I had wanted to say, realising it was ridiculous. Of course these people would take a higher offer if they thought they could get away with it. He nodded, understanding where my thoughts had gone.

'I would have thought it merely bad luck if it had not

happened again a few months later, at the next auction. It took careful investigation to discover that in both instances the buyer had been an Englishman. Not the same gentleman, but both used the same broker for their purchases. A criminal by the name of Ahmet Demir. The Ottoman general responsible for the sale of these girls seems to have a very special relationship with Mr Demir. Thankfully there is little honour amongst thieves, and we used some of our saffron money to purchase information from him. He confirmed that there was a small triad of English merchants making these outside bids, and that, amongst other things, was what led us here.'

'You believe that these girls are being shipped to London?'

'Unlikely. Only a few can be sold at a time, lest some authority discover them. The girls are groomed into the highest order of prostitute, and the men who purchase them have to be wealthy. The sellers must have connections in order to distribute the girls across a number of countries. Unfortunately, in both of those instances, we failed to locate where they had been sent.'

A sick feeling settled in my stomach. More than thirty-six women had been separated and vanished, preventing Erasmus and his crew from being able to find them. That would take no small amount of funds, I thought, considering the ships required to transport the girls and possibly the bribes required for the captains and crews to carry out their criminal work.

'So whoever made those higher offers than you must have been very wealthy indeed,' I concluded, wondering what sort of man would involve himself in a venture such as this. Were my father's merchant friends capable of such disregard for people's lives? For the lives and safety of young girls? I shook my head even as I thought of it. 'And you believe that someone you are in contact with here in London was responsible?'

Erasmus pressed his lips together, as though unsure how much to say.

'We narrowed down the suspects considerably, based on a contact my captain made on Corfu. There are two London merchants we believe are involved.'

I thought of the letter I had found under his mattress. I hoped, silently prayed, that he had been told to seek a position in one of the two companies for money alone. I wanted him to tell me that his battle had nothing to do with Miller, Osborne & Talver.

My godfather could not be involved in this. He had three daughters of his own and would not – could not – condone the practice of girls being ripped from their families and made to fulfil the basest of needs. Talver might not be my favourite person, but I liked to think that the man my father had called one of his closest associates would not stoop so low either. Erasmus's expression was one of apprehension. He could see where my thoughts were taking me and he did not want to be the one to say it aloud.

'Impossible,' I said in response to his unspoken suspicion, sounding far more certain than I felt. 'My father was a pacifist. He convinced Osborne and Talver years ago that they should not do business with those who used slaves to harvest their crops. To think that they would willingly traffic humans is out of the question. Surely you do not think them capable of such cruelty? Osborne can be a little overbearing at times, and I am the first to admit that Talver makes my skin crawl, but they are not *evil*. They were my father's closest friends.' Panic constricted my lungs and I found I could not easily breathe.

'Jenny,' Erasmus said softly, his tone sympathetic, 'the world is not as clear-cut as you might believe. And I am accusing no one directly, but although there are laws in England forbidding the practice, there are still entire countries and nations that have not voted as this government did eight years ago. It is still possible to profit from trading flesh if you know who to ask, sending ships under the guise of selling one commodity when what you are doing in reality is something entirely different.'

'But not my father.' I shook my head. 'He would have shut his own company down and lost his fortune before doing such a thing. Wouldn't he?' I heard the edge of fear in my voice, the doubt and worry that I hadn't known the man I'd loved and looked up to as well as I had thought, even as I defended him.

'Jenny . . .'

'He was honourable. A true gentleman and believer.' I began to sense a note of hysteria in my own words, looking at Erasmus with pleading eyes. He got up off the bed and knelt before me, taking my hands in his own so that I was forced to look at him.

'Jenny, I don't think your father knew anything of it,' he said reassuringly. 'I've spent every spare moment I can trying to find documents at your father's offices that pertain to the purchase of those girls, or any voyages connected to it, to no avail. But if my sources are as accurate as I believe them to be, one of my new business partners is hiding those manifests very carefully, and only finding them will bring him to justice.'

The revelation set my nerves on edge, a peculiar pain catching in my every breath. Even if Jacob Miller had known nothing of it, did that mean that my father's company, my family's fortune, was implicated? Did my mother know?

'It must be Talver,' I whispered, thinking of Erasmus's letter. He had been sent to infiltrate my father's company and Griegsson's – the real reason for him being in London.

'All indications point to him,' Erasmus admitted, 'but he is not working alone. There are other investigations I must make, for I do not see how George Talver would have access to the necessary funds.'

The two thousand pounds? Was this what the amount in his letter had referred to? I did not know how to ask without showing my hand.

'It sickens me,' I bit out. 'He was here in our home. I have known him my entire life and yet had no notion that he could be capable of such despicable behaviour. To think that there are people so willing to flout the law for the sake of money. Talver. Griegsson. Who knows how many others?'

Erasmus became very still, his grip tightening on my fingers.

'Where did you hear that name?'

I felt the colour drain from my cheeks as I realised my slip. I thought of lying, of telling him that of course as a merchant's daughter I would have met Mr Griegsson, but even as I conjured up the fib, I realised that it was no good admonishing him for keeping the truth from me, only to do the same to him.

'I read it. In your letter.'

He frowned, perhaps wondering if there was another meaning to what I had said.

'It is my turn to apologise.' I extricated my hands from his and stood, pacing the room, the skirts of my robe swishing against the floor. 'On the first day you were away at the offices, I felt you were hiding something, and in a momentary lapse of judgement I came in here to search for clues. I wanted to understand who you were and why you had ended up in our lives seemingly by accident. I found the letter mentioning my father's company and Mr Griegsson's, and I thought perhaps you had been looking for merchant businesses that offered high-paying contracts, or those that had positions available. The sum of money, two thousand pounds per month, was so high that only a handful of merchants would be able to fund you. Then I began to wonder if our meeting had been coincidental, or if you had somehow known that I was in need of a husband and had arranged to be in the tavern that night.'

His mahogany eyes followed me around the room as I paced, my hands tangling in the skirts of my robe as I spoke.

'Well I never,' he said, though his tone was light and almost humorous. 'You are full of surprises, little mouse. Is there anything else I should know while we're on the subject of secrets?'

'Is there anything else you ought to tell *me*?' I countered.

He stood and crossed the room in two strides, so that we were barely inches apart. My breath caught in my throat at the proximity, at his black hair limned by candlelight so that the strands shone bronze, the angles of his jaw, his cheekbones. Those dark eyebrows furrowed as he studied me.

'I did not meet you by any design of my own, if that is what you are asking.'

I exhaled, sensing the truth in those words that I had needed to hear.

'You are a remarkable woman, Jenny.' He gave a wolfish smile, and I felt a blush from the compliment all the way down to my toes.

'What do you require such a sum of money for?' I asked in an attempt to remove the attention from my flushed cheeks.

'What do you know of saffron?' he countered, and then added, in response to my scowl, 'I am not trying to get out of answering you, but it is a relevant part of my reply.'

I thought back to what I had heard of it, more over the past week than ever before. 'It is rare, and expensive. I did not realise until you mentioned it that it comes from Greece. But surely it would not be worth two thousand pounds per month? Who on earth would require that much of it?'

'Perhaps only the king and his court,' Erasmus replied. 'But trading saffron is also an excellent way of hiding other expensive commodities. Such as slave girls.'

I blinked, feeling only a little wiser.

'So you require the money to buy these girls?'

'No, no,' he said with a shake of his head. 'These English merchants are using saffron as a way to cover up their purchase of girls. There have to be manifests of some sort, declarations of goods and what have you. Saffron is so expensive in some regions that no one would baulk at that price. If it is George Talver's doing, he will have needed to secrete away something in the order of two thousand pounds per month for at least a quarter of the year to make the purchase. That size of expenditure, or anything near to it, would be enough evidence that he was intending to acquire a small amount of saffron and perhaps four or five Greek girls.'

I thought over this new information. 'I still don't understand why he would go to the trouble. I don't claim to be an expert, but what is wrong with the local . . . women of the night?' I said, not quite ready to refer to them by any other name.

Erasmus wrinkled his nose in distaste, then took a breath, searching for words that would not offend my already assaulted sensibilities. 'These girls are pure. Unadulterated,' he said carefully, gauging my understanding. I nodded. They were virgins. Untouched and free from disease. 'They are specially trained for their work, often drugged so that they are pliable and carefree. A man who purchases one owns her completely without the technicalities of marriage.'

Men like this existed, I knew. I could not help but think someone like Lord Darleston would have relished such an idea, evil as he was. 'Do they not worry about children? About illegitimacy?'

'That is not bedtime conversation, I think,' Erasmus said hastily, and if the matter had not been so serious, I would have found his discomfort amusing. 'I am convinced that you are capable of understanding the truth, Jenny, but it is late and you need your rest. I will not insult you by hiding further information from you if you are willing to trust my lead and heed my warnings when I say that what I am doing is unsafe.' His voice was low, almost hypnotic, and I found myself nodding along.

'Of course, but I want to help you. Your captain. If someone in my father's company is involved in this, I want them brought to justice and my father's name cleared. What do you require of me?'

There was a finality to my declaration. He took in my determined expression, sufficiently satisfied with what he saw there that his next words came quickly.

'I have spent my last few days attempting to befriend my new business partners. Henry Osborne, your godfather as I understand it, seems willing enough to accept me into his confidence. He has a pleasant if rather pompous demeanour, I have found.' He paused to see if I had taken offence at his observation. I nodded, agreeing with his sentiments entirely. 'But George Talver is harder to read. He shows very little emotion and is unwilling to share more than a few words with me when we are forced into proximity with one another. He uses this aloof manner to demonstrate his distrust of me, but I am beginning to sense there is something more to it. The only occasion I have had to determine his thoughts on the matter of slaves was this evening, when I stayed behind to speak with him. When I mentioned my recent voyages to Tunis and Morea, he perked up considerably, and we had a lengthy discourse on the subject of the money that could be made there if we were open to trades of a different sort. I felt as though he was trying to get a sense for where I stood on the matter; he even went so far as to ask what I would be willing to do to keep the company afloat.'

'As I suspected, the man is a viper.' Anger surged through my blood at the thought of him attempting to bully my husband into doing what he wanted. If Erasmus had been any other man, one of the dandies Mother had tried to marry me off to, perhaps he would have fallen for it, keen to please and even more eager to gain Talver's favour. But he was not. He was Erasmus Black, and whether he was a privateer or a captain or a pirate, he would not stand for such a thing.

I wondered if Talver had tried the same tactics with my father, or if he had known that Jacob Miller would never agree to the arrangement, and had instead hidden it altogether.

'What will you do?' I asked.

'Well, I have to gather evidence, ideally catch him in the act. I have a contact in the Saints who is very interested in putting an end to all this.'

'The Saints?' I asked, trying to remember where I had heard the name. I recalled my father speaking of the Christian men who had lobbied for our anti-slavery bills. It was the journalists who had dubbed them the "Clapham Saints", somewhat disparagingly, but they had taken the moniker to heart and continued their work.

Erasmus confirmed as much, nodding as he replied, 'Indeed, the social reformers from Clapham who have worked rather tirelessly to have new laws passed. I believe they can assist us, even though we might be asking that they turn their attention further to the East. We are compiling evidence, putting a new bill together. It is taking a considerable amount of time, which is why I decided to take a more . . . proactive approach to the situation, but the goal is the same.'

A strange pride swelled inside me at knowing this; that he

wasn't just a privateer or a vigilante, but someone with a driving purpose to help everyone, not just his kinfolk. I felt a strange certainty then as I studied him.

'What can I do to assist?'

He gave a soft laugh. 'Ah, there's the lioness.' My toes curled in my slippers at the look he gave me then, as though I were some sort of wonder that he had stumbled upon. It was a look that made me feel ten feet tall. I could kiss him now, and no one could stop me. God knew I wanted to.

'Why are you smiling?' he asked quietly, dispersing my thoughts as I realised I'd been grinning.

I breathed a laugh, running a hand down his arm, my palm tingling with the warmth of his skin. 'To think I wanted to go on adventures before I met you,' I said with a shake of my head.

'Why is that so amusing?' He leaned closer, his pupils dilating in the dark as our breath mingled.

'Well, Erasmus, I think you're all the adventure I'll ever need.'

He inhaled sharply, as though the words had surprised him. Some emotion passed over his face and he closed his eyes as though bracing himself. His was the look of someone who had loved and lost before, I was sure of it.

'If any harm were to come to you . . .'

'I trust you,' I said, squeezing his arm gently. 'Won't you trust me too?'

His hands were suddenly on me, holding my face as he studied me, his thumbs tracing the lines of my jaw, so careful not to touch the bruises on my neck. Slowly he leaned forward, touching his nose to mine as if to see how close he could possibly get without actually kissing me. The agony of being so near to him was a tangible pain in my chest. He brushed his lips on each cheek so softly I barely felt it, before releasing me as quickly as he had taken hold and guiding me to the door of his bedroom. I was too stunned to argue, too caught up in the brief moment of tenderness to complain that I had yet to be kissed.

'You have my trust, Jenny Black,' he whispered into the corridor as he moved to close the door. 'I only pray that I am worthy of yours.'

Chapter 14

ꕥ

THE MIDNIGHT ROSE

I awoke when the morning sun reached between the curtains, striping my room in dark and light and stirring me from yet more troubled dreams. I had stood outside my husband's closed door for several long minutes the previous evening, blinking in surprise and disbelief before I realised that it had been his way of ensuring our conversation was resolutely over.

I groaned as I flipped myself onto my stomach to escape the sunlight and buried my head in my pillow. Had I embarrassed myself last night? Had I seemed so needy and desperate for affection that it had forced Erasmus to push me away so that nothing more could happen between us?

The thought of his hands on my face, the brush of his lips against my cheeks, had me kicking my sheets off and heading to my basin, washing with tepid water from the jug so that I could cool the burning in my cheeks. Edith came to help dress me shortly after, no doubt having heard me stomping about my room as I upbraided myself for being so stupid. I glared at the novel on my bed stand, blaming it for giving me false ideas of heroes and heroines, deciding that I really ought to purchase some books that were more appropriate.

'Not that one,' I said to Edith as she retrieved one of my dresses from the closet. 'No lace today. I should like to walk about the city and visit Oscarson's, so I think the more practical darker blue will do nicely.' I added a shawl to cover the already fading bruises on my neck.

Once I had dressed and Edith had helped to do my hair in a tight bun, leaving a few blonde ringlets loose at my temples, I descended the stairs to breakfast to the sound of my mother laughing hysterically.

I stopped at the doorway of the dining room, mouth agape as she and Erasmus laughed over something to the point where my mother had tears in the corners of her eyes.

'Oh, very good, William. You are quite the wit,' she managed to say as she dabbed her face with a napkin. 'Jenny, good morning. How are you feeling, my dear?'

Erasmus looked up from his breakfast, his eyes darting up and down until they rested on my face. If I didn't know better, I would have thought there was a hint of desire behind that look, but recalling his rebuttal from last night, I gave a perfunctory nod and took my place beside him. I was tired of chasing, of wearing my heart on my sleeve. I would let him do some work for once.

'I'm well, Mama, thank you. I shall be visiting Oscarson's this morning if you can spare Marcus.'

Erasmus answered before she could. 'Fortuitously I have the day free after all my long evenings this week. If Mrs Miller has no objection, I would be happy to accompany you.'

My mother clapped her hands happily. 'A marvellous idea. It will be good to have you seen together out in public. I noted that apart from your marriage announcement, there has been little by way of recognition in the social papers, and it would not do for anyone to question the legitimacy of your betrothal.'

'I was not aware that it had been called into question,' I said with surprise.

'You know how people like to gossip, Jenny. We need only display the two of you together every so often to put any nasty rumours to bed. I had a letter just this morning from Lady Griffiths, feigning distress that she had not been invited to your wedding and wondering why it had not been given proper coverage in the *Chronicle*.' She rolled her eyes at the social games we all played. It explained why she was so keen to throw us together. If I hadn't been intending to avoid my husband today, to put a little distance between us after my embarrassment last night, I might have enjoyed the attention.

'It would be my great pleasure to accompany you if you'll have me, Jenny,' Erasmus said. He tried to make eye contact with me, which I resolutely ignored.

My mother gave me an encouraging nod, almost comical in its enthusiasm, and I restrained myself from groaning. At least there was no sign of her slipping back into the abyss she had fallen into after my father had died. To see her enjoying a jest was enough for me to forgive Erasmus a little.

'Very well. I should like to set off on foot early, if that isn't too inconvenient for you. It feels as though I haven't walked or moved beyond my room in days.'

'Not at all. I know a wonderful spot to take refreshment if you are happy to walk a little further than the bookshop,' he said in some sort of peace offering.

'Take Aristotle with you, won't you?' Mother interjected, and the spaniel perked up at the mention of his name. 'I have so much to do today, it would be better not to have him under my feet, and I'm certain he would enjoy a little adventure.'

I agreed, taking a roll from the basket at the centre of the table and spreading a good helping of butter on it while my mother explained her many tasks for the day.

'Do you know how many invitations we have received just in the past week since you married, Jenny? Four! Four invitations to soirées and dinners. They know I cannot attend, of course, but it is polite of them to consider me. I must say, it is as though your wedding has absolutely eclipsed your father's passing,' she said with a theatrical wave of a hand. 'Before I forget, cousin Beatrice will be visiting, so we shall have to have a room made up for her. Oh, and would you believe that Marie Osborne is holding a ball? A *party*, Jenny, so soon after my Jacob's death.'

I half listened, distracted by Erasmus sneaking a piece of sausage to Aristotle beneath the table.

'It has been more than two months, Mama, and they likely wish to gawp at the fallen-from-grace socialite who managed to marry the mysterious Mr Black,' I replied with a sigh. If Erasmus noted the jab at him, he said nothing, pretending to be engrossed in my mother's every word.

'Osborne mentioned nothing to me at the offices. What is the cause for celebration?' he asked after a sip of tea.

'Henrietta's sixteenth birthday. It is far too young for her to be out, but they are inviting half of London, I've heard,' she said, raising a disapproving eyebrow. Henrietta, the Osbornes' eldest daughter, would no doubt be in the same predicament as I had been if Henry were also to meet an untimely death. I could imagine the many reasons why she was about to be paraded to the eligible men so early. That was the penalty for having daughters, I supposed.

'That is one engagement I do not think it would be wise to miss,' she added, nodding to Erasmus to ensure he was paying attention.

'I'm sure it will be delightful,' he said smoothly, hiding a smile behind his cup of tea that only I could see.

'It will *not*,' Mother said adamantly. 'But I shall have to pretend for the sake of propriety, even if it feels far too soon to celebrate anything. Besides, if you think Henry Osborne is a tad overbearing, just wait until you meet his wife.' She finished off with a harrumph, and I had to kick Erasmus under the table to stop him from laughing.

Marcus stepped into the room at that moment with a letter for Erasmus.

Who brought it? I signed to him.

The young lad, K-I-T. He spelled out the name and I interpreted for Erasmus.

My husband broke the seal and scanned the contents of the letter in almost one motion, too quick for me steal a glance at what it might contain but not so fast that I didn't spot the way he gripped the paper, and the huff of frustration as he folded it back up and slid it into an inner jacket pocket.

'Bad news?' my mother asked with a sweet smile that I knew was a poor attempt at hiding her curiosity.

'Just an update from my crew; nothing to worry about. We may need to make a small detour before we venture home, if that isn't too much trouble, Jenny?'

I was surprised to hear him inviting me along for whatever it was he needed to attend to, but I agreed before he could change his mind.

'Just be home before dinner time, if you would,' Mother said with a meaningful look towards us both. 'Aristotle won't know what to do with himself if you don't make it back by then.'

'Of course, Mrs Miller,' Erasmus replied, stroking the dog's floppy ears as he whined for more food.

*

Oscarson's wasn't my only port of call for the morning, but it was the first place on my list, and the sound of the bell as we entered the old bookshop sent a delighted thrill through me. The scent of fresh ink and paper, dust and leather greeted me, and I left Erasmus and Aristotle at the door as I stepped between the rows of shelves.

We had shared a few congenial words on our walk over, my arm threaded through my husband's as his cane rapped against the cobbled paving stones, Aristotle tugging on the lead in my other hand at every new smell. I didn't want to bring up what had happened the night before. Or, more accurately, what had *not* happened. I was too ashamed at the rejection to raise the subject and found myself grateful for the distraction and promise of more books to take my mind off the obvious fact that my husband didn't wish to get too close to me.

The shop was deceptively large, with floor-to-ceiling bookcases and aisles in between, and a mezzanine floor that could be reached by way of a staircase. The counter ran along the right-hand side of the entrance to prevent would-be thieves from making off with any precious wares, and a bespectacled man in his late fifties sat behind it reading the paper.

'Good morning, Mr Oscarson,' I said as I approached, leaning my parasol against the counter and folding my hands in front of me until the old man looked up.

'Miss Miller!' He dropped the paper immediately and reached across the counter to take my hands. 'I was so sorry to hear about your father, miss. Truly it was a tragedy,' he said, his sympathy stirring some sadness that I had buried.

'Thank you, sir, you are most kind.'

'How is your dear mother?'

'As well as is to be expected. I wanted to introduce my husband,' I said, gesturing for Erasmus to come over, Aristotle making quick business of sniffing out the shelves. 'This is Er . . . William Black,' I quickly corrected myself.

'Husband! Well, congratulations, and how do you do, sir! Much has happened in the past month, it seems. I must have missed the announcement of your engagement and wedding in the papers.'

He took Erasmus's proffered hand in greeting and shook it vigorously. I refrained from explaining that there had been no engagement announcement, allowing him to assume it was an oversight on his part. Mr Oscarson had always been an emphatic sort of fellow, but he felt to me like a kindly distant uncle, showing small kindnesses in ordering books for me and taking in old ones that I had not enjoyed to swap for something else. Because of this, I didn't purchase books from anywhere else.

'You will be glad to hear that I have held on to your requests, Mrs Black,' he said, rummaging around under the counter until he produced a package wrapped in brown paper.

'Oh, wonderful! Might I browse for a few moments before I collect them from you?'

'Of course, be my guest. Mr Black, I would recommend the armchair at the back of the ground floor should you wish to take the weight off your feet. Your wife can spend many an hour amongst these shelves, I'm afraid,' the shopkeeper said with a well-intentioned chuckle.

'Ah, I see. Thank you for the warning,' Erasmus replied, taking Aristotle with him to the back of the room, where bright panels of sunlight stretched across the wooden floor, his steps stirring the dust motes like glitter.

I watched him go, trying to suppress the warm, homely feeling spreading in my chest as he picked up a book, settled into the armchair and began to read, Aristotle flopping down beside him. It was like glimpsing a moment of some other time, where I had a husband who enjoyed literature, who was nice to my dog, and who was more than happy to traipse around a bookstore with me. Except that it was, in part, an illusion. In this time and place I had a husband who led a secret life that he barely wanted me to be a part of, and who would probably rather be anywhere else than here. I could pretend, though, at least for a while.

An hour later, we were back on the street, Erasmus carrying a parcel of books under one arm that was slightly heavier than I had intended. I threaded my hand through his free arm once more, and refrained from apologising for taking so long, or making so many purchases.

Next was the dressmaker's to enquire about a swatch of lace and some buttons. I would not order a new dress for the sake of Henrietta Osborne's party, but I had in mind one that Edith could improve for me. I would have to discuss my plans with her and send her to fetch more fabric later, but the visit had at least sparked some inspiration in me, and a conversation with the haberdasher about this season's Parisian fashions had kindled an entirely new idea.

Then came the tea room to purchase a jar of Mother's favourite.

'Now that we have the important business taken care of,' Erasmus said, nodding to the bundle he carried, 'would you be averse to taking care of some of *my* business?'

With the jar of Earl Grey and the lace added to the books, he had begun to struggle with the weight of my purchases. Not to mention that Aristotle seemed determined to drag us home for a rest.

'I think we should deposit our shopping first, don't you? Though we shall have to be discreet, otherwise Mama will try and keep us back for lunch, I am certain of it.'

'Discretion is my middle name,' he replied.

'I thought it was Bartholomew?'

He was momentarily taken aback that I had remembered. 'Oh yes, Erasmus Bartholomew Discretion Black. It has a nice ring to it, does it not?'

Back at home, we left the packages and Aristotle with Marcus before dashing back down the front steps.

'All right, Mr Discretion Black, where to?' I asked.

The answer to that was another tavern, this one called the King George, situated just south of Covent Garden. We had walked until my feet ached in my pattens and my stomach rumbled from hunger, but I refrained from complaining as we sat down at a corner table where Gar, Kit and Carl happened to be waiting for us behind an impermeable barrier of pipe smoke.

'When my mother said we should be seen about town, I don't quite think this is what she had in mind,' I murmured, squinting in the dim interior.

'Would you like me to take you home?' Erasmus asked quietly.

I shook my head fervently and resolved to stay quiet if I could.

It was noon, and although the public house was not full by any means, it was certainly not empty. Everyone spoke in low, hushed tones, as though their business was all very secret, and Erasmus's crew followed suit.

'I didn't know you'd be bringing your lady wife, Mr Black,' Carl said, looking at me warily. It was true that seeing a woman in a tavern during the daytime was unusual, particularly one who didn't have more negotiable affections, but I simply shrugged and gave the Viking one of my grins.

'Mr Black has realised the merits of having a wealthy wife to wear on his arm. Where he goes, I go,' I replied simply, not looking at Erasmus as I said it. I sensed that if nothing else, the bravado would make me seem as though I belonged, even when doubt continued to rear its ugly head.

'Cap'n is not going to like that,' grumbled Kit.

'Yes, well, the captain is just going to have to get used to it,' Erasmus replied, cutting off the boy's complaints.

Before I could open my mouth to ask why the captain would dislike Erasmus bringing me with him, someone darted over to our table.

'Lei!' I greeted her, patting the seat beside me for her to sit.

'Mr B, Mrs B,' she said, turning the chair around so that her lean legs were straddling it, her chin propped on the back-rest. She wore a dark grey men's jacket done up to the neck and her cap pulled low over her face, making her look more like a boy than ever. 'Some news, gentlemen. You'll never guess who I just caught leaving the Midnight Rose.'

'George Talver,' Kit replied.

'You ruin all my fun,' she said with a scowl.

'But that's who you were told to follow,' he protested.

'What's the Midnight Rose?' I asked, and was answered with a few flushed cheeks and muttering from the men.

'It's a brothel, my lady,' Lei replied, rolling her eyes at the rest of the crew.

'Ah, I see. And you spotted Talver coming out of there? As in, he was a customer?' I asked, my voice dropping to a scandalised whisper.

'It's not all that surprising really. The Rose is quite an upmarket brothel even by Covent Garden standards,' Erasmus supplied, and I wondered briefly why he referred to it so familiarly, and how he knew that it was upmarket.

'Anyway,' Lei cut in, pulling my attention away from that concerning line of questioning, 'that's not all. You'll truly never guess who left the very same establishment moments afterwards.'

She looked at us all with an expectant grin, knowing that we would wait for her to tell us.

'Klaus Griegsson,' she whispered, at which there was a general intake of breath.

'You know the name, don't you, little mouse,' Erasmus whispered into my ear, as though I could possibly forget it.

'But why would they be meeting each other?' I enquired. It seemed an odd thing to do if they wished not to be caught out in their business.

'That's what we're going to find out,' Erasmus said, nodding to each of the men at the table. 'Jenny, you stay here with Kit. The boys and I will see if we can convince—'

'I told you I'd be coming with you,' I said abruptly.

He gave me a startled look in reply. 'You can't come into a *brothel*, Jenny. Good Lord, what would your mother say?'

'Oh, and it's acceptable for me to let my husband go into such a place unattended?'

I felt the eyes of the crew upon us, wondering who was going to win this particular argument.

'It's all right, Mr B. We'll go in and find out what we can, and you can watch the doors with Mrs B to make sure we don't miss any comings and goings,' Gar said helpfully.

I thought I understood Erasmus's hesitation. It was not because he truly wanted to go into the Midnight Rose, but more because he didn't want to send his people in there without him. Or so I hoped.

'We'll be right outside,' I said to him softly. 'If you get the slightest sense that something has gone wrong, we can be ready. You'll be with us too, won't you, Kit?'

The boy looked up at me, surprised, before his face twisted

into a scowl and he nodded sulkily. I wondered why he disliked me so, but there was no time to ponder on it. I would have to question him later, when we weren't about to embark on a potentially dangerous escapade.

We left the tavern in pairs, meandering around the corners of Covent Garden until the Midnight Rose was in sight. Gar peeled off from our scattered group, followed by Carl and eventually Lei, all heading in the direction of the dusky-pink-painted doors and slipping inside with little more than a backwards glance.

'I do not like this,' Erasmus said, looping my arm through his. The three of us stopped a few feet from the doors of the brothel and pretended to read a noticeboard, the front pages of the latest news tacked up on the wall. We were close enough that if anyone else of interest left, we would easily be able to identify them.

'Surely you trust them enough to do this without your supervision?' I tried to reassure him, wishing I could do more than simply thread my arm through his, resisting the desire to lean my head on his shoulder or move closer to him. Kit stood a few feet away, retrieving a small pipe and a box of matches from his pocket.

'It is not that I don't trust them,' Erasmus replied, frowning at the boy. 'Did Gar give you that?'

Kit exhaled a plume of smoke and shrugged. 'So what if he did?'

'Is he always this recalcitrant?' I murmured.

'More so since we came back to England. He wants me to return him to his mother, but it is far too dangerous in Greece at the moment. He'll be drafted into the Ottoman army in a heartbeat, strapping lad like him.'

I looked between Kit and my husband, wondering at the

history between them, and how he came to be the boy's guardian. Kit was surely old enough to take himself back home if he wanted to, but I sensed there was more to it that I had not yet discovered.

Minutes passed, but there was no sign of commotion or difficulty. There was also no sign of the crew, and Erasmus began to fidget in his subtle way, so that I could tell he was nervous.

I pondered on my husband's familiarity with the establishment, wondering if this might be where some of the girls he had been trying to save had been sent. I asked him as much, whispering the question to him even though no one but Kit was within earshot.

'Not likely. The women who take up the West End tend to be rather more voluntary to their line of work, though they are still referred to by their Greek monikers.' He read my perplexed expression and continued. 'Paphians? Cytheraens? Fair Cyprians?' I shook my head, unfamiliar with the terms.

'She's got no idea,' Kit mumbled, in a way that sounded like a criticism.

'They are all terms used to describe different classes of prostitute,' Erasmus explained, whispering the last word directly into my ear. 'Purportedly named after the cities most beloved by Aphrodite, goddess of love.'

I scoffed at that. 'I think very little of what they do for a living has to do with love.'

'True, but if they are lucky enough to catch the heart of some wealthy gentleman, they may be fortunate enough to have a private residence bought for them and be taken care of for life.'

'Or until their looks fade,' Kit added. Erasmus and I both shot him a disapproving glare. Whatever had made this boy so cynical? I wondered.

Ignoring him, I turned back to Erasmus, who loosened his

cravat slightly in the heat. I moved my parasol so as to provide him some shade and received a quirk of a smile in response.

'I suspect that the girls we failed to rescue never made it to London, or if they did, they are far beyond detection now. But the names given to these women do sometimes cause me to wonder for how long Greek slaves have been used for these purposes.'

I could not add my own thoughts to these suppositions, choosing to stay quiet on the matter.

After twenty minutes of reading the same news bulletins, something finally happened. 'Don't look now,' Kit said, pulling his cap low over his eyes.

Without warning, Erasmus turned to me and nuzzled my neck, his hand coming up to shield my surprised face from view. My parasol automatically covered us from behind as my arms moved to make space for him. A surge of heat coursed through me at the gesture, and I found myself leaning into his chest despite how much his rejection had hurt me last night. I wondered what the passers-by would think of us standing so intimately in the middle of the street, and I blushed at the thought of someone spotting us. But this was Covent Garden, and it wasn't unheard of for couples to meet in this way; they just tended not to be of our status. Then as quickly as he had moved towards me, Erasmus pulled away.

'What on earth was that for?' I asked a little breathlessly.

'Apologies for startling you,' he said, not looking at me but rather tracking some movement down the street, 'but I think I've just discovered why Talver and Griegsson were meeting.'

I turned to see the figure of a short man in a grey coat, top hat askew, with dark curls escaping from it, marching away with purpose.

'Who was it?'

'Kaine Clark,' he replied, grabbing my hand and guiding me in the opposite direction.

'Of course the rotten bastard would be here,' Kit said, keeping up with us, stowing his pipe, which had long since gone out.

'Kit, watch your language!' Erasmus chided.

'What? You've said worse,' the boy retorted, at which my husband rolled his eyes. Apparently there would be no winning with this young man.

'There's only one person who can tell us what's going on here,' Erasmus announced as we trotted along, 'and I'm afraid you're not going to like it.'

'Why does that not surprise me?' I replied, pressing my lips into a thin, unimpressed line and allowing him to take the lead.

The Midnight Rose was in the middle of a block of buildings, and we had to walk the length of it to cut through an alleyway and reach what I assumed was a back door. As untrusting as I was of these narrow streets, it was broad daylight, and gripping Erasmus's hand reassured me that we would not have a repeat of the other night. We pressed against the moss-slick walls to avoid walking into dustbins, and I shuddered as rats squeaked in protest at our trespassing on their home ground. Wooden gangways zigzagged along the backs of the buildings, rough-hewn and ugly compared to their ornate whitewashed frontages, while stone steps led to the basements beneath the various establishments. It was one such basement that Erasmus brought me to, Kit taking up the rear.

'Jenny, I won't ask again lest I insult you, but are you certain you would not rather stay outside?'

I looked at the iron door at the bottom of the stairs, aged and coated with rust. Glancing behind me, the alleyway looked no more inviting, and I nodded before I could change my mind.

'Very well,' he replied with a defeated sigh, before rapping on the door with his cane in a complicated series of staccato knocks.

There was no answer for several minutes, and just as I began to regret my decision to go in, an older woman, perhaps my mother's age, opened the door a crack. Vivid red hair fell about her face down to her waist, and her lips were painted the colour of blood, but more noticeable was her ample bosom, which almost fell out of her corset as she moved to open the door wider.

'Captain Ellison! Well, isn't this an absolute pleasure,' she purred, her eyes focused solely on Erasmus. He knew this woman? And exactly how many names did he have?

'Samantha,' he said with a hint of charm that I recognised. Dread coiled in my stomach at the realisation that they were well enough acquainted, and I tried not to think about how or why, no matter how foolish that made me. 'A business call, I'm afraid,' he added.

'It always is with you,' she said with a wink before standing back and allowing us inside, closing the door behind us with a groan of rusted hinges.

The Midnight Rose was far more opulent than I had expected for a brothel. Although the windows were covered and the walls were painted a dark grey, the furnishings and curtains were plush, in deep purples and reds with gold trimmings. Apparently the patrons paid well.

'Your boys came in here, none too discreetly, I might add, and have made themselves comfortable in the Blue Room with your lady.'

Erasmus froze, and I bumped into him, just as the meaning of Samantha's words jolted through me.

'Ah, very good,' he replied, sounding as uncomfortable as I felt.

His lady? He had his own girl here at this establishment? But then what had I expected? As we walked along the wide corridors, passing doors with names such as Ruby Room, Orchid Room and the rather predictable Rose Room, I scolded myself for being so stupid, and so incredibly naïve.

There could, of course, be an innocent explanation for all of this, but I was not so guileless as to believe it. Perhaps *this* was the reason for his distance last night. It would explain why he was so reluctant to be close to me at the very least, even if I felt ill at the thought of him tangled with some other woman.

I prepared myself for the worst, imagining a lady like Samantha but perhaps younger, lounging on a blue settee and surrounded by cushions with very little to cover herself as she waited for Erasmus to arrive. The picture made my stomach turn, and I stumbled more than once on the carpet, feeling the blood draining from my face.

When the madam finally opened the door to the Blue Room, giving my husband a conspiratorial wink as she ushered us inside, I worried that I might throw up what was left of my breakfast.

Gar and Carl were perched on a chaise longue the colour of sapphires, while Lei sat comfortably cross-legged on a pile of cushions, all topaz, cerulean and turquoise. The four-poster bed was the centrepiece of the room, and was grander even than those I had seen in some of the richest houses, with navy satin curtains hanging from the canopy. There, sitting with one leg crossed over the other, wearing men's britches and a white blouse, knee-high boots and a leather waistcoat, was the most remarkable woman I had ever set eyes on.

Her black hair was plaited around her head like a crown, while the amusement in her grey-blue eyes pinned me to the spot. Her face was richly tanned, except for a light pink scar that ran down one cheek before disappearing under the scarf she wore around her neck.

His lady, the madam had called her. And quite a lady she was too.

'Hello, Mr Black,' she said with a voice like butter, dripping with confidence and warmth.

My husband bowed graciously, and cleared his throat before replying.

'Hello, Captain.'

Chapter 15

ꕥ

THE CAPTAIN

My stomach plummeted as the words left his lips, and a dozen questions crowded my mind.

The captain. A woman. And not just any woman.

She uncrossed her legs and stood, walking towards us with feline grace. Although she did not work for the brothel, with her swaying hips and full lips she could certainly hide in plain sight here. Her scar did not detract from her beauty, but rather made it a more precious and unusual thing.

I took a shaky step backwards, surprised to find Kit behind me, blocking the exit. Not that I wanted to leave the presence of this terrifyingly beautiful woman, but I knew that if I did not sit soon, the ground would swallow me. What did one do in front of such a lady? Ask for permission, or wait for an invitation?

I truly did feel like a mouse in her presence.

'Isn't it extraordinary,' she said, coming face to face with my husband, 'that you sent Lei to watch over Talver and he walked right into my lodgings? Clark and Griegsson too?'

'Most fortunate,' Erasmus replied in the same relaxed manner. It was infuriating, considering that my own stomach had tangled itself into knots and my breathing was shallow. 'Although your choice of lodgings is somewhat conducive to our efforts. Have you already questioned the girls about the meeting?' he asked, oblivious to my discomfort.

The captain smiled, but it didn't reach her eyes. 'I thought I'd leave that to you. You are remarkably persuasive, after all.'

There was something deceitful in her words, but I was too distracted to discern the lie in what she was saying. I was not stupid enough to think that my husband had never been with a woman before. He was handsome, older than I, and a well-travelled seaman, but hearing about his ability to persuade women to talk to him felt all too personal.

'Don't be ridiculous, Mira. They'd much rather gossip to you or Lei than to someone they've never met,' came his retort.

'Well, be that as it may, I think we already know what they're going to tell us, don't we?' she answered matter-of-factly.

'Now is not the time for assumptions. We need actual evidence, papers, witness statements, something to take to the Saints that is actionable. Without that, we shall be chasing contracts in the hopes of catching these men unawares for evermore,' Erasmus replied with a thump of his cane against the floor, the taint of frustration in his voice.

'Anyone would think you've tired of the life, Bart,' she said, her steely gaze settling on me. I blinked in confusion. Why did she call him that? I remained where I stood, straightening my back despite my desire to sit on the nearest pouffe and quail under her scrutiny.

'It is not wrong to want to stop hiding,' Erasmus said, pulling her focus back to him.

The captain took a step back so that she could encompass us both in her glare, the storm-cloud blue-grey of her eyes missing nothing. I threaded my fingers together before me and tried not to fidget. She placed her hands on her hips and arched an eyebrow.

'Hiding? You are not hiding.' She gestured to the both of us. 'Between parading yourself around town, eating at Rules and fraternising with our enemy, you appear to be quite comfortable.'

A strangled sound came from my throat at the word 'enemy', for although she could have been referring to my father's business partners, I felt as though she included me in that group. She gave a disdainful sniff, examining her nails as though nothing could be more interesting, as she said, 'And despite all of that, as far as I can tell you are making little progress. Unless you have some new information that might help us?'

Erasmus didn't even bat an eyelid at her tone, which only brought home to me how familiar they must be with each other.

'Osborne gives me only menial jobs,' he said with a sigh, 'drawing up bills for whalebone, spices, sugar, while Talver watches my every move like a hawk. Anyone would think he was hiding something.'

The captain laughed drily. 'Perhaps your skills would be put to better use elsewhere?'

'I only need more time,' he replied quickly, his tone growing more urgent. 'This is a game of patience. It was part of the plan,' he added indignantly, 'and we are making progress.'

'It was part of *your* plan,' she corrected. 'I was content to press for more contracts. Catch them in the act. Crack some heads, bend a few rules. *You* were the one who wanted to take them down from the inside, to gain a foothold in one of their companies. After Jacob Miller turned you away, I would have thought you'd have given up that silly notion.'

My head twisted so quickly towards Erasmus that I felt something click. A wash of cold came over me, a wave of understanding at how and why Erasmus had entered my life. I had known he was looking for contracts, and that he'd paid particular attention to anything coming from my father's company or Griegsson's. I'd surmised as much from the moment I'd read that letter tucked under his mattress. But this revelation was something altogether different, and hurt far more. Even more than him rejecting that kiss.

'You *knew* my father?'

The others in the room seemed to hold a collective breath, having watched the exchange thus far with little more than morbid curiosity.

Erasmus threw a scathing look towards the captain before turning to me.

'It is not how it sounds, Jenny. Mira has a way of making me look exceptionally bad in front of company when she wishes, but please allow me to explain myself before jumping to conclusions.' His tone was level, even reasonable, but it did very little to assuage the sick feeling in my gut that had started the moment we stepped inside, nor the anger that began to bubble beneath my skin.

'Will you, though? Explain yourself?' I took a step away from him, my fists balling by my sides. 'Or will you just dance around the matter as you normally do, leading me into some false sense of assuredness?'

A chuckle came from the captain's direction, and I tore my eyes from my husband to pin her with an undisguised hostile gaze.

'It seems married life isn't all you hoped it would be, Bart,' she said with a sardonic grin, 'though if it's any consolation, Mrs Black, I am amazed that he brought you here to see me, and that he allowed you to meet our crew without consulting me first.'

'Who my wife chooses to meet is entirely at her discretion,' Erasmus growled, his usually well-reined temper fraying with each word from his captain.

'I am also perfectly capable of speaking for myself,' I snapped in response, feeling that irritability that came when I hadn't eaten in a while. Breakfast had been an awfully long time ago. 'Would anyone mind if I sat?' I asked, while already moving towards an unoccupied settee near where Lei was ensconced on her cushions.

'Are you all right?' Erasmus asked, but I had already closed my eyes, pinching the bridge of my nose as an ache formed behind my eyelids. 'You are very pale, Jenny. I knew it was a mistake to bring you out when you had not fully recovered.' He came over to press the back of his wrist to my forehead, but I pushed him away.

'I am not ill, only hungry,' I replied, just as my stomach growled.

The captain clapped her hands. 'Gar, go down to the market and bring us some lunch, please. Lord knows we shouldn't be having this conversation on empty bellies,' she added, throwing a bag from her belt at him, clinking with coins as it landed in his palms.

'Aye, Captain,' he replied, before dashing off, taking Carl and Kit with him.

'Are you sure you're all right?' Erasmus asked me again, kneeling before me, his face creased with worry.

'Positive,' I replied flatly, leaning into my anger and ignoring the tug at my heart that he was showing concern for my welfare.

'Quite the delicate flower you've married, Bart, with her parasol and her gloves and her pale complexion,' the captain said, shifting her weight to one leg and tapping her foot impatiently as she appraised me with the look of a cobra waiting to strike.

'Why do you call him Bart?' I asked before I could think better of it.

If she was surprised by the question, she did not show it. 'It is the name he gave when we met some years ago – another alias, of course,' she added, looking pointedly at him.

'It is short for Bartholomew, Jenny. My middle name,' he added, as though I needed reminding.

I frowned at them both, too hungry to be polite, even if social events with my mother should have taught me some self-discipline.

'Considering how familiar you are with each other, dare I ask how you met?' I aimed the question at the woman, who seemed to be making it her mission to drive a cleft between my husband and me, wondering if she would twist the tale to serve her own ends or if she would tell me the truth. Thus far I had sensed that most of her words were true, but like Erasmus, she might have her own way of deceiving.

I was not so blind as to have not noticed that no matter where Erasmus was in the room, the captain's body seemed to angle towards him like a magnet. They shared a look that spoke volumes as Erasmus replied, 'A story for another day, perhaps.'

The air in the room was heavy and unbearable. The high windows were covered with thick velvet drapes that blocked out the daylight, giving the illusion that it was always night-time. I imagined it was conducive to the trade that the women ran within these walls, and tried not to think about the things that the furniture I was perched upon might have seen.

But it was the perfect hiding place for a woman like the captain, who could remain anonymous while Erasmus put himself at risk by showing his face in town. For that was obviously their ploy, I realised, as I sorted through everything I knew.

No one would give high-paying illegal contracts to a female

captain, but a man like Erasmus would command enough respect and authority to get the work. It was a perfect plot, save for the fact that his face was now known by too many merchants. A small surge of exasperation at their boldness coursed through me, though I realised it was unfounded. Why wouldn't he have put himself at risk, after all? He was his own man, and until just last week he had had no wife to worry about. Even if his grand plan had involved infiltrating my father's company, it was I who had insisted on getting closer to him. Until but a few days ago, the only family he had truly had were the crew, the captain included.

It must have all been written upon my face, for Erasmus looked at me with some sadness.

'I wrote to your father under a different name, having been informed that he was known in the Quaker community. It was a risk, not knowing for certain that he wasn't in on the operation, but I observed him to be an honourable man,' he said softly as he remained kneeling in front of me. I wondered how long he, or one of his crew, had watched my father before drawing that conclusion. 'I simply made some subtle suggestions that someone in his company might be involved in illicit trades occurring under his nose, and that I would be willing to aid him in sniffing them out. He wrote back explaining that if there were anything untoward happening in his business, he was quite capable of dealing with the matter himself, or words to that effect.'

I slumped in my seat, easily able to imagine my father's reaction to receiving such a communication. He'd be far too cautious to accept help from outside, no matter how well intentioned.

'Every time I think I have got to the bottom of you, I discover something new,' I said wearily.

Lei shifted on her cushions, while the captain retrieved a

small dagger from her boot and began cleaning her fingernails with it.

Erasmus opened his mouth, perhaps to say 'I told you so' or something similar, but I silenced him with a wave of my hand. 'Later. I cannot possibly think on an empty stomach.'

'A woman after my own heart,' Lei chimed in, in an attempt to defuse the bitter tension in the room.

Erasmus seemed to heed the message, taking a seat beside me whilst keeping a small distance. I rested my hand between us, and as though reading my thoughts, he placed his on top of it, saying nothing.

Perhaps it was the hunger, or the many revelations of the morning, or even the vestiges of my fever, but sitting next to him like this caused an ache in my chest that I couldn't quite name.

Whatever it was, I imagined it had a lot to do with the fact that no matter how much I seemed to learn of him or think I knew him, he remained forever out of my reach.

Chapter 16

ꕥ

AN ALLY

The door opened and food was brought in, dispelling the hum of discomfort in the air. It was simple fare: a loaf from the baker's oven, hard white cheese and some sour apples, but I was too hungry to care.

We squeezed around a low table, sitting on cushions, our elbows almost touching. Erasmus watched me carefully as I helped myself to an apple and tried not to wince at its tartness. The captain sat at the head of the table, directly opposite me. I felt her gaze on me more than once but kept my eyes averted, instead leaning towards Lei, who had taken a spot on my left and was more than happy to rest her arm against mine – the only comfort she could offer under the circumstances.

Gar and Carl managed to make a few jests that lightened the mood, and the more I ate, the better I felt, though I had far from forgiven Erasmus for putting me in this awkward position. I wondered what my mother would do, and then changed that thought. What would *I* do to come out of this situation without completely losing face?

'Captain, it appears we have got off on the wrong foot,' I

began once I felt fed enough to hold a conversation and no longer had the desire to cause violence to anyone who might reveal something new to me. 'We have yet to be formally acquainted.'

The captain was just as quick to preserve dignity, standing and coming round to me with a hand outstretched.

'Captain Miranda Hodgson, at your service.' She too had an accent, mild as it was, but with her light eyes and tanned complexion, I could not place her origins. She could have been half Greek like Erasmus, but just as easily she might have been Latin. The hair that was not plaited and pinned to her head curled naturally at her temples.

'You may call me Jenny if you wish,' I said in return, taking her proffered hand and gripping it just as tightly as she held mine. A flash of respect glinted in her eyes, and she gave a nod – an opponent acknowledging a fellow player.

'I've heard rather a lot about you, Mrs Black,' she said with a knowing grin, ignoring my offer. I wondered what it was she had heard, and from whom.

'I admit that I know little of you,' I said, putting more power into my voice, 'but I caught rumour of your existence. It is an honour to finally make your acquaintance.'

Her eyes narrowed as she tried to decide whether I was being insolent. If she had had my ability, she would know that every word I said was true.

'You are most kind,' she said dismissively, 'but I'm afraid it is rather inconvenient of you to have stolen away my first mate. It seems he has already told you all about our mission.'

'Oh, not all, Captain, I assure you,' I replied modestly, 'but some of it I have managed to work out for myself. You two, for instance,' I gestured to her and my husband, 'were clearly lovers in the past.'

Erasmus coughed in surprise, while Gar almost choked on a

mouthful of cheese. I was satisfied to see momentary shock on the captain's face.

'You are shrewd, Mrs Black,' she replied, and the confirmation made my eyes burn. 'What else have you deduced from these brief moments of being in my presence, might I ask?'

She addressed me as though she were an aristocratic lady asking a parlour fortune-teller to read her palm, but I felt ready to oblige.

'My husband goes by many names, it seems. I would presume that he pretends to be the captain and applies for the contracts that gain you access to the slaves, while you command the crew. Your ship belongs to him,' I added, recalling that he had told us as much the night we had met, 'so perhaps he is also a benefactor for your mission, coming from a little money as he does.'

'Jenny,' Erasmus choked out, 'how did you—'

'Don't insult my intelligence,' I replied sharply, 'for you have not tried to hide any of this from me. I did not understand your meaning when you told me that you were only a captain when you needed to be, but this,' I pointed at Captain Hodgson, 'makes much more sense. You have already confirmed to me that our marriage was not part of your plan. My only question now is whether you had any intention of seeing the rest of our arrangement through, or whether, as soon as you had attained your goal, you would disappear on a ship and sail into the horizon, leaving the fate of my mother and myself in the hands of Osborne and Talver.' In the process of my discourse, my voice had taken on a hard edge, just like the one my mother used when she was scolding someone.

Erasmus looked as though I had slapped him. Captain Hodgson watched us both carefully, but she was shrewd enough not to pass comment.

That he didn't answer only further fuelled my anger. Perhaps I was being unjust, but discovering that the captain was a woman – a fact he had most definitely kept from me – had only diluted the trust I had been building in him. And it hurt far more than I wanted to admit.

'Perhaps,' she said finally when the silence had stretched to the point of discomfort, 'you would allow me a few minutes alone with you, Mrs Black? There are things we can say in private that we cannot in company.'

Erasmus looked alarmed. 'That really isn't necessary . . .'

'As much as I appreciate your intentions, Erasmus, I would be delighted to speak to the captain alone,' I said softly.

'Mira, you can't give me orders to leave and you know it,' he appealed, looking between us as though he did not know which of us would survive being unsupervised in a room together.

'That is true, but I would like to have a conversation with your wife where you do not assert your view every other word,' she replied acidly.

'I will be fine,' I added, a little more kindly. 'But do not think I have forgotten that our own conversation is yet to reach a conclusion.'

He nodded with reluctant understanding, then gathered the other men and gestured for Lei to follow.

'She can stay,' the captain said, looking to me for confirmation. I was happy to give it, feeling relieved that I had a familiar face with me, even if the girl was hardly less of a stranger than the woman sitting opposite me.

When the door closed, the captain seemed to relax, gesturing for us to take more comfortable positions. I sat on the chaise longue while Lei stayed where she was across the room from me. The captain herself returned to the bed.

'Finally,' she said, tucking her legs under her on the quilt. 'I was beginning to tire of all the masculinity in the room. Now, Jenny, you are welcome to call me Mira. After all, you are not a part of my crew, so you are not obliged to call me anything else.'

I liked this change of countenance, even if it was sudden. She had become more relaxed and in turn it put me at ease, even if I knew that I should not let down my guard entirely. She was no doubt a wanted woman for a reason, after all.

'Don't get the idea that I trust you,' she said, one of her scarred hands spreading on the quilt, 'but I hope that by the end of this conversation I can determine whether I should.'

I shrugged, feigning nonchalance. 'I have nothing to hide. I only hope that you can provide me with the answers my husband has been so unwilling to give.'

'We both have questions, it seems. Perhaps we can take it in turns to oblige one another.' She inclined her head as if inviting me to speak first.

'Very well. You and Erasmus were indeed lovers,' I said, the final word uncomfortable on my tongue, 'but you are not any more?'

She gave me an appraising stare, as though my first choice of question was one she had not predicted.

'Oh, you know these Mediterranean men, so dramatic.' She waved a dismissive hand. 'We fought constantly. It did not last very long, if that is what you are wondering. Besides, we were better as business partners. He had the money and the ship, I had the mission and the guile.'

I pondered on that, seeing that the two of them were strangely similar. I could understand that perhaps it would be exhausting to be in any sort of relationship with another who was so closely matched in temperament.

'So you do not hold feelings for him still?'

'No,' she said, almost too quickly. It was a lie, but I chose not to press the matter as I noted her discomfort. She waited to see if I was satisfied with the answer before asking her own question.

'Why did you choose Erasmus of all people to marry?'

'Do you ask me because you think I contrived it somehow?'

'I do not believe in coincidences, if that helps.'

'Neither did I, until Erasmus told me it was by chance that he crossed my path that day.'

'You mean to tell me that it was fate that had a hand in your meeting?' She practically scoffed as she said it.

'You believe me a spy, Captain,' I laughed, shaking my head at the realisation. 'I must say that surprises me, but I understand you cannot be too careful. Fate, coincidence, whatever you wish to call it . . . I did not contrive to marry him on purpose, no. The matter is quite simple really. My father, as you know, was Jacob Miller.' I felt a splinter of loss open up at my mention of his name. 'He and his business partners had an agreement that should one of them die, their son, or in the case of a daughter, their son-in-law would take their share of the business. I had no husband, nor was I promised to anyone. Had I not found a husband in time, my father's portion of the business would have been divided between Osborne and Talver, and my mother and I would have been left near-penniless.'

'An interesting contract, is it not? I wonder who devised such a thing,' Mira said, almost to herself. It was true that I too had felt the arrangement to be irregular, but it was only her repeating it aloud now that made me wonder how much of it all had been contrived. She prompted me out of my line of thought when she said, 'And how did you meet Erasmus?'

'He has not told you? Well, my mother arranged a dinner at the Hand and Anchor, inviting only unmarried men in the merchant trade. Erasmus had resolved a misunderstanding between myself and an inebriated gentleman earlier in the day, so when he arrived a little late for the dinner, my mother immediately had him in her sights. She laid out the terms of the arrangement and he accepted. But surely you know all this?'

She shook her head and sighed. 'No indeed, Jenny, for I have not seen him since last week. He has ignored my messages, and the only way I have been able to communicate with him is via the news my crew brings me.'

I felt a peculiar warmth at the realisation that Erasmus had all but shunned his captain since we had been married. I thought of his half-packed trunks. Had the captain ordered him away from me only for me to convince him to stay? It seemed likely.

'What will you do now that he is tied to me? Will you insist that he leave with you when the tides are right?'

The captain and Lei shared a look, and I saw something like pity on the girl's face.

'I have already arranged a new contract for us using Mr Atkins as my cover,' Mira said. 'We are due to set sail in a few weeks, before the tides down to Africa become impossible to navigate. I intended to have Bart . . . Erasmus travel with us, but I am beginning to wonder where his allegiance lies.' Those grey-blue eyes were open and honest and all too telling.

'You resent me for having married him.'

She shook her head and smiled sadly. 'I only wonder if he knows what he is doing. You may not wish to hear this, but I know him well enough to worry that he will tire of the comfort and ease that your life provides him. He has spent the past eight years at sea. It changes a person, seeing what we see, the cruelties of humanity as well as its beauty. I am surprised he has managed to last these few days without resorting to sleeping on the ship.'

A cold doubt spread through my limbs as she spoke, for I knew that she was telling the truth, as far as she was concerned at least.

'You believe he will leave me,' I murmured, and with it I felt an ache in my chest so acute I pressed my hand to it.

'I . . . I do not know. I feel that perhaps now he wants the warmth of your house and the comfort of your bed,' she said, and I reddened, 'but who is to tell if he will tire of it in a week? A month? A year? When you hear of his exploits at sea, you will understand why I mention it. I mean it not as a discredit to you, you must understand,' she added hastily, seeing the anguish on my face. 'I only want you to be prepared. For it is quite obvious that you love him.'

The words snapped at me as though she had clicked her fingers in front of my eyes.

'I did not say I loved him,' I bristled.

'Jenny, please. As a woman who has known what it is to be in love with Erasmus Black, I am too familiar with that look. I do not say you are some fawning adolescent, lust-drunk and stupid with emotion. On the contrary, your affections for him are so subtle that I doubt even he has noticed yet.'

I felt the world teeter, the room turning as though I were falling, and I closed my eyes against the dizziness. Lei was by my side in an instant, concern in her expression, her black eyes full of pity.

'Mrs B,' she said softly, taking my hand in her small callused palm, 'the captain only warns you to guard yourself. We women tend to forget that we are deserving of real love, thinking that we need to wait for some gentleman to come along and confirm our worth.'

I looked from her to Mira, who nodded gently.

'You think Erasmus will betray me?'

Lei shrugged. 'Mr B is a good man from my experience, but I don't confess to be an authority on good men.'

If what I had surmised was correct, Lei preferred the company of ladies, and I could not entirely blame her if half of what I had inferred were true.

'I do not love him,' I said firmly. It was a preposterous idea. Attached to him, without a doubt. Vexed by him, certainly. Perhaps more than a little desirous, if I were honest with myself. With his virtuous principles and those rare moments of solicitousness shown for me in between the deceit and well-disguised dishonesty, it was too easy for me to fool myself into thinking he cared. And then there were those mahogany eyes that one could almost drown in, and that scarce smile – the one that illuminated the room when he was genuinely happy. But I could not love him.

I mentally shook myself and pushed it all from my mind, realising that it would do me no good now to examine those feelings – not if what Mira said was true and Erasmus might grow bored and abscond at any moment.

She shrugged, as though it did not bother her either way, but I sensed she did not believe me.

'I think it is your turn to ask me a question,' I said, patting Lei's hand and moving up on the chaise longue so that she could sit beside me.

I was grateful that Mira did not push the matter further, instead returning to business.

'My next question is, what do you intend to do with the information you are now privy to? You know of our mission, you know our faces and names. What's to stop you from betraying us at the first opportunity?'

The question caught me off guard, but only for a moment. If our roles were reversed, I would have thought the same thing.

'I have no intention of betraying you, Captain . . . Mira,' I corrected, 'for now that you have brought it to my attention, I feel that George Talver may have more to answer for than dealing in these Ottoman slaves. If he managed to purchase so many women, and at vast expense, as Erasmus has led me to understand, then what else has he got away with?'

'You intend to find out?'

'I will certainly try. And as to what I plan to do now that I know all of you, well, I hope you will allow me to provide assistance in whatever way I can.'

It was Mira's turn to look surprised, her brows shooting upward.

'No disrespect intended, Jenny, but how could you possibly help?'

'I believe I could be invaluable to you if you do not dismiss me on account of me being young and rich.'

'Neither are sins, nor your fault, but you must realise that what we do is dangerous.'

'I'm not sure why everyone speaks to me as though I am simple, but I am entirely aware of the dangers.' I absently fingered the faded bruises at my neck, knowing that what I was about to say might sound ludicrous to a woman of her stature and experience. 'There are a number of ways in which I can be of service to you, Mira. Your mission is valiant, and one that I feel strongly about. If you can find it within you to put your trust in me, I think you will find my skills indispensable.'

A small ember of delight ignited in those grey-blue eyes of hers at that. 'What can a proper young lady such as yourself do for the likes of us?' She gestured around the near-empty room.

I took a breath. I had already resolved to assist Erasmus in whatever way I could. Just because the person he worked for was not a man, but instead this ferocious, fearless-looking woman, why would my decision change? In fact, I thought as I fortified myself with the intention of pleading my case, it was *because* she was a woman, aiding other less fortunate girls, that

I wanted to help. For what was the alternative? To hide in my house and go back to my books? I cleared my throat and tried to match her confidence.

'You are conducting an investigation that intimately concerns my father's business partner. You may, as Erasmus said, continue to chase contracts and help to release these girls one ship at a time, but why not have true evidence? Documents proving your claims? A confession, even?'

'You are beginning to sound a lot like your husband,' she said, 'but I'm listening.'

I recognised the hunger of someone who was being offered something they needed, and I gave it to her.

'What if, instead of breaking into offices after hours, I could get into the very houses of the quarry you chase? My family is well connected, and although Erasmus could perhaps tag along to a dinner or two, nothing will replace the way that women talk at salons, over tea and cakes, or the access I can gain to their homes. Certainly Lei is skilled at her trade,' I nodded towards her, and she gave me an appreciative wink in reply, 'but much more can be done when one is in receipt of an invitation. If nothing else, it will reduce the risk to your crew considerably.'

The room was silent as this proposal sank in. I might be laughed at for how preposterous it was, but similarly I felt it had some merit. For it wasn't just the desire to help this woman that drove me, but the knowledge that I could be doing something worthwhile on a grander scale. A selfish part of me would even call it adventurous.

'Let us be clear,' Mira said, crossing her arms and cocking her head to one side so that the scar stretched silver in the light, 'you would take the risk of bringing us evidence that certain families in society are dealing in the illicit sex slave trade by gaining access to their homes?'

'My mother has been in receipt of party invitations all across town. Surely someone useful will be opening their doors, since these affairs are ordinarily filled with anyone and everyone important in society. And it would not be impossible for me to smuggle a few of your crew in to do their own investigating,' I added, feeling immensely proud of my quick thinking.

Mira studied me for a moment, the seconds stretching out before she spoke again.

'This will not be without considerable risk to yourself, you realise. Not just your person, but your family's fortune could be forfeit if the Saints decide to take action against Mr Talver and, by association, the business.'

My heart stuttered in my ribcage, for of course Erasmus had said as much to me before, and the reality of it was beginning to strike true.

I thought of my mother, and what we would do if the business was seized. But how could I continue to do nothing, knowing what I did? I steeled myself for whatever outcome I brought upon us, for I knew that Erasmus would not give up his plan whether I helped or not.

'I shall just have to worry about that if it comes to it,' I said after a moment's hesitation.

'You are certain?' Mira asked, unfolding herself from the bed and coming over to me, holding out her hand.

I nodded, tired of repeating myself, as I accepted the handshake.

I knew the risks.

I knew it was dangerous, but I would do it anyway.

Chapter 17

℘ ℘

THE STRAWBERRY SELLER

I blinked in the sun as we left the Midnight Rose, surprised to find that it was still daylight. The cosy dimness had lured me into believing it was evening, but the clock in the market showed that it was only mid afternoon. It had been so warm inside that I found myself chilled when a summer breeze cooled my cheeks and neck.

Erasmus had been waiting for us outside the door of the Blue Room, unwilling to venture further into the halls of the brothel. I imagined I was supposed to be grateful for that small mercy, but Mira's words rattled around inside my mind like a pair of dice, never landing, only tumbling over and over and worrying me with the uncertain outcome. She had explained our hastily devised plan to him, and we had not uttered a word to each other since.

We walked in heavy silence, even though I wished desperately for him to call a sedan. My hem was ruined from the walk over here in spite of my pattens, the grime and other unmentionable things on the street dirtying my dress so that Edith would have kittens when she saw it. Not to mention that the whole ordeal of meeting the captain had left me weary.

Children ran in front of us, some barefoot or with holes in the soles of their shoes, cackling with joyous laughter despite the dirt on their faces and the clothes that required darning. Hawkers tried to sell us their wares from small makeshift stalls or even from their hats, while the air was heavy with hops from Combe & Co.'s Brewery as we crossed Long Acre towards St Giles in the Fields.

So much had happened of late that every hour felt like a day, compared to the empty weeks before Erasmus entered my life. Was this what it would be like now? I couldn't say that I very much minded the change of pace.

I shielded us from the afternoon sun with my parasol as I studied him from the corner of my eye, gauging his mood. I was still angry with him, but it was a deflated sort of annoyance now. He, on the other hand, looked as though he had been punched in the gut and was waiting for the next blow to land, so furrowed was his brow.

A woman's call to my left startled me. She was selling strawberries from a crate at her hip, a babe swaddled and tied to her other side with a dirty shawl.

'Fresh strawberries! Picked jess this mornin'!' she cried in her thick East London accent, proffering the crate to us with sticky hands, the juice running down her arms.

It wasn't just the sweet aroma that had me stopping, but the tiny fist that reached out of the blanket. Having spent my pin money this morning, my reticule devoid of anything of use to her, I had nothing on my person to offer. Instead, I smiled and nudged my husband into action. Fishing around for a coin, he pulled out a clean handkerchief for her to load strawberries into. The coin vanished as though into thin air before she scooped up a cupful and dumped them into his outstretched hand.

'Is it a boy or a girl? The babe.' I nodded towards the child, realising up close that under the grime, the woman was perhaps even younger than I.

'A li'l gel, madam,' she replied proudly, the baby fussing quietly in her swaddling clothes. 'Comes wiv me everywhere, does my Mariah.'

I felt a small tear in my composure at the thought of this young woman getting up at Lord knew what time, strapping her child to her and travelling out of the city to pick strawberries, returning in the afternoon to sell her wares before trundling home at dark to start the whole thing again the next day.

I nudged my elbow gently into Erasmus's side once again and looked up at him pleadingly. He did not need to ask me what my request was, a welcome warmth spreading in my chest as he retrieved half a crown and handed it to the strawberry seller. It was more money than she would make in a week, and she gave a small gasping sound.

'I've not enough strawberries for that much money, sir,' she said thickly.

'Ah, not to worry,' he replied, the first words he had said since we had left the brothel. 'If it is agreeable to you, I shall relieve you of your crate and send someone later to replace it with a basket. Perhaps one with a carrying strap to make things easier for you and little Mariah,' he added, giving her that smile of his, the one I didn't know I'd missed until now.

'God in heaven above,' she exclaimed, grateful tears filling her eyes. 'How can I ever thank you?'

'The strawberries will be more than adequate,' I said, clearing my throat as I fought back emotion of my own.

Erasmus asked for an address so he could send someone to

bring the basket, and then we turned down Bloomsbury Street towards Bedford Square and home, the crate under his arm.

'Thank you for doing that,' I said when the young lady was out of earshot.

He chuckled drily, and I glanced up to see affection in his gaze. My toes curled when he looked at me that way, and I had to remind myself that I was annoyed with him still.

'I think you would have made a very good liberator, Jenny, so attuned as you are to people's feelings,' he said, the tap of his cane echoing in the quieter side street.

'You have seen worse, I'm sure,' I replied.

He hummed in agreement. 'Sadly that is true. It would not be too difficult for you to imagine, though, seeing people work twice as hard as that poor girl and receiving no pay. Knowing that if you had a child there was every chance it would be sent to a workhouse, killed, or worse. That should you contract any one of the terrible diseases that women in the skin trade are susceptible to, you would more likely be turned out and abandoned than healed.' Giving a heavy sigh, he shook his head, and I knew he had seen all of this and more.

'I notice how the wealthy pull curtains over their carriage windows so as not to see the state of our city,' I said quietly, my thoughts going to the young men and women I had attended balls with in the years past. They would drink and eat more in one night than a poor family would see in a month. 'How do you manage it? Seeing so much suffering and not going mad with it?'

He was quiet for a time, considering his reply.

We stopped at the edge of Bedford Gardens, the little patch of greenery that stood almost on our doorstep. I rarely walked through it these days, but Erasmus pushed the gate open and gestured for me to step inside. The grass was cut to precision, with plane trees, rhododendron and pyracantha bushes planted around the perimeter for privacy. Carefully tended flower beds framed a large pond in the middle, where a statue of a robed woman poured water from her jug. It was a bench beside the pond that Erasmus guided me towards, placing the crate of strawberries down and ignoring the juice stains on his jacket.

'It is difficult to say how anyone manages to endure the things we do. How does a doctor cope, knowing that he cannot save all of his patients? Or a soldier, knowing that many of his brothers in arms will die before the war is over? I believe they tell themselves that you cannot help everyone. But I view it altogether differently.' He picked up a pebble from the ground, smooth, grey and no larger than a robin's egg, and ran his thumb over it.

'Look at the pond,' he said, pointing to the clear water, the glint of goldfish swimming under the surface visible between lily pads and pond weed. I watched a mayfly hover over the surface, alighting upon a leaning sword lily, iridescent blue against the fiery red petals. 'Now, you see the flow of it, the way the water cycles, creating ripples all the way to the edge, continual and unchanging?'

'Of course,' I replied, wondering why he had brought me here. As lovely as it was, I could have seen it from my bedroom window. He threw the pebble in suddenly, upsetting the pattern of movement in the water.

'Imagine the pond is the world, the water being the running of things, the ever-turning wheels of humanity. The pebble is our actions. Doing one thing differently, no matter how insignificant,' he said, picking up a much smaller stone and tossing it somewhere to the right, where it made a *plop* as it landed, 'will make a difference.'

I looked from the pond's surface, waves lapping at the edge from the disturbance, back to him.

'How does one ever know what truly makes a difference, though?'

He seemed to think on this for a moment, picking up a strawberry from the crate and putting it in his mouth, pulling off the stalk with his teeth.

'Some years ago, my ship had stopped in Jamaica to resupply.' His voice took on the faraway quality it sometimes did as he recounted a tale from his mind's eye. 'In those days, it was anything from picking up cargo to selling on plunder – under official mandate, of course,' he added hastily. 'I was looking for work wherever I could find it, my crew often changing from one port to the next, and I had just acquired a contract to deliver a shipment of sugar to England when the most curious thing happened.

'My lodgings were a mile from the very plantation we were to collect from. The landscape was constant, with flat fields and almost nothing but sugar cane and the bent backs of workers visible for miles, hills and mountains some way off in the distance. And oh, the heat! It was unforgiving. Your shirt would stick to you after just a moment in the midday sun, so I took to walking early in the mornings or after sundown, finding it too hot to go out in the brightness of the day. It was on one of these late evenings that I heard a cry from a boiling house. When I arrived, a boy, no older than ten, had scalded his hands badly when lifting a drum, blisters on the pads of his fingers, layers of skin gone in moments.'

I sucked air between my teeth at the thought of it. 'What happened?'

'Well, I was certain that his master, a horrid man I had had the misfortune of meeting, would punish the boy, or worse. His hands needed tending, and he would be in bandages for weeks, unable to work.' He paused, his eyes seeing another landscape altogether before us. Relentless sun, the air humming with insects, the tang of sweating bodies and sugar alcohol. This was all I could imagine, but I was certain the reality was much worse.

'What did you do?' I whispered, forgetting where I was for the moment, as though I was right there with Erasmus, in a stuffy boiling house in the West Indies.

'I stole the boy away. What else could I do? His parents had died and Ode was sure to be killed, so he became my responsibility, and as a result he has helped me to save hundreds of lives.'

I recalled the name, vaguely, from my first meeting with his crew.

'He works on your ship?'

Erasmus smiled then, with a fondness I rarely saw. 'He grew up on it, and has been an invaluable crew member. But all this is to say that you should never underestimate your actions, no matter how small. That strawberry seller? Perhaps the half-crown will buy medicine to nurse a sick loved one back to health. Perhaps it will buy her daughter better clothes or save them from starving next week.

'You ask how I face the horrors I have seen. I tell myself that I can always do *something*, and the ripples of whatever course I take will stretch further than perhaps you or I could ever understand.'

He exhaled a great deep breath, as though it had been a relief to tell me all this, and the change in the air was tangible.

'Thank you,' I said, leaning into him as we watched pond skaters dance across the surface of the water. A pigeon landed nearby, eyeing the strawberries from a distance.

'For what?' He stood, holding out a hand to help me up. Although I did not need it, I took it, straightening my skirts and grimacing at the state of my shoes as he collected his cane and the strawberries in one arm.

'For telling me. I realise that you are not used to sharing so much about yourself with someone who isn't your crew,' I said with a knowing look, 'and I doubt even they know everything of the elusive Erasmus Black. If that truly is your name,' I added meaningfully.

'Is this your subtle way of asking me if I married you under an alias?' There was suspicion behind the hint of humour in his voice.

'Well, if so, we would not really be married at all, and you have no cause to stay, aside from your own agenda, of course.'

In a few words I had turned a tender conversation into an accusation, and I kicked myself for it. But I could not leave it alone, so agitated was I by Mira's suggestion that Erasmus would disappear at the first opportunity.

A flash of hurt crossed his face, but was so quickly masked I wondered if I had imagined it.

'Would you like that? For me to leave so that you can marry some wealthy dandy who will do everything that Osborne and Talver tell them to do?'

I scoffed, the deflated anger of earlier swelling up like a balloon inside me at the idea.

'You do not truly think me so vapid as to want an agreeable, docile husband, do you? One who would simply carry my books and tend to my every need? That I would value my own comfort and wealth over what you are trying to do?' I kept my voice low so as not to attract eavesdroppers, but there was no less venom in the words.

'I am rather good at the carrying part,' he quipped, nodding briefly to the strawberries that now dripped onto the path. He pinched the bridge of his nose with his free hand, something I realised both of us did when we were frustrated. 'I do not know what to think, Jenny. Truly I do not. May I be frank?'

'I would expect no less,' I replied, gripping the handle of my parasol with both hands.

'Well, when first we met, you were a quiet, thoughtful girl. There was a spark in you, though. I saw it when you stood up to that drunkard in the tavern, and I admit that you piqued my curiosity. At the time, your mother's proposal seemed almost too good to be true. I would have immediate access to the very company I was investigating, safe lodgings away from the threat of Kaine Clark and his men, and a well-bred and pretty wife. By your own admission, you had barely left the house for years, and were accustomed to solitude and your books. It was an error on my part that I believed myself to have married someone with little ambition, happy just to be seen wearing the latest dress, or to know the most recent scandals of society. Lord knows it probably would have been easier that way.'

He put the crate back down and ran a sticky hand through his hair, dislodging it from its thong so that strands hung around his face. It reminded me of when I had first seen him, coming to my defence.

'But then you followed me that night to the tavern. When I introduced you to the crew, I honestly expected you to run away, or at least to be terrified of them. But instead you worked your way into their hearts and minds. Do you know the first thing Mr Atkins said to me after he met you?'

I shook my head, wondering what the sour old man could have thought from a few minutes of conversation.

'He said, "She's alright, your new wife. There's a little fire in her, though, and if you're not careful, son, you might burn yourself."'

'That doesn't sound so bad,' I said uncertainly. Was it a compliment? I couldn't tell.

'That's just the thing, Jenny. Mr Atkins is notorious for hating *everyone*.'

I smiled to myself, but it was clear that Erasmus was not finished. He took a step forward, whispering fiercely, 'And then you offer your services to Mira of all people! As if being kidnapped by Clark's men was not enough to scare you away!'

I frowned at him, the fear in his eyes, the desperation in his tone.

'I don't understand why this upsets you, Erasmus. Surely it is better for us to be fighting on the same side than for you to be doing all of this alone and trying to hide it from me? Or are you simply finding excuses to push me away?'

His eyes roamed my face, taking in my confusion, seeing that I would not give up.

'It upsets me because I never wanted this for you.' He shook his head and his hair came completely loose. 'And because I still do not understand why you are helping me, knowing what you do of my intentions towards your father's company.'

I understood, though. The certainty of it clanged through me like a church bell. It was as though I had known the feeling all along, like a distant image that the captain's words had only brought into clear view. I had formed an attachment to him, and though I would not be so bold as to call it love, I wanted to be near him – felt better, in fact, when I was in his presence. Even when he drove me to distraction with his secrets. That alone felt like reason enough to push me forward and keep him by my side.

I did not say this, of course, for if she was right about that, then who was to say that her understanding of Erasmus was not also correct. That he would leave as soon as he tired of me.

Besides, how could I go back to life as it had been knowing what I did now? Aware that somewhere out there girls were being taken from their families and sold into servitude to be playthings for men who wanted nothing more than the satisfaction of conquest? No, even if Erasmus left on a ship tomorrow and never returned, I would do what I could to further his cause.

I shook my head and moved in the direction of our house, exhaustion clear in my voice as I replied. 'I do wish you would give up trying to be a martyr, Erasmus, and just accept my help. Chalk it up to boredom if you wish – a socialite in need of a new project for lack of something to do.'

'Going up against the men we are dealing with is hardly a pastime for a lady,' he scoffed, picking up the strawberries again and holding his other arm out for me to take, slowing our pace.

'But if I am to constantly be a lady, it will be impossible for me to make even the tiniest ripples. Well-behaved women don't change the world.' He gave a hum of amusement but didn't disagree, so I continued my argument. 'I do believe you will do whatever you can to avoid leaving my mother and myself in complete destitution. She is rather adept at handling the business, you know.'

'I did notice that, yes,' he said quietly, some thought occurring to him and distracting him from our argument. We took the gate at the far end of the gardens, only a few paces from our door.

'Maybe,' I said as we finally reached the front steps, 'you can find it in yourself to believe in me. Have faith that I will not let you down and allow me to be of use as the captain has, rather than coddling me like an infant all the time.'

'You know that it is not that I do not believe in you, little mouse,' he said, and I was oddly relieved to hear the moniker, a sign that his mood was lightening. 'It is that I worry what will happen to you if you put too much of your belief in *me*.'

The door opened at our arrival and Marcus took the crate of strawberries without instruction. I headed straight for the stairs in the hopes that I could change before Edith or my mother noticed the state of my dress.

'Oh, Erasmus,' I murmured to myself as soon as I was in my room, 'it is far too late for that.'

Chapter 18

A VISITOR

I spent the rest of the day dutifully avoiding Erasmus, which was simple enough as he had a message from Osborne that some business could not wait. He left for the offices and didn't return until the late hours.

I ignored the little thrill I felt when I heard him finally arrive home, sensing it was well past midnight. For although every part of me wanted to be in the same room as him, to rest my hand on his arm and give him cause to smile, the more time I spent alone, the more the captain's warning ate at me.

Sunday was quiet after church. My mother had me accompany her for a walk while Erasmus disappeared off somewhere in the afternoon, but little more was said between us on the matter of the captain or our plans. I threw myself into being my mother's companion in the hope that it would aid me in pushing the doubts out of my mind.

Monday found me sitting in my window seat watching the bustle of the square detachedly, unable to even enjoy one of my newest purchases from Mr Oscarson – a story of a young man falling in love with a wealthy heiress and his quest to win her heart. I had ordered it long before I'd sworn off novels to do with romance, and it struck a little too close to home. The heiress's distance and coolness, the hero's desire to do whatever it took to convince her to marry him for love. In the end, I shelved it and picked up something far more dry.

Every so often I admonished myself for growing too attached to Erasmus, only to find it ridiculous that I could not become attached to my own husband.

But I did not want a husband who would not love me back.

I had almost told him in the gardens, when he had asked why I offered my help despite knowing who he was and what he intended to do.

Because I have feelings that, if I allow them to continue, will surely make things more complicated for us. Because I want nothing more than to allow myself to fall for you, knowing that you do not want the same. Because I care for you in a way I didn't think would be possible.

I did not need to say the words aloud to him to know what his reaction would be. Surprise, sadness, perhaps a little wry humour, after which he would tell me that I could not possibly have such feelings for him, despite his handsome roguishness, or words to that effect.

I almost threw my book across the room with frustration, but was saved from doing that most regrettable thing as the doorbell pealed from the hall. I had been so distracted in my thoughts I had not even noticed the carriage that had pulled up outside the house, or the familiar figure standing on the stoop.

I leapt out of my seat, my slippers sliding on the waxed floorboards. Aristotle, who had been dozing by my feet, was startled into action by the commotion, paws scrabbling to catch up with me.

'Beatrice!' I cried as the front door opened to reveal my

young cousin from my mother's side. She had grown considerably in the few years since I had seen her – no longer a girl, but a woman now. She wore a dress of cream and pink, a bonnet holding back her blonde curls, which had always been tighter and more unruly than my own, while her skin was a shade darker thanks to her mother's Spanish heritage.

'Jenny, my goodness! I am so glad to see you!' she replied, pulling me into an embrace. Marcus stepped away, taken aback by the sudden commotion, while Aristotle danced around us, no doubt hoping that our visitor had brought food.

'I hadn't realised you were arriving so soon, or I would have been more prepared,' I said, taking her hands and drawing her into the hall.

'My father did write to Aunt Katherine. I assumed it was all arranged?'

I reassured her that it was my own absent-mindedness at fault as I ushered her into the drawing room.

Would you arrange for her trunk to be fetched? I signed to Marcus, who gave a single nod.

'I did write to you as well, Jen, after Uncle Jacob's passing,' she said as soon as he had gone. I thought guiltily of the stack of letters of condolences addressed to me personally that I had chosen not to reply to. 'I was truly sorry not to be able to attend the funeral, but we were in Spain when the news first came and I only arrived home after it had taken place.'

'It is not you who needs to apologise, Bea,' I said. 'My mother and I . . . It was a difficult time for us, and by the time we felt capable of responding to anyone, there was far too much happening to get round to it.'

She rested a cream-gloved hand on my own and gave it a gentle squeeze just as my mother arrived, interrupting with an uncharacteristic shriek of excitement.

'Beatrice! I thought we weren't going to see you until teatime – had I known you were here, I would have been at the door to receive you, my dear.' She embraced Beatrice, who responded with a kiss on each cheek, which had my mother giggling. 'I do love how very effusive the Spanish are with their greetings. You must have picked up some of their customs while on your travels,' she said, holding my cousin at arm's length so she could look her up and down.

'Indeed. Aunt Katherine, you look so well. It feels far too long since we've seen you at Toughton House,' Bea replied, referring to her childhood home on the outskirts of Buckinghamshire.

'You are too kind, and quite right too. Once Jenny and her husband have settled in properly, perhaps I can come and visit that wayward brother of mine,' my mother said with a forced grin. I wondered why my uncle Victor hadn't come to visit her himself upon the family's return to England, to comfort her after the loss of her husband. My father had no living relatives, and Victor Stanton, his wife, Luisa, and my cousin Beatrice were the only family we had left. I tucked the thought away for later, intending to subtly question Bea about it when we were alone.

'When do I get to meet this mysterious husband that you wrote of to my father, Aunt Katherine?' Beatrice asked, looking from my mother to me with her wide doe-like eyes.

'Soon enough,' I cut in a moment too hastily. 'Perhaps Beatrice might like to get settled first, and surely some tea is in order before delving into that particular story, Mama.' The suggestion was in part because I dreaded the tirade of questions that would come in the retelling of all that had happened since my father's passing, but also because Beatrice had likely been travelling for a good part of the day. I needed time to gather my thoughts, and to decide how much, or how little, to confide in my cousin.

Growing up, we had received regular visits from my uncle

and his wife. As I understood it, although my mother had married below her station and my maternal grandparents had been less than impressed, Uncle Victor had forgiven her. Perhaps my father's income hadn't hurt either. Beatrice, only three years my junior, had been like the younger sister I had never had, and we wrote to each other regularly. Until . . . Lord Darleston. I shoved the thought away and gave my full attention to our visitor.

After her luggage was fetched from the carriage and she had been given a chance to catch her breath, we all settled down to tea and some light provisions while I tried to recount the events of the past week, avoiding saying anything too revealing about Erasmus. Aristotle paced around Beatrice's chair, snuffling up any errant crumbs from her dress, before settling down at my feet and whining every so often. I was not as much of a messy eater.

'Goodness me, Jen,' Bea said once I had finished with my brief account, 'it sounds to me like you caught a bout of good fortune in settling down so quickly with someone who could take care of Uncle Jacob's business.' There was no true jealousy in her tone, but a hint of longing and the slight envy of a young unmarried lady speaking to someone who had recently left those ranks.

'But what about you, Beatrice?' Mother prompted. 'I believe you attended your first debutante ball closer to home last year, did you not?'

Bea took a polite sip of tea and nodded. 'In all honesty, the prospects are not all that good for me up in Buckinghamshire. It was one of the reasons Father sent me down here to stay with you this season, although I'm aware I am a little late. I think the news of Jenny's wedding prompted my hasty arrival.'

'Well, thankfully we have been invited to many a ball and party, haven't we, Jenny?' Mother asked rhetorically. 'I'm certain that with a little luck, we can find you a suitable husband that even your father would approve of,' she added pointedly.

There was a moment of uncomfortable silence. Beatrice replied with a strained smile, and I endeavoured to change the subject, giving Aristotle a stroke of his floppy ears.

'How is Uncle Victor, and dear Aunt Luisa?' I asked, noting that my mother hadn't enquired.

'Oh, you know. Mama insists that we spend more time with my grandparents in Spain, while Papa is always vying for more time at Toughton. He says that the Spanish cuisine gives him indigestion and he frets over the way our tenants leave the house when we're away for more than a few months.'

'Which do you prefer, Bea?' I asked, having always wondered what it must be like to live partly overseas and to spend so much time on a ship.

'Oh, I love it over there, truly I do. The air is different, and it is so much warmer than England. The sea is the brightest shade of blue and the food is delicious. The people are friendly if you speak to them in Spanish, though they do tend to penalise Papa for being English, and I am often grateful that I inherited my mother's looks and colouring when speaking to the locals,' she replied wistfully.

'I sense a "but" coming.'

'But it isn't England.' She gave me a small smile.

'There you have it, Jenny. All that travelling your cousin does, and England is still home,' my mother said, as though trying to prove a point.

'At least Beatrice has something to compare it to, Mama,' I replied tartly.

'Jenny wanted to travel before she was married,' she ploughed on, 'though thankfully we have managed to disabuse her of that idea now that she has a husband.'

'Mama, I would appreciate it if you would cease speaking of me as though I were not present,' I said with some affront. 'Besides, I am not disabused of anything. I would still like to travel one day, and surely being married to a man who owns a ship is conducive to that desire.'

'A discussion for another time, perhaps,' my mother said, breezing over the topic about as subtly as a hurricane.

Beatrice seemed to take the hint that another talking point was in order, and began to tell us about her itinerary for the few weeks she would be staying with us. I filed away the names of those who were hosting salons or parties that might warrant an extra invitation or two for the captain's crew, while keeping a pleasantly blank look plastered across my face.

My mother took the opportunity to ask about various associates she had known from her childhood home before changing tack and rambling on about the latest engagements, the balls we had in store for Beatrice, the fact that Mr Bane had lately bought a house in Bath while Mrs Georgia Riley had become a wealthy widow as there were no male heirs for her husband's estate to be entailed to. None of it was of interest to my cousin, I was certain, but she was agreeable, making the correct sounds at appropriate moments so that my mother exclaimed how lovely it was to have a nice young lady in our midst. I couldn't wait for the moment when I could steal my cousin away and speak with her in private.

'I should like to give Beatrice a tour of the house, Mama, now that we have finished our tea. It's been years since she visited and I wouldn't want her to get lost during her stay.'

Mother's expression fell a little at losing her captive audience. She could get quite carried away by the life of a socialite, reliving her days before she was married to a merchant.

'It is not half as grand as Toughton, I assure you, although twenty rooms is considerable for a town house, and Mr Miller kept a wonderful collection of paintings,' she said with a little sadness.

'I have always loved this place, Aunt Katherine,' Bea said kindly, though I sensed the slightest twang of a lie in the statement. She gave my mother's shoulder a gentle squeeze, before I managed to tug her away.

'I'm so sorry about that,' I said to her as soon as we were out of earshot. 'She loves a gossip and I think I've been remiss in my social duties of late. She knows I don't have the attention or interest for it, and she misses other female companionship.'

'Not at all,' Beatrice replied, giving me an understanding smile. 'I imagine that she must be quite lonely now that you are . . . what did she say? Off gallivanting with your husband?'

We fell into a fit of giggles as I took her upstairs to the first floor and cursorily toured the rooms. I would open a door, wave a hand to show her what was inside and move on to the next.

Our house was, I would admit, beautifully furnished. Every item had been hand-picked by my parents, chosen specifically depending on the direction the windows were facing, the paper on the walls, or the function of the room. I tried to look at it all now through a visitor's eyes, and appreciated my mother's efforts to create an aesthetic home. Each guest bedroom held an ornate bed frame, a matching bureau and wash stand, a Turkey rug, and suitable pictures adorning the walls. In one room was a small sculpture my father had picked up in Italy, while in another, painted plates from a journey to the Orient adorned the wall. Some of his own studies hung in the halls, though he had always been too modest to display his paintings downstairs, where most guests would be received.

'I suppose there has been a little bit of gallivanting,' I said quietly, opening another door and gesturing around the room before carrying on our tour.

'Only a little?' She quirked her eyebrow and twisted her mouth into a smile that would put the ladies at the Midnight Rose to shame.

'Not *that* sort!' I felt my cheeks heat at her hidden implication. 'There has been very little of anything of that kind, as it goes,' I replied meaningfully. We were in my room now, and Bea ran a finger over the walnut dresser, toying with the handles on the drawers as though itching to open them and see what was inside.

She raised an inquisitive eyebrow, but as I ventured no more information, she changed tack. 'I must congratulate you again on such a fortunate match, Jen. Though you do seem a little reserved in your description of the mysterious Mr Black. He is not dismissive of you, is he?'

'Oh no, not at all,' I said automatically, his brief moments of warmth shuffling in my mind's eye like a deck of playing cards. Him accompanying me to the bookshop. The way our fingers brushed over the table at Rules. His eyes in candlelight. The way he had used his hands to guide me on landing a punch. The almost kiss that had left me wanting.

I turned away from her, looking out at the garden square. A boy leaned against the railings opposite, a small pipe in his mouth, and it was only when he spotted me looking, touching his cap in acknowledgement, that I realised it was actually Lei in her usual male guise.

Erasmus evidently still did not trust Kaine Clark or his men not to come looking for us. The idea that they might know where I lived sent a shiver down my spine, even if I was grateful that he had not neglected to keep me under watch.

I gave Lei a smile and turned back to Beatrice, who was

admiring the selection of clothing in my closet, filled as it was with dresses and shoes, petticoats, hats, bonnets and shawls. Lord Buckface was well concealed beneath his shroud, and I doubted she would be so bold as to disturb the covering.

'It is not that he is dismissive, more that he is . . . complicated,' I said eventually, hating the doubt in my tone.

'Do not tell me that you have not . . .' she dropped her voice to a whisper as she chose her words, 'enjoyed physical company from him?'

This was my younger cousin, and if I had not been so mortified at admitting the truth, I would have questioned where her knowledge of such things had come from. Perhaps her parents had been a little more liberal in their discussions of post-marital affairs. I instantly dismissed the idea that my uncle would condone such talk, but my aunt was Spanish, and perhaps they did things differently.

'In all honesty, our meeting was so sudden that my mother thought it imprudent to enforce any physicality between us,' I said tactfully, hoping that I was hiding my blush well enough by standing at the window. 'As I said, things are complicated at the moment.'

Beatrice made an unconvinced humming sound, and I felt guilty for placing the blame entirely on my mother. It was not her fault that Erasmus and I hadn't consummated our marriage. She had only been trying to protect me, as I had asked. And now that we had accepted him into our family a little more, it was not she who was stopping things from going any further.

I longed to tell Beatrice the truth, about both his character and his plans; that he was brave and dangerous, equally rugged and handsome, so that this combination made him almost untouchable. But I could not betray his trust, even if my cousin was possibly the closest thing to a friend I might have.

'I don't believe people are as infinitely complicated as they like to think,' she replied pertly, in an attempt to perhaps make me feel better about my husband.

'You're probably right,' I replied, forcing myself to sound light and airy. 'Would you like to see my father's study? I have not been in there for weeks, but he truly does have a beautiful collection of paintings.'

She nodded, following me up the stairs to the floor I rarely frequented, and the room I had not set foot in since the funeral. Which was why I was surprised to find that it had recently been used.

One of Erasmus's cravats sat on the desk – I recognised it as one that he had worn the day before, deep purple with an intricate gold stitching along the hem. I had eyed it over dinner, even though I had looked away whenever he caught me admiring him.

The fireplace had been lit and was yet to be cleaned out. A glass of rum sat beside a pile of paperwork, a finger of liquid at the bottom.

When my father had been alive, the place had always been immaculate, so it shocked me to know that my mother had allowed Erasmus into the room, and had not ordered it cleaned. Or perhaps he'd come in here without her permission.

The paintings that adorned the walls were mostly pastoral scenes or still lifes, although my favourite had always been a large depiction of a ship crashing over waves, the sun breaking through the clouds in the distance, as though the sailors only had to ride the storm a little longer before they would reach calmer waters.

An elegant vase sat on the windowsill. During my father's time it had always been filled with flowers at my mother's orders, and it looked bereft without them. A momentary panic seized me that I could not recall exactly where it had come from. He had told me the story of its origin once, and I believed I was the only one privy to it. Had he told my mother as well? And if I had forgotten, then who was there to keep these pieces of him? The stories and anecdotes that he would share over an evening meal or sitting by the fire? What was one's legacy if those one held most dear could not keep the memories alive?

'Oh, this is rather grand,' Bea said, taking in the family portrait that hung above the fireplace, distracting me from my worries. Other than a small portrait in the parlour, this was the only other image of my father in the house, and something throbbed in my chest at the sight of us all together, even if it had been painted almost a decade ago. He had ordered it to be hung behind him so that he my mother and I were always watching his back. I must have been twelve when it was done, and the doll-like girl with porcelain skin and straw-coloured hair looked nothing like me now. She held a puppy, for Aristotle had only just arrived with us when the painting was commissioned, and I recalled him sleeping in my arms as I sat for it, fur soft as silk and still smelling of milk.

'I remember you then,' Beatrice said, stepping closer to examine the details. 'I was always so envious of you.'

A surprised laugh escaped me. 'Why on earth would you be envious, Bea? You would only have been about nine back then, and I remember you had already visited your mother's family in Spain at least once. I had never even ventured further than to visit you at Toughton.'

'Ah, but you got everything you wanted. New dresses, dolls, even special sweets brought from your father's shipments.'

'And you scoffed them all one day in my bedroom,' I reminded her pointedly, recalling how angry I had been at the time at something that was so trivial to me now. We both giggled.

'That was the first time I realised you could tell when I was lying,' she said.

'Well, we used it to our advantage, did we not? I shall never forget you asking me to investigate where your mother had concealed your Christmas presents by asking her questions until I detected a lie.' We shared a sly smile, before her expression became serious.

'I was still jealous, though. Most of all it was the friendship with your father that I never had with my own that made me despise you as much as I loved you,' she said with a sigh.

I watched my cousin carefully as she looked up at the family portrait. In it, my father rested a hand on my shoulder, his eyes on me even though his head tilted towards my mother, who stared out of the canvas with eyes a shade darker than my own. The way we had been positioned showed that there was much affection there. I had never thought of it as something to be jealous of until I heard the way Beatrice talked about her own father.

'Things between yourself and Uncle Victor are . . . strained?' I asked cautiously.

She shrugged and turned towards me. 'He would forever set you as the example I was to follow. "Your cousin Jennifer is already out . . . Jennifer has had three proposals . . . Jennifer is an accomplished dancer and a skilled artist."'

I huffed a laugh at the last statement. My rough sketches were acceptable, but my watercolours and general artistic ability were nothing in comparison to my father's.

'You laugh now, Jen, but it was all I heard between your summer visits to us. I used to dread coming here, knowing that when I returned home, I would have your latest exploits shoved under my nose as though I had somehow failed.' There was no mistaking the bitterness in her tone.

'Bea,' I said with a gasp, 'how could you possibly think you'd failed at anything? You are three years my junior, which is nothing as an adult, of course, but as a child? You couldn't be held to the same standards as someone older than you before you'd even had a chance to shine.'

She waved a hand dismissively. 'Oh, it is no matter now. After your fall from grace, my father never mentioned your name in our house again—' She stopped short, clapping a hand over her mouth as she realised that she had misspoken.

I felt the heat creep up my neck and into my cheeks with familiar shame, which quickly turned to anger at myself for feeling that I had done something wrong. It was Lord Darleston who had ruined me, not the other way around.

My voice was full of quiet hurt as I said, 'Uncle Victor believed the lies? The rumours that other people spread?'

Beatrice turned to me apologetically, grasping me gently by the arms. 'I'm so sorry, Jen. He only heard the news second-hand. As soon as the story reached him, he felt it best to refrain from communicating with you all in case our reputations were ruined by association.'

I pulled out of her grip and slumped in my father's old chair, keeping my mouth firmly closed lest I say something I might regret. Suddenly the fact that Uncle Victor had been out of touch with my mother made sense. It was only the news that I was married, I realised, that had changed his position on being associated with us and prompted Beatrice's sudden visit. By marrying Erasmus and re-entering society as a legitimately wedded woman, I had restored us in his eyes. It was a wonder he had allowed Beatrice to occasionally write to me.

'I really must apologise for his behaviour,' my cousin said, and I sensed she truly meant it. 'At first I admit I was as bad as the rest, only believing what I'd been told by others. But the more I thought of it, the more I realised that there was always more to a story than the gossip-mongers might like us to believe. That was why my mother used to help me sneak letters out to you, and I'm so glad we stayed in contact, no matter how sporadically.'

I waved her apology away, but as I did so, my eyes fell upon the papers in front of me.

'Don't apologise on his behalf, Bea,' I murmured, distracted. It was as though the work had been left in a hurry, now that I looked at the scene from my father's seat behind the desk. The cravat hastily torn off. The rum almost finished. The documents scattered or stacked haphazardly.

I sifted through them, surprised when I found bills for the house. I wondered if my mother had given up on training me and had instead passed the task of looking after the household accounts to my husband. That seemed unlikely, however, and when I peeled away the first few pages, I wondered why Erasmus had been studying them.

Beneath the bills were chits – statements clearly showing how much my father had been paid after the last few voyages. I felt a tremor run through me at the realisation of what Erasmus had been trying to determine as I scanned each one. Measures of silk, tobacco, crates of spices, sugar, groundnuts, even a few pineapples. My family received a large percentage of the profits. There was no mention of payment for anything suspicious, although I had not expected Talver to write out a receipt for 'a dozen women' or 'sex slaves'.

My father's ledger sat closed, a corner of paper poking out from between the pages. I flipped it open, something twisting in my gut when I saw his handwriting, as fresh as the day he wrote it: *Missing receipts for twenty pounds of saffron. Unknown vendor. Ask Osborne.*

Saffron. Erasmus had mentioned this rarity as a way for Talver to disguise his purchases. If saffron were worth its weight in gold – I attempted some quick arithmetic in my head – twenty pounds of it might cost upwards of two thousand pounds. The missing receipts would have alarmed my father immediately. More importantly, if he had known about the missing money and confronted his business partners about it, who was to say that Talver, finding himself backed into a corner, wouldn't do something treacherous in response?

'Jenny?' Beatrice's voice broke into my thoughts, and I found her looking at me, her light brown eyes wide with concern.

'I'm sorry,' I said, shuffling the paperwork together with shaky fingers. 'I hadn't realised that the room was being used.'

'It shouldn't matter, should it?' she replied, perplexed by my sudden alarm, before stooping down to pick something up that had fallen from the desk and handing it to me.

I stiffened at the cursive handwriting, so feminine, but also erratic in its nature, and completely unfamiliar to me. The letter was dated a few days ago – the night Erasmus had been so tormented, when he had almost left. And when he had almost kissed me, my thoughts reminded me.

B,

I did not wish for it to be this way, but I cannot pretend to agree with your plan. You put everyone in danger with the risks you are taking.

Juliet and I are leaving in a fortnight, whether you are with her or not. She is impatient, unforgiving, and she will despise your abandoning her, but I can deal with the consequences, and the crew, if you choose to stay.

I have a new assignment, and the chance to save many more souls. I cannot wait any longer with this many lives at risk. You already know you are being watched, and Kaine will have you killed, along with that wife of yours, if you remain in London.

I suggest you leave the girl lest the same fate befall her as your last conquest.

M

My heart stuttered.

'B' was evidently short for Bart, Captain Hodgson's name for Erasmus, while the letter was clearly from her. She hadn't made her feelings for me or my husband a secret, and I had to forgive her manner of writing, considering that this note had arrived before our recent meeting.

But who was Juliet? Another crew member? One of the girls he had saved? Or, more likely, a lover he had jilted so as to marry me? I shouldn't be surprised, as secretive as my husband was, but the realisation did not hurt any less. In the short time I had spoken with Captain Hodgson, I had noted that she had a tendency to twist her words to suit her intentions. I had seen it in the way she had tried to pit me against Erasmus with her revelations about my father, and this letter took a similar tone. Was it intended to mislead the reader? I wished that my ability to tell truth from lie extended to reading a person's words on the page, but it did not, and I was no more informed by a second look at the letter.

I gripped the flimsy parchment in my hand, tempted to scrunch it up or burn it or tear it to tiny fragments.

'Are you well?' Bea asked me, drawing closer and glancing over my shoulder at the letter, which I hastily stuffed into the stack of papers.

'Fine!' I answered too quickly, rising and turning my back on the desk and its many secrets, wanting nothing more than to escape the room.

'Jenny, you are quite wan. I hope it's not because of what I said earlier?' She put a gentle hand on my arm to stop my retreat.

'No, no. I am fine, truly,' I replied, trying to sound more convincing, 'but I have suddenly recalled why I never come up here. Too many memories.'

I made to leave, and she followed obediently, her disbelief obvious in the way she watched me cautiously. I turned to look at the desk one final time, almost able to picture my father sitting there, humming away to himself in a cloud of pipe smoke as he sifted through ledgers and worked until his candle had burned down to a stub. More than once I had sat with him here in companionable silence, curled up on the floor by his desk with a book, but not for many years. As I grew older, my only interests had been men and parties, while after that I had preferred to be alone.

How much would I give to sit there one last night, reading by his side while he worked?

All that was now impossible because of one lunch, at a chop house only a few doors away from the office he had shared with Talver. It gnawed at me as I turned from the room and descended the stairs with Beatrice in tow, and I began to sift through the pieces of information I had learned in these past few days. Something Mira had said about my father's arrangement with his business partners. It was altogether too convenient that he should die before there was a suitable man from the Miller side of the family to take up the business. I wondered when that contract between the partners had been signed, for surely my mother would have known of it. And then there was Erasmus's correspondence with my father before he passed, alerting him to something untoward going on beneath his nose. Sick dread tightened around me, closing in little by little as I wondered if my father's death had not been the terrible accident that it had been made out to be.

Suddenly, I needed to know.

'Are you very weary, Bea, or would you be willing to accompany me out this afternoon?'

My cousin stalled at my sudden change of tone, but seemed relieved that I wasn't holding a grudge for what she'd revealed earlier. 'I should love an excursion, if it isn't too far. Are we going to meet your husband?'

It occurred to me that Erasmus would be at the offices right now. If I were to call in and drop the name Juliet in his lap, I wondered what he would make of it, or how he would react. My stomach twisted at the thought of the confrontation, but I hardened my resolve. No matter what I found, or didn't, it would not be a wasted journey.

'Yes, something like that. I'll order the carriage now. We should be back in time for dinner.'

Chapter 19

ꟸꟹ

THE UNWANTED TRUTH

The three of us stood outside the chop house, breathing in the scents of roasted meat and stale ale and the underlying fragrance of the city.

Despite my earlier efforts to evade Erasmus, I had realised as soon as the carriage pulled up on the street that I wanted him with me for this. No matter how conflicted I was about our relationship, his presence was much needed. I had relished the surprise on his face when Beatrice and I had entered the offices of Miller, Osborne & Talver, which had been oddly quiet this late in the afternoon. I could see the thin form of Talver behind the distorted glass of his office, while Erasmus had been elbow-deep in papers, his jacket slung over a chair while he moved from one desk to another, muttering under his breath. Beatrice had taken one look at him and given me another one of her brazen smiles, causing me to blush. I could admit he was rather striking at first meeting, and a peculiar swell of pride inflated in my chest when she whispered, 'A fortunate match indeed, cousin.'

Erasmus had greeted her with polite warmth, agreeing to join us for a short time at the chop house. He threw on his jacket and called out to Talver that he would be back within the hour, before escorting us down the road on foot, a lady on each arm as he and my cousin exchanged pleasantries.

But now I felt a sense of detachment, standing outside the very place my father had died, and only the reassurance of my companions kept me from bolting in the opposite direction.

'Remind me again why you wanted to come here, Jen?' Beatrice asked as we stared up at the door. The buildings in this part of the city had been constructed on hills and uneven ground, so there were four short steps leading up to the establishment, which was nicer than the worn grub houses and cheaper meat shops surrounding it.

'I'm not entirely sure,' I answered honestly, ascending the steps into the smoky interior before I could change my mind. I'd explained in as few words as I could that I had an uncomfortable feeling about the last meal my father had taken. As well as Mira's comment about the oddly convenient death clause in the business's contract, Erasmus's recent conversation with Talver about doing what it took to keep the business afloat had aroused my suspicions. The fact that my father might have confronted Talver right before his death had me desperate for answers.

Erasmus held me back for a moment as I scanned the restaurant.

'Would you like me to ask some questions, little mouse?' he whispered. I looked up at him, his brows drawn together in concern but his eyes open and honest. He understood why I had needed to come here, to find out for myself if there had been anything more to my father's death than a simple reaction to the food, and for that I was supremely grateful.

'Alert me discreetly if you sense anything, won't you?' he added.

I nodded in silent thanks. It was the first time he had made mention of my abilities in this way, and something warmed inside me.

The restaurant was relatively empty, being as it was at least an hour before dinner, and there were several free tables to choose from. I wished that I had known where my father had sat for his final meal, finding myself automatically searching for a spot by the windows that was bright and airy. After some deliberation, I selected a secluded booth overlooking the street facing east. In the early afternoon the sun would have hit somewhere there, and I could picture Miller, Osborne and Talver huddling over their plates, talking business and eating stew or legs of mutton or ham. My heart gave a sudden twinge at the thought that I might sit exactly where he had, the last place he had drawn breath, maybe laughed or smiled. Erasmus and Beatrice followed my lead and settled onto the benches beside and opposite me, the former watching me discreetly while my cousin carefully surveyed the room.

'What can I get ye?' A moustached man with a dirty apron came over as soon as we were settled.

'Three ales, good sir, and some information,' said Erasmus smoothly, sliding coins across the wooden surface that were eyed suspiciously by the server.

'Not in the business of information, I'm afraid.'

'Well, perhaps you should start now. It could be profitable for you, and would help us greatly in our investigation. Now,' Erasmus slipped another coin onto the table, 'if you'd be so kind, I'd like to ask you a question.'

'Depends on what the question is as to whether I'd be kind or not, sir,' he said, making no move to take the money.

Erasmus gave him his best predatory smile, eyes glinting with the challenge.

'Three gentlemen sat somewhere here about two months ago,' he began, to which the man immediately scoffed.

'Don't expect me to remember naught beyond this mornin', sir, for we gets so many round this way I'll forget your own faces just as soon as you turn your backs.'

'I think you might remember these three,' Erasmus pressed, 'for one of them died no sooner had he begun his meal.'

The server paled at the mention of it and took a step back. The coins remained exactly where they were, between us, like an offering.

'Why, y-yes, I do so recall such an instance. M-most unfortunate. Think he must have had an sensitivity to s-something,' he stuttered. The air around me hummed with his lie, and I gripped Erasmus's arm, daring him to challenge the man.

'It seems your memory isn't as bad as you thought then, is it, sir?'

The server seemed to back away a step, but Erasmus was close enough that he could grab him if needed.

'Did these men frequent this establishment often, sir?' I asked in a gentler tone, thinking that any sane man would be afraid of the keen look in my husband's eye.

'Once a week or so, ma'am,' he said with a wary look at me.

'And did you ever hear of an altercation between any members of the party?'

'You ain't from the Runners, is ya?' he asked nervously, eyes darting left and right to see if anyone was eavesdropping.

'No, no.' Erasmus chuckled, which seemed to relax the man slightly. 'We are merely concerned citizens. I work nearby, and wouldn't want the good name of your establishment to be dragged through the mud just because something untoward happened here. There are rumours that the quality of meat is below standard, and that is what killed the man.'

'Th-that's impossible!' the server replied indignantly. 'The gentleman who died never ate the meat besides. He only ever ordered the vegetable stew.'

I looked down at the polished table in front of me, picturing my father's last meal, my heart picking up a quicker pace.

'I should like to order a vegetable stew,' my cousin chimed in, and I looked at her in surprise. 'But being from out of town, I'd very much like to know how it is cooked. Do you make each portion individually, perhaps, or a large pot that you serve straight from as and when it is ordered?'

Erasmus, myself and the server all gave her varying looks of confusion, and I tried to see the reasoning behind her line of questioning.

'I'm not sure why it matters, miss, but we make it first thing in the mornin', and then Sal in the kitchen sets out a few bowls when we get customers so he can get on with other orders. There's always at least two or three requests for it durin' a midday rush.'

'Ah, in that case, could I have it served straight from the pot?' Beatrice asked sweetly. Something prickled at the back of my neck as I began to understand why she had asked. If anyone were to interfere with a person's meal, it would be when a plate or bowl had already been sitting there for a while.

'I'll 'ave to see if there's any left, miss. And, er, three ales, was it?' The gentleman turned to the kitchen before we could stop him, and the three of us huddled a little closer.

'That man is lying, Erasmus. All it took was one mention of my father's sensitivity to the food for me to notice it. He's hiding something.'

Erasmus nodded, resting a hand on my own on the table, his palm warm on my gloved one. 'Jenny, if you and Miss Stanton are thinking the same thing as I, is it possible that your father's death was not in fact some cruel twist of fate, but by design?'

I swallowed as I agreed, gripping his fingers in mine, more grateful than ever that he was here, and that he understood my suspicions.

'I know it sounds far-fetched,' I said, looking from him to Beatrice.

'Only a little, Jen, and not if everything you were saying earlier is true – that one of Uncle Jacob's business partners was up to something illegal.' My mouth opened in surprise at how quickly she had caught up, and she gave a soft laugh. 'I'm not just an insipid socialite after all, am I?'

'No, indeed,' I replied, thinking about our server's nervous disposition as soon as my father's death had been mentioned. 'Whatever you do, if that man brings the stew, *don't* eat it,' I added.

'Oh, I had no intention of consuming anything from here, though I would imagine that if it had been something in the food, someone would have had to pay very highly to bring that about.'

Erasmus nodded in agreement. 'Money that only a few gentlemen might possess, knowing that if they eradicated a particular obstacle, they would be in line to make more,' he said, his voice taking on a frightening edge. 'I must confess something, Jenny, which may only solidify our suspicions.'

He kept hold of my hand, shuffling closer so that our heads were almost touching over the tabletop. 'Just this morning, I was sifting through ship manifests from the weeks prior to your father's passing. I would have worked faster, but Talver has been breathing down my neck all week, and today was the first opportunity I had to pull out the records. It took me a while to note a pattern, but I think I may have it.' He looked at me as he explained, our faces so near I had to resist the urge to rest a gloved hand on his cheek. 'All the shipments coming from

Brazil, Spain, even Asia were signed by your father. But there were three ships for which the cargo was always inspected by Talver. They usually came from the West Indies, but occasionally other locations. Greece, for example. Yet it was always the same ships. Going back *years*. I questioned Osborne yesterday when I first noticed it. He mentioned something about Talver having a special relationship with the captain.

'That could have been entirely plausible, of course, but then this morning I found an exception. About a week before your father died, he had signed the goods receipt. Whether Talver had been away that day, or your father decided to take it upon himself to examine this shipment, I had to wonder . . .'

'That he perhaps saw something he didn't like?' I offered.

'It's possible, isn't it? That there was something in that cargo, or some evidence left behind, and he confronted his business partners about it.'

'He did,' I said, quickly explaining my father's note in his ledger. Erasmus nodded along, having seen it himself a few nights before.

Beatrice jerked upright in her seat. 'You think Uncle Jacob confronted this George Talver, and Talver decided it wasn't worth keeping him around any longer if it would jeopardise his operation?' she said excitedly. I hushed her, looking around to see if anyone was near enough to eavesdrop, though the only other patrons were on the other side of the room.

'It's a lot of "ifs", isn't it?' I said doubtfully.

'Well, I know a very quick way to determine whether our suspicions are founded,' Erasmus said, nodding towards the server, who was approaching with a large wooden tray containing our order. I had to admit that the stew he set down before Beatrice smelled divine, and the ale was served in real glass mugs.

'Ah, there you are,' Erasmus said, feigning joviality. 'We were wondering where you had got to. Perhaps the ale keg was empty, or you'd run out of poison for our drinks and had to fetch more.'

The man was so surprised, I could see the whites of his eyes, his pupils becoming small brown circles as he stared at us in horror.

I heard a familiar snick and realised that Erasmus's cane was armed, ready and pressed gently to the man's foot so that, should he try to run, the blade would likely slice through his boot before he got the chance.

'I-I d-don't know what you m-mean, sir,' he said, leaning so far back that it was a wonder he didn't bend over backwards.

That was a lie too, of course.

'I think you do,' I said acerbically. 'How much did they pay you to do it? What was it, hmm? Cyanide? Strychnine?'

He gave a fervent shake of his head, tears forming at the corner of his eyes as Erasmus pressed his blade a little harder against his toes.

'Would you like to make a wager, Mr . . .?'

'B-Blythe,' the man blurted, too afraid to lie this time.

'Mr Blythe, how much would you like to wager that my knife is sharpened daily, and that only this morning I confirmed that it is honed enough to slice through bone? How much is your toe worth to you, Mr Blythe?'

Perhaps I should have felt revulsion or fear at my husband's words, but at that moment, all I could feel was the cruel need for justice to be served. This man might have had a hand in my father's death. A man ten times greater than he would ever be. Some dark, terrifying part of me wanted to see him suffer for it. I glanced at Beatrice, suddenly worried that she would think less of me for condoning such violence, but I needn't have been concerned. She pinned Mr Blythe with her own deadly glare, alert and ready to act if need be.

'It weren't me!' Blythe cried, holding his hands up as though it would ward us off. 'It weren't me! I din't know until well after. 'Twas the cook, I swear it,' he sobbed. The point of the blade had already penetrated his boot; when I glanced down, there was a small trickle of blood seeping through the hole Erasmus had made.

My husband looked at me as though for confirmation, and I nodded. It wasn't a lie, or at least Mr Blythe believed it to be the truth.

Erasmus stood, causing Blythe to yelp, torn between wanting to leap away from him and wanting to keep his toe.

'Be so kind as to take me to this cook, good man,' he said, his voice laced with danger.

I got up out of my seat and skirted around the table so that I stood on Blythe's other side, Erasmus holding the knife to his foot on my right, the kitchens, and exit, to my left. If there was any chance of the server running, he would find me blocking his path. I didn't think what would happen if he hurt me in the process.

I noticed that the other patrons in the chop house had disappeared at the first sign of commotion, leaving the four of us to our business.

'Mr Blythe, I would recommend that you escort us to this man, lest I begin taking fingers as well as toes,' Erasmus threatened.

'He's g-gone. Left a day after it all happened, sayin' he was gonna make a name for hisself w-with the c-coin.'

I released a frustrated groan.

Of course. Anyone willing to poison a customer would

require handsome payment – enough to be able to escape lest he be suspected of murder.

'You don't happen to know *where* he decided to make this name for himself, do you?' Erasmus asked.

It was then that Mr Blythe made his biggest mistake. He lied again.

My anger and grief stretched inside me until I felt I would snap, and the final lie struck them like a bow slicing across a violin string. All it had taken were three simple words: 'I don't know.' My fist came out reflexively and cracked directly into his jaw, sending him sprawling across our table and upsetting the ale. Erasmus had the sense to pull the knife out of his shoe, otherwise he would have lost the toe as well.

Mr Blythe yelped, trying to scramble away, but Beatrice stood firmly in his way, hands on her hips. 'Good sir, I suggest you begin telling the truth immediately. If you had not already noticed, my cousin here can determine when you are lying, and the man your cook was so heinously paid to poison was her father. Surely your life is not worth less than a murderer's?'

My hand was throbbing from the impact with Blythe's bony face, and I tucked it under my arm in the hope that I could stop it from hurting. But it was a good sort of pain, one that would take my mind off my own murderous thoughts.

Erasmus guided Blythe, almost gently, to his feet. 'Now, shall we start again?' he said, fixing the man's collar and brushing down his sleeves as though it would repair the damage we had done. Blythe held his cheek, his eyes darting between the three of us as though we were crazed, and I wondered how we must look to him; three finely dressed well-to-doers with knives and fists and dangerous questions.

He nodded glumly, pulling a rag out of the pocket of his

apron and throwing it onto the ale that had spilled over the floor around our feet.

'The man you're lookin' for is Sly Fairfax. Worked 'ere for almost ten years, but I knew he wasn't above doin' a bit of the dirty on the side. I overheard him saying he'd picked up a job that'd set him up for life if he could pull it off. Never realised he was gonna kill a bloke or I'd have . . . well, I dunno. I'm no tattler and Sly was a friend of sorts, but it was wrong what he did. Heard him say he was going to get hisself a plot out in Clapham and that's all I know, I swear it.' He held up his free hand before thinking better of it and tucking it away, lest someone try to poke a hole in that too.

'Did you ever see with whom he dealt? Anyone unusual who came to the kitchens, perhaps, to supply him with the poison?' Erasmus insisted.

'Nah, that was the thing. He'd just use the stuff that kills the rats – don't taste like nothin', and easy enough to buy. Untraceable too,' said Mr Blythe, yapping freely now that the truth was out. 'But I know he picked up most of his jobs from the King's pub down on St Martin's.'

The King's? What were the chances that this was the King George public house, which I had sat in with Erasmus's crew, so close to where Talver had been spotted coming out of the Midnight Rose? Unless there were two pubs on St Martin's with similar names, it was no coincidence. My entire body was cold, despite the warmth of the afternoon. It was circumstantial, perhaps, but I felt in my gut that my father's murder had been paid for by the very man he called a friend and colleague. It should have been painfully obvious to me, I suppose.

Erasmus continued to question Mr Blythe for several minutes, but all I heard was the roar in my ears as I thought over the sequence of events. When he was satisfied, he said, 'Very well, Mr Blythe. If there is anything else of note you recall, please contact one of my associates here.' He handed over a small card with an address on it, though whether it was the Midnight Rose or some other hideout his crew used, I couldn't see. Then he scooped up the coins from the damp table and slipped them into the man's apron pocket, wiping his fingers with his handkerchief afterwards.

I leaned back against the wall of the booth as I pulled apart what had happened. My father, noticing the peculiar missing receipts of funds for saffron, would have confronted Talver about it. As if that wasn't enough, he had also inspected one of Talver's ships, most likely expecting something innocuous – day-to-day staples, sugar, linen and the like. I could not recall him ever speaking of saffron as a commodity we traded in, but my mother would know better than I. What if, during his inspection, he had discovered something more, though – evidence of people being transported under inhumane conditions? He would have been outraged. That, along with Erasmus's anonymous letter warning him that something untoward was happening beneath his nose, would have been cause enough for him to take it straight to Talver.

And rather than refrain from committing further crimes, Talver must have realised that with my father out of the way, not only would he be safe from persecution, but he would also gain a larger share of the legitimate business, as I had had no husband and there was no son to take over.

Outside the grubby windows, people milled about on the street. Carriages trundled past. Hawkers called out their wares to passers-by. Life continued. Yet here I was, feeling as though a wound that had just begun to heal had ripped open all over again. I forced back the tears, swallowing the ache in my throat and turning to find two pairs of eyes on me, both filled with wary concern.

'From the look upon your face, I believe you may have drawn the same conclusions as I, Jenny,' Erasmus muttered.

'That Talver is responsible for all of this, yes,' I replied gravely. 'You must warn Osborne somehow without arousing Talver's suspicions.'

He put an arm around my shoulders to pull me closer, tucking me into his side as though it would protect me from the information we had just gathered.

'That alone may be too dangerous. This will change things dramatically for us,' he said, his lips close to my ear.

'I know, I know. How are you to work beside him now knowing . . . knowing what he did?' I pressed my head to his shoulder, feeling heavy with fresh grief. Beatrice had found something particularly interesting to look at outside, allowing us this moment of privacy as best she could.

'I shall do what I have to every day when I shake his hand in the morning. You shall have to do the same so as to keep him unawares. We pretend. We act, we play our parts, and then we do all we can to take him down.'

I looked up to find that fire in his eyes, and despite the captain's letter and all of my many doubts, I felt such a deep understanding of him, of his need to repair whatever he could in this broken world of ours, that speech failed me.

At some point, Erasmus and Bea must have escorted me from the chop house, for I found myself being bundled into our carriage even as I was mulling over the discoveries, the fierce rage I had felt earlier simmering down to a cool wrath in my veins.

'Jenny,' Erasmus said, laying a hand upon mine, 'I must return to the office. I'm in the midst of a dozen different things and need to give Talver no additional excuse to watch over me.'

'But you're in danger,' I exclaimed, stopping him from backing out of the carriage door.

He smiled softly, giving the fingers on my good hand a squeeze. 'When am I not?' He leaned forward, brushing a light kiss against my cheek before retreating. 'Excellent right hook, by the way, but do make sure to put something cold on those knuckles when you get home,' he added, before closing the door and thumping the side of the carriage so that we were pulled away.

I watched him out of the window for as long as I could before he was lost to sight, retreating up the steps of the building that housed Miller, Osborne & Talver Merchanting Ltd.

I found Beatrice assessing me carefully, a grim smile playing across her lips. 'Well, all in all, I think that was rather successful, don't you?'

Chapter 20

ဢဢ

THE REAL JULIET

'How's the hand?' my cousin asked, watching me across the parlour table. The cook had given me a slab of cold meat to reduce the swelling, but it would surely bruise, and I would have to remember to wear gloves in public. There were so many parties my mother had accepted invitations to on my behalf, and it wouldn't do to look like a common brawler.

I had come home in a state and escaped to my room for a time while Beatrice distracted my mother. The cracks across my heart had reopened, fresh as the day I had learned of my father's passing. I allowed myself to weep, knowing that I must harden that grief into anger. Just because I had never liked Talver did not make the betrayal hurt any less, for it was not just my own trust that had been violated, but my mother's and father's too.

If my hand had not hurt so much, I would have spent some time with Lord Buckface, but as my knuckles were already turning a shocking shade of violet, I had cleaned myself up, put on a brave face and joined my cousin in the parlour.

'Jen?'

I blinked back to the present. 'Pardon?'

'I asked how the hand was faring.' Beatrice pointed to the peculiar medical device.

I shrugged in reply, favouring my left hand to drink my tea. 'I'm certain it will heal. It's the pain in here,' I tapped my chest gently, 'that will take longer.'

She gave me an understanding smile.

'I cannot tell you how grateful I am that you were there, although I imagine you did not expect events to unfold quite the way they did.'

'Nonsense.' She shook her head. 'I am only glad that I could help. I am worried, though, for you and Mr Black.' Her eyebrows furrowed as she took a sip of tea. 'When I first pieced together what you were discussing, your suspicions about Uncle Jacob's death, I thought you were being ridiculous. But hearing that server speak of it . . . it all became very real to me. Your husband is working with your father's killer. Does that not terrify you?'

The tea tasted bitter in my mouth and I set my cup down with a clink. 'There is more at stake here than just a bit of illicit cargo, Bea. This has been Erasmus's life for years now, and I trust that he knows what he's doing, even if he never intended to drag me into it,' I added, echoing the words he had used many times. I understood now why he had been trying to hold me at arm's length, particularly if he had suspected Talver of more than just illegally buying and selling girls. The thought that a man I had known most of my life was capable of murder filled me with a particular type of dread. Certainly I had had my suspicions, but they had been nothing more than an observation of his character, a feeling that he did not have anything but selfish interests. How could greed force a man to order the murder of one of his oldest friends? Grief and pain and anger warred within me. I wanted to take our discoveries to the nearest Runner and order them to arrest Talver. But I knew from my own experience that the word of a young woman would not hold up against that of a man. They would just as soon laugh at me and send me on my way with a pat on the head, for without genuine evidence they would not dare to go up against a man like Talver.

And as much as I wanted to see justice done, in a dark part of myself I admitted that I desired to cause him the same hurt he had inflicted upon my family. I thought of the captain. If Miranda Hodgson was the woman who had been wronged in this instance, I had no doubt she would take matters into her own hands.

'But here's the question,' Beatrice said, pulling me from my dark thoughts. 'What do you and he intend to do now that you know who's responsible?'

I let out an exasperated breath. 'I wish I knew. Erasmus has a plan, I'm sure, but whether he'll let me help is another matter.'

'He's quite the charming rogue, isn't he?' she said with a dreamy smile that sent that sense of satisfaction through me again. 'And he's obviously besotted with you.'

'What? Hardly,' I scoffed, feeling my cheeks redden. 'As much as I would delight in knowing he felt that way, he is far too cryptic and aloof to ever be besotted with anyone.'

'Don't be silly,' Bea replied with a roll of her eyes. 'It is very clear to anyone with the ability to see that he's in love with you. Surely that is not a bad thing, considering you are married?'

I opened my mouth to say that his ex-lover had warned me not to get my hopes up and I should probably follow her advice, but shut it promptly as my mother swept into the room.

'Ah, there you are,' she said, before spotting the ham on my hand. 'Good gracious, Jenny, what did you do to yourself?'

'Shut it in the carriage door,' I lied, barely thinking about it.

She paused for a moment at my explanation. Between the

marks on my neck from last week and now this, perhaps she was revising her decision to let me wander freely outside the house. 'Dear me! Does it feel broken?'

'No, Mama, just a bit tender,' I said honestly.

'Well, you'll have to wear gloves for the parties if it is still unsightly.'

The parties. Talver would be at Henrietta's ball, of course. I could barely stomach the idea of facing my father's murderer in a setting such as that. God knew how Erasmus was managing it at the offices, though I imagined he had already suspected the worst of the man. Could he find the evidence he needed to bring Talver to justice before then? I wondered.

'Not to mention Anna Griegsson's salon tomorrow,' my mother continued.

'Anna Griegsson?'

'Klaus Griegsson's wife? The merchant? Jenny, do you not listen to a word I say?' Mother gave me an exasperated look as she threw the invitation down on the parlour table.

'Of course, of course,' I said, staring at the gilded card before me. Anna and Klaus Griegsson were presenting their newest painting collection, which meant there would be other merchants present as well. This could be the perfect opportunity . . .

'I have just the dress for you, Beatrice, for although this is no dance or ball, it would be a wise idea to have you already introduced to some of these young merchants,' my mother continued, while I wondered how gaining access to Griegsson's house might benefit Erasmus and the captain.

'Oh, and these are for Henrietta Osborne's ball,' she continued, producing an envelope with a flourish. 'The two additional invitations you requested,' she said proudly, sitting herself beside me, 'although you will have to give them strict instructions should anyone ask their relation to us.'

My mother had become so proficient at lying of late that I had to stop myself from being surprised. I had told her that two of Erasmus's crew wished to attend the ball to make their own connections, and my mother, sensing that I would not take no for an answer, had delivered. I wondered if I ought to bring her into our confidence regarding Talver's involvement in my father's death, but that would lead to questions about Erasmus's life that I had promised not to speak of. And if Talver and his connections were as dangerous as Erasmus suggested, the less my mother knew the better. As soon as I could have his agreement, though, I would tell her. I had to.

'What did you say to Mrs Osborne?' I asked, wondering what tale she had invented this time.

'Oh, just that William's cousins were visiting, and that one of them was a sailor of great renown. I also told her that he was handsome and seeking a wife, which made her eyes light up like kindling, so please, let's hope that at least *one* of his guests will fit the description.'

I found myself chuckling in disbelief at her ingenuity.

'I've also managed an invitation for Beatrice,' she said, handing another envelope to my cousin.

'Oh, Aunt Katherine, thank you! I have *longed* to go to a proper London ball since the beginning of the season,' Bea replied, taking the invitation gratefully.

'Well, you aren't an eligible bachelor, which is all Marie Osborne seems interested in at this point, but I told her it couldn't hurt to have another debutante at the event, even if it is just to dance with the young men waiting in line for Henrietta. Though we all know that Beatrice will easily steal all the attention,' she added in a stage whisper, clearly pleased with herself.

'Mama, I didn't know you had it in you.'

'Yes, well,' she straightened herself, pursing her lips and giving me a beady look, 'you're not the only one who can fib, Jenny.'

I looked at her sharply. What did she mean by that? I wondered briefly at her intuition.

'I saw the family portrait in Uncle Jacob's office,' Beatrice butted in, coming to my rescue. 'It seems a shame to have it up there where no one can see it. Perhaps you will consider bringing it down and hanging it somewhere in here?'

Mother accepted the distraction, immediately looking about the room for a space where it would fit, asking Bea's opinion of the best location based on the way that Toughton was furnished.

With their attention focused elsewhere, I stood, peering out of the window to see who was on guard this late in the afternoon. It took me a while to spot him, but Kit was sitting on the edge of the pavement, smoking and occasionally glancing at the house. I scooped up the envelope and excused myself, leaving the cold meat on the table and testing out my sore hand on the front door handle.

I'll be back in just a moment, I signed to Marcus, who obligingly held the door while I darted across the square.

Kit looked up, surprised to see me approach him, but made no move to get up.

'Invitations to the Osbornes' party next weekend,' I said, dropping the envelope into his lap as discreetly as I could. 'Whoever attends will have to say they are cousins of Erasmus's.' I relayed Mother's instructions.

'Very good, ma'am,' Kit replied flatly, sliding it inside his jacket before taking a deep pull of his pipe. I dawdled, knowing that I should return to the house before I was missed, but feeling the nagging pull of a question on the tip of my tongue.

'Why don't you like me, Kit?' I blurted out before I could think better of it.

The boy frowned at the directness of my question, glancing at me from the corner of his eye. This close, he appeared no older than fourteen, the beginnings of a moustache on his upper lip still soft and lighter than the dark hair on his head, swept haphazardly from his face.

'Who says I don't?'

'Well, by your every action and tone when I am in the same room as you, it isn't difficult to make the assumption. I only wonder what it is I did to offend you, and how I can possibly make up for it.'

With a final puff, he tapped out the remainder of his pipe in the gutter and shook his head, exhaling in a grey cloud.

'S'not that I don't like you specifically, Mrs B. It's more . . . what you represent.'

It was my turn to frown. 'I don't quite understand your meaning.'

'Well, you're rich, yeah? And your money came from the backs of other people working twice as hard for less than half the pay.'

'You dislike me because I was born into wealth?' I said, a little affronted. 'I'm afraid that was hardly under my control. Unlike some of the other residents of this square, my father built his company up from meagre earnings and the fortune of good sailing. Just because we live a more comfortable life does not make us the enemy.'

'Well, Bart . . . Erasmus was rich too once. But he gave it all up to do something right in the world, din't he? I suppose there's not many wealthy folk who can say that they traded comfort because they saw something broken and wanted to fix it.'

I gathered up my skirts and crouched on the balls of my feet, not wanting to sit on the ground as he did, but feeling that I needed to get closer to him somehow. He was important to Erasmus, and it felt right that I should try to gain his trust, though I did not have enough understanding of his life back home to know the source of his anger; whether the wealthy there were contributors to the oppression of his people or if it was just rich British folk he took umbrage with.

'I'm trying, Kit, truly I am. In fact, I believe that if it were up to me, I'd have joined your crew some time ago, for I wanted to travel long before I met Erasmus. I had plans to run off to Sussex, and from there to Portsmouth and beyond. Sadly, things are never that simple.'

He raised his brows appraisingly. 'How so?'

'Well, I have obligations. My mother, for one, who needs me here.'

A storm cloud seemed to pass over his face. 'My mother needs me too, but I'm all the way over here, aren't I?' he said resentfully.

'As I understand it, she'd rather you be here and safe than home and fighting for an army that you can't leave. Did I get that right?'

He gave a half-shrug, but it was enough of an acknowledgement of the truth for me to know I had made my point.

'I have a feeling that if we had met on a ship in the ocean, rather than here,' I waved at the town houses towering above us, 'you and I would have become great friends.'

He gave a non-committal nod, working loose with his boot a clod of grass that had grown between the cobbles. 'Maybe, but either way you're going to take him away from me, aren't you?'

'Who, Erasmus?' I said with a bemused smile. 'Oh, Kit, nothing I do will make a difference to him. If he wants to leave, he'll leave. If he wants to stay, he'll stay, but I'd never try and take him away from you. In fact,' I said, leaning a little closer so that he had to stop fidgeting and listen, 'I wouldn't be surprised if he's already got a plan for all of us. Whatever he chooses, he'll try to do right by you all, I know it. We only need to trust him.'

Maybe I was only trying to convince myself, but it seemed to appease the boy. Perhaps he had needed reminding as much as I did what we already both knew: that Erasmus Black was a good man, no matter his methods.

I stood, straightening my skirts, and gave his shoulder a gentle squeeze before heading back to the house, where Marcus watched me from the shadow of the doorway.

'Vinegar,' Kit called out before I had gone too far.

'Pardon?'

'For your hand – vinegar will pull out the bruise. My mama swears by it,' he said, the hint of a smile playing on his lips. I nodded with gratitude before turning back to him as an afterthought.

'Do you know who Juliet is?'

A bemused look passed across his face as he answered. 'She's not a who, ma'am, she's a ship. Mr B's ship.'

Relief washed over me at his answer, and a nervous laugh escaped my lips.

Juliet was Erasmus's ship, and she was leaving with or without him. That was what the captain's message had meant. If I hadn't been so comforted by that news, I would have chastised myself for jumping to conclusions, but as it was, I had to dart out of the way of an oncoming carriage.

I gave Kit a wave with my good hand as I returned to the house, in search of vinegar.

Erasmus came home in time to join us for supper, looking slightly frayed at the edges but otherwise unscathed. I found myself stealing glances at him while we ate, trying to read how the rest of his day had unfolded, but he was as courteous and polite as ever. His temper had not got the better of him then, despite having to work with my father's killer all day.

With my doubts about *Juliet* having been assuaged, I found myself thinking more and more of the captain's note, and wondering if perhaps her forewarning was tainted by the vestiges of her own feelings for Erasmus. She did not seem the type to be jealous, but had rather been pitying of me, as though she thought my feelings of attachment for him were unrequited.

Yet as I caught his eye over our meal, the warmth of his smiles sending a pleasant flush through my cheeks, I could not help but wonder whether Bea's earlier comments were accurate.

Perhaps we were not in love in the traditional sense, for nothing about Erasmus was truly traditional, but I would enjoy his company while I could, whether he tired of me tomorrow or ten years from now. It would be the only way to stay sane if we were to continue our facade and carry out his plans.

After a meal of roasted game, baked potatoes and boiled carrots in sugar, and a pudding of pear pie with cream, my mother suggested that my cousin and I retire while she discussed business with Erasmus. She had been receiving almost daily reports from him, I discovered, on the state of affairs at my father's company. It did not surprise me that she would want to keep a close eye on things whilst my husband was still so new to it, and she was more than qualified to understand it all.

But Erasmus gave his most charming smile and suggested that we all retire to the drawing room, where the four of us could spend the evening in companionable conversation. My mother agreed, swayed by the presence of Beatrice, who longed for Erasmus's tales of adventure as much as I did. Aristotle, full of scraps, slipped stealthily from the table and warmed himself on the Turkey carpet by the hearth, his gentle snores and snuffles just audible over the crackle of the fire.

'I'm sure Jenny has told you of their meeting, Beatrice.' My mother gestured to Erasmus and me, sitting side by side on a low couch, while she herself took up her usual armchair and my cousin sat in what I would always consider my father's seat.

'Well, I did hear that there was a certain defending of Jenny's honour,' Bea replied with a meaningful glance in my direction.

Erasmus chuckled wryly at that, and the sound sent a tingle up my spine. 'Oh, not at all. I believe that if I hadn't stepped in, the gentleman might have left with more than his pride bruised.'

I shook my head. 'Marcus is not prone to violence,' I protested. 'If anything, he would have made a few choice gestures and the drunk would have been on his way. You were the one who made it all very dramatic.'

Erasmus placed a hand on his chest as though I had wounded him. 'Dramatic? Me?' He gave me a wry smile. 'I was not speaking of Marcus, my dear wife,' he murmured, leaning closer to me, the scent of the wine he'd drunk with dinner on his lips.

There was a heartbeat of silence as I wondered what it would be like to kiss him here, in the cosy warmth of the withdrawing room, only inches apart on the seat. The subtle perfume of burning logs and liquor had made everything comfortably blurry. His eyes were dark pools in the firelight, deceptively black, with licks of flame reflected in them.

Someone cleared their throat noisily, and I realised it was my mother, snapping me out of my trance.

'You speak little of your family, William,' she said, continuing to insist on using the name she had created for him even in such close company. 'What of your late parents?'

Erasmus pulled his attention from me slowly, almost reluctantly, as he focused on my mother. It was hard to tell in the dimness, but I imagined that his cheeks were more flushed than usual.

'They have been dead a long time now, Mrs Miller,' he replied quietly. A strand of sympathy threaded through me at those words, so heavy were they with emotion. It was true that he rarely mentioned his parents, but the inscription in his copy of *Aesop's Fables* gave me the impression of a loving mother, one who cared deeply about her son.

'Perhaps you would indulge us with a story, Mr Black. Jenny says that you tell them so well,' Bea added gently.

He looked uncertainly between us, all waiting expectantly for him to speak.

'You do not have to,' I said quietly, for although I was sure Beatrice had meant to change the subject, it was clear that a story of his family was what plagued him.

He gave a small smile in response and cleared his throat.

'It would be my pleasure,' he lied. I knew that the telling of it would bring him no joy, but despite me squeezing his arm to signal that he did not owe us any of his pain, he gave a deep sigh and the faintest hint of a smile.

He looked down at his hands, slender callused fingers wrapped around each other, as though the tale was written somewhere in the lines and creases, and only he could read from them.

And then he told us.

Chapter 21

ꕥ

A BRIEF HISTORY OF ERASMUS BLACK

'My mother was an apothecary, selling medicines and herbs from her shop in Nafplio,' Erasmus began, his voice low and sonorous, 'one of the very few places in Greece where the Ottomans had no stronghold. My father was first mate of a ship named *Helena's Glory*, waylaid en route from Portsmouth to Arabia, where they were forced to dock due to unnavigable storms. He was a trader, much like I am, and had years at sea under his belt before they met.

'One night, as my mother walked home from her shop, she passed a tavern where pirates and sailors were often known to meet and deal. Her pace was always faster on that road, for although it was the swiftest route home, it was still beset with danger for an unmarried woman.'

I pictured her as he spoke, a woman with olive skin and dark hair hurrying down a paved road, the lights from taverns spilling gold onto the shadows, her steps quickening as she neared the sounds of men drinking and shouting.

'Just as she passed the door of the tavern, she tripped on something soft, cursing the name of all that was holy, until she realised that it was a man and that she had trodden on his hand. I believe the only reason she dragged him out of the gutter and to her house was her guilt at having broken one of his fingers when she stepped on him. There she tended his wounds, even while she admonished him for picking a fight and getting thrown into the street in the few English words she knew. I cannot tell you the particulars of how they came to fall for one another, but my mother, being of Mediterranean temperament and a fiercely beautiful woman, always told me that she did not expect to find herself in love with a brown-eyed English sailor who had an inclination for getting himself in trouble and starting fights that he had no right to win but often did.'

His words were soft and so full of love, and I could clearly imagine these two strangers who had found each other despite their differences in background and upbringing.

'My father always insisted that the only reason he lost that particular altercation was because fate was trying to throw him into her path, both figuratively and literally. Whether fate had a hand in it or no, on this occasion he had not only come out the loser but had suffered two broken ribs, and so was bedridden for some time. In exchange for her healing and hospitality, he taught her more of his language and told her stories of home, and at the month's end, *Helena's Glory* sailed without him, to the chagrin of his captain. Instead, they were married, my mother continuing to attend to her apothecary while my father became tirelessly involved in the politics of the Greek revolution, in the hope of one day aiding an uprising against their oppressors.

'But when my mother discovered she was with child she became fearful. Young boys had always been fodder for the Ottoman army from a young age, and she feared that if she bore a son, he would not be able to escape that fate. I think she prayed for a daughter every day, for if she could teach her the skills of being an apothecary, she might be spared the fate of so many women there. But none of the poorer families were truly safe, and any child could be at risk if an Ottoman company swept into their town.

'I was born in Greece, in my mother's very apothecary, the scent of olive groves and the sea in the air, but the fear kept my parents awake at night and tainted every early childhood memory of mine. They were torn between their love of the country that she had been raised in and he had grown to treasure, and the future of their family. Rebellions were constantly instigated and quashed before they came to fruition, and with neighbouring countries refusing to give assistance, my parents decided at last that they had no choice but to flee. They supported the rebellions as far as possible, but in the end, my father persuaded my mother that he would do whatever he could to help her people from afar.

'We came to England before my third birthday, where my father took up his inherited estate at Crawbridge.' His expression grew soft in the firelight as he began to recall those early years. 'We were a happy trio, sitting, much like we are now, around the fireplace after dinner. My mother would tell me a Greek legend, recounting the dramas and tragedies, my father a story from his travels or childhood, and I would be asked to make up a tale of my own. From an early age I was educated in the history of my mother's people, and she constantly drummed into me the fear of soldiers coming into homes and tearing children away, forcing people into slavery or drafting them into the army. I'll never forget that fear, nor the desire and need to fight for freedom on behalf of those who couldn't do so for themselves.'

The thread of sympathy that had woven through me tugged

tight at his revelation. I wanted to throw my arms around him and comfort him, so full of sorrow were his words. I understood now how he had come to so fiercely believe in the cause for which he fought; rebellion was the food on which he had been raised.

'It was seven more years before my younger brother, Adrian, arrived, but as he entered this world, my mother left it, taking her stories and her tales of myth and legend with her.' Erasmus's voice grew very low as he spoke, his eyes fixed on the flames in the fireplace rather than on any of us. I wanted to tell him to stop, to keep his grief to a time when we were alone, but I sensed that it was as cathartic to him to speak of it as it was for me to hear the truth.

'My father, in his grief, resolved to petition for British involvement in the Greek rebellion, but no one would listen to him, for he was neither a politician nor a naval officer. So, being a sailor at heart, he resolved to join the navy. While he worked his way up the ranks, I was left at Crawbridge to raise my younger brother with the help of a nursemaid and the few staff in our employ. My mother had always said that our family was Greek by nature and English by circumstance, and Adrian was no exception. He had my mother's temper and my father's stubbornness, but I did my best by him until he was old enough to decide for himself what he wished to do. Every night I would recount our mother's stories, our father's history lessons. I tried to paint a picture of our parents that would make up for their absence, but in doing so I raised his expectations too high. For despite barely knowing our father, he idolised him in a way I could never compete with.' He shook his head, a sad smile on his face.

I wondered how lonely it must have been to raise a brother ten years his junior in an empty house. With his father leaving after his mother's death, they would have been no different to orphans really. I tried to envisage a young Erasmus regaling his brother with stories and instilling in him the same lessons their mother had taught him, the two boys running wild on their large country estate. The responsibilities that would have been placed on him from such a young age must have been incredible. He had inherited his desire to fight for others from his parents, I could see, but still I felt a sense of outrage that a father could leave his son in such a way. Perhaps Erasmus also took his impulsiveness from him.

'Adrian joined the navy to follow in our father's footsteps, and I, no longer able to bear the emptiness of Crawbridge, found my own path to the sea, and to lands where I witnessed another sort of oppression. One I could not ignore. That was when I vowed to help others however I could.'

I was grateful for the gentleness in my mother's voice as she asked, 'But your father passed away?'

Erasmus sighed, nodding in reply. 'A letter that took almost a year to find its way to me told news of his death in the line of duty. Thankfully my brother is still alive, to my knowledge, although he was there when it happened.'

I pressed my lips together, holding back my own questions. I did not want to push him, and I sensed that he did not desire to speak more of it. To my surprise, he placed his glass down and took my good hand in his, brushing a rough thumb over my knuckles, warm where our skin touched.

'It is not a happy story, I'm afraid,' he said apologetically, giving a small smile.

'On the contrary, Mr Black,' Beatrice said with a smile of her own, 'it is a beautiful story. One of love and family, of fighting for what one believes in and keeping promises. What could be better than a tale such as that?'

Erasmus looked up at her with a fondness I had seen him reserve only for his crew. 'You are too kind, Miss Stanton, but I am glad you enjoyed it.'

Mother placed her hand on the armrest of my father's chair as she said, 'I believe that you would have been great friends with my Jacob, God rest his soul, for he too had strong opinions on the very same subject.'

'I have no doubt,' Erasmus replied sincerely.

'My husband's father was raised as a Quaker, and the whole family were strong advocates for the laws that passed eight years ago on the banning of slave keeping and transportation. Much like you, Jacob abhorred the idea and was until his death in regular correspondence with men from Westminster,' Mother continued.

Erasmus and I looked up at her at the same time, surprised.

'Mr Miller had a contact in Parliament?' he asked.

She stood, smoothing her skirts as she did so. 'Or someone who had Parliament's ear, reformers and the suchlike. He didn't trouble me too much with the specifics of the politics, but I knew he had friends higher up. He had become quite animated on the matter in recent months . . .' She trailed off as though just recalling something, but blinked it away rapidly. 'I warned him not to involve himself too heavily in anything that might mar the family name, but I know he signed more than one petition on the matter. I only wish he had lived to see it through.' She fell silent, clasping her hands in front of her in contemplation.

I looked to Erasmus, who appeared as alarmed as I felt at this sudden news. If my father had a contact at Westminster, perhaps he had already told them of Talver's dealings. But if so, why had nothing been done about it?

My mother clapped softly, waking Aristotle as she announced her departure. 'Well, my dears, I'm afraid I must bid you goodnight. You have Mrs Griegsson's salon tomorrow, and the invitation says to be there for seven, no doubt so that she can avoid having to serve her guests with dinner,' she said a little haughtily. 'I would advise an early night for you all,' she added, looking pointedly at me. My eyes widened at her implication, and I looked away quickly.

'I too should retire,' Beatrice said, rising from her chair and pulling me into an embrace. She brushed a strand of my hair behind my ear as she whispered, 'If you do not see that he is in love with you, cousin, then you ought to get spectacles.' I laughed quietly, her curls brushing my cheek as I held her close, the smell of lavender water and face powder lingering as she said goodnight to Erasmus and followed my mother upstairs.

'You know, they say that you can best judge a man by his friends,' Erasmus said as we stood before the hearth, our only company Aristotle, who had gone back to snoozing.

'Is that so?' I replied, resting a hand on his arm. He seemed buoyant now, despite having recounted the story of his parents' lives. I hoped that in learning this little piece of himself that he'd revealed to me, I was finally beginning to complete the puzzle of him.

'Absolutely.' He gestured towards the door, following closely behind me. 'I imagine the same rule applies to your sex.'

I turned to him as we ascended the stairs, pausing halfway. 'And?'

'Well, your cousin seems charming, kind and witty, much like a certain someone I know,' he said, flashing me a smile before I continued my way up.

'Are you saying that you like my cousin as much as you do me?' I asked pointedly, allowing my lips to tug at the corners.

'Not at all. I am merely saying that it appears we both have excellent taste in companionship.'

'That sounds awfully as though you are complimenting yourself, husband,' I said, narrowing my eyes at him as we reached the first landing. He stopped on the second-to-last step so that our faces were level, his hands coming to my waist, where they rested gently. The heat from them seeped through my dress and into the skin beneath my underclothes.

'Perhaps I am,' he replied, his nose just inches from my own, his smile within reach of my lips.

I found myself hypnotised by the dark hunger in his eyes, by the proximity of his face, by the warmth of his hands, placed so reverently above my hips.

He closed the gap between us slowly, taking his time, enjoying every second of agony that it caused me to have him this close and not be touching him. I wondered if he would hesitate this time; if he would grip me as though his life depended upon it only to push me away as he had done a few nights ago. His gaze breezed over my face, as though taking in every detail, before landing on my mouth with a questioning look. *Is this what you want?* he seemed to ask. My nod was almost imperceptible, and when he leaned in, a small gasp left me.

As his lips met mine, my hands smoothed over the lapels of his jacket, up his broad chest, to twine in his hair and the back of his neck. His sea salt and rum scent filled my lungs as we kissed, his hands never roaming further than they should while managing to pull me flush against him. I worried we might teeter off the stairs if we weren't careful.

'Wait,' I said, my breath coming fast as I broke away. 'Did you inadvertently call me charming, kind and witty?'

He made a low sound in his throat somewhere between a laugh and a moan. It was a sound I would delight in hearing again. '*That's* what you are fixated on? Whether I gave you the admiration you are due?'

'It so seldom happens, I just wanted it to be recognised,' I said, pressing my lips to the corner of his mouth, a gesture that was rewarded with another low moan.

'Well, then I have been terribly remiss in my duties. If I were to tell you that you were charming, kind, witty, intelligent *and* beautiful, would that appease you?'

I pretended to think about it, my fingers still in his hair, pulling him closer to me so that the tips of our noses were touching.

'Now you're just saying things to make me happy.'

'You would know if I were lying, little mouse, so let me tell you another truth.' He closed his eyes, his dark lashes casting shadows on his cheeks. 'When I first saw you, I was fascinated by you. I wanted to know you better, more than anything else.' It wasn't *I love you*, but the sincerity in his words was like the harmonious plucking of harp strings, and my heart thrummed with it.

'I don't understand,' I said, shaking my head so that our noses brushed.

'Well, I hope you'll give me the rest of our lives to adequately explain,' he said, pressing his forehead to mine, a hand roaming up my back to cup my neck.

My breath hitched in my throat. I was blissfully aware of all the places where he touched me, everywhere our bodies met, the layers between us. I could almost believe Beatrice's assessment of his feelings for me. In fact, in the darkness of the stairwell, I could almost believe that I felt the same.

Desire, flaming and sudden, sparked in my chest, and I didn't hesitate when he led me past my room to his, stopping just outside the door. Now that we weren't on the stairs, he had to bend down to kiss me, but he did so once, gently, before turning the handle and opening the door to his room.

He froze as we entered, and a match sparked to life across the room, illuminating the face of the woman within.

'Sorry to interrupt,' Captain Hodgson said quietly, booted legs crossed on the edge of the bed as she lit a candle on the bedside table. 'But we have a problem. Kaine Clark appears to have left town. I sent you a missive.'

It was like being doused with a bucket of cold water, and my hands slipped from Erasmus's as he swiftly closed the door behind us.

'For goodness' sake, Mira, is this how you got the notes onto my desk? By breaking into my rooms?'

She pouted, which on anyone else might have looked sullen but on her only accentuated her full lips. Her scar was almost invisible in the dimness.

Seeing her here, on his bed, reminded me that they used to be lovers, and that she knew of his previous trysts. Likely she had heard the sad story he had recounted to us this evening. Perhaps they had shared everything, and her being here was her way to tear us apart.

I tried to dismiss those thoughts as quickly as I formulated them, for whether she still had feelings for Erasmus or not, what we were embarking on was a dangerous thing and she had every right to be cautious, yet I was not entirely convinced that she was here out of the goodness of her heart.

'You didn't reply. I had little choice but to come myself and ensure that you had not lost sight of the plan,' she bit out, keeping her voice to a whisper.

'On the contrary, Jenny's mother obtained the extra invitations. You need only pick one of the lads to accompany you and the rest should be relatively straightforward.'

Mira snorted, a most unladylike sound. 'Straightforward, Bart? Nothing about your convoluted plan is straightforward.'

'It is just as we discussed. I will keep up my end of the bargain, I assure you,' Erasmus replied, unable to hide his frustration.

I wondered what more Mira's unanswered letter had said, other than the news of Kaine Clark's escape, and whether Erasmus's failure to reply was what had angered her. Her mood had certainly soured since Saturday.

'Attending one party is not going to upend the entire broken system. Nor will it find my sister.'

I paused at this revelation. Not that anyone's eyes were on me to notice. What had Erasmus said when he first mentioned the captain – that she was looking for someone important? A missing sister would make an awful lot of sense.

'You insist on dancing around the gentry to glean scraps of evidence so that you can lay them at a politician's feet, but that will take for ever.'

Erasmus stalked further into the room, our passion forgotten, tearing savagely at his cravat and flinging it onto the chest of drawers.

'I do not mean to sound insensitive, Mira, but what about the poor girls captured and sold next month? Or the month after? If we do not bring the men responsible to heel, you will spend the rest of your life chipping away at the mountain. With my method, we will bring the mountain *down*.'

'That is unfair. You know that if it were someone *you* held dear, you would move heaven and earth to get them to safety,' Mira replied, jabbing a fierce look in my direction. 'I have been as patient as I can, Bart, but I cannot keep an entire crew here for months on end while you . . . hold up your end of the bargain.'

Erasmus inched back towards me, as though trying to shield me from her verbal attack. I did not begrudge her anger, though.

If I had a sister and she had gone missing, sold to one of these slavers, I would have been just as determined as Mira to get her back.

'We are on the same side, Mira,' Bart said, his impatience showing.

'And if she is, as we speak, being transported to yet another master in another country and we miss our opportunity, how do you justify your plan then?'

'It was your intelligence that brought us back to London in the first place. I do not think we have exhausted all avenues here yet.'

'And how long would you have me wait before you are willing to move on, hmm?'

Though they spoke in near-whispers, their voices both began to take on an edge that would be heard outside the room, and I shushed them quickly.

'You are both right,' I said quietly, stepping between them so as not to be ignored. 'Mira's priority should be her sister.' She looked at me in surprise, as though in the heat of their argument she had forgotten I could speak. 'Your method of seeking out these ships and freeing the imprisoned women on them is fast and effective, but mortally dangerous,' I acknowledged. 'Erasmus, your plan is sound, provided we are not caught in the process. It is lengthy, however, and will require more than a few weeks to see through. I see no reason why you cannot both continue on your chosen paths, if Erasmus is willing to gift you his ship and crew in its entirety.'

Erasmus gave a dismayed huff, and I truly wondered what he had been intending when Mira's few weeks here were at an end. Had he really planned on leaving? I ignored the stab of betrayal I felt at that thought.

'What say you, Bart? Would you willingly hand over *Juliet*

to me so that you can continue this . . . arrangement?' Mira asked in a needling tone, standing up and placing her hands on her hips, leaning her weight on one leg.

'It would be a logical plan,' Erasmus said, not directly answering the question. I wanted to shake him by the lapels of his fine jacket and demand that he tell it to me plainly, but I refused to lose my temper in front of the captain.

'And what about you, Mrs Black? Have you held up your side of the bargain and found us anything useful?' she said with a derisive hint in her tone. She was not truly angry with me, I knew, so I did not hold it against her.

'Don't speak to my wife like that,' Erasmus cut in, dangerously low.

I gave him a look that I hoped said, *I can take care of myself*, then turned to the captain.

'Aside from the intelligence that my father was poisoned, that a man by the name of Sly Fairfax did the deed and that he has removed himself to Clapham? That it is entirely likely that my father was on to Talver's involvement and that his business partner most likely decided to have him killed rather than face the consequences? I would consider that information "useful".' I willed my voice not to crack as I said it all aloud.

She pressed her lips into a thin line and nodded. 'I am sorry for that, Mrs Black. Bart passed the news onto Lei earlier today and she in turn relayed it to me. I did raise my suspicions when first we met if you recall.' There was the hint of sympathy there that was, I suspected, unfamiliar to her. I accepted her brief condolences and drew myself up, rallying my courage. 'Well, you'll be pleased to hear that Erasmus and I have an invitation to Klaus Griegsson's wife's salon tomorrow evening. She will be showing off some of their new paintings and, knowing these events, he will be gathering his gentlemen friends in his parlour to discuss whatever it is that men talk about when their wives are out of earshot. I'm certain that Erasmus will be able to pick up something while I provide an appropriate distraction.'

Mira narrowed her eyes, but I could see she was impressed with my suggestion.

'That is all very well, but even presuming George Talver is there, I don't think he will be discussing buying slaves with Griegsson in front of a room full of gentlemen,' she said, looking to Erasmus for support.

'Actually, that is how many business transactions take place,' I replied. 'They may be discreet, but you would be surprised at what men will reveal with a bit of liquor in their bellies in the company of friends.'

Erasmus raised his eyebrows in pleasant surprise and the satisfaction of it warmed me, even as Mira tried to poke another hole in my idea.

'Your contact in the Saints won't be interested in overheard conversations, Bart. If they are to press charges in front of a judge, you'll need physical evidence to implicate these men.'

'I shall search Griegsson's study,' I said abruptly.

'Jenny—'

'Erasmus,' I interrupted him in his protest, 'if you are found searching a man's study, they'll have a Bow Street Runner on you in a second. If I get conveniently lost in his house and someone finds me in the wrong room, they'll merely chalk it up to feminine absent-mindedness or some other nonsense.'

He opened his mouth to argue, but closed it when he realised that I was right. I looked to Mira, a smug smile playing across her lips.

'Well, well,' she crossed her arms and moved to sit on the bed, 'it sounds as though we need a proper plan if you're to succeed in this little deception.'

'And you want to hash it out now, in the middle of the night?' Erasmus asked, exasperated that she would not be got rid of so easily.

'There is no better time, surely, unless . . . you had other business?'

I shared a look with him that could have meant any number of things, but it was obvious that Mira Hodgson was not a woman to be deterred so easily.

'You want a strategy, Captain, I shall provide you with one,' I said, sweeping past her as elegantly as I could and sitting at the writing desk.

'What are you doing, Jenny?' Erasmus asked, sounding a little mystified.

I pulled a pen and paper from the drawer, opening a pot of ink.

'Going into Griegsson's unprepared would be like walking into the wolf's den. You do not know these people as I do,' I explained, beginning to write names of individuals I was certain would be there, and the details of how these events usually unfolded.

I wrote until I ran out of space on the page and ink in the pen, answering Erasmus and Mira's questions when asked and revising where necessary. Then, moving on to Henrietta's ball, Mira asked for some sort of a map of Osborne's house, explaining that she didn't like to go to parties without knowing where all the exits were. It was a peculiar request, but I obliged with a rough sketch of the lower floor. When I finally finished, I looked up to see them both studying my drawing and words with awe. I could not help but feel a little pride at that.

'This is fantastic, Jenny,' Erasmus said, picking up the paper and blowing on it to dry the ink. 'How do you remember it all?'

I shrugged, stretching out my cramped hand. 'You have your

skills, I have mine. Memorising names and locations happens to be one of them.'

'You would have made a remarkable thief,' he replied with utter sincerity.

Satisfied that we had some semblance of organisation for tomorrow, I noted down the Griegssons' address so that Mira could station one of her crew nearby just in case there were any unpleasant surprises.

'Not bad at all,' was all she said, tucking the slip of paper into her blouse. It was as close to a compliment as I would ever get from her. 'This had better work,' she added to Erasmus, 'for if not, we could all end up in Newgate.'

My stomach plummeted at the thought of him, or any of his crew, in prison. Was stealing paperwork from a criminal truly considered a crime? Without another word, Mira slid open the window and climbed out, much as Erasmus had done on his first night here.

He released a frustrated sigh before closing the window, leaving me still sitting at his desk, our kiss all but forgotten. Even with Mira not in the room, her presence hung over me like a spectre. Of course, she had the best interests of her crew – and her missing sister – at heart, and was concerned for the cause for which she and Erasmus had worked so tirelessly. Yet I could not shake the feeling that she, like Kit, resented me for taking him away from them.

'I must apologise, Jenny,' he said, removing his waistcoat and hanging it in the wardrobe. 'Mira has a tendency to forget that etiquette on land is quite different to that at sea.'

'I don't believe forgetfulness has anything to do with it,' I muttered, getting up to leave but finding his hand on my arm before I could get very far.

'Stay,' he whispered. 'Please?'

The contact brought back all those feelings on the staircase. The rush of desire, the aching need, the thrill as our lips had met. But the captain's arrival had once again clouded my emotions with doubt. What was he asking of me exactly, in this request for me to stay?

I hesitated. 'Just to sleep?' I asked, frozen in place by my desire to embrace him and yet to run from the room lest I be hurt again.

It was not only Erasmus's fickleness that scared me, but the thought of being so open with him, taking that next and very final step in our marriage, knowing that he held the power to utterly destroy me if he so wished it. For if I did spend this night with him and he then left, I felt sure that it would break me beyond anything that Lord Darleston had accomplished all those months ago.

'If that is all you want,' he said, his voice a shade deeper.

Heat licked up my insides as I realised that it wasn't all I wanted at all, but I was too scared to admit it. He must have sensed my hesitation, for he closed the distance between us, pressing a kiss to the top of my head as I curled into his chest, his arms settling around me as though this space had been made just for me.

'Just to sleep,' he said, his voice rumbling through us both as the decision was made.

It was the sensible thing to do, I thought, as I attempted to force all sensations of physical need from my mind. Today had been traumatic for us both, and I was still coming to terms with the revelations from the chop house. But just because it was sensible was not to say I didn't question my decision at every moment.

Deftly undoing the clasps on my dress with those clever long fingers, he helped me out of it and hung it neatly on the back of the chair. I removed my petticoat, climbing under the blankets in just my chemise, while he stripped down to his shirt, then blew out the candle and came to lie beside me, clasping my unbruised hand in his, turning me towards him with a gentle tug so that our noses touched and our lips met once more. Mira's appearance might have temporarily quashed our moment of desire, but it was still there.

Erasmus closed his eyes without saying another word, our hands still entwined as he seemingly somehow managed to put all the fear and worry from his mind. He was used to this, of course; accustomed to standing on the precipice of danger. I watched him for a while, the moonlight shining through a crack in the curtains lining his features in silver, until his breathing evened out and I waited for sleep to take me too.

My final thoughts before I drifted off were for the event tomorrow. If anything were to go wrong, for so much could, who would take the fall?

And if it were Mira or their crew, would Erasmus ever forgive me?

Chapter 22

ᘓᘐ

A MOST DELECTABLE LITTLE THIEF

When I awoke, it was to the gentle brush of fingers stroking my cheek. I batted them away and pulled the covers over my head, but rather than take the hint, Erasmus laughed, tugging them back down and planting a kiss on my cheek.

'It's not morning already, is it?' I groaned, rubbing the sleep from my eyes.

'It surprises me that you are a grumpy riser, little mouse,' he rumbled, throwing open the curtains and letting the sunlight in.

'Argh.' I held my hands over my face to block out the light. Goodness knew what I looked like, my hair wayward, my undergarments dishevelled. I supposed that was the good thing about marrying a sailor. He would have seen people in a worse state than I at closer quarters – I hoped.

'I have been summoned for breakfast already,' he added, busying himself getting ready before my eyes. I observed in fascination as he shaved at his basin while I fought to stir myself from the bed. 'As much as I enjoy you watching me, it might be a sensible idea to return to your room before your mother sends Edith up to fetch you,' he pointed out, straightening his cravat before pulling on a waistcoat. I never ceased to be surprised by his attire, for despite having been at sea for nearly a decade, he dressed like a true gentleman.

I sighed, reluctantly dragging myself from the softness of the bed before catching a glimpse of my hair in his mirror. To say it resembled a bird's nest would be too kind.

'Good gracious,' I muttered. 'I'll be down in a moment,' I added, pushing him out of the door and resting my back against it, willing myself into action.

This time less than a fortnight ago, I had been preparing for my wedding. In such a short time I had taken a new name, been kidnapped, discovered my father was murdered, begun to fall for a pirate and found out that my husband was planning to dismantle my family's business. And that was just the beginning.

When had this become normal for me?

I scurried to my room before anyone could come searching for me and dressed in a simple day dress before going down to breakfast, knowing that I would have to change before leaving for the salon in the evening.

The sound of my mother's voice reached me from the staircase. She was already in full flow as she advised my poor cousin on which young gentlemen attending later were available, who had the greater fortune, and whom I had been to visit when searching for my own husband. I gave Beatrice an apologetic look as I took my seat beside Erasmus, but her only response was an amused quirk of her mouth as she listened carefully to Mother.

Perhaps she was happy to be in receipt of so much attention, I mused, as I recalled her words from yesterday. Although I had not been married for long, Mother seemed to enjoy the idea of having someone new to order around and find a suitor for, while Beatrice appeared to relish her aunt's interest. My new status as a married woman was bringing them closer together, and I couldn't complain.

'How is your hand?' Erasmus asked, leaning towards me and giving my knuckles a gentle brush with his fingers, an intimate gesture that he disguised by reaching past me for the butter.

'Aching, but better than it was yesterday. Kit told me to put vinegar on it,' I replied quietly, picking up the teapot.

'I'm sure it will heal faster than Mr Blythe's face,' Erasmus replied with a hint of laughter in his voice.

'I shall send Edith up to dress you at four, Jenny,' Mother interrupted.

'Very good, Mama,' I replied, last night's nerves settling in my stomach as I remembered what we had to do today.

The hours of the morning and afternoon appeared to vanish, and before I felt truly prepared, our carriage was pulling up outside the Griegsson residence in Belgravia. Much like our own home, their terraced house stood in a grand square of identical buildings with a gated communal garden in the centre. A chandelier hung in the colonnaded entrance, both ostentatious and completely impractical, below which a steward stood, checking our invitations as we entered. I gripped Erasmus's arm a little tighter, trying desperately to look the picture of relaxation while my insides somersaulted. Glancing up at him, I noted his keen eyes taking it all in – the marbled hall with a chandelier twice the size of the one outside the front door; the double doors to the left that appeared to open to some sort of parlour; the door to the right ajar, the smell of pipe smoke and men's voices drifting out through the gap. The grand staircase before us had doors beneath it on either side, one of which was open, with smartly dressed staff bustling in and out.

'Mrs Black! I was so sorry to hear about your father,' Anna Griegsson said with a curtsey that I returned, waving a server over to offer us champagne from a silver tray. I was surprised to be addressed so familiarly by a woman I had never met before, but the sad smile that found its way onto my face was genuine.

'Thank you, Mrs Griegsson. I appreciate your kind offer to invite us into your home so soon after losing him,' I said, hoping it did not sound like an insult. Had the loss of my father and my subsequent marriage forced the incident at Lord Darleston's party from everyone's minds? Or would I be confronted once again by thinly veiled barbs and hushed sniggers?

Anna Griegsson pursed her lips in a peculiar sort of smile, her pinched features and fine bones giving her the air of someone sharp but quite delicate. Her thin frame was exaggerated by the many layers of skirts she wore beneath a tight stomacher. She had evidently kept to the fashions of her own country rather than adapting to the attire of London, and I felt rather plain by comparison in my white dress overlaid with an embroidered light blue fichu.

Without my mother here to make introductions and move the conversation along, I realised that that duty now fell to me. 'I've heard much of your husband's success as a merchant from my dear father. As a lover of art himself, I'm certain he would have delighted in seeing your collection,' I said. The truth was, I didn't know how much Mrs Griegsson knew of her husband's secret work. Was she aware how close he was to my late father's business partner? Could it be possible that she secretly condoned what he did, and was privy to his every secret? I hoped not, and chose to give her the benefit of the doubt.

She smiled agreeably at the compliment, then angled her

head at Erasmus. 'You must be Mr Black,' she observed, 'the captain turned merchant.'

'It seems my reputation precedes me, madam,' he replied with a bow.

'Well, the tale of your very fortunate match has been heard in most circles. It is not every day that a company such as Miller, Osborne & Talver loses a prized member of their company, only to gain a replacement so quickly.' There was no animosity in Mrs Griegsson's tone, but it was a peculiar observation, I thought. I wondered what else had been told about us in 'most circles' and was immediately grateful that Kaine Clark was no longer in town, for his presence at the salon would have immediately jeopardised both our plans and our safety.

'Mrs Griegsson,' I cut in, 'allow me to introduce my cousin, Miss Beatrice Stanton. It is her first season here in London.'

Beatrice gave her sweetest curtsey before distracting our hostess with a compliment about her dress. I was grateful that Mrs Griegsson's attention was briefly diverted, giving Erasmus and myself a chance to move into the parlour without appearing rude.

There were some ten other guests already there, sipping their drinks and making polite conversation, but no sign of Mr Griegsson himself.

'Did you observe the room to the right of the entrance hall?' Erasmus leaned down to murmur in my ear as we stood in front of a painting, a bucolic scene of a horse drawing a plough painted by a lesser-known Cornishman.

'It must be Griegsson's smoking room or something similar,' I replied with a nod, smiling at a couple as they walked past, my face falling as they bowed their heads to murmur to each other whilst keeping their eyes steadily fixed on us. Whether it was an observation about our marriage or some disparaging remark about my fall from grace, I didn't know, and I tried to push it from my mind. 'I wonder what it might take to secure an invitation into that inner sanctum?'

'Oh, don't fret about that. I shall be in there before the hour is up, squeezing them for all they're worth,' he reassured me. 'It is what you will be doing when I leave you that I am worried about.'

I exhaled on a small laugh, casually moving away from the painting when someone came to stand near us. We crossed the floor slowly, sauntering over to a miniature statue of a nymph draped over a tree trunk. The detail in the carving was exquisite, with so much emotion caught in the simple white stone.

'I have that in hand. As soon as I see an opening, I know exactly what excuse I shall be making,' I replied, taking a sip of my drink.

Erasmus had been correct, of course. Within a quarter of an hour, one of the gentlemen stewards came to extend an invitation to him from Mr Griegsson himself, and my husband took his leave of me with a certain *see, I told you so* look.

My own opportunity to extricate myself took slightly longer to arrive. Anna Griegsson wanted all the ladies in her presence to know exactly where each of the paintings had come from and the difficulty her husband had had in obtaining them. There were biblical depictions from Italy, Ottoman tapestries and French sculptures positioned throughout the lower rooms of the house, and we moved from the parlour to the music room, from the drawing room to the dining room, all while I found myself looking for some sign that might indicate where Klaus Griegsson had his study. After almost an hour of listening to stories of his great exploits from our hostess, I was beginning to think that Mr Griegsson inflated his many stories when retelling them to his wife. If her pride in all he did was not a sign of love, I didn't know what it was.

It wasn't until we reached the back of the house, a conservatory that opened out to a pristine garden with more statues than Medusa's lair, that I took my chance.

'My apologies, but might you have a retiring room?' I whispered to a servant who stood with a loaded tray of champagne flutes by the door.

'If you return to the main entrance hall and go up to the first floor, there is a lady's maid stationed just outside the door to assist you, madam,' he said with an understanding smile.

I wasted no time in following his instructions, passing the smoking room on my way to the grand staircase. I spared a brief thought for Erasmus and hoped that he was coping in a den full of men who could just as easily be foes as friends, but then stopped myself. Of course he was coping. He had been carrying out these grand charades for far longer than I had.

A long corridor greeted me at the top of the stairs, but thankfully the maid was nowhere to be seen – perhaps she was assisting another lady within – and it gave me the chance to check each door to see what was behind it.

The first and second were bedrooms, exquisitely decorated but leaving me with the impression that I was in a museum rather than a home. The third was the retiring room, and when I heard the telltale sounds of someone relieving themselves behind the decorative screen, I retreated quickly to check the next.

I withheld a whoop of joy when I finally encountered what had to be Mr Griegsson's study. Its large French doors overlooked the garden beyond, and I shrank back from them lest one of the roaming guests down on the lawn spot someone lurking upstairs. The days were shortening inch by inch, and already the sun was beginning its descent, filling the study with rich golden rays. I knew I would run out of light before long, so with nerves thrumming through my body, I began to search.

The room was twice the size of my father's study, with bookshelves behind the large desk, maps hanging on the walls, and dark leather furniture. A painting of Mr Griegsson hung over the unlit fireplace, a sword in one hand while the other rested on his hip in some tribute to a past conqueror or army general, I thought. I resisted the temptation to spin the globe that sat like a centrepiece on the drinks cabinet, memorising instead the layout of every item on the desk. Documents pertaining to the purchase of a shipment of slaves would not be lying in full view, I was sure, but seeing how the Dutch merchant organised his belongings might enable me to understand something of his character.

Evidence. I needed to find some evidence of Griegsson's dealings with Clark and Talver, whether it be a letter or a note, a record of a meeting or . . . well, anything at all. I inhaled deeply, trying to steady my quivering fingers as I started on the desk drawers, studying the contents of each one before returning it exactly as I had found it and moving on to the next.

Minutes ticked past, marked by a large clock on the mantelpiece, but there was nothing of interest. The dockets in the drawers looked much the same as those Erasmus had been reading in my father's study. Sugar, crates of spice, silk, groundnuts. Griegsson had organised them by date, and I steadily progressed backwards in time.

I thought back to what we had realised only yesterday. If my father had discovered some evidence – perhaps some sign of human captivity, such as manacles, blood or who knew what else – on a ship he was inspecting, that contract could have easily been forged nine months to a year ago. I did not know if the girls being sold by the Ottoman army were being transported directly to Europe, or if they were hidden alongside cargo that had to make a long, circuitous journey to other continents. That left a rather large window of time for me to investigate, and some contracts might take over twelve months to complete. Although I had usually had my head in a book when my parents discussed the business, a few valuable pieces of information had slipped through. If Griegsson was dealing in the sex slave trade, and Erasmus had been foiled in his recent mission this spring, perhaps he had something from last winter – some directive ordering his ships to sail, or a requisition order. I needed to look earlier.

The paperwork in the drawer I was searching only detailed up to six months ago – too recent to be useful. Just as I was set to return it to its original place, something gave me pause. An ink blotter rolled back and forth as I moved the drawer, knocking a bottle of ink to the side, revealing the corner of something small and white. I carefully lifted the bottle to find myself looking at a piece of paper folded to the size of a wax seal. Prising it from its hiding place with a fingernail and unfolding it, I was unsurprised to see that it was a handwritten note, and I moved closer to the window to read it.

Fairfax in Clapham.

KC

A sharp wave of nausea roiled in my stomach. Fairfax was my father's poisoner. It could be a coincidence, but the initials at the end of the note were unique enough to tie it all together. *Kaine Clark.*

Possession of this note would imply that Griegsson had had a hand in my father's death. They were all in it together. Of course they were.

It was perhaps not the firm evidence I had wanted, but I would not allow my discovery to go to waste. I folded the note back up and tucked it into my glove, but then thought better of it. Sweat, cold and slick under my clothes, could easily ruin such a small thing. Instead, I placed it under one of the folds of fabric in my fichu, protected between the bodice of my dress and the scarf that covered my décolletage, hoping it would stay in place long enough for me to get home. Would Griegsson notice it was missing before we had a chance to act on it?

I cast about for a blank sheet of paper, and tore a small piece off the bottom of it, folding it and placing it under the ink pot. If Griegsson were to make a quick check of his desk drawer, he would see it there and hopefully not take much of a closer look than that. I folded the remainder of the blank page as small as I could and slipped that into my glove.

The note was still not enough proof to tie Klaus Griegsson in with the illegal trading, however, and I began checking for false drawer bottoms, and then searched the cupboards behind the desk, my ears pricking at the slightest sound outside the room. I had never been more aware of the seconds ticking by, my thunderous heartbeat marking the time in my chest.

The sound of a lock clicking had me leaping upright and trying desperately to look innocent. I scurried over to the painting above the fireplace as though I could pretend I was simply admiring it, and glanced back at the desk. Thank goodness I had had the forethought to replace everything after I had examined it. But the door to the study remained closed. Then the curtains at the balcony doors rustled, and a small, lithe figure stepped out from behind them.

'Mrs B, it's a nice office and all, but I don't think studying the artwork is going to find us what we want any faster,' Lei said, her teeth shining in the dimming twilight. I exhaled a relieved laugh, running over to scoop her up in an embrace. She was the only member of the crew smaller than me, and her bony shoulder dug into my neck as I held her.

'I thought you were Mr Griegsson. No offence,' I added when she pulled a face.

'None taken,' she replied with a grin. 'Found anything at all?' she asked.

'Only a note that I suspect confirms that Kaine Clark worked with Griegsson and Talver to murder my father,' I said, hating the way my voice cracked as I spoke.

Lei whistled quietly between her teeth. 'But nothing on the girls or the shipments?'

I shook my head, and she grimaced as though she'd been expecting as much.

'The note is a start, but we really need something else,' she replied, looking hopefully at the desk.

'Well, I've searched the drawers.'

'Checked for false bottoms?'

'Of course.' I allowed myself a fleeting moment of pride. 'The only promising thing is ten years of records, but there's no way we'll be able to get them out of here without them being missed.' I walked over to the cabinets I had started searching and opened the door of the nearest to demonstrate my meaning. Ledgers going back years were neatly stacked on each shelf. Not only would Griegsson notice their disappearance, but there was no easy way to get them out of the study either.

Lei checked the other cabinets, glaring at the offending volumes as though they might transform into something useful. Then she made a thoughtful noise, turning about the room suddenly. 'I wonder . . .' she murmured, her brow furrowed as she placed an ear to the wall nearest the bookshelves. She tapped with a fingernail, concentration etched across her face as she moved up and down, tapping, listening, moving, tapping, listening, moving again. She obviously didn't find what she was looking for, as she strode over to the other side of the room and did the same.

'Ah,' she said finally, standing back to look accusingly at a framed map of the Americas. 'A little obvious, I suppose, but you wouldn't mind lending me a hand, would you, Mrs B?'

Between the two of us, we managed to lift and unhook the picture, placing it gently against the skirting. Lei grinned from ear to ear, while I let out an impressed laugh, for there, set within the wall, was a metal safe. I never would have found it without her.

'Now we just need to open it,' she said, cracking her knuckles exaggeratedly and stretching her neck from side to side as though limbering up.

As safes went, this one was reasonably straightforward; all that was required was the right key, or in Lei's case, a good set of lock picks. She produced a small leather roll and selected her tools before going to work.

'Is this how you got in through the balcony doors?' I asked, but she shushed me gently. Apparently lock-picking was intricate work.

Perspiration ran down my back, and I wondered how anyone could possibly lead a life of crime without dying young of heart failure. Every sound from without, every echo of steps in the corridor outside had me tensing, just waiting for discovery. If Griegsson came in now, there would be no hiding what we were doing – no admiring the artwork or pretending we had got lost – for it would take us too long to return the map to its rightful place on the wall.

An agonising seven minutes later, she had the safe open to reveal a carved wooden box of precious stones, velvet pouches that clinked with gold, and a stack of banknotes. These were of little interest to me, however. What I sought was the mundane-looking ledger, bound in worn black leather, that was tucked at the back of the small space.

'Is that it?' Lei asked, pressing against my arm so that she could take a look.

There were no words for what was inside, and I found myself unable to speak. Contracts for voyages, sums of money that astonished even me, and receipts for every man, woman and child that Griegsson had bought and sold.

'This won't fit under my dress, Lei,' I said, hefting the book and putting it into her hands, ignoring the way her face fell when I closed the safe door on the jewels and money.

'That's what I'm here for,' she replied, helping to return the map to its rightful place before tucking the ledger under a slender arm and heading for the French doors. She gave me a small two-fingered salute as she slipped onto the balcony and dropped one-handed into the darkness below.

I waited until she was out of sight, lost to the lengthening shadows of the garden, where it had grown so dark that the guests had all retreated inside, before making my own exit. The clock told me it was well past nine, and with no candle to see by, I had to be careful not to knock against any precious antiques or pieces of art in my haste for the door.

But just as I reached it, the handle turned and the door opened. I leaped back, startled, knowing that it would be no good trying to hide.

'As I was saying, Osborne, it is quite unfortunate about those two ships of yours—' Klaus Griegsson pulled up short when he spotted me.

'M-my apologies, sir,' I stuttered, dropping into a curtsey, 'but I was looking for the retiring room.'

Griegsson was just as tall as I remembered him – as tall as Erasmus, perhaps over six feet – with a dark blond moustache and thinning hair.

'The retiring room is down the hall, madam, but that does

not explain why you were in my office with the door closed behind you,' he said, narrowing his dark eyes at me.

'Jenny, is that you?' My godfather stepped around the imposing Dutchman so that he was positioned between us. 'Mr Griegsson, this is my goddaughter, Mrs Jennifer Black. Her father was my dear friend and business partner, Jacob Miller, if you recall him?' Although my legs shook beneath my dress, I gave a weak smile as Osborne threw an arm around my shoulders. 'She is quite the art aficionado, just as her father was,' he added, though it was a considerable exaggeration of my level of knowledge.

'Is that so?' Griegsson replied with an arch of an eyebrow. I sensed he was waiting for me to speak for myself, and I nodded eagerly, continuing the ruse. I had not missed the way his eyes had flicked to the desk and then the map on the wall.

'Indeed, sir. It was the remarkable painting above your fireplace that caught my eye, and I must have lost track of the time while studying it. The likeness is striking, I might add.'

Griegsson didn't seem like the sort of person who would give in to flattery, but my pandering must have worked, for his expression softened slightly as he moved to light the candles nearest the picture, illuminating the preposterous portrait. I supposed that if a man could tolerate standing in that pose for hours on end, he might like his efforts to be applauded by a virtual stranger.

'Ah, yes. It was painstaking work to find an artist who could capture the essence of my intentions for this piece, but after several trials I found this extraordinary man,' the merchant replied, happily taking up the invitation to speak about himself while I threw my godfather a grateful smile.

When I finally extricated myself, explaining that I truly did need to find the retiring room, Osborne showed me to the study door. Enveloping one of my hands between his large paws, he kept his voice quiet so that only I could hear. 'Jenny, dear, we will be discussing this later, I assure you.'

I looked up to see only concern on his face, and withheld a wince as he squeezed my bruised knuckles gently.

'Of course, godfather. And thank you,' I replied with as disarming a smile as I could muster.

Scooping up my skirts, I almost ran downstairs, catching my breath in the entrance hall before re-entering the parlour, where ladies and gentlemen had been reunited and were beginning to say their goodbyes.

Erasmus slipped beside me, taking up my arm and threading it through his own as we waited our turn to take leave of our hostess.

I managed to say a few words to Anna Griegsson, Beatrice taking the lead and expressing her gratitude for what had apparently been a wonderful evening. It was only as we walked through the marble hall and out into the fresh night air that I thought I might be able to relax.

'Everything all right? You look as though you might be sick,' Erasmus said, his words easily concealed under the din of the rising conversation of departing guests and the clatter of carriages outside the house.

I blew out a steadying breath, relishing the warmth and solidity of him beside me. Searching a man's office, discovering that he had been complicit in my father's murder, and then narrowly avoiding being caught had all taken its toll.

'I might still be. The sooner we can be home and speak, the better,' I replied, giving a little nod of my head so that he stooped lower. 'I believe I've found what we need. Lei has the ledger, and I have a rather condemning communication about a certain poisoner in Clapham.'

His dark brows shot up in pleasant surprise. 'Goodness, Jenny. Aren't you a most delectable little thief?' He gave me one of his cunning smiles, the kind that set my skin tingling and an altogether different set of feelings quivering in my insides.

'As you said, you may make a pirate of me yet,' I replied, matching his smile with my own.

'Privateer,' he corrected, his look filled with promise.

'If you say so, Mr Black. If you say so.'

Chapter 23

ꙮ

A GRAVELY CONCERNED FRIEND

Mr Osborne is here, Marcus signed to me as I sat in my favourite spot, curled up with a book.

I frowned, searching for some sort of page marker and having to settle for slipping in my handkerchief for lack of something better.

Show him to the drawing room and I shall be right there, I replied, straightening my dress and darting to the nearest mirror to check that I looked presentable, before pulling on a pair of gloves to disguise the bruises blossoming on my hand.

It was the afternoon following the Griegssons' salon, and I was home alone save for Marcus and the staff. Mother and Beatrice had gone for a walk in the garden square, and Erasmus was at the offices. I knew he would be working late, having planned on meeting with his crew to discuss presenting Griegsson's ledger and the note regarding Sly Fairfax as evidence to his contact in Parliament. He had also decided to send one of the crew to find the cook-cum-poisoner in the hope of pressing a confession out of him before Kaine Clark's thugs got to him.

I entered the drawing room to find my godfather studying the bookshelf, ignoring Marcus who stood in the corner watching him.

'Jenny, my apologies for not sending word. I was in the area and thought I had better call in,' Osborne boomed, giving me a bow.

'Not at all, but I'm afraid my mother won't be back for another hour,' I replied with a curtsey.

'It is you I wished to see. Is there somewhere we might sit?'

I suppressed the nerves that had begun to rattle inside me at the thought of lying to him. Erasmus had made it quite clear that it would be treacherous for me to bring someone else into the investigation, not because he didn't trust Osborne, but because a simple wrong look or misspoken word could alert the dark circle of slave traders that we were on to them. Not to mention that Talver was already suspicious.

'Please,' I said, gesturing to my parents' armchairs, where we both took a seat. 'If it is about yesterday, I am truly sorry that you had to intervene as you did. I had got lost, and I hope I didn't interrupt something important.' I hoped my quick apology might deter any further questions regarding the encounter.

'Ah, yes. I did wonder what made you choose Griegsson's study of all places to pause in your quest for a bourdaloue.' He gave a knowing grin. 'You forget that I have known you all your life, Jenny, and that look you gave Klaus Griegsson when he discovered your presence was just the same as when you convinced Henrietta to help you steal biscuits from our kitchen when you were a child.'

My eyes widened in surprise that he remembered such a thing. 'I-I'm sorry about the biscuits, Mr Osborne, but I assure you—'

'No need to fret, my girl. I imagine that husband of yours sent you to locate something, perhaps thinking that Griegsson would forgive a young lady but would not take kindly to one of his competitors worming his way into his private rooms.'

I was momentarily lost for words. Did Osborne already know of everything that was going on? Was he secretly on our side?

'I see I have rendered you speechless, but allow me to explain. I noticed your new husband's particular interest in a set of voyages that should have returned to us two weeks ago. In fact, it was one of the first true problems that arose after your dear father's death, and I had set Mr Black to planning how we might recover from the loss of so much cargo. I believe that he suspected foul play, however, for he said something to the effect of making commodities scarcer so that the prices would go up. He even mentioned that Mr Griegsson might be involved in some way, though I couldn't understand his interest in the man.

'It was my intention at the salon yesterday to get Griegsson alone so that I might question him discreetly on the matter, and I noted your husband becoming increasingly interested in the conversation. When we found you up in Griegsson's study, I assumed that your beau had asked you to search for evidence of any ship tampering or similar, but I presume from the look on your face that you were unsuccessful.'

My mind whirred. Perhaps there was something to this theory, particularly if a commodity as scarce and valuable as saffron truly was involved. It would be harder to drive up the prices of more common commodities. It could be, though, that my godfather was just trying to find his own way to rationalise Talver's odd behaviour, and the missing goods receipts.

I almost wanted to blurt it all out there and then, tell him he was on the right path but that his suspicions should start with his business partner. I bit my tongue, instead saying, 'I was indeed unsuccessful in finding such evidence.' Not strictly a lie. 'But perhaps you should take William into your confidence and work together with him to bring Klaus Griegsson down for his crimes.'

Osborne gave me a pitying look, one that I didn't understand at first. 'That was the other reason I came to see you personally, my dear Jenny.' He braced his hands on his knees as though steeling himself to give me bad news. 'A few nights ago, Mr Black was working late at the offices – I assumed he was finding more information regarding our aforementioned missing ships. When I approached him, however, he hastily hid a letter he was writing beneath one of his ledgers. I thought perhaps it was something to do with his various investigations, and so I dismissed it as him being overcautious. It wasn't until he stepped outside for a few moments that . . . well, I'm afraid to admit I went looking for the letter.' He had the grace to look ashamed at the confession. 'If I knew the man any better, I would not involve myself, nor be so bold as to bring this to your attention. After all, he is your husband, and in the short week I have known him, I have observed him to be a diligent worker and a guileful businessman. Under other circumstances I would confront him directly on the contents of the letter and demand that he confess everything at once, but I fear I would have no sway over him.'

To my surprise he slipped a folded piece of paper from within his breast pocket and handed it to me without another word, allowing me to read it silently.

My dear Jenny,

It is more difficult than you can possibly know for me to write these words, but I must. I am unworthy of all that you have given, and all you are willing to give: your faith in me, your confidence and trust, your very heart.

I have no doubt that you were warned by my crew that we are scheduled to set sail before month's end, and this letter is only to say that I intend to go with them. Please do not think that this is due to any doing of your own, but rather that my soul belongs at sea, and that with all that has unfolded in the short time I have had the great honour of knowing you, I have brought more danger to your doorstep than one person has any right to.

Please know that you are more precious to me

The letter ended abruptly, presumably when Osborne had interrupted Erasmus in writing it. My fingers trembled as I read it again, trying to sense the hidden meaning, the deceit or the lie. But my godfather was telling the truth. He actually had caught Erasmus writing this, and had given it to me thinking that it would be a better alternative to confronting him.

'I am so sorry, my dear. I only brought you this because I wanted to make sure you did not risk your own safety on this man again, and that you understood his true intentions. Obviously I had no business reading the contents, but my thoughts were only for you and for our company, the empire that your father built. I wanted to hope that William, although never a true replacement for dear Jacob, would manage to at least maintain our success. It appears that he may be leaving sooner than we think, however, and I would not wish you to become entangled in the web he has created in order to trap one of our competitors, who may or may not be guilty, might I add.'

I hated the fact that my eyes were stinging, and I quickly blinked away any tears before they formed, folding the letter back up and placing it on the table between us.

'Thank you for bringing this to me,' I said, clearing my throat, and with it, the emotion from my voice. 'I will certainly take heed now that I know my husband's intentions to leave.'

Osborne stood with me as I rose from my chair, pulling me into a fatherly embrace before grimacing sympathetically.

'You Miller women are stronger than stone, Jenny. After everything that has happened to you, I know you will come out on top of this.'

'Thank you, godfather,' I replied walking with him to the hall, hesitating before I opened the door. 'I . . . I would be remiss in not giving you a warning of my own.'

His eyebrows pinched together as he waited for me to explain.

'I wish to be honest with you, and I am aware that this may be difficult to hear from me, but I'd ask that you be wary of Mr Talver. I shan't go into details,' I added, seeing him straighten, readying a protest. 'All I can say is that I don't believe he is the man you think he is. I realise you are the firmest of friends, but would you guard yourself around him? For me?'

Osborne peered at me with those small black eyes of his beneath furrowed brows, as though he understood the words I had spoken but found them to be disturbing.

'Very well, Jenny. I shall keep my wits about me when dealing with both Mr Black and Mr Talver, though if I am honest, I know that George would not harm a hair on your head. He has known you as long as I have, after all.'

I wanted to say it wasn't me that I was worried about, but something else had struck me as odd at that moment, and I simply nodded, opening the door to let him go. He gave me a small wave before climbing into his carriage, and I pressed my back against the door and closed my eyes, willing myself to take deep breaths.

A gentle touch a few moments later had me opening them to find Marcus standing before me, the picture of concern.

Are you all right?

I shook my head, my lower lip quivering as I quickly clamped down my panic and returned to the drawing room to retrieve Erasmus's unfinished letter.

'How much of that did you see?' I asked him.

Enough to know that Mr Osborne does not trust Mr Black, and that you in turn do not trust Mr Talver.

I gave a mirthless laugh. 'So everything, then,' I replied, handing him the letter and letting him read it for himself.

He pinched his brow as he deciphered the words, looking back at me with concern once he had finished. In the afternoon light, I realised that with his honey-coloured eyes and light brown hair, broad stature and rarely shared smile, Marcus was a handsome man. If people had been able to look beyond his disability, he might have found himself a wife and be living with children of his own rather than guarding my mother and me.

I hoped he never felt taken for granted by us.

You believe Mr Black wishes to leave you? he asked.

I shrugged, signalling back with my hands as I replied.

'This was written a few days ago, and Erasmus changes moods as quickly as the summer weather. I truly believed that he might wish to stay for good after all that had happened between us in such a short time, but perhaps I was foolish to think it.'

What will you do?

It was an excellent question. Just at that moment, I felt split in two. I wanted Erasmus to come home so that I could fold myself into his arms and kiss him and weep all at the same time. I also wanted never to have to speak to him again, so weary was I of being disappointed and hurt by men. I felt the tiny fissures of heartbreak that threatened to deepen if I let myself think about it all too much.

I didn't realise that I had started crying until Marcus stooped before me and offered his handkerchief, which I took gratefully.

'I will make the most of the time I have with him, I suppose. I would hate for him to leave at the end of the month only for me to have wasted our final days together being angry about it.'

You are wise for one so young, and a stronger woman than most, Miss Jenny, he replied, using the old sign for the name he called me growing up. He gave one of his precious smiles, no more than a small lifting of the corners of his mouth, but it transformed his usually serious face.

'Oh, I don't know about that,' I replied, dabbing my eyes. 'Some might call me foolish for falling in love with a man like Erasmus Black.'

As soon as I said it, I ascertained it to be true. I felt I had seen all his sides now. The privateer, the crew member, the gentleman and the thief. And despite any better judgement on my part, I realised that I loved every part of him. If he left, I would not love him any less, I would only be more destroyed. But if he stayed . . . I would savour every moment in his presence. The pain doubled in my chest at the recognition of my feelings. It was as though the knowing of it had stolen the breath from my lungs. As I looked up at Marcus with blurred vision, I saw only sympathy there, and some hint of understanding.

You love him.

'I do,' I whispered, the feeling solidifying as I said it aloud.

The letter might have been a ruse? Marcus phrased it as a question, and his hope warmed me.

'Yes, or it might be that he truly does intend to leave. I cannot say I blame him with all I know now. And a life behind a desk is not for him, of that I am certain.'

He seemed to think on that for a moment.

If you truly are in love with him, it would be ill advice indeed to let him go without putting up a fight.

I nodded, knowing he was of course right.

'When did you become so wise?' I asked, half jesting.

Around the same time a young, headstrong girl who wanted to be a pirate princess when she grew up entered my life, he replied.

Before he could move away, I stepped forward and threw my arms about his middle, causing him to stiffen in surprise before patting me gingerly on the back. When had he last been touched, or held? Such a small, important thing, human contact, and I was sure I had not embraced him since I was a little girl, before parties and boys and dancing became my infatuation.

'Thank you,' I murmured into his chest, and though I knew he could not hear me or read my lips, he squeezed me in response as though he understood.

I am always here for you, he said when we broke apart, and in that moment, I had never felt more fortunate to have him as a friend.

Mother and Beatrice returned in the mid afternoon, and I distracted myself for a while with their talk of which eligible gentlemen they had seen during their brief promenade, and how many had offered to call upon Beatrice this coming week. Soon, however, growing tired of the incessant talk of the forthcoming party, I retired to my room.

It was just before dinner when Erasmus returned. I could sense him searching the house for me, wandering from room to room until he knocked softly on my door and I beckoned him in. The ache in my chest throbbed a little at the sight of him, and I had to remind myself that I was not going to raise the subject of the letter, safely hidden in my bedside drawer with my father's sketches. After all, he had not actually given it to me, or even finished it, and I felt it would only ruin the comfortable companionship we had begun to form in recent days.

'How was your afternoon, little mouse?' he asked, removing his jacket and placing it on the back of my writing desk chair.

'It was eventful,' I replied cryptically, 'but more importantly, how was yours?'

'Well, Mira was delighted with your discoveries at the Griegsson household. I have arranged a meeting with one of our contacts in the Saints, and from there we will look for an appropriate way in which to put a stop to Griegsson and Talver's activities.'

'And Sly Fairfax?' I asked.

'Big Don, Gar and Carl set off last night in search of him, so let us hope that they locate him before Kaine Clark's men do,' Erasmus replied, sitting on the bed beside me. 'Everything is in hand, though I don't know if we will be able to do much more before Osborne's party.'

'So we shall have to pretend to enjoy their company for a while longer. Mira was right, this way does take a long time,' I said, letting him take my hand, enjoying the tingle that spread up my arm when he touched me. If I only had a couple more weeks of this, I wanted to remember every second of it. The way his mahogany eyes roamed my face, the calluses on his palms as they brushed my knuckles, the dimple on his chin.

'I think we can find something suitably diverting in the meantime to make up for it,' he said, his voice catching as my gaze met his. 'But something is the matter, Jenny. I can see it in the way you hold yourself, and in the way you look at me, as though I have hurt you in some way. What is it, little mouse?'

I shook my head, recalling what had bothered me so much about earlier, aside from the unwelcome letter.

'Osborne visited me today while everyone else was out,' I said, looking away from him so as not to fall apart completely at the expression on his face.

'Did he now? And what did your godfather have to say for himself?' Was that an edge of panic in his voice, or just my imagination?

'He came to warn me not to put too much trust in you,' I said, nudging him with my shoulder playfully so as to assuage his worry. 'But the oddest thing was when I told him to be on his guard about George Talver. I asked him merely to be wary of him, and he told me that he knew George would not harm a hair on my head.'

'That does not seem so odd, considering the man is his closest friend. He is bound to believe that Talver's intentions towards you would be pure.'

I shook my head, finally acknowledging what I had sensed earlier. 'It wasn't the words that were the problem, Erasmus, so much as what was behind them. I can swear here and now before you that it was a lie.'

Chapter 24

NOW WE DANCE

The next couple of weeks passed quickly, the days blending into one another as Erasmus worked late at his offices while I entertained my cousin, accompanying her to various teas and soirées in the lead-up to the final event of the season: Henrietta Osborne's party. Beatrice had her fair share of male callers after each event, meaning that I spent the rest of my time being hostess. My mother, I noticed with a small sense of satisfaction, had come to wear varying shades of purple rather than her black dresses of the previous months – a sign that she was slowly coming through the stages of mourning. I was grateful to have Beatrice in the house as a friend and companion, but more so when I realised how refreshing she had been for Mother. She was as vibrant and filled with enthusiasm as I had been when I first came out, before I had become afraid and jaded by society.

Meanwhile, I tried my very best to enjoy my husband's company whenever possible, despite feeling as though every minute of it was a grain of sand falling through an hourglass, and that if I wasted a moment feeling angry or distraught by the knowledge that he might be leaving, I was somehow cheating myself.

We shared chaste kisses in the morning, passionate ones before bed, almost always giving a little more, touching a little more, sharing a little more. But I hadn't yet given all of myself to him, certain that if I did that, I would not recover from his departure. I felt almost sure of his affection, though. I saw it in the way he smiled at me, the way his eyes softened when I entered the room. Every night that I slept in his bed, I found myself aching with an unfamiliar need while he slumbered beside me. My body screamed out to touch him, and at times I thought it might be easier to be apart rather than entertain the possibility of being rejected if I were to act on my impulses. I let myself imagine it instead, knowing that at least my thoughts could not refute me. For his part, Erasmus never forced the matter, or hesitated when I gave him a final peck on the lips before turning over to sleep. A truer gentleman I had never found.

I was given a few days of reprieve from chaperoning my cousin when my monthly bleeding began, and for one blissful afternoon I was able to tuck myself away in my own room and read. But in the night, Erasmus slipped into my bed, heedless to my warnings, and held me close, soothing my aching back and abdomen with warm, gentle hands. If my mother, or anyone else, had noticed our changing sleeping arrangements, nothing was said.

Sly Fairfax had still not been found, but nor had there been any reports of his death in the papers. Big Don sent word to inform us that they would continue their search. In the meantime, Erasmus had been putting his case together for his contact in the Saints. He would secrete himself away up in my father's study before disappearing for an hour in the evening to hand over his letter to whoever it was that acted as messenger between them.

'This politician is working you very hard,' I observed the

evening before the Osbornes' party. Erasmus had missed dinner but had arrived home in time for supper. Beatrice and my mother were playing an after-meal game of cards while my husband and I sat together close to the fire.

He sighed, swirling the rum in his glass as though it might conjure up an answer for him.

'I understand why,' he said eventually. 'If we can supply enough evidence to prove that British ships have been engaging in . . .' He paused, glancing over to where my mother and cousin sat across the room. 'Well, you know. I may be able to do more than simply bring down Talver, Griegsson and Clark. It could result in the support of the navy, a possible end to all of this. The fight could be truly over.' I noted a bittersweet tone to his voice.

I had not thought of that, I realised. I had only given thought to the immediate problem of Talver, and of bringing my father's murderers to justice.

'You believe that a few letters to the right person could do that?' I asked.

He smiled at me over his drink. 'The smallest stones can make the furthest-reaching ripples, little mouse.' I thought of our walk through the gardens the other week and the point he had been trying to make even then.

'What would you do? If your fight was over,' I clarified.

He thought about it for a moment. 'I suppose if we can salvage some of your father's business, I would have my work cut out for me with Talver gone. Osborne may wish to bring on another partner, but I imagine it would be a challenging first few months. Then there is the matter of Mira's sister.' He tapped the side of his glass in slight agitation. 'I would have to give Mira *Juliet*, but I would miss the crew something awful. And if we truly did succeed, if British attentions moved to the Ottoman Empire in earnest, it might be safe to take Kit back home at last.'

I tried not to let my disappointment show, for it had been selfish to think that he could possibly forget all those people he had lived and worked with for nearly a decade, and his concern and care for them all was one of the reasons why I loved him.

'But I should like you to see Crawbridge,' he added, unaware of my inner conflict. 'And we have not honeymooned, which seems a terrible oversight considering I am a traveller and you a would-be adventurer.' His smile was teasing, but there was something earnest and almost vulnerable in it, as though he expected to be contradicted.

The breath caught in my lungs, my heart like a humming-bird in a cage. 'You truly mean to stay?' I asked on a whisper, my fingers bunched up in the fabric of my dress to stop them from quivering.

Erasmus gave me a quizzical look. 'Of course. If I were to go anywhere at all, I would have you by my side,' he added, extricating my hand and tangling his fingers with mine.

He was telling the truth. My traitorous thoughts reminded me of the captain's words. *He will tire of the comfort and ease that your life provides him. He has spent the past eight years at sea.* Even with his assurances, I could not kill that worm of doubt.

He seemed to read something in my expression, for he put his glass down and tilted his head towards me. 'Jenny, do you recall our wedding day?'

It was only three weeks ago, but still the memory was hazy with all that had happened since then. I nodded anyway.

'Do you remember what I said? When the vicar asked if I would have and hold you, honour you and forsake all others, and whatever else was demanded of me?'

I thought back to the ceremony. I had been so caught up in it that the details had blurred, but I remembered his promise. 'You said "I will."'

'And did you detect a lie?'

I blinked away the sting of tears. I did not know why it had not occurred to me, but he had promised, and he had intended to keep that promise. All this time, he had wholly intended to give his life and his heart to me.

Perhaps now he wants the warmth of your house and the comfort of your bed, but who is to tell if he will tire of it in a week? A month? A year? I tried to erase the captain's words from my mind, focusing on Erasmus's voice, his handsome face, the sincerity in his eyes.

'I do not have your same set of skills, but I hope that your own vows were said in earnest, as mine were.'

I nodded, and he cupped my cheek.

'Little mouse, I—'

'We are retiring,' my mother announced from across the room, standing abruptly. I bit my tongue and rose with Erasmus, who kept his hand in mine.

'Goodnight, Mrs Miller. Miss Stanton.' He bowed, waiting for them to leave. I murmured my own goodnights, catching the devilish smile my cousin threw over her shoulder at me.

'I should like to continue this conversation. Perhaps we too should retire upstairs?' he suggested.

I followed, holding onto him as though I would be lost without the certainty of our fingers entwined with one another, as though if I let him go, he might suddenly vanish and this would all have been a dream. He led me to my room, whether because it was further from where my cousin would be sleeping or because it was nearest to the top of the stairs, I couldn't say.

'Erasmus . . .'

'Jenny . . .' He spoke at the same time, and I bit back a smile.

'Allow me to go first, if you would,' I said, satisfied with the nod he gave me. 'I realise we have had an unconventional marriage. I know you have seen far more adventures than I could ever imagine, that you have likely been with dozens of beautiful women.' He opened his mouth to say something, but I pressed my fingers to his lips. 'I do not want to make you say things you think I want to hear. I don't want to demand promises from you that you cannot keep, even if you believe you can.'

He took the fingers that were gently pressed to his lips and brushed a kiss to them. The gesture ignited desire in me so quickly it took me by surprise.

'Then what *do* you want, little mouse?' The words were low, his tone serious. I knew it then. That I was ready, and that if I could have one perfect thing from him, whether he left in a week, a month, a year, I would have this night.

'You,' I breathed. 'Right now, there is nothing more I want than you.' There was no question of what I meant.

'I have waited a long time to hear you say that,' he said, leaning down to press his lips against mine. There was something different in this kiss, a depth that I had not felt before, an urgency and a promise.

He trailed a line of them down my neck, each one painfully slow and perfect. And then my fingers were unbuttoning his waistcoat, his shirt, pausing only to let him unlace my dress. We removed layers from each other as though we were pulling off armour after a battle, our clothes pooling on the floor around our feet as we moved step by step towards my bed. And then there was nothing between us but skin, hot and sensitive and aflame with need.

I released a gasp as his lips found my collarbone, my breast, and I took the opportunity to pull the thong from his hair, tangling my fingers in it. Erasmus scooped me up suddenly, carrying me over to the bed and placing me gently upon the sheets. 'Let me look at you,' he said, his voice breathless with want as his eyes roamed my body, finding places that he wished to explore and placing kisses there over and over again.

I took in the hardened muscles of his chest, the dozens of scars that had healed and not quite faded across his body. He was magnificent.

'You are perfect,' I murmured, and his expression softened. When was the last time someone had told him that? Had told him they valued him, or that he was all they could ever want? I resolved to do so every day if I could, just to see this look upon his face.

'Are you ready?' he asked. *Are you sure?* he seemed to imply.

I nodded. I had never been so sure about wanting anything as I was right now, and all I wanted was him.

'If at any point you are not, if you change your mind, you tell me,' he said, and I loved him even more for caring, for knowing that the only time I had been touched before was a wound that could reopen at any time. But what had happened that night all those months ago was so far from my mind, I did not want to bring it into this space we had created.

I nodded once more, drawing him to me, knowing that with every movement, with every sigh and breath and frisson of pleasure, and with our eventual release, he was leaving an indelible mark upon my heart.

Afterwards, I curled up in that space between his arms, my head resting against his chest as I begged sleep to take me, and for my thoughts to give me some reprieve.

'What troubles you, little mouse?' Erasmus murmured into the darkness.

'Sorry if I've disturbed you. I thought myself perfectly still.'

'Too still. And your mind is loud tonight.' There was a smile in his voice, and his words rumbled through me as he tightened his embrace. His fingers found my hair and gently began to stroke it, relaxing me a little.

'Tomorrow. The party. I have not seen Talver since I found out he . . .' I could not say the words. 'I do not want to taint this night with talk of it, but I cannot help but think I might do something terrible if I see him.'

Erasmus's hands travelled from my hair to my face, and he looked down at me where I lay cocooned in the safety of his embrace.

'You have every right to be angry. To be hell-bent on revenge, to want to curse him, to hurt him. I do not know your pain, Jenny, but I am familiar with the form it takes. We will stop him. All of them,' he added, pulling me closer. 'But for now, think of nothing but the fact that you and I are here. I have sailed oceans and travelled thousands of miles, but I have never been happier than right at this very moment.'

'Truly?' I said, with disbelief that I could be the cause of so much emotion in someone.

'Did you sense a lie in my words?' I heard the smile in his voice.

'No, I did not,' I replied, pressing a kiss to his throat.

And then he showed me just how happy he was all over again.

I awoke to an empty bed, though I knew that Erasmus had been with me until not long ago, for it was still warm where he had lain. The morning light had already broken through the curtains and my room was streaked with sunbeams, patches of warmth between the shade. My dress for tonight had been hung in front of my closet, and I was temporarily waylaid in getting ready by my urge to admire it.

The entire thing was made of satin, trimmed with lace at the hem in a light blue-green that reminded me of the colour of the ocean. There were three diaphanous layers of skirts, each one tiered with silver and aquamarine stitching at the bottom, which caught the light and gave the effect of rippling water, while the bust and capped sleeves were studded with beads that matched the blue of my eyes. The neckline of the bodice was straight, sewn with tiny silver and blue threads styled in the pattern of cresting waves. Lord knew how much it had cost to make.

My mother was already finishing her breakfast when I arrived downstairs and planted a kiss on her cheek. 'You approve of the dress then?' she said with a smile as I took my seat opposite her, Erasmus on my right. I squeezed his hand under the table in greeting and nodded eagerly, helping myself to a small bread roll and some jam.

'It is beautiful, Mama. I've not seen anything like it, and the *colours*,' I gushed, unable to hide my pleasure, 'are so perfect, it is a true masterpiece.'

This was what it had been like when I was younger, attending parties and balls; always a new dress, or a new pair of shoes, or jewellery to complement an older outfit and bring it new life. My parents had never truly denied me anything, I realised now. Or at least nothing that was important to me. I did recall requesting a Pegasus one birthday, which, being a mythological creature, was beyond even their means.

'Marcus helped me pick the fabric, didn't you,' she asked the steward, who had tried to blend into the corner of the room and had almost succeeded until she called attention to him. He nodded a little shyly, and I signed, *Excellent choice*, which only made him look more bashful.

'I believe we are expected to be there by six, so we shall have an early dinner before we ready ourselves. I doubt that Osborne will be intending to cater for so many guests, and I would not like you to go hungry.'

'Very good, Mama. And what will you be wearing tonight?'

She stirred a teaspoon of sugar into her tea, the china clinking softly. 'I do not know if I will go, if I am quite honest.' It was the sadness in her tone that gave me pause. My mother had been in mourning these three months, and although it might be acceptable for the rest of the family to be seen out in society, I could understand why she might have second thoughts.

'I do not think Mr and Mrs Osborne would frown upon your attendance,' I said.

She gave a little snort as she said, 'I care not about being frowned upon, my dear. I have kept up propriety because it was how I was raised, but a few wealthy working class are not going to stop me from doing something I wish to do.' She took a sip of tea before continuing. 'It is only that . . . the last time I attended such an occasion, your father was still with us.'

The ache of loss was an unhealing bruise, almost forgotten until pressed upon as it had been now.

'Of course,' I whispered, leaning over to take her free hand, attempting to comfort her in the only way I knew how, despite my efforts never feeling adequate to stem the flow of her grief.

She blinked away the silver lining her lashes and cleared her throat, giving my fingers a squeeze before extricating them.

'But you are right, the Osbornes would bear no ill will towards me for putting on a dark dress and at least observing the festivities. If nothing else, I should like to witness my daughter and her husband having an enjoyable evening,' she said with a tenderness that I had forgotten I missed. 'And you, William? I assume you have a suitable costume to wear?'

I stopped listening, my mind once again on the evening's

event and the fact that Erasmus still had not managed to finalise a meeting with his contact at the Saints. We would have to parade around as a happy couple, greeting Klaus Griegsson and George Talver as though we knew nothing of their dealings with Kaine Clark and the illegalities they were involved in, not to mention the fact that they had been entirely responsible for my father's death.

Erasmus rested a hand gently on my faintly bruised knuckles. 'Don't look so worried,' he murmured in my ear. 'This will be the last time we will have to pretend.'

I gave him a weak smile, grateful for his assurance but not entirely convinced.

'And your friends, William? Will they be meeting us at the party or riding in convoy with us?'

'I believe the intention is to ride behind us, so that we may be announced together when we arrive.'

'They are welcome to join us for dinner and to ready themselves in one of the rooms here, should they wish to,' my mother invited kindly. I nearly blurted out a no, for I did not want to prepare myself for tonight with Mira in the same building, as childish as that was.

'Not to worry, Mrs Miller. My "cousin" has access to all the things a lady might need for such an occasion,' he replied casually.

I had asked why his crew still needed to attend if we had everything we needed by way of evidence against Talver, but Erasmus had replied that he wanted all the support he could get for us, considering the company we would be keeping at the party. I could not help but picture Miranda Hodgson dressing in her finest gown, the ladies of the Midnight Rose perfuming her and adorning her with jewels. Perhaps she would see tonight as a competition, and I did not wish to be upstaged.

A squeal from upstairs distracted me from silly jealous thoughts, and we looked at each other in alarm.

'It seems that Beatrice also approves of her gown,' my mother said, hiding her satisfied grin behind her cup of tea.

The day passed quickly, the party looming on the horizon like a battle, as I readied myself while trying in vain to push down my nerves.

Edith helped me prepare, tightening my stays, making small adjustments to give me more freedom to move. When finally I was ready, pulling on blue silk gloves, I spun around in the mirror, admiring the way the aquamarine set off the colour of my eyes. Edith had divided my hair into complicated plaits, before pinning it all together with tiny gold hairpins, a white pearl at the end of each one. My mother entered holding a necklace of topazes and pearls to match, and placed it around my neck.

'Oh, Jenny,' she said to my reflection as she stood behind me, 'I forgot how much I enjoyed seeing my little girl dress up like this.'

'I too had forgotten,' I said, placing a hand on the cold gems that hung at my throat. This dress was far grander than anything I had worn while chaperoning Beatrice, for I had not wanted to upstage her under any circumstances. But tonight was different – this was a ball hosted by my husband's business partners. Tonight I had to shine.

Beatrice sauntered in with Aristotle on her heels, running circles around her slippered feet. I gave a small gasp when I saw her dress, a pale rose that made her light-brown eyes and tanned skin stand out. The bodice had been embroidered with tiny pink flowers, an iridescent bead sewn into the centre of each one, and a string of freshwater pearls caressed her collarbones, the colour matching her long silk gloves.

'Goodness, Jen, if that gown was my colour, I'd want to steal it right off you,' she said, looking me up and down.

'Don't be silly. You are the very image of perfection, Bea,' I replied, giving her a playful nudge with my elbow. 'I'd be surprised if your dance card isn't full within minutes of us walking through the door.'

There came a knock at the door and Erasmus poked his head around it, his eyes widening when he saw me. He had dressed in dark blue velvet, but the colours of his cravat echoed those of my dress so that we looked like a matching pair. I noted his expression in the mirror, suppressing a smile as he seemed to flounder for words.

'Edith, Beatrice and I require your assistance in my room,' my mother said suddenly, marching out with my cousin, the dog and the maid and leaving Erasmus and me alone.

I turned around so that he could see the dress in full, and enjoyed the way his mouth fell open slightly.

'Shall I infer from your silence that you approve, husband?'

He cleared his throat as he stepped towards me. 'I believe that I shall have to be especially careful tonight,' he said quietly, placing his hands on my arms as he took me in.

'Why is that?'

'Well, if I turn my back, someone will certainly try to thieve you from me, and I could not possibly allow that.'

I laughed and rolled my eyes. 'I believe *I* am the one who will have to be careful with Mira around,' I said, wrapping my gloved arms around his neck so that I could look up into his eyes.

'What do you mean?' The line of a frown formed between his brows.

'Oh, don't act the oblivious male. Even you must sense that she does not like me stealing you away from her.'

'Well, it is far too late for that. She must consider me stolen and be done with it,' he said, tracing his fingers down my arms to my waist.

My body responded as though it understood only his call. As I looked up into his face, I recalled what a mystery he had been to me only a short time ago, one I sometimes felt I was still trying to decipher. The past weeks had given me a glimpse into what life could be like with him permanently at my side, a team of two against the rest of the world. Even as I reminded myself that it was better to enjoy these short moments together than spoil them with my own sadness, I had to admit that I wanted more for myself, and for us.

Misreading my expression, he said, 'I did not come here to talk about Mira.' He slipped something out of his pocket. It was a small silver object, almost cylindrical, with a beautifully etched pattern, but with the press of a button, a blade flicked from within it, much like the design of his walking cane. He took one of my hands from his neck and placed the object in my palm.

'You think I need a weapon?' I said, examining it carefully.

'I am merely loaning it to you in case something should happen if we are separated tonight. I would feel happier knowing that you have something to protect yourself with. After all,' he added, seeing my troubled expression, 'you said yourself that we were walking into the wolf's den.'

I nodded, even if I didn't feel entirely comfortable carrying a knife, and slipped it into my glove.

'I thought I could just punch someone if they bothered me,' I replied with a nonchalant shrug.

'That does have a certain efficacy,' he agreed, 'but let us give your fist a rest if we can help it.'

*

Despite our jesting, my nerves still jangled like discordant pianoforte notes in the carriage all the way to Henry Osborne's Mayfair home, and I had to resist the temptation to bombard Erasmus with my concerns as we sat side by side, my hand in his, my mother chatting idly to Beatrice opposite us. Marcus rode with the driver, but I felt reassured to have another ally with us for the evening. The bulge and weight of the switchblade in my glove became oddly reassuring as we pulled up outside, the captain's carriage stopping just behind ours so that we all alighted together.

Miranda Hodgson had brought Carl along with her, for despite their dissimilarity, they could hopefully pass for cousins of Erasmus's without too much speculation. Very, *very* distant cousins.

Her dress was dark red, the colour of wine or drying blood, with a high collar of lace disguising most of her scar. I would not have been at all surprised if she wore weapons under her skirts, for she seemed to pat herself down every now and then as though checking they were still in place. She had kept her hair tied back simply and away from her face, as though she was preparing for war. In some ways I imagined she was. She was stunning, I had to admit, with her naturally olive skin and light eyes, and I noticed more than one guest stop to admire her.

Carl had dressed in a simple black suit, his beard trimmed and hair combed, so that to anyone else he would look like a reasonably wealthy sailor, which was just the disguise he intended.

I gave the captain and the Viking a nod of acknowledgement while Erasmus made the formal introductions. Mother knew that they were crew members of my husband's, but had suggested the ruse of family so as not to alarm Henry Osborne. As she commented on Mira's beauty, and my cousin flushed at

Carl's attentions, I wondered at what a peculiar party we might form. Despite Mira's breathtaking appearance, I was reassured to have her there.

The Osborne town house gave the impression of a large manor, despite being crowded on either side by neighbouring buildings. The balustraded balconies were detailed with marble cherubim, and I could just make out a huddled figure crouching between two angel babes. I allowed myself a smile at the knowledge that even without an invitation, Lei was keeping guard.

The front door loomed before us, framed by white-painted columns. Marble steps led up to it and pruned bay laurel trees stood like sentinels on either side. Already I could see people milling around inside.

Carl offered one arm to the captain, the other to my cousin, who took it bashfully.

'Shall we?' Erasmus asked, following suit by handing me his cane and taking my arm and my mother's, guiding us towards a steward in coat and tails who checked our invitations.

The entrance hall was just as I remembered it: deep red carpets and dark teak wood panelling, with a grand staircase to the right that led to a gallery of sorts. Paintings depicting generations of Osbornes glared at us haughtily; the largest of them was one of my godfather's predecessors mounted on a huge black stallion, looking down his nose at anyone who passed him.

Free-standing candelabras held fresh candles, pointing guests through double doors on the left to the ballroom. During our last visit, a dinner almost a year ago, we had only passed through this room, instead sitting in the ornate dining room, large enough to seat forty. Now that I studied it in in detail, I appreciated its size and wondered how often it was used. A string quartet played pleasantly by the bay windows, but nobody had yet mustered up the courage to take to the floor.

'Katherine!' my godfather boomed from across the room. He was dressed in a yellow jacket with a gold-stitched waistcoat stretching across his belly, and I tried to push the image of a canary out of my mind. 'I am so glad you decided to attend. Delighted to see you all, I'm sure,' he added, beckoning us over to where he stood with his wife and daughter. Our party made for a large crowd, and one not to be quickly dismissed, for I felt several sets of eyes upon us as we approached our hosts.

Henrietta Osborne was a pretty young thing with plump cheeks and her father's colouring, and her pink dress looked as though it had been ordered in especially from Paris. Her mother, Marie, might have been a quiet and mild lady if she were not constantly competing with her husband to be heard. She had always been pleasant to us and greeted us effusively.

'It was so kind of you to extend your hospitality to my niece, and to William's cousins,' Mother said as she allowed Henry to kiss her hand.

'Not at all,' he interrupted before Marie could reply. 'Any relation of yours or William's is as good as family to us, eh?' He jabbed Erasmus in the ribs, and my husband miraculously kept his features neutral.

'And,' Marie added at the top of her voice, looking at Carl purposefully, 'we are simply delighted to provide Henrietta more introductions.'

Erasmus accepted the hint. 'Indeed. Henry, Mrs Osborne, Miss Osborne, may I introduce my cousins, Amanda Black and Carl Jonsson.'

I tried not to flinch at Mira being referred to as a Black, even though we had rehearsed it as such. Carl, I had been told, would be awful at remembering a fake name, but the captain was more than used to it. Amanda Black had been one of her many aliases over their time together, I was rather dismayed to discover.

'Charmed,' Osborne said, planting a wet kiss on Mira's gloved hand. I caught her eye as she discreetly wiped it on her dress, and quickly hid my smile.

Beatrice cleverly sank back from the group so that her hand was well out of reach of Osborne's lips, making do with a polite curtsey in his direction.

'Jenny, dear, you look radiant,' he said as he greeted me, before stepping aside to give his daughter the spotlight. Henrietta cast me a wary look, which I ignored by putting on my best smile and embracing her.

'Many happy returns, Henrietta. May this year be your happiest yet.'

'Thank you, Mrs Black,' she said with a slight frown, returning the embrace, as though she hadn't expected so much affection from me.

'George hasn't arrived yet?' Mother asked, looking around for the weasel. I was grateful I could not lay eyes on him as I glanced about the ballroom, noticing a few of the socialites I had partied with some years before.

'He's around here somewhere with a few associates of ours.' Osborne waved his wine glass, the contents sloshing against the side. 'We do still have some business to attend to, I'm afraid, even while the rest of you enjoy yourselves.'

'There you are, Henry,' came a familiarly sinister voice from behind us, and I whirled to see George Talver pushing his way into our company without so much as an acknowledgement of anyone other than his business partner. I had not had the displeasure of seeing him since discovering his part in my father's death, and now I instinctively reached for the knife in my glove.

Calm yourself, Jenny, it would do no good to ruin the evening by committing a murder of your own here and now.

If Erasmus noticed me falter, he said nothing, but he placed his free hand over mine for reassurance.

Mira noted my discomfort as well, and leaned in to whisper something to Carl. Instructions, apparently, for he nodded to her, murmuring something about finding a drink, when in truth I knew he must be off to seek out wherever the business Osborne spoke of was going to be conducted.

Osborne, looking somewhat put out that the only bachelor in our party had left, was thankfully distracted by some newcomers, excusing his family so that the rest of our party were left alone.

But not for long.

'Miss Jenny Miller, is that you?'

I did not recognise the voice at first, turning slowly to discover where it had come from. My skin prickled with sudden familiarity as I spotted the red-haired man stalking across the room.

'Nigel,' I said, hating the way the breath had left my lungs as I said his name. The first boy to break my heart.

'You are a sight for sore eyes,' he said enthusiastically, looking over his shoulder ruefully at a group of merchants' daughters he had just extricated himself from, and who were now exaggeratedly fanning themselves while shooting me daggers.

The room became very hot all of a sudden, for seeing the young poet, I was reminded of another Jenny from a different time. One whose only interest was ball gowns and cotillions, boys and falling in love. That Jenny had let herself become disgraced. My back straightened as he approached, my chin lifting as though that alone would make me look more mature, even as I felt a strange twisting in my gut.

'I-I have not seen you in years, Nigel. How have you been?'

'Can't complain, although you likely heard the news about my engagement,' he said, practically pulling me from Erasmus's grasp, ignoring the fact that I was in company. My mother had drawn Beatrice away, wandering off to speak to one of her friends, and I hoped she was not watching the exchange from wherever she was.

'I had not,' I replied cautiously, wanting more than anything to get away from him.

'Oh, well, I had to call it off when I discovered she had no dowry to speak of. Very sad business. She was devastated, of course, but that is the way of things, I suppose,' he said without a hint of remorse. 'But it means that I am now seeking a wife, Jenny Miller.' The sparkle in his eyes made my punching fist tingle in anticipation.

'It's Black now, actually,' I said, freeing myself from his grip and taking Erasmus's arm. 'Nigel, this is my husband, William Black.'

I wished there had been an artist nearby to capture the expression on the poet's face as he looked up at him, for Erasmus stood almost a head taller. Indignation traded places with recognition as he realised that he had met his match.

'How do you do,' Erasmus rumbled, voice laced with threat.

'Ah, I see. How do you do,' Nigel mumbled, 'I did not know you had married.'

'It is recent,' I conceded, 'but it feels like we have known each other for ever, doesn't it, Mr Black?'

The smile Erasmus gave me almost set my legs wobbling. 'That it does, my darling.'

Nigel recovered quickly. 'And who is this fine lady?' He turned to Mira, who levelled a look at him that would have made any sane man turn and run.

'This fine lady,' she said in her rich tone, flicking at his flopping fringe with a gloved finger, 'is not even a little interested.'

At that moment, I wanted to hug them both for being wonderfully ruthless, but contained myself as Nigel turned on his heel and retreated to the group of simpering girls. They all deserved each other as far as I was concerned.

'Anyone else you need us to terrorise before the evening is through?' Mira said, watching the poet's back as she came to stand beside me.

'There is no shortage of people, I'm afraid, but I'll inform you when I'm in need of a little intimidation.'

'I can't say I think much of your old friends,' Erasmus commented, looking at the gaggle of girls all vying for a dance with Nigel.

I shook my head ruefully. It was as though the other side of the room was a portal into the past, one that I would rather leave behind. I let out a breath as I said, 'Honestly, neither do I.'

A server approached us with a tray of drinks and we each took a champagne flute, although none of us would be doing much drinking tonight. Just then, Carl returned with a report that he had spotted Griegsson playing cards with several gentlemen in the parlour, and it looked as though he wouldn't be moving any time soon.

'Wouldn't it be better to go and search the study now?' he suggested, bouncing on the balls of his feet nervously.

'Search the . . . What are you all up to?' I asked, eyes narrowed at Carl, who appeared to immediately regret opening his mouth.

'We're going to stick to the plan,' Erasmus told him, before turning to me. 'Mira and Carl are acting on a hunch that Talver may have hidden something in your godfather's study as some form of alibi. Nothing you need concern yourself with.' Despite his encouraging nod, I didn't feel any more reassured. He turned back to Carl and Mira. 'We wait for the dancing to begin in earnest, and for the gentry to be drunk enough that they won't remember our comings and goings, then we get the carriages ready. To act now would be folly.'

'So what do we do now?' Carl insisted, taking a sip of his own drink before apparently remembering he ought to remain sober.

Erasmus grinned, looking from the string quartet to the empty floor, then resting his cane against the wall and offering me his hand. 'Why, now we dance.'

Chapter 25

A GRAVE MISTAKE

I had not forgotten the dances, though I hadn't remembered how much I enjoyed them. The cotillion, the waltz, the Scotch reel, made all the better for having a partner such as Erasmus. His fighting skill, his coordination, and the muscles that worked beneath his suit were demonstrated when he moved. Despite his old injury, which meant that he led with his left rather than his right leg, he moved more gracefully than many dance partners from my previous life. Raised as he was with no mother after the age of ten to insist on an education in society, I imagined that his nursemaid or governess had been responsible for his skill. And she had taught him well. As we took to the floor, other couples finally mustered up the courage to join us. I almost warned Henrietta when Nigel approached her, but I needn't have worried, for she was led onto the floor by a young man I vaguely recognised as the boy with the formaldehyde mice that I had escaped from. Beatrice had found a partner just as quickly, a young man I hadn't met before but whom I would be certain to question if he got too close to her.

Dancing was as much to be seen in public together as it was

for our own enjoyment, I surmised, as Mira and Carl too took to the floor. If we could all be remembered by other guests, interacting and milling around, no one would pay much notice when one or other of us slipped away, provided that some of our party was always visible.

When the second dance ended, I was already hot and breathless, and feeling wildly happy, despite the company I knew we were in.

'You still dance beautifully, I see,' Beatrice said, panting after dancing with two different gentlemen. 'And Mr Black isn't so bad either.'

'I was impressed myself,' I said, shooting Erasmus a wistful look. 'I had no idea he had it in him to move so gracefully.'

'I like to keep some surprises up my sleeve,' he said with a knowing smile.

Mira, who had filled her dance card within a few minutes of our arrival, sauntered across the floor towards us. Had I not known any better, I would have assumed her grace and strength came from a wealth of dancing experience rather than years of sailing and fighting and piracy. I wondered where she had learned to dance so perfectly, and what had led her to take on the role of captain, saviour of lost girls, leader of rebellion. If she did not leave London before I had the chance to speak with her properly, I thought I should like to hear her story.

She certainly turned heads everywhere she went, and I wondered if I wouldn't have been a better candidate for searching my godfather's study, if only because no one would suspect little Jenny of wandering the home of a childhood friend. But as I had been kept from the details of this particular mission, I would have to remain here, in sight of the guests, while the others risked life and limb for some unknown key piece of evidence.

'Where has that Dane got to?' Mira asked irritably, looking across the floor to find Carl in deep conversation with a young lady I dimly recognised as the daughter of some lesser lord. 'Oh, gracious,' she said, rustling over to extricate him before nodding at us from across the room and disappearing through one of the doors.

I looked around the ballroom, taking note of those who were already drunk on champagne or engaged in flirting voraciously with one another, my eyes always darting back to the bright yellow figure of my godfather. At least he was easy to spot.

'I hate to leave you here, ladies, but I have a card game scheduled with a certain business partner of mine,' Erasmus said, which I knew to mean that he would be keeping an eye on Talver and Griegsson while Mira and Carl searched Osborne's study.

'Oh, what a shame. Who shall Jenny dance with if you are playing card games, Mr Black?' Beatrice asked, oblivious to the layers of planning that had gone into this evening's activities.

'I am sure that my wife is free to dance with whomever she wishes, though if anyone so much as treads on one of her toes, they will have me to answer to, Miss Stanton,' Erasmus said with a wink, leaning in to place a kiss on my cheek before threading through the guests in search of the card table.

'What is the matter, cousin?' Beatrice asked, studying my expression as I watched my husband's retreating form.

'Nothing, nothing,' I said, abruptly ceasing the worried chewing of my bottom lip to give her a calm smile. She saw through it immediately.

'Is this what I think it is?'

'That depends on what you think it is.'

'The great plot. The plan to bring your father's murderer to justice.' She whispered the last part so that only I could hear it, but still I looked over my shoulder furtively.

'Nothing gets past you, does it?' I asked rhetorically, impressed that my cousin was able to think of more than filling her dance card. In her position a few years ago I certainly wouldn't have cared for much else. I briefly panicked as I lost sight of Osborne's yellow-clad form, only to find him in a circle of ladies and gentlemen I believed had come up from Brighton specially to see him. 'Honestly, I don't know if that is what this is. I didn't realise there was any plotting going on until just now, and I have the terrible sense that something could go horribly wrong.'

Beatrice waved away an approaching gentleman with a quick flash of the card around her wrist, and I admired how much command was in the dismissal.

'From what little I have gleaned while staying with you, Jen, your husband and company are somewhat adept at this sort of thing, are they not? Not to mention you disappearing off at Anna Griegsson's salon to go in search for something. I'd say you too are quite good at sneaking around.' She looked rather pleased with herself at that, and I had to match her amused look with my own.

'All right, Bea, either you are very shrewd indeed, or I am not as discreet as I like to think. But if you're willing to lend a hand this evening, I have a favour to ask you.'

Her eyes lit up as she came closer, our heads bending together. 'Of course, Jen, anything.'

I caught sight of Mr Osborne breaking away from his group, trying to extricate himself from the ballroom.

'If anything goes wrong, I need you to take Mama home. Your sole duty will be to get her to our carriage and away from any commotion.'

She hid her disappointment that I wasn't asking her to break into a locked room, or similar, quite well, I thought. But her words from the day she arrived had resonated with me – my uncle had tried to remove us from their lives because of my fall from grace. If we were to be found connected to anything else that might damage our family's reputation, I wanted Beatrice to come out unscathed.

She nodded once, and I tugged her towards the door that I had just seen my godfather leave through. 'Good. Now we have to make sure that whatever happens, Mr Osborne doesn't go into his study,' I added quickly, swishing across the ballroom as quickly as I could whilst trying to make it look as though Beatrice and I were nothing more than two ladies, arm in arm, off to find some fresh air or a mirror to check our appearances in.

The few people I recognised were content to keep their greetings short, although we were waylaid once by an older gentleman banker who had known our family for years and, as he continued to remind us, could not believe how big we had grown since last he saw us.

When we finally reached the door, I was cold with sweat and sick with worry that I had lost Osborne, and that he would arrive at his study before I had a chance to warn Mira and Carl. But when we rounded the corner, there he stood, in the corridor outside the parlour, in deep discussion with a man I did not recognise but who wore the blue uniform of a Bow Street Runner, top hat between his hands. The door to the parlour was open, and from within I could hear the distinctive clamour of male voices, the clink of glasses and guffaws of laughter that had disguised our footsteps. I pulled Beatrice out of sight, gripping her hand in mine as I pressed my back against the coolness of the wallpaper.

'I need you to distract him while I go and tell Mira and Carl to get out of the study,' I whispered, feeling her fingers trembling in mine before realising that it was actually me that was quivering. Perhaps someone had seen them break away from the party, or Osborne had detected some intrusion and had sent for the watch. Whatever the reason for the Runner's presence, it could not be good. If anything happened to any of Erasmus's crew, if they were caught and arrested . . .

I shook the thought from my head as I separated from my cousin, knowing from memory that I could reach the back staircase from where we were and access my godfather's study without running into any more guests. Osborne had back passages and staircases for his servants and enforced the rule that the staff not be seen, which on this occasion suited me well.

Thankfully my gift for recall served me well. When I finally reached the double doors that led to Osborne's study, I knocked gently. 'Mira,' I whispered through the crack, hating the way my voice echoed in the hallway. 'Mira, Carl, it's Jenny.'

Several seconds passed before the lock clicked and the door opened from within, Carl's face a pale oval against the darkness behind him. He pulled me inside before I had a chance to protest, closing the door behind me with a soft click.

'You scared the life out of me, Mrs B,' he said, nodding over to where Mira stood at the windows, hidden in the shadow of the curtains. It took me a moment to realise she was talking to someone, and another to recognise the petite crouched shape on the windowsill.

'Lei? What is it?' I asked, walking across the room to where the women conferred in the dark. The study overlooked the street, and below I could see the carriages of the gentry waiting around the square. The light boys had the street lamps lit and everything appeared the picture of calm below, the scene at odds with what I felt coming off the girl before me in waves. I saw her eyes flick to Mira as though asking for permission before saying anything.

'I was on lookout on the top of the house, Mrs B. I came as soon as I saw him, but it took me a good time to find the study windows and stay out of sight of the footmen below.'

'Saw who?' I pressed, looking to Mira for support.

'Kaine Clark,' Mira replied, her flat tone betraying the concern I could see breaking through her hard exterior.

'Kaine . . . Oh dear God,' I cursed, clutching my fist to my chest as though it would stop my rising panic. 'Carl, you must find Erasmus at once. If Clark is here and recognises him, everything could be lost.'

Carl nodded and turned back towards the door, but he was beaten to it by my cousin, who stood breathless in the hall outside.

'Jen, I have to get you and Aunt Katherine out of here,' she said, hesitating only for a moment at the sight of Lei crouched in the window.

'Where's Erasmus?'

'It's too late. The place is swarming with Bow Street Runners and watchmen. Is there a back door we can use?'

'Carl, find Erasmus *now*,' I bit out, ignoring Beatrice's warning. 'Mira, use the servants' staircase to the kitchens below. There's a door behind the large plant pot down the corridor to the right that will take you there, and if you run into someone just pretend you're drunk. Lei, I assume you can make your way out?'

Lei nodded in reply, and surprisingly, no one protested my sudden decision to take charge.

Beatrice spoke again, more urgently. 'You're not listening. When I approached Mr Osborne to speak to him, he waved me away, and then a man he called Clark turned up with a host of watchmen. I tried to waylay them, but there were more than I could count. I thought they were coming up here, but they went straight into the parlour and came out dragging Mr Black with them.'

'What?' Carl, Mira and I all exclaimed at the same time.

'They have Erasmus, Jen. He's been arrested.'

Chapter 26

ஐ ௸

FIVE WORDS

I ran down the opulent corridors, bereft of guests now that something of interest was happening at the centre of the party, although a watchman dashed past me as I approached the open double doors of the ballroom and elbowed my way through the crowd to the scene at the heart of it all.

My mother, raised to her full height, was currently dishing out threats to George Talver, while the man I realised must be Kaine Clark spoke in hushed tones with Osborne. I had only seen the back of his head before, the dark curls escaping his top hat as he walked away from the Midnight Rose. But now I saw him in full, his long face pockmarked, his eyes like chips of ice against pale skin. His mouth moved rapidly as he conferred with Osborne, pouring poison into my godfather's ears. I wondered whether it was he, Griegsson or Talver who had been the one to decide that my father had known too much and was better out of the way.

Griegsson stood with his wife a little further off, a bemused expression on his severe face as though he had walked into some organised evening entertainment.

Anger fizzled in my veins like hot oil on a skillet. I wanted to pull the pocket knife from my glove and brandish it at them, thrusting the knowledge of their crimes at them in front of the watchmen and telling them that they had the wrong person. But I had to be careful, for one wrong move now could cause irreparable damage to Erasmus's plans.

The music had stopped and the constant hum of voices made me want to scream for quiet, but instead I nudged closer, searching for Erasmus amongst the throng.

Carl and Beatrice had caught up with me, but I hoped that Mira and Lei had escaped. I had not even entertained the idea of leaving as Bea had ordered, despite her desperate pleas that had followed me all the way from Osborne's study.

Nudging a couple out of the way, I finally spied my husband, who, despite his hands being held behind his back by a watchman, looked the picture of calm. He didn't struggle against his captor, nor complain, but I recognised the look of disappointment on his face when he saw me approach. No doubt he had hoped that I would leave at the first sign of trouble.

'What on earth is going on?' I demanded, ignoring everyone else and making a beeline for him.

'These gentlemen seem to have mistaken me for someone else, my dear. Nothing that cannot be clarified with ease, I'm certain.'

'This man is a liar and a fraud,' Clark rasped, breaking off from whatever it was he was saying to Osborne. 'Nothing he says can be believed.' His voice was the brittle sound of churning gravel, coarse and guttural.

'Nonsense!' my mother spat, pulling away from Talver. 'My son-in-law is a more decent man than all of you put together.' She gestured to them emphatically as I stared at her in shock and gratitude for coming to Erasmus's aid. 'Now, unhand him this instant and we will bid leave of you all, for there is no use staying where we are not wanted.'

'Don't you dare,' Clark called to the watchman, who until now had been happy to do no more than hold Erasmus's arms behind his back. In response, he gripped my husband even tighter, causing him to wince.

'I'm afraid you have been as deceived as we have, Katherine,' Osborne said, alarm and sympathy written across his face, 'for it seems that Mr Clark here knows William from previous dealings.'

I searched the faces in the room, the air feeling hot and stale as so many people looked on, women whispering to each other behind their fans while men silently judged us. I balled my fists in an attempt to keep my composure. Their sniggers and gasps were too much like the night I had left Lord Darleston's house with my face tear-streaked and my dress torn. Beatrice and Carl were still at my shoulder. Someone must have sent for Marcus, for he towered above the throng, forcing his way towards us as though he alone could stand against the watch on our behalf. And Mira had now appeared too, ignoring my instructions to leave, vengeance in her eyes.

'He is a pirate and a thief!' Clark continued, striding closer. I wondered how he expected this to play out, for if he accused Erasmus of buying slaves or trying to fix sugar prices, surely, *surely* my husband and his crew were in the right? How could any accusation against him bear weight in front of a magistrate?

I held up my hands as though they would ward the man away before turning to Erasmus, who bent his head down to hear me.

'What do you need?' I whispered to him.

'Just for you to be safe,' he murmured, looking me up and

down as though this interaction was somehow causing me injury. I shook my head, unwilling for him to try and get rid of me now. 'Jenny, I need you to let them take me away. I don't want you in Clark's sights any longer than necessary.'

I opened my mouth to reply, but Clark, as though sensing what we were discussing, interrupted. 'Don't let them confer, man! What if they are in league with one another?'

'Don't be ridiculous, sir,' my mother snapped. 'My daughter and her husband are not *in league* about anything.'

I tensed as Clark narrowed his eyes at her. He had already taken one of my parents from me; what would stop him from taking the other?

'Mama,' I began, wondering how I could make her leave. As much as I appreciated her arguing on our behalf, I did not know what I would do if anything happened to her as a result.

'This is all very upsetting,' Osborne boomed, looking distraught, 'but I would appreciate it if you would allow Henrietta to continue her birthday celebrations. Take young William away until we can clear this business up.'

My hand was moving towards the knife in my glove before I could stop myself, but a warning look from Erasmus gave me pause.

'I will go willingly, sirs,' he said, sounding calmer than the rest of us put together. 'There is no need for restraint or theatrics. I shan't fight you.'

Clark bent and picked up Erasmus's cane, which had landed on the floor at some point during the kerfuffle.

'Indeed you won't,' he rumbled. 'Take him away!'

Panic-stricken, I looked between Erasmus and our enemies.

'But he's done nothing wrong!' I cried, finally finding my voice as two Bow Street Runners burst through the crowd and more watchmen moved to flank their colleagues.

Marcus signed to me frantically from where he stood at my mother's side. *Shall I fight them?* I caught sight of Mira's wine-red dress in my periphery, the glint of metal in her hand. If we had to, we could.

But Erasmus was shaking his head urgently at her, then at Marcus, and finally at me.

'Jenny, dear, don't worry. He'll be safe and sound in a holding cell tonight and we can clear all of this up in the morning,' Osborne said reassuringly. But it wasn't reassuring at all, because the lie struck the air between us like a discordant note. That was the second time I had been lied to by my godfather, and I looked back at Erasmus in a panic. I knew about prisoners mysteriously dying before they had the chance to make it in front of a judge. I could not hide the fear from my face as my eyes met my husband's, resignation in their dark brown depths.

'I can't let them take you,' I said, stepping towards him as the watchman tried unsuccessfully to pull him away.

'Don't worry about me. This will all be over soon,' he said softly, so that only I could hear.

'But they'll kill you.'

He gave me a wolfish smile, the one I had been nervous of when I had first seen it but that now filled me with an ache of longing. I gripped his lapel, as though that would stop the man holding his arms from taking him away.

'Worse men have tried. Let me go, Jenny.'

Before anyone could stop me, I reached up to press a kiss to his mouth, ignoring the mutters of dismay from the guests and the disapproving grumble from Kaine Clark.

'That's enough of that,' the watchman said, pulling us apart.

'I love you, Jenny Black,' Erasmus said, before he was jerked away.

My mouth fell open at his words as I watched them

manhandle him away. I knew that he was hiding his true strength. He could have broken free of their grip and had them on the floor in an instant even without his cane, so why was he allowing himself to be arrested?

As he disappeared through the crowd that parted to make way for him, I barely heard my mother coaxing me away, or Beatrice murmuring sympathetically. I was vaguely aware of Mira snatching Erasmus's cane out of Kaine Clark's hands. Of someone guiding me into the chill night.

I love you, Jenny Black.

Five words that had punctured my heart as though it had been shot with a pistol.

'You heard the man, we must find a way to clear his name by morning,' my mother was saying to Mira, who had joined us in the carriage.

'Mrs Miller, it is best if you don't involve yourself. These are dangerous gentlemen,' the captain replied, not unkindly. She knew what those monsters had done to my father, and although it was not in her interests to protect my family, I felt a surge of gratitude to her for trying.

I took Erasmus's cane from her, twirling it in my fingers thoughtfully, wondering how he felt without it.

'That may be so, Miss Black, but I am not going to simply stand by while they drag my family through the mud. Jenny is a Black too. She will be disgraced if her husband is imprisoned.' My mother used Mira's false name, as she did not know of any other way to address her.

'That is the least of our worries, madam,' the captain replied. I should have been annoyed that she had little care for my reputation, but in all honesty I agreed with her. 'And you may call me Mira. I am not a Black and never have been,' she added, her voice quietening.

I glanced sideways at her to find her looking back at me, her emotions for once evident in her expression. Regret, perhaps, but certainly sadness. Not the hint of jealousy I had expected.

I love you, Jenny Black.

The words thrummed through me, the truth in them clear and bright.

When we finally arrived home, Beatrice was sent to bed despite her protests, but insisted that I call for her if she could do anything at all to help. My mother echoed my own worries regarding her involvement. The less Beatrice had to do with it, the better for her reputation.

I was tempted to send Mira to her lodgings as well, not particularly wanting her in the same room, the same building, but I could not shake the idea that if I sent her away, she would only climb back into the house through Erasmus's window and wait for me upstairs.

'Would you like me to have a room made up for you?' my mother asked her, ever the hostess.

'I do not think I shall have time to sleep, madam. I have much to discuss with Jenny,' Mira replied, keeping her voice level despite the urgency I sensed in her words. *We need a plan. Fast.*

'I should like to speak to my daughter alone if it is all the same to you,' Mother began, but I interrupted her before she could make any more decisions on my behalf.

'Mama, you may speak frankly around Mira. She already knows everything about us, and is closer to Erasmus than any other. There is no point in excluding her from our conversation.' I didn't bother to hide the weariness in my voice.

'If you say so, Jenny,' Mother replied uncertainly, sinking down into her armchair. I sat in my father's to be near the warmth of the fire, resting Erasmus's cane beside me. Mira perched on the chaise, right at the edge, as though she might need to stand at any moment.

I beckoned Marcus from his usual post by the door, gesturing for him to sit. He recovered from his surprise well, settling awkwardly on one of the rarely used stools so that he could read everyone's lips as we spoke.

Mother sighed, resting an elbow on the armrest and cradling her head. 'This is a terrible mess we have got ourselves into.'

'I care not about the mess we are in, Mama. What of Erasmus?'

'The marriage could be annulled. I know you are fond of him, but it has not been consummated,' she said, and I heard the question in that statement. Anger flared hot and bright inside my chest.

'If you are suggesting that we leave him to those beasts that Father took up business with, you are mistaken,' I snapped.

Her eyebrows shot up. I rarely spoke out of turn to her.

'I suspected you would feel that way,' she said, her gaze inscrutable. 'But they could ruin us, you know. Although we have lied to Mr Osborne and Mr Talver by telling them you had known him longer than you had, it is this other identity of his that seems to be the real issue. If we can convince them that he hoodwinked us, we may come out of this no worse off than when we started.'

'And what, leave him to be murdered in prison?'

'Who said anything about murder, girl? Just because that horrible man this evening . . .'

'Kaine Clark,' Mira supplied.

'Indeed. Just because this Mr Clark objects to some of Mr Black's previous activities doesn't mean he's going to murder him, for goodness' sake. If we were to cut ties with Will . . . Erasmus,' she corrected, no longer needing to keep up the pretence, 'we might still be able to salvage a share in the business. Hear me out, daughter.' She held up a warning hand when I began to protest. 'You have been married less than a month. If we were to annul the marriage, we might still be able to buy ourselves some time, at the very least, and I am sure Henry and George will be accommodating if we deny all knowledge of Mr Black's unscrupulous past.' She leaned forward and took my chin in her grip, forcing me to meet her gaze. 'But if you insist on continuing your affiliation with him, not only will they take his share of the profits and wipe your father's name from the company, but our reputation will be dragged down with his. Is that a risk you are willing to take? Do you truly believe that your father – God rest his soul – would take the side of a near-stranger at the risk of our ruination after everything he did for us?'

Her final words caught me off guard, but I pulled my chin from her grasp and shook my head. 'Erasmus has done nothing wrong. To the contrary, if Father had known half of what I do, he would have taken my husband's side without question.' I wanted to rail at her, to throw something across the room, anything to make her understand what she was asking of me. But of course she didn't, because she still thought that my father had died from a food sensitivity, and that his business partners were two of his oldest friends.

'Erasmus may or may not be guilty, Jenny, but if he truly loves you, he'll understand that your best chance at a future is to let him go.'

I stood, too agitated to remain seated, and paced in front of her.

'I refuse to abandon him. You may not comprehend the dangers, but I know for a fact that they will try to kill him tonight if we don't take action now.' I turned to Mira imploringly. 'Is there anyone on watch outside?' I had to hope that one of their crew had been left to keep an eye on the house just in case, although the chances were slim considering we were all supposed to be out at the party.

She frowned before crossing to the window and peering through the curtains.

'Watching the house? Why would anyone be—'

'Kaine Clark is a far more dangerous man than you realise, Mama,' I said, as Mira went to the front door, her fingers already in her mouth to whistle. The sound was loud enough to wake the dead, and it brought Kit dashing across the road from where he'd been hiding. Quick instructions were relayed, and then he was off, running across the square as though his life depended on it.

'If Clark's men come for us tonight, we've just got rid of the only person who knows where to find the rest of the crew,' Mira said as she came back.

'I'm sure we'll manage between us,' I said, grateful that Erasmus had left me with the pocket knife. I never wanted to have to use it, but as I tore off my gloves and flung them onto a table, I held it in my palm like a talisman.

'Why would someone come for us? I've never even met the man before today! What business would Mr Clark have at the house?' Mother protested indignantly. My eyes darted to Mira with every question. 'All this talk of killing and murder is making me feel quite ill. I think I am owed an explanation!'

The captain returned to her seat, a blade in her hands that had materialised from somewhere, as though she suspected that Clark and his henchmen might burst in at any moment.

'Do you want to tell her, or shall I?' she said, flipping the knife end over end, making my mother flinch each time.

'Tell me what?'

I took a deep breath. There was no escaping it now.

I signalled to Marcus, who stood at my word. 'We'll need drinks. Strong ones.' He nodded, finding three glasses, filling them with dark liquid and passing them to each of us. 'You too,' I added. He gave an inquisitive quirk of his eyebrow, but I insisted, gesturing for him to take his drink and sit back down. 'If we are to save my husband, Marcus, we're going to need all the help we can get, and it would benefit you to know how my father was killed.'

'Killed?' my mother echoed, the colour draining from her face as I turned to her.

I placed Erasmus's pocket knife in my lap, taking a sip of my drink for courage. Rum, my husband's drink of choice. Just the scent of it filled me with longing and gave me courage.

'Yes, Mama, killed.'

It took me more than an hour, signing to Marcus as I explained, Mira supplying details where I fell short. My mother bombarded me with questions, once she had recovered from the shock of hearing that the man my father had called a friend had been in league with those who had had him murdered. But when midnight finally struck, I had told her everything. Now it was time to make a plan.

Chapter 27

ꕥ

LIES LIKE WOUNDS

None of us slept that night. Even if we had wanted to, there was far too much to do.

I paced the withdrawing room, bile rising in my throat every time I thought of Erasmus alone, perhaps chained up in a cell, or being beaten by Tommy, Little Tom and Medium Jim, with not even his cane to defend himself. Time and again I pleaded with Mira to go and find him, to make sure he lived through the night, but she insisted that she had her best people looking out for him.

What felt like hours later, a knock at the door sounded, and Mr Atkins, the oldest member of the crew, was shown in, bearing the news that they had found where Erasmus was being kept and would prevent Clark's men from getting within ten feet of the cell. Only then did I stop my pacing, sagging with relief and allowing myself a brief moment of respite.

'We cannot leave the poor man at their mercy for long,' Mother said as I closed my eyes for a moment, resting my head on the back of the armchair. 'Now that we know what they are capable of, we shall have to act quickly.'

'That is all very well, Mrs Miller,' Mira replied, taking my place pacing in front of the fireplace, 'but you must understand that Erasmus is the one with the contacts in the Saints. He is the only person who knows the identity of the man building a case for us, and even with this mystery gentleman's aid, progress has been painfully slow. We have been waiting on a meeting date to bring evidence to him so that Talver, Clark and the rest of their dark network can be arrested, but Erasmus refuses to send anything with a messenger, not trusting the ledger Jenny discovered in Griegsson's study to anyone else.' Her last words were weighted with frustration, and I imagined she had held conversations with Erasmus about such things many times before. Heated conversations.

'She is correct, I'm afraid,' Mr Atkins added, the old sea dog sitting ill at ease on the chaise. 'We can certainly try and locate Black's contact, but if we leave it up to the politicians, they will be arguing about it for years. We will undoubtedly win our case against Clark and the others, but Erasmus will be either dead or in the colonies by then.'

'Thank you for that helpful exposition, sir,' I quipped, pinching the bridge of my nose against the onset of a headache, 'but I would be delighted to hear a suggestion that doesn't result in my husband being deported or executed.'

Mr Atkins shot me an irritated glare, but thankfully kept his mouth shut.

If only we could find out with whom he had been corresponding . . .

I thought of the surreptitious meetings, the passing of notes and letters in taverns, the mention of the two companies he had received. The messages were coming from someone, and that someone might lead us straight to the person who could help to free him.

Erasmus had left that letter under the mattress in his room. Perhaps there were other things to find that could help us, if only I knew where to look.

Standing abruptly, the blood rushing to my head, I beckoned Mira upstairs with me. If anyone knew where Erasmus might hide something, it would be her.

The room felt cold and lifeless without him, and as she lit the candles, I couldn't help but run my fingers over his possessions scattered around the room. The cravat that he had flung onto the bureau; his books, so precious to him that they had travelled all around the world with him; the little trunk under the desk . . .

I paused, struck by something odd.

It had been peculiar to me that this was the one item he had never opened in my presence. I recalled him unpacking on our wedding night, nudging it out of sight with his toe, and the evening I came in and found it closed, but in the middle of the room, as though I had disturbed him while going through it.

I knelt down and pulled it out from under the table, managing to manoeuvre it onto the bed despite its weight. It measured less than two feet across and one foot deep, certainly large enough to hold correspondence, but from its weight it could also contain coins, jewels or any manner of things.

'Do you know what's in here?' I asked the captain, who looked up from her task of rifling through his drawers.

She frowned. 'Paperwork, I think. I don't recall ever seeing it open.' Nudging the drawer shut with a hip, she came over, taking the padlock in her fingers and examining it.

'If only Lei were here, she could probably have us inside it in a few minutes,' I sighed, slumping onto the mattress, the chest bouncing up and down beside me.

Mira waggled her eyebrows at me cunningly. 'I make it a

point for *all* of my crew to learn how to pick locks, Jenny, lest they find themselves in a . . . compromising situation that they need to escape from.'

'Or lest they find themselves in need of breaking into a safe?' I ventured, narrowing my eyes at her.

She shrugged, retrieving two tiny pins from the bodice of her dress and going to work on the lock.

'Doing what we do, we have to take money where we can get it. I do have a crew to feed and a ship to run, after all.'

'But *Juliet* is Erasmus's ship, yes?' I dared, knowing that I shouldn't be distracting her from the task at hand.

She crouched down, her skirts splaying around her as though she were sitting in a pool of spilled blood, and paused in her work to look up at me. I was surprised to see something that looked an awful lot like regret on her face.

'I must apologise to you, Jenny,' she murmured, as though she wasn't proud of the fact.

'Whatever for? Threatening to take my husband's ship and leave him here?' I thought of the terse note up in my father's study, and the ultimatum she had given him. Heat rose to her cheeks, her scar turning white against the flush of her skin.

'I do not have many close female friends. Well, none who would be considered proper in society. Please do not make this more difficult than it already is.'

I supposed that the ladies at the Midnight Rose could hardly be called her friends; rather they were a distraction, drawing attention from her hiding there. I could not imagine what it would be like to command so many people. Was it lonely? I wondered. Was that why she craved Erasmus's company? Because he was someone who understood what it was like to be in charge, and could share some of the burden as her first mate? I understood so little of her and her motives, but I acquiesced, holding my tongue and nodding so that she could finish what she was saying.

'You must think me wretched and jealous, telling you that Bart would leave you at the first opportunity,' she mumbled, taking her eyes from me as she manoeuvred the pins in the padlock, 'but you must understand that I was only speaking from experience. He is not a man to give his love freely nor wantonly, and when we separated at first, I did not see him for nearly a year.'

I didn't bother to hide my puzzlement. 'So you did not remain working closely immediately after you . . . broke things off?'

She hummed a laugh and shook her head. 'You make it sound as though we were something lasting, or that we were promised to each other. No, Jenny, there was not much breaking off to be done. He found me attractive, most certainly, and we shared a common interest in wanting to free the oppressed women of his mother's homeland, but I think I fell for him harder than he for I. We were never going to last with such a disparity of affections.'

Something clicked inside the small lock, but still it did not open, and I thought it might have something to do with her only being half-minded about it. It was clear she needed to unburden herself of whatever it was that weighed on her conscience, even though I didn't truly believe I was owed any sort of apology at all.

'You worked together successfully for years, though. He even took on false identities to protect you,' I pointed out.

'To protect the mission,' she corrected, 'and I think out of guilt for this.' She let go of a pin to point to her scar, lifting her chin so that I could see it better.

I felt a twist in my stomach at the thought that Erasmus had

had something to do with disfiguring such a beautiful face, even though it didn't make her any less attractive in my opinion.

'What did he do?' I croaked, unable to imagine my husband, as strong and wild as he was, ever inflicting such a thing upon a lady.

She shook her head. 'It is not a short tale, and I don't know how much of all that we do has been explained to you.'

'Enough to understand that the Ottomans have been taking girls from their homes and selling them to brothels across Europe.'

Mira raised a brow. 'That is a little simplistic, but yes. Many slaves are treated well if they serve the Ottoman army. Boys are militarised, but girls are often domesticated, taught to read and write, and given a finite contract of nine years of service. They may just as likely become serving staff as concubines, or governesses or nurses. The difference between them and your own staff is that the Ottoman girls are not paid for their service.'

I considered this new information. 'What does that have to do with you?'

The corner of her mouth picked up in place of a smile, but quickly fell as she continued to poke at the lock with her pins. 'A story for another time, perhaps.'

'Your sister is missing, from what I gathered.'

The glance she threw my way was cold, but I gave her a steady look of my own. I would not back down now when I was so close to understanding more of her, and in turn, more of my husband. She huffed, stopping her work for a moment and handing her pins to me so that she could flex her aching wrists.

'My earliest memories are of my sister. Elora and I were born minutes apart, but only with the similarities of any other pair of siblings. Our mother rarely spoke of her past, but I knew she had come from a small island off the coast of Greece and was brought here, to England, when she was nine. She and four others had been sold into prostitution before they had even begun their first bleeding.' Mira's tone had taken on a bitter edge, one I could not blame her for. 'My mother fell pregnant with us when she was fifteen. She should have got rid of us when she still could, but she believed our father to be a sailor who had visited her every month, and of whom she had grown fond. She gave him the news that she maintained herself to be expecting his child, and to his credit he agreed to help her escape. Other women at the brothel did it often enough, and although there was the risk of being followed, there was little anyone could truly do to stop her. That is how myself and my sister came to be born on a small island near Gibraltar.

'We thought ourselves safe when we were small. I did not know then that my father had dropped us on an island known for its annual *yesir* – a marketplace where slaves were sold to the highest bidder. Perhaps he did not know either. I like to think that he did not intentionally choose to discard his lover and daughters in a place where women were likely to be dragged from their beds at night and thrown into the slavers' paths when they had insufficient goods to sell.'

I swallowed the lump that had formed in my throat, anger and despair for her warring within me as she continued.

'All we had growing up were my mother's stories of a home she was still young enough to remember, and the efforts of the locals to protect their daughters. My father had left before we were a year old, and my mother went back to prostitution to support us – the only work she knew well.' She gave a long exhale through her nose as she hardened herself to speak her next words. 'I will not explain how the village came to be raided, nor my mother killed, my sister taken from me while I was hidden away,' she said, closing her eyes against the pain.

She had lost so much, and her voice had taken on a darker shade as she recounted her story. It felt wrong to push her further, but she seemed just as aware that she had not yet answered my first question.

'As for Bart, we first met in a tap house in the port of Marsaskala in Malta. I had acquired a ship that was bringing saffron from Greece to Spain but that also contained a group of slave girls. My intention had been to land in Malta, turn the ship around and deposit the girls somewhere closer to safety.' The way she said 'acquired' made me believe that it was perhaps synonymous for 'pirated' in this instance. 'I was reckless, though. In Bart I found a man desperate to visit his mother's homeland and equally terrified to know what he might find there. He had some of my sympathy for that, and I told him a little of my mission. He was in awe of me, a pirate taking the law into my own hands, and pressed me for information as to how he might do the same. It was there that we first . . . well, you know.'

I looked away, embarrassed. Unfortunately, I *did* know.

'He admired my daring and achievements, while I was so enamoured of him, this English gentleman who had grown weary of loneliness and had set off across the sea, that I did not think twice about bringing him onto my crew. We had two ships then. I renamed mine *Romeo* to his *Juliet*.' She cringed, even though to my ears it sounded ridiculously romantic. 'But I had secrets of my own. *Romeo* had contained not only the slaves and the saffron, but an exceptionally large shipment of opium that was worth almost as much as the souls I'd released. I was young and foolish, thinking I could sell it or offload it without ever having it traced back to us.

'I hid it from Bart, spending more time with him on *Juliet* than I ever did on my own ship, trying to keep him away from the cargo and the potential danger it might bring. Instead I plotted a course for us to sail down to South America, where I could get rid of the opium safely, telling him I had heard rumours of an Ottoman ship that would be trading there, and that I suspected we would find more girls to save.

'But on that very first voyage together, we ourselves were set upon by pirates in the Western Ocean who had heard rumours of a stolen British ship with a valuable cargo. I was with him in his chamber on the *Juliet* when they climbed aboard in the night. They pulled us from our bed and cut me from heart to jowl in front of his eyes, all so that he would reveal the location of what they sought. Bart, of course, knew nothing of it, but through my bloody haze I told them where to find the opium.

'I still do not know how he managed to convince them to spare the crew of *Romeo*, bringing them over to his ship and allowing the pirates to make off with my own and all it held. He left us as soon as we made land, and it was eleven months before I found him again.'

I slid off the bed and knelt down beside her. Looking at me with eyes the colour of grey London pavements after fresh rainfall, she said, 'I lost him that night, if I had ever truly had him in the first place. He blamed himself for my injury, but he never forgave me for the lie.'

'You did what you thought was best for him,' I replied, understanding why she had acted the way she had, even if I would have perhaps taken a different course in her situation.

'I did what I thought was best for *me*,' she corrected. 'Lies and wounds are much the same. Time may pass and wounds may heal, but both leave scars that can never be truly forgotten. I think that's why he never felt for me the way he does you. He loves you, Jenny, I see it now, and I cannot in my true heart say that I believe he would willingly leave your side.'

Despite having been both intimidated and terrified by Mira,

I took her by the arms and pulled her into an embrace, feeling her stiffen at first before relaxing, returning the affection. Perhaps she had never been held like this before, by a friend and confidante.

'There is no need to apologise, Mira,' I murmured, her hair falling in dark spirals around her shoulders and tickling my cheek. 'You have my gratitude, for making me guard my heart long enough to know when it was time to let him in. Thanks to your warning, I could not be hurt by hearing he intended to set sail with you at the end of the month, or at least not as much as I would have been otherwise.'

She pulled back with a startled expression. 'He has no intention to leave with me, I assure you.'

I huffed, handing over the lock picks and getting up to fetch his letter from my own room. Her eyes scanned the words quickly and she shook her head.

'There must be some mistake. Where did you get this?'

'My godfather brought it to me. He said he'd spotted Erasmus hiding it under his work one day and thought I should see for myself.'

'It must be some sort of decoy. I can assure you that Erasmus has no plan but to stay with you. You have his heart, Jenny, just as much as he has yours. Not even the sea herself could pull him away from what you have.'

I swallowed back my emotion and nodded. Perhaps she was right, and Erasmus had written this as a way to throw his business partners off the scent. I still didn't understand why he would have felt the need to pretend that he was leaving, but hopefully all would become clear before it was too late.

'Well, we had better open this chest or we'll never get him back,' I replied, taking the letter from her and placing it on the bed while she returned to the lock.

I let her work in silence, crouched beside her on the floor, my blue-green dress against her dark red skirts. Sea and sky and metal and blood, I thought as I watched her wriggle the pins in earnest, coaxing the mechanism to come loose. When she finally succeeded, I wanted to cheer, but instead I gasped as she prised the lid open to reveal the chest's contents.

Stack upon stack of folded letters, some of them with a familiar seal, others adorned with the emblems of embassies or the government, were jammed into every corner. There were documents belonging to slaves that Erasmus and Mira had relocated, proving that they had been forced into servitude even after the law was passed. There were letters from his contact in the Saints, and a small ledger containing the names of ships, the dates they had sailed and, subsequently, the dates that Mira and her crew had freed their human cargoes. With Griegsson's own ledger, they might finally have enough to bring the three men down. Surely all that remained was a witness, and if Big Don and Gar could locate Sly Fairfax and force a confession, the case would be won.

'Bart, you clever dog,' Mira said, poring through the papers. 'I always made great fun of his meticulous record-keeping, but if this doesn't help us, I don't know what will.' She gestured for me to take the other side of the chest so that we could bring it downstairs.

The window slid open in Erasmus's room suddenly, letting in a gust of night air, and Lei stooped to pass through the gap, the black ledger stuffed under her jacket. I couldn't imagine how she had climbed the guttering with it.

'Lei, was there a problem with using the front door?' Mira asked in mock surprise.

The girl gave us her signature grin, freeing a hand to touch her cap. 'There were lots of people in the front room, Cap'n. Thought it better to come and find you directly.'

The captain rolled her eyes but gestured for her to follow us down to the withdrawing room with our own precious cargo.

If anyone wondered how we had gained another member of our party, they didn't say, but I introduced Lei to my mother all the same, explaining how she had been instrumental in our success thus far. Whatever Mother thought of the girl dressed as a boy with a smile that could make a vicar blush, she kept it to herself.

When Mr Atkins laid eyes upon the papers, he almost rubbed his hands in delight, while my mother picked one up curiously, humming to herself as though a thought had just struck her.

'What is it, Mama?' I came over to her, glancing at the paper in her hand, her finger running over the initials 'T. C.' at the bottom.

She frowned at it, reading the brief message several times before looking up at me.

'There is something awfully familiar about this,' she said, pointing to the writing. 'Something your father worked on while he was alive.'

I jolted in surprise. 'Do you think . . . Could the man Father was writing to in Westminster be . . .'

'The very same that your Erasmus was corresponding with on a similar matter? I believe that might well be the case.'

If it were so, it could be the key to it all. To freeing Erasmus, to stopping Talver, Griegsson and Clark for good. To aiding Mira and her crew in their mission of almost a decade. But time was not on our side.

'Mama, if Talver is involved in this, Osborne may wish to disband the company. We may have nothing left. No fortune, no livelihood.' I said it quietly, not wanting to be overheard by the others. Although I had no consideration for it myself, I knew it would ruin her to lose everything that my father had worked for.

She gave me a smile I had never seen from her before; one that reminded me distinctly of Erasmus when he was plotting something.

'Marcus,' she signed as she spoke, 'be a dear and see if you can find any letters of Jacob's that resemble this.' She gave the steward the piece of paper she held, and he bowed and left the room. 'Don't you worry, Jenny, my dear.' She turned to me, patting my hand. 'I believe I have a plan.'

Chapter 28

ഗ്ര

IN THE FACE OF MONSTERS

The dining table was set for a dozen. I marvelled at the sight, each place carefully laid, late summer roses and geraniums arranged tastefully at intervals down the long table, the candles lit, making the entire space feel warm and welcoming. No hint of the true intentions behind the evening's meal. It had been three full days since the Osborne ball, each one utter chaos as we made our plans.

My cousin had been dispatched to one of Mother's friends first thing this morning, with no explanation as to why but with the condition that if we did not send for her by the evening, she was to return home and breathe not a word of what had transpired to her parents. I knew she would hate being excluded, particularly as she had been so integral in finding out about Father's poisoner, but her reputation by association with us was so precarious already that I did not wish to make it worse.

'Are we ready?' I heard my mother asking Marcus just outside in the hall. I didn't see his reply from where I stood, but I wondered about the steward. He had looked hurt and infuriated when I explained what I had discovered at the chop house, his eyes clouding with pain and an unmistakable desire for revenge that I knew was mirrored in my own. Marcus was more family than staff, and once all this was over, I thought I'd make a point of letting him know that, giving him the credit he was due for watching over us. Provided everything went as we had devised and we all made it through this dinner unscathed.

Mira swept in wearing a dress she had borrowed from my mother – a simple gown of white fabric, bunched under the bust, with long capped sleeves. She lifted her skirt and gave me a wicked smile, for beneath it she wore her britches and boots, a knife tucked into the top, ready for a fight should the need arise.

When the doorbell rang, I choked down the nerves that rose in my chest, but it was only more of the crew. Gar and Carl looked impeccable in their suits, although there was no taming Gar's wild red hair, and the Viking looked as short of sleep as the rest of us. Mr Atkins soon followed, along with Lei and Big Don, the girl stowing herself behind one of the curtains at the rear of the room, the giant giving me a quick bow before stealing off to another part of the house to await orders.

'Don't look so worried, Jenny,' Mira said, walking over to the drinks table and pouring us each a glass, before handing one to me. 'Your mother's plan is almost infallible.'

I knocked back the rum, savouring the taste and smell, if only because it reminded me of Erasmus. It did nothing to calm me, but I tried to compose myself, knowing I would be expected to play hostess for our guests. At least I could *try* not to look like the little mouse my husband always insisted I was.

'It's the *almost* that worries me,' I muttered, before straightening my skirts as our first guest was shown in.

'Mr Clarkson, thank you so much for coming at such short notice,' Mother exclaimed to a tall gentleman with an impressive countenance. Thomas Clarkson's wispy light brown hair was combed neatly from his face, and his prominent nose and large forehead indicated a man of extreme intelligence, as could be seen from the way he looked thoughtfully at the assembled company. My mother had called in more than a few favours to have him here this evening, and as the key contributor to the Clapham Saints' case against British-owned slaves, he was the most important person in the room as far as we were concerned. He was also the mysterious correspondent that my father, and Erasmus, had been writing to. A man they had had in common. I had to wonder if my path might have crossed with Erasmus's in some other way if my father had lived, for they had more of a common interest than any of us had realised at first meeting.

'I thank you for inviting me, Mrs Miller. I was awfully sad to hear of your husband's passing, for I very much enjoyed our correspondence during the short time that we were in contact.'

Mother thanked him, then signalled to me to take her place so that she could greet our final guests. Mira joined me, and together we kept Mr Clarkson engaged while we waited.

'I am truly glad that you accepted our invitation, Henry, George,' I could hear my mother saying from the hall. The sound of their names alone had me stiffening, even while Mr Clarkson spoke modestly about his latest essay, which apparently Mira had read with some fervour.

'We are grateful to be invited, Katherine. Jacob was a friend to us for so long that it seems a shame to have any rift between us,' Osborne boomed.

I had not eaten at all today, but the rum I had drunk turned sour in my stomach as Talver entered, smiling serpentinely to one and all.

I averted my eyes, keeping them fixed on Mr Clarkson's face instead as everyone was introduced before being shown to their places.

My father's seat at the head of the table remained empty. Mira took the chair beside me, the crew interspersed between Osborne, Talver and Mr Clarkson, who sat at the other end with Mr Atkins. I wished that I did not have to be within line of sight of Jacob Miller's murderer, but there was no avoiding it. Every time I stole a glance at the man, I saw my father's face the morning before he went to have lunch with them, his smile as he agreed to let me travel, our moments together reading or riding in the carriage, and quickly lost my appetite.

Everyone seemed to be behaving as though the incident at Henrietta's party had never happened, even though Erasmus was still absent. No one made mention of this in the company of Mr Clarkson, although I noticed a few curious looks in his direction. We had not explained nor expanded upon why he was here, my mother wishing to reveal it at the right time.

'I must ask,' she said as the first dish was served, 'did you find a suitor for Henrietta?'

The question was aimed at Osborne, who had immediately started on his cold soup of creamed artichoke and onion.

'Ah, I thank you for your consideration, Katherine, but I am not certain that I agree with her decision at present. She has become rather taken by the young man who first asked her to dance, but his . . . personal activities are somewhat worrying. He calls himself a scientist and I do not like the idea of such a man coming into contact with our business, should anything happen to me.'

I caught my mother's eye and hid a smile, dabbing a piece of bread into my soup.

'I recall the young man in question,' she replied tactfully, before pretending to think it over. 'You could always have Henrietta marry George here – that would keep it within the family, so to speak. Surely there is no one more competent to look after the business than Mr Talver, wouldn't you agree?'

Osborne coughed loudly in surprise. Talver seemed pleasantly taken aback by the suggestion, but his partner shook his head fervently. We all knew what Talver was capable of. It would not be a stretch of the imagination to realise that Osborne might meet a similar fate to my father, should Talver wish to take the lion's share of the company.

'As sound as that suggestion might be, Henrietta has rather made up her mind,' he replied hastily. Talver looked about to open his mouth to argue his case when he was interrupted. 'This soup is quite marvellous, Katherine,' Osborne exclaimed, hoping to change the subject, no doubt.

My mother's face brightened at the compliment. 'That is wonderful to hear, Henry, for we have recently employed a new cook, and he would be delighted to know that you take pleasure in his craft.'

'Well, you chose well. Such a use of herbs as I have never tasted before! The man has my respect,' he replied, waving his spoon emphatically.

'Marcus, go and fetch the new cook, would you? I think he should like to hear such compliments with his own ears.'

The steward obliged, returning moments later with a reluctant-looking man, arms as thick as tree trunks, a face like a slab of meat.

Talver was the first to recognise him, dropping his spoon with a clatter in his bowl.

'Oh dear, George, you look as though you have seen a ghost,' Mother said, managing to suppress her smile. 'Henry, this is Mr Sly Fairfax. We were lucky to find him at his home in Clapham just a few nights ago.'

Osborne blanched at the name, looking from the cook to Talver, who appeared quite ill. 'You don't say?' he murmured, for once lost for words.

'It was fortunate that we found him, in fact. We had heard of his excellent reputation, but there was quite the disturbance at his home when my son-in-law's men arrived. As it transpired, Mr Fairfax was being attacked by some ruffians. We are certain they would have caused him grievous harm if it weren't for our intervention and a small band of parish constables.'

Talver made a spluttering noise, as though he was choking on his soup. It was not poisoned, of course, but I enjoyed watching him think it for the moment.

'Mr Osborne here was just complimenting your soup, Mr Fairfax,' my mother continued, as though nothing untoward were happening at all.

'M-much obliged to you, sir,' Fairfax managed, bowing as he ducked out of the room, no doubt uncomfortable in the presence of his previous employer and would-be murderer.

'George, are you quite well?' Mother continued, taking a mouthful of soup herself to demonstrate that no one was dying today. Not yet, anyway.

Talver, evidently realising that he was not about to suffer the same fate as my father, nodded angrily, as though we had caused him offence in our ruse. He glared at my godfather, some secret communication passing between them. I could hazard a guess at his worry, though. If we had managed to produce Sly Fairfax, then surely, he must have realised, we knew about the rest of the tale too? It could be no coincidence that we had brought him here and paraded the hired poisoner in front of him like an animal at an exhibit. I savoured the emotions that flitted across his face; the doubt, fear and indignation at being made a fool of. He seemed to conclude that he had had enough of the game, for he threw his napkin down on the table, aggrieved.

'I have just recalled that I have another engagement,' he announced, his voice like slick oil. Osborne seemed to be wavering, and I wondered if now was the time to reveal our hand.

'Surely not, George?' said Mother, pretending to be insulted. 'You cannot go yet. We have a wonderful surprise for you both.'

'What surprise?' Talver insisted, no politeness in his tone now.

'Well, I had hoped it could wait until dessert, but as you are so insistent on having it now . . .' She turned to Marcus and gave him a nod of her head. 'I would just like to make amends for the scene created by my family at Henrietta's party.'

'No amends or apology is needed, Katherine,' Osborne answered too quickly. 'We all make mistakes, and I am certain that we can come to an agreement about the company shares, even with Mr Black out of the picture.'

'That is such a shame to hear,' a deep, smooth voice said from behind me, sending goosebumps running up the back of my neck, 'for if I am honest, I had intended to take the company from *you*, gentlemen.'

I resisted the temptation to turn around, savouring the shock and horror on Talver and Osborne's faces.

A warm hand rested on my shoulder, and I finally allowed myself to look up at Erasmus, my heart fracturing at the sight of his black eye and the bruises along his jaw. Despite the ordeal he had suffered in prison, he had made time to dress impeccably as always in a black velvet jacket, maroon waistcoat and matching silk cravat, his hair tied back neatly so that I could see every line and angle of his handsome face.

'Y-you!' Talver spat, standing so abruptly that he almost knocked his chair over.

'Yes, indeed, Mr Talver, 'tis I.'

'But you're *dead*,' Osborne said, and the word made me want to launch at him with claws and teeth.

'And yet here I stand before your eyes, alive and well, save for a few knocks and scrapes,' Erasmus conceded, gesturing to his eye. His free hand rested on his cane, which I had returned into his possession yesterday, when he had arrived from the prison, beaten and bloody, before ordering him a bath and a change of clothes. It was only thanks to the quick actions of his crew that he hadn't been killed that night; they had managed to intercept Kaine Clark's men before they could do any permanent damage. I was grateful that Tommy had gone into Erasmus's cell alone, ordering Little Tom and Medium Jim to keep guard outside, thinking that they would be any match for the crew. They would not be capable of causing any harm for a good long time.

'As you can see, gentlemen,' my mother said, patting her mouth daintily with her napkin before placing it down, 'we have been rather busy since last we saw you. It appears you were very certain of your ability to murder my husband and get away with it, but I think you'll agree that this is not the case.'

Osborne's face fell. 'What is this talk of murder, Katherine? You know that Jacob was my very dearest friend.'

'Oh yes, you were a very dear friend indeed, Henry. One who planned to take the business out from under him with Mr Griegsson and Mr Clark.'

My mother held out a hand, into which Marcus placed a slip of paper. It was a receipt for two thousand pounds' worth of saffron, with Osborne's clear signature along the bottom. Apparently there had been several similar receipts hidden in his study, which Mira and Carl had managed to retrieve at the party last night. All this time we had been looking just to George Talver for evidence of misdeeds, not realising that my godfather held the vital piece of evidence. My father's handwritten note in his ledger should have been the clue. *Missing receipts for twenty pounds of saffron. Unknown vendor. Ask Osborne.* He had confronted Henry, only to meet with his demise shortly afterwards.

My mother flung the receipt down in the centre of the table with a flourish, my godfather's complexion blanching as he recognised it.

'Y-you broke into my house?' he spluttered indignantly.

'Actually, no, you invited us,' my mother replied with vitriol of her own.

Talver scowled, his lips twisting so that he looked as though he had swallowed a lemon.

'You can prove nothing!' he shouted, and my mother's eyebrow shot up at his tone.

'On the contrary, George, I can prove everything.' She clapped her hands and Sly Fairfax entered the room once again, this time with a meat cleaver clutched in his huge grip.

'What, this commoner's word against that of a gentleman?' Osborne said, now standing up so that he and his partner were shoulder to shoulder.

I retrieved the note that I had discovered in Griegsson's desk and laid it delicately in front of my soup bowl.

'Actually, I think it would be your word against Klaus Griegsson and Kaine Clark's, if this is anything to go by,' I said, keeping my voice steady.

Talver recognised it immediately, his piggy eyes bulging in his skull. 'You *stole* from us?'

'I merely came upon this by accident while attending Mr Griegsson's salon, Mr Talver,' I said innocently, before tucking the paper out of harm's way once more. 'But there is far more evidence where that came from.'

Talver seemed to have tired of our conferring. Pulling out a slender, sharp-looking knife from his jacket, he stepped back from the table, searching the room for an escape. But the door to his right would quickly be blocked by Erasmus should he desire to run, while that on the left was barred by Sly Fairfax and his meat cleaver.

'Oh dear, George, a blade! Must you be so *dramatic*?' Mother said, rolling her eyes. 'It will do you no good. At this moment there are Bow Street Runners and constables waiting just outside the house for you, ready to take you to Newgate. You could at least sit down and finish your meal before you go, for I understand the food is rather awful in prisons these days.'

Mira chuckled at my mother's words, and I reached my hand under the table to squeeze hers, grateful that she could find a moment to laugh despite the events unfolding before us.

'Prison? You would treat us like common dogs after all we have been through together?' Talver said, doing himself no favours, for even Osborne could see that the situation was lost, shaking his head at his friend.

'All we have been through, George?' Mother said rhetorically. 'You mean to insult me further by accusing me of betraying our friendship? Jacob refused your offer to trade slaves, but you carried out your plan anyway, and when he discovered it, you had him murdered in cold blood.'

'Katherine, please,' Osborne protested. 'Jacob would not see sense. He would have lost us thousands of pounds—'

'My husband's life was worth more than thousands of pounds, Henry! He was a father and a philanthropist, a wise and kind heart, and he is gone because of *you*.' She pointed at them both, giving them a glare that threatened to burn them where they stood.

Osborne had the decency to look ashamed. Talver merely sneered. I couldn't resist having the final word.

'You will find that the little skiff you have moored at the docks, the one stashed with money and rations enough for one,' I added, almost able to see the ideas flitting across his face as he formed them, 'has been appropriated by the *Juliet*'s crew.'

'You can't do that!' Talver protested.

'In fact we can,' I replied, sharing a knowing look with Mira beside me, 'for the boat was purchased with company money, and as my husband is a partner, he has deemed it appropriate that it be put to use for company purposes.'

'I've had enough of this,' Talver muttered, clambering onto the dining table, sending dishes and cutlery flying as he chose his escape route, believing perhaps that Erasmus would not be able to put up a fight in his state. He took a diagonal path across it towards the door, and the room held a collective breath at his audacity.

But it was not escape he intended. Time seemed to simultaneously speed up and slow down. Talver's knife shone silver in the candlelight as he plunged it towards his nearest target: me.

I heard the snick of Erasmus's cane at the same time as my switchblade came out of the folds of my skirts, while to my right Mira had pulled her own blade from her boot. There was an almighty clash of metal as Talver brought his knife down towards me and all three of ours came up to meet it.

I had asked Erasmus once how he remained so calm in the face of monsters. His reply had been that he believed that even the monsters thought they were doing what was best, and that there was some vestige of good in every man. Those words came to mind as I strained with the weight of Talver pressing down upon me, the point of his knife inches from my face, hatred and alarm in his eyes. If there was any good left in this man, it was so buried, so hidden beneath the layers of evil that I did not know if he could ever be redeemed.

I was aware of a large shape reaching around Talver's waist and heaving him away, throwing him from the table to the floor like a rag doll. I blinked to see Marcus disarming him and cuffing him around the head hard enough to render the man unconscious.

In the moments it had taken Talver to both attack and be knocked down, Gar, Carl and Lei had restrained Osborne, who, seeing that the battle was lost, put up no fight as they pinned his arms behind his back before escorting him from the room to the waiting prison cart outside. Marcus threw the prone form of Talver over his shoulder and followed them.

'Are you all right, Jenny?' my mother, Erasmus and Mira all asked me at the same time. I realised that I was still clutching the switchblade, my knuckles white on the hilt, and my entire body shook with adrenaline.

'I-I am fine,' I managed, allowing Erasmus to gently prise the blade from my fingers. I watched him in a slightly detached way, unable to quite believe all that had just transpired.

'Do you have everything you need, Mr Clarkson?' my mother asked our guest, who had watched the entire exchange with some interest.

'That was as good as a confession, Mrs Miller. With your permission, I shall bring all you have documented to the Clapham Saints, and to Mr Wilberforce himself, for I am certain that he will find it of great interest in our cause.' He gave me a sympathetic smile. 'You were remarkable, mesdames, all of you,' he gestured to the room, 'and I can say without a doubt in my mind that we will be able to press charges against these men for their crimes.'

Erasmus, who could not help but idolise the man who worked with Mr Wilberforce and who had been working towards the anti-slavery bill for much of his life, cleared his throat gently.

'What of Kaine Clark? I'm afraid I was otherwise engaged and have yet to hear what happened to him.'

'While you were busy relaxing in a prison cell,' Mira replied, none too kindly, 'Big Don managed to track him down at the docks and bring him to a constable first thing yesterday morning. He will be standing trial for murder and slave trade on British ships along with the rest of them.'

My body relaxed at her words, for I too had not heard of Clark's fate, and had been expecting that perhaps he might find some other henchmen to torment us if he managed to escape justice. As it was, I felt both exhausted and elated, even after having my life so recently threatened. With Griegsson's ledger and Clark's note, Sly Fairfax's testimony and the fact that he owed Erasmus's crew a life debt and so would be loyal to us to the last, the tension in my stomach eased like an over-tightened spring finally uncoiling.

'It is a shame to waste such wonderful fare,' Mother said, looking a little forlornly at the broken dishes and upset table arrangements.

'It is not too late to have dinner, madam. I am not one to turn down a good meal, should you wish to continue,' Mr Clarkson said congenially.

She seemed to think on it for a moment before she eventually nodded. 'Very well, but I think we shall take it in the parlour if it is all the same to you.'

Chapter 29

ꕥ

AN ENDING AND A BEGINNING

The weeks following that evening proceeded in a heady sort of chaos.

Beatrice, upon hearing about the events of the dinner from which she had been excluded, admonished me severely, but she carried out the rest of her visit before returning home to Toughton with two potential proposals and a wickedly knowing smile at myself and Erasmus as she left.

Aristotle, on the other hand, had not been the least upset about being neglected, for he was permitted to clean up the leftovers after the meal and given extra treats when it was discovered he had bitten Osborne's ankles on the way to the prison cart.

There had been some doubt that Sly Fairfax might refuse to testify against Talver, for fear of implicating himself in my father's murder. Yet although my mother had not forgiven him for his part in it, she cleverly negotiated that we would not pursue prosecution, provided it was made clear who had paid him to carry out such a heinous act. He did not live out his days without impunity, however, for as soon as the magistrate heard his tale, he discovered that several other gentlemen had been victims of Mr Fairfax's 'special services', and he was immediately sent to Newgate as punishment. He would likely hang before the year was out.

Mr Clarkson and the Clapham Saints used the evidence Erasmus had gathered to bring the culprits to trial, as well as reinforcing their case for eliminating all British involvement in the slave trade once and for all. His intention, he told us one afternoon when visiting for tea, was to travel across Europe and the Americas in the hope that he could bring his campaign to the rest of the world.

Mr Gallows, of Gallows & Enwright Solicitors, was instrumental when it came to deciding the fate of my father's company.

As Talver had no wife or surviving relatives, it was deemed that his shares should be divided between the Osbornes and the Millers. So it was that Erasmus, my mother and I spent many an afternoon meeting with the solicitor, Mrs Osborne and Henrietta, now engaged to the young scientist, to decide how best to proceed.

'I'm afraid that I do not bring good news, madam,' Mr Gallows announced to Mrs Osborne one afternoon in our parlour, at the same table where all of this had begun in the summer. His peculiar moustache quivered with fervour as he spoke. 'With Mr Osborne now permanently indisposed, and Henrietta not yet married, per the company by-laws the remainder of your shares should be bequeathed to Mr Black.' As Henry Osborne was in a gentlemen's prison of sorts, and George Talver and Kaine Clark were on a ship somewhere on their way to the colonies, none of them would be arguing this point.

'But we shall be penniless!' Mrs Osborne protested, clasping her daughter's hand in hers and dabbing her eyes with a lace kerchief.

'Not quite, Maria,' my mother said softly, giving the woman an encouraging smile. 'If it is agreeable to you, Mr Black and I will run the company until such time as Henrietta is married, providing you with twenty per cent of the profits as a sleeping partner for the time being. Should you, Henrietta or her future husband wish to involve yourselves in the merchanting business, we shall split the profits three ways, as they were divided prior to . . . all this misfortune.'

It was more generous an offer than Osborne and Talver would ever have given us in their position, but my mother was not interested in ruining a woman and her daughters for the sake of spite.

'Y-you would do that? After everything Henry did?' Maria gasped, her eyes already swollen from tears. Henrietta too had not stopped sniffling since they had entered the room, but now paused in her blubbering to look at my mother with a mixture of reverence and awe.

'I do not believe you should suffer on account of his proclivity for dishonesty, no. Besides, if you have managed to learn as much about the trade as I have over the years, we may make quite the success of it yet,' Mother added, looking knowingly between myself and Erasmus.

'I'm afraid I do not know the first thing about ships, nor tides, nor the market,' Maria admitted. Perhaps she had spent too much time organising salons and attending parties to pay much attention, but Mother did not punish her for it.

'No matter. I can more than make up for it.'

'You would truly give up your freedom for the sake of the business?' Maria looked stunned at the prospect of a woman of Mother's age and stature actually *working*.

Mother chuckled, waving a hand dismissively. 'Not at all! For doing something you enjoy for a living is surely a freedom in itself, is it not?'

Mr Gallows, who until then had spent the conversation opening and closing his mouth, looking for a moment when he could contribute, slapped a contract onto the tablecloth.

'With that settled, may I ask for a witness?'

Marcus stepped from the shadows so abruptly that I started in surprise.

As he, Maria Osborne and my mother signed paper after paper, I looked at the surrounding company and allowed myself a moment of relief. Things truly were going to be all right. The recognition of it made me giddy, and for a moment I was overcome. I found Erasmus's hand in my own, a smile playing across his lips as he watched me, his eyes signalling that he wished to speak alone.

Over an hour later, when our guests had been shown out, I sat on the bed in my room, the only place that would allow us some semblance of privacy.

'What now, Jenny?' he asked, settling onto the mattress beside me and threading his long fingers through mine. I rested my head on his shoulder, tucking my legs underneath me, my eyes on the blue new-autumn skies and the beginnings of turning leaves in the square outside.

'Well, I suppose you will have much to do in reorganising the offices now that we are to reopen them,' I said with a sigh. 'And Mira will be itching to leave soon, no doubt. It's a wonder she stayed another month to see things to an end.'

'That woman has brine running through her veins, there is no doubt,' Erasmus agreed, but I felt he had more to say.

'Then there's the matter of *Juliet*, and everything of Osborne and Talver's that was seized at the docks. Mother will refuse to use those captains who took on the slave contracts, so new ships will need to be contracted, and there is of course going to be the problem of rough seas at this time of year—'

'Jenny.' Erasmus silenced me with my name and a squeeze of my hand. 'My question was not aimed at what we should do with the business, for I believe that is all in hand.'

'How so?'

'I am not certain if you noticed, little mouse, but your mother is a very capable woman, and has every intention of running it herself. With Marcus by her side, of course.'

I raised my head from his shoulder to look at him, the quirk in his lips, the brightness in his dark mahogany eyes. Puzzling this for a moment, I realised that what he said was true. Marcus *had* been by my mother's side, a constant for the past few months and even more so in recent weeks. The recognition of it stirred a conflict of emotions in my chest.

'But what about you?' I asked him.

His expression was perplexed, and I stood up from my place on the bed beside him to retrieve something from my bedside drawer. I unfolded the letter Osborne had given me all those weeks ago, trying not to think about the words it contained.

His face fell as he read it. 'I wondered where this had gone,' he muttered before looking up at me. 'Osborne gave it to you, and you kept it all this time?' I nodded, ashamed not to have confronted him about it sooner.

'Oh, little mouse,' he said, putting the letter down on the bed and pulling me towards him, so that my skirts were bracketed by his legs, his face level with my breastbone. 'I understand now. All those times you thought I would vanish. I realise how it must appear to you, but this was merely a decoy.' As Mira had suspected, I thought, but I waited for him to explain himself further. 'I knew that if Talver thought I was about to leave you, he would drop his guard. My business partners would not need to worry about me if I was preparing to set sail, and I hoped they might grow careless. When I returned to my desk to find the letter gone, I thought Osborne might have merely shown it to his business partner as I had originally intended. I had no idea he had given it to you.'

The relief of hearing this confirmation was heady, like the lightness of too much champagne, and I found my hands twining around his neck, pulling him closer to me so that his head rested against my chest, anchoring myself to him.

'It was foolish of me not to ask you about it sooner, but after everything Mira had said, I could not bear to be misled.'

'Surely you would have known if I had been lying to you?' he said softly, listening to my heartbeat as his arms came around my waist to pull me closer to him.

'Not if you did not know you were lying. If you had had the very best intentions to stay, and then had been pulled away by the call of the sea or some duty, I would have had no way of knowing. I can only tell if someone is purposefully lying to me.'

Erasmus sighed, pulling his head back to shake it. 'Do not bear these burdens of worry, little mouse. I am here with you. I will always be here with you. Of course I have plans to travel, but they only ever depend upon whether you will come with me on my journey.'

'Journey?' I echoed the word a little breathlessly.

'Well, honeymoon, holiday, whatever you wish to call it,' he said airily, 'but it would involve a ship, and some far-off lands, and most certainly at least a little romance.'

I gave a small gasp, unable to fathom it for a moment. For these past weeks I had not entertained the idea that we would go anywhere together. If anything, it felt as though Osborne and

Talver's arrests had forced me to stay by my mother's side, forever her companion. But it seemed she now had Marcus for that.

Did this mean I was truly free to do as I wished, and as I had wanted all along?

'Jenny Black,' Erasmus murmured my name and slid his hands along my arms to take both of mine in his, as though he were a gentleman proposing, 'will you go on an adventure with me?'

I laughed then, and planted a kiss on his lips before I could stop myself. 'Oh, if you insist. Yes, I shall.'

It was another month before we left, for there was the matter of the ship and the crew. Erasmus gifted *Juliet* to Mira, and although the crew were loath to separate from us, they were ever faithful to their captain. The only exception was Kit, who had finally begun to warm to me and would not leave Erasmus's side.

The cargo that Captain Hodgson and her people had so faithfully protected contained enough silk and saffron to pay for another ship, which she in turn gifted to Erasmus and me as a belated wedding present, insisting that we name it *Miranda*. I did not enquire as to where the precious goods came from, nor why they had been hiding them. Some things, Erasmus reminded me often, were better left unknown.

Our final parting from the crew was bittersweet. We stood upon the London docks one calm September afternoon, the sunlight coruscating off the Thames, surrounded by the people who had been family for Erasmus for nearly a decade, and who had become some of my dearest friends.

'You look after him now, won't you, Mrs B,' Big Don said, pulling me into a bear-like embrace, blinking back tears that I gave him the dignity of ignoring. Although I only came up to the man's chest and my arms could barely make it around his middle, I gave him a squeeze and a promise. Gar and Carl both bowed, each placing a kiss on the back of my hand, while Mr Atkins merely gave me a nod of respect from the gangplank as he hobbled up it, wishing to be away as soon as possible. Erasmus was on the deck, speaking with the crew I had not been able to meet more than once or twice during their stay in London, mostly for discretion. He came down now, tailed by Lei, who practically skipped behind him, along with a young black man and two other women.

'Jenny, this is Ode,' he said, and the young man gave me a flash of teeth and a deep bow.

'I have heard so much of you,' I said, stepping forward to take his burn-scarred hands in my own. He did not flinch or even seem to mind, and I was grateful for the warmth in his demeanour as he greeted me.

'And I of you, Mrs Black,' he replied, before moving aside for me to be introduced to the two women behind him.

'This is Anastasia,' Erasmus said, putting emphasis towards the end of the name as he introduced a girl of about eighteen, lithe and sinewy like the other sailing women I had met. Her dark eyes were bright and intelligent as she took me in, giving me a nod of regard. 'And Pelagia,' he added as he gestured towards a tawny-haired girl whose bright green eyes shone with intrigue as she looked at me. The two of them did not bother to hide their curiosity about this stranger who had stolen the heart of their ship's first mate, and although I felt no animosity from them, I could not help the guilt that settled in my stomach that they were losing Erasmus from their ranks.

Lei stepped forward last, pulling me towards her and placing a soft kiss on my cheek as she whispered, 'If you ever tire of travelling with Mr B, you'll always be welcome on our ship.'

I chuckled, pulling back to look at her, this girl who had seen and suffered so much that I still could not comprehend, who had taken a place in my heart. 'I'll remember that. I might even threaten him with it if he misbehaves.'

'Ah, there you are,' the captain said, emerging from the ship and joining us on the quay. 'I hate to break up the party, but the tides are in our favour if we leave now.'

She focused on Erasmus, her eyes betraying so much more than she would ever say, and I moved to leave them for a moment. Her hand shot out before I could go, taking my arm and pulling me towards her in an unexpected embrace.

'Farewell, Jenny Black,' she murmured, releasing me as quickly as she had grasped me.

'Safe travels, Mira,' I replied, meaning it with every ounce of my being.

'You will hire your crew from my list of recommendations?' she asked Erasmus, her tone businesslike, though I knew beneath it she must be warring with her emotions.

'It is all in hand,' Erasmus replied, stepping forward to place a kiss on each of her cheeks. 'Be safe, Mira.' He did not notice the way she stiffened, nor the little breath she took in, as though committing his scent to memory. Had our roles been reversed, I would have done the same.

And then they were leaving.

We stayed beside the water as they pulled up the anchor and unfurled the sails, as Mira navigated the ship down the river to the sea beyond, and I wondered if we would ever see them again.

Weeks later, with our own vessel finally manned and a course plotted, my best travelling clothes packed and a promise to my mother and Marcus that we would write at every available opportunity, we set our course for Greece. Erasmus wished to visit his mother's home town, the place where his parents had first met, and I, of course, was happy to go anywhere so long as there was some adventure involved. Kit, whose mood had lightened considerably knowing that he would be reunited with his own mother at least for a time, had made an excellent companion in recent weeks, while Erasmus was still finalising the voyage.

As for books, I brought a trunk exclusively for my favourite volumes, despite being told by my husband that I would sink the ship before we had even set sail.

A week into our journey, we lay in the captain's quarters, my head resting upon his heart, his arm around my shoulders, holding me close. I ran my fingers over his bare chest, turning my head so that he could kiss me before he blew out the lantern. I had found it difficult to sleep at first, with the constant crash of water against the hull, the cramped spaces, the plain fare at mealtimes, salt in my eyes, my nose, on my clothes. But I would get used to it, for the sake of adventure.

Just as I began to drift off, the up-and-down lull of the waves easing me into slumber, Erasmus spoke.

'May I tell you a story?' he asked, his voice a rumble beneath my cheek as it pressed against his skin.

'Of course. You know I'll never say no to a story,' I mumbled, fighting sleep for a few more moments.

'It's one my mother used to tell me when I was a child, from *Aesop's Fables*.'

I thought of the volume that sat on his desk nearby, of the words his mother had written there all those years ago.

'A lion lay asleep in the forest,' he began, 'his great head resting on his paws. A timid little mouse came upon him unexpectedly, and in her fright and haste to get away, she ran across the lion's nose. Roused from his nap, the lion entrapped the tiny creature, intending to kill her.

'"Spare me!" begged the mouse. "Please let me go, and someday I will repay you, have no doubt."

'The lion was amused to think that a little mouse could ever help him, but he was feeling generous and finally let her go. Some days later, while stalking his prey in the forest, he was caught up in a hunter's net. Unable to free himself, he roared and roared, filling the woods with the echo of his ire. The mouse knew his voice and quickly found him struggling in the net. Running to one of the great ropes that bound him, she gnawed it until it parted, and within minutes the lion was free.

'"I laughed to think that you could ever repay me," the lion said, "but it seems that even a mouse can help a lion, and no act of kindness, no matter how small, is ever wasted."'

All those weeks ago, in the garden in Bedford Square, I recalled him throwing pebbles into the pond and telling me words to the same effect. That had been the day I had begun to fall in love with him. It made my heart full to realise how much had changed since then.

'And then,' he continued, to my surprise, 'the lion fell in love with the little mouse and they lived happily ever after.'

He kissed me again, his lips gentle against mine, and I frowned even as I felt him smile in the dark.

'I don't recall that part of the story.'

'I may have changed it slightly, although similarities to anyone you may know are purely coincidental,' he said smoothly.

I huffed a laugh and kissed him again.

'Well, I like your version better.'

Acknowledgements

Thank you, reader, for reaching the end of my second book! My thanks go to you, first and foremost, for picking this story up and taking this journey with Jenny and Erasmus. Whilst writing *The House of Lost Wives* I knew that Jenny Miller needed a story of her own, and some justice for what had befallen her. She deserved a happy ending and I'm so glad that I could finally provide her with one, even if getting there wasn't without its trials and tribulations.

As it takes a village to write a book, I must give huge thanks to my wonderful agent, Vanessa Holt, for constantly championing my stories, and to my marvellous editor Nicola Caws, for asking all the right questions so that we could make this book the best version of itself (and for laughing at my jokes!). To the editorial team at Headline Accent and everyone involved in putting this book into your hands, my deepest gratitude.

As the dedication implies, my parents, Tom and Tabitha Hardy, have forever been the cochairmen of my fan club, happily reading every scrap of writing I put out. My gratitude for your unwavering faith and confidence in me can never be overstated.

Thank you to my Greek friends, and the incredible Greek people who welcomed me and my family there on our visit in 2016, that kindled the beginnings of this story in me. To Tatiana Gabilondo for always being willing to go on a research trip with me, for being my sounding board, and for loving Jenny as much as I do. And to Olivia Elmiger for reading the first draft of this and for falling in love with Erasmus too. To Gillian Greenwood, for constantly comparing my writing to other much better, much more famous authors, and for reading every first draft without bias or judgement. To my Grays team, you're all far more than just coworkers. Thank you for your encouragement and support.

To Daniele, for being incredibly patient with me despite being married to an author, and to Zack and Damon, for forcing me to take a break from the keyboard every so often.

And to Mamgu, my Grandmother. There's a little bit of you in everything I do.

Author's Afterword

ꕥ

By 1800 the population of Earth had reached 1 billion. Of that, it is estimated 1 million people were enslaved. That means 0.1 per cent of the entire world's population were in some form of slavery, according to The National Archives.

Although this is ultimately a love story, Erasmus's mission is inspired by true events and history. Barbary pirates bought and sold somewhere in the region of a million Europeans over a 250-year period, and while the Ottoman Empire had dwindled in power and activity by the beginning of the nineteenth century, and the 'child levy' system (Devshirme) had officially ended in the seventeenth century, there were many overlapping occurrences throughout history that could give credence to a story such as this one.

Unfortunately, slavery is not only based in history. According to Anti-Slavery International, there are 49.6 million people enslaved today that we know of. That is more than the entire population of Spain (48 million) or the state of California (39 million).

To find out more or to show your support I highly recommend visiting antislavery.org and youthforhumanrights.org.